MW01420442

The Diaspora Returns

My Brother's Keeper

&

Hong Kong by Moonlight

To Valerie

The Diaspora Returns

A Healing For The Soul

Hope you enjoy

O. F. Willisomhouse

O.F. Willisomhouse

Library of Congress Control Number: 2013902467

ISBN:	Hardcover	978-1-4797-9212-2
	Softcover	978-1-4797-9211-5
	Ebook	978-1-4797-9213-9

This book was printed in the United States of America.

Rev. date: 03/06/2013

To order additional copies of this book, contact:
Xlibris Corporation
1-888-795-4274
www.Xlibris.com
Orders@Xlibris.com
129562

Contents

Max and Milani's Prayer

Thank you God for this day, again,
tomorrow I will pray
And just in case I forget so later on, I won't regret
Focus my eyes to stay on you and
teach my lips to tell the truth
Tame my tongue so I may speak words
of wisdom and not defeat
Instruct my mind, sins to confess
train my hands to do their best
Guide my feet on righteous path
protect my spirit from evil wrath
Heavenly Father high up above teach
my heart how to love, Amen

"My Brother's Keeper" Oath

The Lord God is my Shepherd; therefore
I am my brother's keeper
I will do everything in my power, with God's
help, not to become a slave to sin
I will meditate often, so I will recognize
the Shepherd's voice when he speaks
I will attempt to restore all the lives I have disrupted
I will reward all whom I have inconvinenced
I will not judge my brother, for
his journey is not my own
I will embrace and appreciate our differences,
and allow God to chastise his faults
I will pray to overcome my fear of death,
for death is only another phase of life
I will respect my body, as I respect the
Temple, for it is not mind to abuse
I will shield my spirit from greed, lust,
arrogance and unjustifiable acts of survival
For each and every life is precious
I will focus on my purpose and not my past,
for it is over and I can never go back
I believe great self-sacrifice will
reap great spiritual rewards
Therefore I shall forever be "My Brother's Keeper"

"When Monique Came Out To Play" Song

It was a warm April day when
Monique came out to play
Her cheeks were red as fire and
so filled with life that day
But her mother never heard her cry
And her daddy never wiped a single tear from her eyes
And that is how this story all began

Chorus
*You have to find a friend you like
and love them-don't quit.
And when the two of you fight, just
learn how to grin and bear it
Keep all your heartfelt secrets for a very rain day
And that's how it was when Monique came out to play*

Well months turned into years as
the days just rolled away
Monique grew up and found a new role she had to play
Some how she found a friend and
loved them to the end
And that's how her story all began

Chorus
Well her father just grew old and
the story was never told
And everyone just prayed that
that day would stay away

But old hearts can't take much pain
When there are lies between friends it leaves a stain
And this is how the story always ends

Chorus

Now the hearts have all been broken
and the friendship is just a token
Of an oath taken on that warm April day
Now the truth has to be spoken, to mend
hearts that have been broken
About that day that Monique came out to play

Preface

In book one **'My Brother's Keeper, Secrets of Tarnished Shields'** the tale begins as several unlikely souls paths, while on very distinctive and different journeys, somehow manages to cross. Helen, one of the main characters and the story's voice is once again attempting to heal from her second companion's death. Alex is focused on his career and hopes to fulfill his contract with the bureau and staying alive. Alex had long given up on ever sharing his golden years with a lady that he had fallen in love with as a boy. Then to complicated things more, Alex's best friend unknowingly, has desiring eyes for the same woman. It's now decades later since Alex fell in love with her, yet Tate is in hope that she will be able to heal his wounds of a great lost as well. The characters are all seasoned adults and time is of the essences to enjoy whatever remaining life God chooses to grant them. The stage is set as a group of secret servicemen form an illegal high-stakes bounty hunting business while remaining under the bureau's radar and the public's criticizing and judgmental eyes. Lies that have stood the tests of time are all about to be revealed as they scatter for protective-cover, while investigating a mishap that has happened much to close to home for their comfort.

As the story continues in **'Hong Kong by Moonlight, Exiled to the Orient'**, a portion of the assembly and some of their love ones hideout while the agents in the group investigate the unexplained mishaps. More personal enlightenment is retrieved and their exiled numbers increase along with deep hidden pain as truths raises to the top. Loyalties are questioned as priorities shifts, while each person search for a way to lessen their own pain and began his or her individual spiritual healing.

In the following chapter, **'The Diaspora Returns, a Healing for the Soul'**, the healing begins as the characters grasp the concept that coming-clean with their family, friends and themselves is the only positive way to move forward with the time they have left in this life. This work allows the reader to explore more of the character's past and understand how they arrived at this point in their lives. Plus reveals some of the regrets that they are forced to live with while moving forward.

The Diaspora Returns II, the Healing Continues' illustrates how embracing these truths have assisted with the healing process and has provided them with new hope. The sub-agency is now closed and everyone seems to be concentrating on getting their lives back on track, with the help of divine intervention; as they struggle to shed the disappointing remnants of their past. Renewed relationships are formed and the next generation will be keeping a close eye on their caretakers as become mature enough to ask some important questions that would seem difficult to understand if all the facts were made available to them now. Please shadow the results of these changes and flashbacks in a possible episode in titled **‘Beneath the Kintai Moon, Next Generation’.**

Introduction

'The Diaspora Returns, a Healing for the soul' is the third book of a fictional series that allows a glance into the lives of a small and possibly an insignificant group of people, by sociality's standards. The word 'Diaspora' is usual reserved for a large group of people that have been forced into a far distant land with their language, culture, and family members intact and with the hope of returning one day to their ancestral origin. This small entourage, in spite of its size, has been forced to face some of the similar uncertainties as a correctly labeled Diaspora. They are scattered, in exile and embrace the hope of returning to their established homeland. While in exile, they are enlightened by more truths about themselves and other members of the assortment. During the exile period, of the falsely labeled Diaspora, the group increases in size as they discovered others that have migrated to this place. Some had arrived years before they had, for various reasons. This amalgamation of friendships has created a renewed spirit of hope in them, as the Irish Catholic priest continues to pray and anoint them while he demands that they improve their relationships with each other and the Divine One as well. Please continue to track their enlightenments as the story unfolds in **'The Diaspora Returns, a Healing for the Soul'.**

Chapter One

A Legend Returns

The journey back home almost always, seems to be a long and hard one, especially when you have spent a portion of your exile status searching for the truth while exposing others for the lies they have insisted on protecting.

My foster-father was finally laid to rest and more truths had come to light about my past. I, in spite of everything, had not taken the time to have that very important dialog exchange with my foster-mother; the discussion to do so would fill in the gaps that my biological father, Uncle Oscar, was unable to complete.

My father, Uncle Oscar, and I stayed on for a few more days. As a matter of fact, I left my father behind to help my foster-mother with some of the endless paperwork. The boarder that my foster-parents had taken in had continued to live there and would prove to be a more stable assistant to my mother, later on, than we initially thought. He was a lifelong friend of my foster-father. He had moved in a few years after

I left home and just before my foster-father retired from work. The boarder assumed that my parents needed the money, but the truth was that they only took his rent to allow his pride to remain undamaged. Whenever one was incline to deal with my foster-parents, for some reason or another, you very seldom got all the details about any situation. I wasn't sure at this point if it was because they were private people or if they felt that secrets held some unspoken power for them. I knew I had to ponder these thoughts and others like them longer, but at a later time, for the true understanding and perhaps ask some more questions about this unique aspect of their personalities. During those first few days, of this initial trip back to the States, while remaining in an exile status; I called back to Hong Kong everyday to check on my step-son, Max, and to inquire how Slapp and his mother's renewed lifetime-of-waiting relationship was coming along. Gayle was unable to tell me much, but at least no one was screaming at each other. Max on the other hand was having the time of his life. The embassy's staff was catering more to him than they ever had to the ambassador. I'm not sure what the big attraction was because he was only a seven-year-old kid with no job and no money of which to speak. Although, he was extremely handsome and he had a way about him that suckered you in every time he made a request, in which usually wasn't too outside the norm, at first glance. But when you thought about it later, and added up all the little things, that's when you realized that a professional manipulating seven-year-old had taken you for a ride.

The embassy's kitchen staff had even adjusted the menu in the cafeteria to accommodate him more. Mr. Charlie, the inside roving patrol night watchman; had given Max a master-key to all the rooms on his temporary assigned residential floor so Max could wonder around from the bunkroom, to Mrs. Carrington's [Miss Beasley] room and then back to Miss Gayle's sleeping quarters. Each area carried its own appeal for Max. The duty bunkroom had the most space and cable TV channels. Miss Gayle's room had the best view of the city. While Mrs. Carrington's room, better known as Nana Carrington to Max, had a full size refrigerator that was always well stocked with things that he liked. Max had even been granted permission to make a few runs with his Uncle Slapp and someone had found him a chauffeur's cap in his size to make his front seat shotgun-ride-along look more official. Well, Slapp wasn't really his uncle. He was a good friend of his father's and an ex-boyfriend of his deceased mother.

Each day I became more and more afraid to call back to the American Embassy, Hong Kong branch, for an update on how this guy had charmingly shifted protocol even further away from the norm, with simply a wink of an eye. The only thing I could conclude, for Max's powerful influence, was that the ambassador had taken a long trip and the second in charge had gone off island, as well.

A week and half later, we received word that the men that had attacked and beaten Slapp had been identified. One was the son of the man that Miss Beasley had testified against, nearly thirty-five years earlier, while the other two where merely hirelings [hired hands] for the job. It seems that only three weeks before the man was to be released, he had consequently died in prison. His son, who was now a forty-year old man, blamed Miss Beasley for not having his father around when he was growing up. He had found out that she was now in the witness protection program for testifying against his father. The security computer man that Slapp had made arrangements for his home to spring a gas leak and blow-up after he had been warned not to go inside the house, of course; had in fact sold the dead prisoner's son some information that linked Slapp to Miss Beasley. Now all Alex and Tate had to do was figure out if the other two men knew what they were getting into or was it just a-job-for-pay, when they had beaten Slapp near death, temporarily blinding him, and left in a cold wet alley near death. This would influence the decision; of how much jail time they would get, or if they would even survive the misunderstanding, in which they had managed to, possibly had unknowingly, become a part of. The other dilemma was if they would live long enough to receive a trial. After all Slapp had strong reservation about leaving an enemy breathing after such a serious confrontation. Once again, this had been the very reason that Slapp had been instructed to stay back and protect the love ones that we all had to leave behind. Due to this fact and the strategic plan, the illegal mission was now one agent short.

This was where all the men agreed that Mr. Dexter Allen Burney would come in handy. Agent Burney was considered a legend by many and was now retired from the bureau. We had heard that he had remained physically fit and active, but we didn't know in which line of work had he chosen to spend his days. Alex and Tate needed him to work a few bartender gigs and become a listener. The son of the man that had died in prison was known to be a heavy drinker. They knew where he lived and were familiar with a couple of watering holes that he frequented, so all they had to do was plant someone and wait. The new computer analyzer of the downloaded copies, removed from the computer surveillance security man's computer, prior to the gas leak and fire, had revealed all of this information. Mr. Dexter answered three advertisements, from various locations, in hope that one would be where the dead man's son would discuss his plot to kill Miss Beasley for revenge or get drunk enough to brag about the plan. Alex and Tate wasn't sure if the decease prisoner's son knew where Miss Beasley had been placed by the witness protection program, but they were positive that he knew she was alive and that Slapp was her son. Twenty plus years ago, Miss Beasley had to be moved because someone had recognized her and had followed her home, to her first placement. The bureau was sure back then that it was the partners of the man that she had help put in prison. This is when Tate first came into the picture and had escorted her to the airport, soon after her facial reconstructive surgery. Facial reconstruction was a part of the program's package and at first Miss Beasley had declined to take it. She wanted her son to be able to identify her if there were ever any hope that they would be reunited in the future. Alex started to worry a little more now about what would be the outcome, after they gathered all the evidence of fact. He wanted to turn them in, but he knew Slapp and possibly Agent Burney wanted all of them dead. I was pressed to doubt that Miss Beasley wouldn't be a part of this fan club; that believed the son should pay for the sins of his father and later on, his sins as well. It seems that three lives had been altered and derailed forever; just because someone had tried to do what they thought was right even though the reasons had an initial selfish element attached, at first. This trait seems to surface in all of us from time to time, which I believe makes the closer-walk with the Divine One more of a daily struggle than we would like to admit.

Perhaps it was karma or just a couple of people who had taken a bad turn early in life. No one knew better than I what a bad decision could do or how many lives could be altered by one egotistical thought, put into action. It seemed that Miss Beasley's mother was an alcoholic who had a few kids that sort of raised themselves.

Sarah Lynn Beasley was the oldest and wanted to escape her situation. So at sixteen she got a job in a bar, after school. She finished high school and realized that she had no money for college. She then became a pole dancer in a nightclub to pay for her tuition. Her name on stage was Pocahontas. She was pretty, thin, with thick auburn curly hair and had very nice legs. She was the full package. Everyone that knew her loved her, because she was there for a good reason and a short season. The owner of the smoky joint guarded her like a watch dog on steroids. He was aware she was a student because he had a daughter only two years younger. He allowed her to study in the back and take the earlier entertaining shifts, during happy hour. She cleaned up the place on the weekends for the establishment and she helped with the accounting books as well. No one doubted that she knew that she was going places.

She majored in foreign languages and caught on very quickly. One night she over heard a plan-of-crime, so she thought that perhaps this might shorten her work-time at this gloomy strip club. So she called the tip hotline for a monetary reward. She later testified and had to be placed into the witness protection program. Sarah Lynn was forced to give up the one thing that she loved the most and the only thing that she was able to call her own, her son at the age of two and a half.

When had Sarah Lynn altered her path? Was it when she desired to escape poverty, by any means necessary? Perhaps it was the night she over heard the criminal's plan and called to turn them in for the reward? Or was it the night she started to date and later formed an intimate relationship with one of the secret serviceman, while they staked out the location. Maybe it was shortly after that, while becoming pregnant to complicated matters further. It could have been any number of things that had driven her to these early, but not-well-thought-out resolutions. There is no simple answer, just a lot of questions that had caused all of us to end up here in Hong Kong hiding out, at this very moment.

Agent Burney agreed to meet with Alex, before he took the assignment. Their first meeting was at the National Botanical Garden, in downtown Washington D.C., one of agent Burney's favorite locations. Alex found Mr. Dexter Allen Burney in the middle of the atrium on the second level, watching him closely from above; probably so he could read Alex's body language before he was able to observe him and read his. Mr. Burney was standing on the back wall that looked out over the rear garden. There he stood facing the open-view metal cage elevator doors, at an angle. He was very tourist-camouflaged-ly dressed wearing a two-or-three-day old unshaven beard. His clothes were wrinkled as though they had been taken right out of the suitcase. He wore a pair of worn-out tennis shoes with socks that were knapping around his ankles from lost of elasticity. Agent Burney had done such an excellent job of fading into the crowd until it made Alex feel out of place and feared he would blow Burney's cover, just by speaking to him in such an open and public location. Alex quickly took the open metal elevator to the second floor of the atrium. Burney walked towards Alex with his hand stretched out to the full length of his arm, as he gave him a complete body scan, with his eagle eyes. Agent Burney smiled to himself which manifested into a grin as he wondered what part of the Camouflage Lectures, which he had taught for years at the F.B.I. academy, had Alex missed in regards to blending into your surroundings. Alex knew instantly what the smirk on Burney's face was about; nevertheless he attempted to explain his oversight of standard protocol whenever two or more undercover people called a public meeting.

"Hello Alex, it has been a long time and I'm glad to see that you are still in the game, after your career started later than most of our field agents." Alex grabbed hold of Agent Burney's hand and held on to it as he replied. Alex wasn't sure if a shoulder-tap hug was in order, but he was so overjoyed that Burney was in such good health and willing to help them with their one-man-short predicament, that he was willing to take a chance that the gesture and attempt wouldn't be an over-kill.

"Hello Mr. Burney, how have you been? It's a pleasure and an honor to see you after all these years sir. You look fit, that's good." Then Alex nervously pulled Mr. Burney in for a one-arm hug, aided by a handshake and shoulder-to-shoulder contact press. While in shock at Alex's openly public affection, Burney's smile turned into to a stunned chuckle as he slowly pushed Alex away and released the hand grasp between them.

"Hey, hold-up there stud. I have already agreed that I would help you guys. Let's not get too carried away with the friendly reciprocated contact and please, I think we both should drop the sir handles." They both turned toward the area that Agent Burney had just arrived from, which was deeper and closer to the back second floor atrium's wall of the fully enclosed greenhouse. Agent Burney continued as they slowly strolled away from the view of others.

"You know I'm not that much older than you are Alex and I'm pleased to see you too. I settled on meeting you here for three reasons. I wanted to size you up, ask you some personal questions about your friend and partner-of-crime, Alvin." He hesitated briefly. "And because this is one of my favorite places in the city. Can I let you in on a little secret? There are a few fulltime maintenance men working here; I think one is a horticulturist. I believe that's the proper title for a man in his line of work. Well anyway, whenever they prune the plants they save me all the clippings, well perhaps not all, but more than I have a right to receive. I built me a greenhouse on my two and a half acre lot and now after ten years, I have almost every plant on my property that they have here." Agent Burney peered over at Alex to observe what his response would be to what he had just revealed to him about his personal life. Agent Burney informed Alex about his little hush-hush with the pride of a strutting rooster-cock in the barnyard after the arrival of a fresh new purchase of seasonal hens. For the first time Alex remembered something about Agent Burney that he had forgotten. Alex noticed the country-ness in him. Perhaps it had moved more to the forefront because he was now retired or it could have been a part of his persona's new cover. Alex also remembered that one of Agent Burney's top attributes had been profiling and that body language reading had also made the top five on that list. Alex was extremely confident that if given the time and opportunity, which Agent Burney recently had a lot of on his hands, that he had probably improved his skills ten-fold. Growing flowers wasn't his only hobby, after retirement. Alex remembered what Slapp had informed him about how Mr. Burney came across slightly introverted and suspicious and at times, now that he had been selected to retire, perhaps paranoid would be a better choice of words. Slapp had also warned Alex to play it straight and not to leave out anything if the old man asked him any questions about him, or the mission. Slapp was relatively sure that he would ask Alex about him, and that was the part that none of us had figured out why, at this point. We were all reasonably sure that Miss Beasley and Tate knew more than they were telling the remainder of us, but the fact that Agent Burney had agreed to help us was all that mattered for now.

Alex stood perfectly motionless and waited for Agent Burney to give him an opening to ask a question or perhaps listen to another little secret that Alex obviously didn't give a damn about. Alex stared down at the steel grated walkway beneath them and took short breaths as he waited. Agent Burney hesitated then spoke again.

"So Alex, aren't you going to ask me why a middle-aged retired F.B.I. instructor is now stealing clippings from the National Botanical Gardens while spending more time here than the overseer of this place? Well, let me help you out with that. I love to see things grow and change. I needed something to do that would take a long time so I wouldn't lose my mind and where else can you study such a wide slice of the world's pie of people, without anyone questioning your motives. To be honest, I work here part-time as a group tour guide for the school kids." Alex started to smile a little as he was grateful that Agent Burney had let him off the hook, by answering his burning rhetorical question, before he was forced to answer it and possibly piss Burney off in the process. They both laughed out loud as Alex brought his eyes up, once again, to Burney's eye contact level.

"What I'm trying to tell you Alex is that you have no idea how much I wanted to get back into the field, just one last time. Alvin's phone call saved my life, so to speak. I realized a few years ago that I had made some grave mistakes during my existence about what was important. You see Alex; you have to plan for old age, just in case you reach that time in your years of living. You have to respect others and how they may feel about you. You should always consider those things when you make decisions that might become very hard to readjust later. Back when I was in the secret service. That was my life.

I think I became even more neurotic when my partner got killed. After that, I didn't want another sidekick and I started to take the most dangerous assignments that I could. I guess I felt guilty that my friend died and I lived. In the meantime, I've ruined two other lives that I'm aware of. That brings me to Alvin; tell me Alex, what you know about him?"

Alex laced his fingers together as he remembered that Slapp had warned him that Burney would ask about him. He wasn't sure he understood Agent Burney's area of questioning, so he started out with information that he knew that Agent Burney already had access to. Alex looked downward, took a few steps away from Burney and wrung his hands together as he decided where he wanted to start.

"Well, as you know Agent Burney, Alvin is my double when we are on the street. We are about the same size and he can be made-up to look like me or I him, with very little effort." Agent Burney stopped Alex.

"Please Alex, call me Dexter. This line of questioning is strictly personal." Alex resumed his response.

"He is a very good field agent and I trust him with my life. It has come down to that more than a few times. He's one of our very best profilers and he continues to improve." Burney interrupted Alex again.

"No Alex, you don't understand why I'm asking these questions. The things you're telling me, I can find out on my own. I still have a few friends at the Bureau that I can call in a favor, if I need to. I want to know the personal stuff that won't show up in any files. You know, the things that a friend would know and never tell anyone else about." Alex became anxious that Agent Burney would ask him to betray a friend's confidence. Alex turned quickly to face Agent Burney while he read Alex's angry body language. Alex was annoyed that this could possibly be a deal-breaker if he didn't answer the old man's questions, in the manner he desired.

"Wait, Alex I know this is confusing to you about why I want to know so much about Alvin's personal life. Perhaps if I told you a story that has never been told aloud before, then you will understand." They moved near the elevators and rode it down to the ground level. The two of them found a bench on the first level in the vicinity of these huge trees and large leaf plants that was still inside and out of the elements. The bench was located near and slightly beneath a set of stairs that lead to the second level of the atrium. The area provided them a bit of privacy as Agent Burney began the complicated tale. Alex watched him closely as Burney contemplated just how far back he wanted to start with Alvin's story, which mysteriously intertwined with his own. He gave Alex one quick glance and realized that from the beginning would probably be the safest place to start, if he wanted to remain healthy and physically out of harm's way. Alex had been like a big brother and father to Slapp and believed that Slap had endured more than his share of disappointments and personal pain. After all, Slapp had just learned that Mrs. Carrington was Miss Beasley and in fact his mother that he had thought for thirty-five years, was dead or believed that she didn't want him. He had fallen in love with a woman that in turn left him for another agent, and then before he could heal from that lost; she had gotten killed in a bombing. To add to that, three guys had beaten him near death to draw out his estranged mother from the witness protection program, for revenge. Now retired Agent Burney shows up with questions about Slapp, for his best friend to answer, without any concerns of the impact that they may cause to a long forged relationship. It was true that Agent Burney was reading Alex correctly, he was pissed off that retired Agent Burney appeared to have attached the answers about his friend Slapp as a contingency of whether or not he would help them. Alex was an impatient man at times with somewhat of a bad temper, to say the least. Agent Burney knew all of this because Alex had been one of his students, during his initial training. He also assumed that time and pressures of life and the age factor, over the years hadn't improved Alex's personality traits, in these areas. Agent Burney decided to start at the beginning, just in case his analysis of Alex's mood was accurate.

"Alex my man, it was almost thirty-seven years ago and I was still a freshman on the payroll of the agency. Alvin J. Madison was my partner's name. We met the first week of training and were inseparable from that day on. We had a lot in common and had similar interests. We were both single, and had made a break from our families for safety reasons of course. Back then; you had to be the best to continue to be promoted. We both had our eyes set on being the president's bodyguard one day. We thought it would be real cool to go to all those parties and meet all those people that we would never come into contact with otherwise. Chasing the scum of the earth wasn't glamorous enough for two country boys like ourselves. We were a good team and moved up the ranks pretty quickly, considering this was our first time in the city, or any metropolitan area for that matter, so to speak." Burney then looked down and away for a brief moment as if this part of the story had brought back painful memories. He thought that he had buried the pain long ago, or at least had come to grips with its impact. Alex didn't flinch because he was patiently waiting for the portion of the story that explained his line of questioning about his long time partner and friend, Slapp. Agent Burney swallowed hard before he continued. "The day that my partner, Agent Madison, was killed we were on stakeout at this strip club. I left my partner out front and went in the back to talk to our tip-off witness, with whom I had formed a romantic affair. She was supposed to come out and do her dance and signal us which guys had been talking about making a hit. Just before it was her turn to take the stage and right before I left her in the back, we heard shots coming from the main area of the club. She and I were in the back getting our signal codes synchronized when all hell broke loose out front. I pulled my weapon, ran out onto the stage and screamed my partner's name. The shooter had come in and just sprayed the entire place down with bullets. It was a dope-ring's middleman that had accused one of their mules [drug seller] of skimming off the top. The dancer had overheard the plan to kill this person. He was the one that had come into the club to shoot them first. Three other people were shot that night, but my partner was the only one that died, besides the gunman. I took him down with one shot, but I was still standing over him pulling the trigger on my empty weapon when the policemen arrived fifteen minutes later. I knew my partner was dead, the moment I screamed his name from backstage of the club." Burney eyes were wet with tears as he stared straight ahead into the heart of a large water-lily plant; just across from the two of them in this makeshift pond in the middle of the large lushly planted area. He then quickly looked around to see if anyone else had noticed his emotional moment of weakness. Now as he gazed back in Alex's direction, while wiping his tears to the side of his face with his thumb, he resumed his explanation. "I was forced to take a long desk job and that worked in my favor, because now that I had a girlfriend and a baby on the way. Sarah did testify and received the reward. She used the money for college and now she no longer had to work in that sleaze strip club. After she had the baby, we learned that she was a target of revenge, so we arranged to place her into the protective witness program. By this time, I had been given a complete clean bill of health by the shrink, and was allowed to return to full-duty status. This meant that I could return to the field. Everytime I was assigned a new partner I found something wrong with him or her. I became a very private person and I masked my guilt by taking dangerous assignments. I believed for a while I was hoping that I would be killed, so the pain of my guilt would go away. Then to complicate matters and increase my remorse factor, just before Sarah left for her first placement location, our son got sick and she had to leave him behind. I promised to take care of him and I kept that promise. I legally changed his name to Alvin J. Madison after my partner for safety reasons, now that he had to be separated from his mother. Another reason that I changed his name to my partners was because I felt so guilty for being backstage when he got shot, while leaving him alone. I knew the name change of my son would force me to remember him every single day." Burney turned to an angle to face Alex, as they both continued to sit on this short wooden bench, tucked underneath this canopy of giant leaves that would remind anyone of a tropical paradise vacation. All they needed was a couple of coconut drinks with the little umbrellas, and this would have been a perfect picture, minus the fact that they were both men. Now as Burney was about to make the final statement, that put everything into perspective, Alex was one step ahead of him because he had used the word 'our' earlier in his recount.

"So you see Alex, Alvin J. Madison Jr. is my son and Sarah Lynn Beasley is his mother. Where do we go from here? How can I tell him, after all these years? He must have asked me fifty times or more to tell him something about his father. I was more afraid to tell him after he became an adult. As a child, he just knew me as a friend of the old lady that worked at the orphanage where he grew up. The fact is that she is my mother and one of his biological grandmothers. To Alvin, she probably just appears as an old Caucasian woman that worked at the orphanage where he grew up. I'm sure that he never put the two together, because I took on my father hue." Agent Burney paused again while taking in full breaths, as if he was waiting for all of this to soak into Alex's consciousness. Alex was so relieved that he wasn't about to give Slapp's personal history to a non-family member or an outsider. Agent Burney went on with his story.

"Sarah was moved the second time to Hong Kong and I've been flying out there twice a year to visit her for the last twenty five years. During her second placement, I believe that was when she met Agent Thaddeus Romano. He wouldn't have remembered her, because she still had some of her bandages on from her reconstruction surgery. She has also been traveling back here, twice a year to be with me and get a closer look at Alvin. We both have hundreds, if not thousands of photos of him. I guess you could call us stalkers." Agent Burney laughed briefly as he gave their surroundings a quick safety glance. "You wouldn't believe the photograph equipment that we own, between the two of us. We were able to catch all the highlighted events of Alvin's life. A few times, he looked directly at us, but never did put it together. I knew he recognized me from the academy training, but with Sarah taking the facial reconstruction option and he being so young when she had to leave him, there is no way he would remember. When he graduated from training, he rode down on the elevator with her, without knowing. I can't tell you what I had to do to pull that off. Anyway, that's my story."

Agent Burney and Alex met two more times to go over the details and possibly talk about Slapp. Alex was now thoroughly convinced that Agent Burney was onboard with the plans a hundred percent. Alex was also apprehensive about his reactions when they discovered what they now believed to be fact; that the dead man's son had tried to draw out Miss Beasley [Sarah Lynn] by having Slapp beaten up. Alex's other notions had very much been on target. It seemed that Tate knew more about the connections and Slapp's family history than he was willing to share with the remainder of the group. At this point, Alex didn't have the time to tap into the archives for the full story. Everything was happening too fast.

Mr. Dexter started his three part-time positions, bartender jobs, about two weeks after he had applied. It was as though time was repeating itself. Thirty-seven years ago someone had overheard a conversation in a club. This time we were hoping that life was replicating itself and possibly be able to indirectly correct what had gone wrong before.

Agent Burney rotated between the three locations. Each location was only a few hour gigs, to fill-in when the regular bartender's assistant didn't show. Nevertheless, this allowed retired Agent Burney to stakeout three known locations at once and this made him feel like he was back in the field, like in the old days.

Father Caleb and Bruce continued to cover the office at the old warehouse that the unit had rented, as their office for their side business. It was many things in one. It served as a hideout when the pursuit of a perk made it to dangerous to go home. There was a chapel on one floor and Father was running a soup kitchen out of one of its wings, partially as a cover to all the other illegal activities. The soup kitchen for the homeless was still running smoothly. The website charities were holding their own. There was only one thing remaining for the unit to do and that was to round-up the men responsible for the bombing of the Clinton Satellite office, wait for the dust to settle and then bring everyone home. However, this return from exile could take another year or so. When you are dealing with this type of dangerous situation, you never want to rush things.

Alex and Tate had split-up for a few days, while Tate flew out to do another secret visit to his girlfriend's daughter in college. He wanted to tell her how the relationship was progressing and that he had promised to marry her mother, Gayle, when all of this was finished. His second stop, on the West Coast, was to check on Jerome and to establish if he had been cleared of all misconduct and misuse-of-position charges that had remained in a pending mode, until the long investigation was completed. I returned to Hong Kong after three weeks. As I said before, my father, Uncle Oscar, agreed to stay on and help my mother to settle things. I arrived at the airport. Slapp and Max were waiting curbside to pick me up. I exited through the double automatic sliding glass doors of the Hong Kong airport and there stood Slapp leaning up against the driver's door in his uniform and with his chauffeur's cap pulled low over his brow. I heard him instruct his assistant.

"Max, open the rear passenger's door and stand still and quiet, just like we rehearsed." Slapp had his legs crossed at the ankles and his arms folded over his chest. He reminded me of a bodyguard on a cigarette break, when and only when his partner had taken over. Then I looked and saw Max standing tall motionless next to the rear door of the limo, looking straight ahead and away from my approaching direction, as he held the door widely open. I stopped about thirty feet from the car and dropped all of my bags to free up my arms to hug him as I instantly began to cry. He was so handsome; and even though it had only been three weeks or so, I could have sworn that he had grown, just a little. Slapp stood up quickly and ran over to pick up all my bags and my purse as I screamed Max's name. "Maximilian!!!" He turned to look in my direction as his face exploded with happiness and in surprise that it was I that he and his Uncle Slapp were scheduled to pickup. The only thing that I could gather, from his reaction, was that no one had informed him that I was due to return. He started to run towards me, while crying as well.

"Auntie Ma," he screamed as he came charging in my direction. He leaped into my arms and held me tightly as if he had just awakened from a bad dream. I kissed the side of his face and neck as he held on for dear life and cried. I realized then that Alex and I had performed poorly as new parents, while explaining to him about what was going on before we left. I also became aware that all the people that usually took care of him, except for his Uncle Slapp, had all departed at the same time. I promised myself that I would never allow that to happen to him again. Max and I climbed into the backseat as we both tried to pull ourselves together. I imagine both of us were surprised at how our emotions had taken on a personality of their own. In the backseat of the limo, we dried our faces and laughed through the tears as Slapp loaded my luggage into the trunk and tipped the luggage-cart man. He jumped in the driver's seat quickly as he passed my purse over the front seat. He gave Max a quick glance and smiled as he spoke to him in jest.

"Hey big guy, I guess you forgot all about your training as a chauffeur, once you saw that the pickup was your mother.

I thought I told you that you are to remain invisible and you can't get personally or emotionally involved with the passengers. We are only here to provide a service to the client, not any emotional stimulation in the form of hugs and kisses." Max was smiling the entire time, because he was finally getting a handle on his Uncle Slapp's bizarre sense of humor.

He responded quickly, "But Uncle Slapp this was different. It was my mama coming back home." Slapp adjusted the rear-view mirror so he could see both of us as he drove.

"You want to know the truth Sport," as he hesitated and let out a grin? "Can you keep a secret? I even shed a tear or two when I saw you running towards Miss Helen as she dropped all her bags to pick you up into her arms. It was just like a scene from one of those classic girly tear-jerking movies. You know the ones that come on late at night when it's to late for anyone, except perhaps God, to still be up. You know Max, you can't mention a word of this to your father or Uncle Tate, because they will never let me live this down."

Max threw up his thumbs-up-sign gesture as a symbol that he could keep a secret and that he wouldn't whisper a word. I was totally convinced that if Slapp and Max's mother, Stacey, would have made a successful run, at their relationship, Slapp would have made an impressive step-father. "Hello Lady Thore," said Slapp finally. "How was your trip? I'm sorry to hear about your dad. How is your mother holding up?" No one had called me Lady Thore in a long time. Max wrinkled his brow, because I'm sure that he hadn't heard anyone address me with that title in a very long time or could remembered if anyone had ever done before, in his presence.

"Hello Slapp, the trip was okay. My father, Uncle Oscar stayed on to help my foster-mother settle things. I think that Max and I will stay at the resort, in my father's room until Alex or Tate returns. I know that you have to stay close to the embassy. So tell me, how is it coming along between you and your mother, Mrs. Carrington?" Slapp glanced at me in the mirror as if he hadn't expected me to question him about this so soon after my arrival. He licked and then chewed his bottom lip and stalled for a moment before he answered.

"Well," he responded with a pause. "We haven't shot each other yet; you do realize that the old girl carries a gun in her boot everyday." Slapp answered as he chewed his bottom lip, again. "I was forced to sleep in the room with her and Max the first night when you all left for the States because Gayle was with Tate, and the watchman's bunkroom was too dusty to occupy. I do believe now that she is my mother. I just wish I could remember something so I can have some type of connection to her. I guess me remaining infuriated as hell that she didn't tell me the moment I arrived, months ago, isn't helping my memory either.

"Well Slapp", I said after a brief hesitation. "I heard you were pretty young and sick at the time your mother had to leave you. I'm sure that some memories are locked in the back of your mind and that if you continue to spend time with her, something will come back to you when you least expect. I say, just give her a chance. Her life was just as hard without you as yours was without her." He smiled just a little as we drove towards the resort. Then I turned to Max. "Max, are you staying with me or are you going back to the embassy?" Max looked into the reflection mirror into Slapp's glance before he answered.

"Well you know that I have been sleeping in the bunkroom with Uncle Slapp, when he comes in early enough," replied Max. "If he's not afraid to sleep in that big room alone, then I can move back to the resort tomorrow. I didn't know you were coming Ma, so all of my school backpack and clothes are at the embassy." Slapp titled his head downward quickly so Max wouldn't see him laugh at him. He responded to Max's inquiry.

"I'm sure that I will be fine Max, and if I get scared I will sleep in the room with Nana Carrington." Max looked with a surprise stare.

"Uncle Slapp, did she tell you that it would be alright to call her Nana Carrington too," replied Max with a puzzled look on his face? Slapp and I both laughed as Max waited for an explanation.

"No little buddy, she is my real mother." The car went silent as Slapp spoke those words out loudly, probably for the first time in his life.

Chapter Two

Milani's Dream Team

The date finally arrived for the ambassador and the local officials to have a meeting about the legal custody of Milani, who was the daughter of Alex's deceased twin brother, Austin, and my former husband. The meeting was held in the conference room on the second floor of the American Embassy, Hong Kong Branch. In attendance for this meeting was the American Ambassador, Miss Beasley whose name had been changed to Mrs. Carrington when she entered the witness protection program, Miss Gayle, a local attorney, the Chief of Police and me. When the great-grandmother and great-aunt initially had arrived, the great-grandmother appeared very frail, but proved to be strong enough and was willing to do what was best for the child. The great-aunt, on the other hand, wanted whatever was going to give her the largest financial reward for the child's release into our custody. These facts were apparent to everyone in the room, no matter what language you favored or spoke. Miss Beasley was our translator and I'm sure the Chief of Police was checking her every translated word. I was informed later that he and the attorney each spoke at least three dialects themselves. The Chinese Ambassador had picked this team to represent him. Something had come up and he was unable to attend the meeting. He didn't want to cancel the engagement because he was unaware of how long we would be in the country. Plus he had no idea that we were using his country as an exiled location. I'm sure that these facts would have had strong barring on the proceedings that was about to take place, if all parties had been privileged to this information. Just as we were about to begin, the Chief of Police stood up and went over to the door to introduce his recorder to the board. His recorder was none other than the same lady that had sat in on the interview when Alex was applying for the consulting position, with the Hong Kong Police Department. The attorney informed us that our statements, due to their serious nature, would be considered declarations under oath and would be recorded as such, for public availability. Since I was representing the person who had activated the petition, I spoke first. "My name is Helen Jones and I was married to the child's deceased father, shortly after the child was born. I am now married to the brother of the deceased father of the child, who is a joint requesting petitioner of custody for the child in question." The recorder started to record my words as Mrs. Beasley turned to the great-grandmother and great-aunt to translate my words in their language. The great-grandmother nodded her head slowly, up and down once or twice, as she stared at me with the glance of understanding. In spite of the language barrier, I felt that the two of us had a heart-to-heart understanding. The great-aunt didn't seem as agreeable as her demeanor shifted to one of disappointment. The child had been left in the care of the great-grandmother. The grandparents had been injured during the same disaster as the mother in Thailand and had no interest in fighting to keep the half-breed child in their family. The great-grandmother had also kept this correspondence of fact that she had received from her daughter and son-in-law. Shortly after that, Milani's grandparents had both succumb to the harsh conditions that had been created by the tsunami that had struck Thailand, December 25, 2004. Their letters also reflected that they had been willing to give the child every opportunity, for a better life than the one they could provide. The next to speak was Miss Gayle. She informed the counsel that the great-grandmother had contacted the American Embassy and requested that we help locate the father after the mother had been killed by the tsunami that struck Thailand. The attorney stopped the proceedings and requested that all supporting documents be turned over to him at his time. The Chief of Police pulled some records from a folder that confirmed that the mother had flown to Thailand, during that time with a roundtrip ticket and had never returned. He also had a list of names of people that had been killed in the tsunami, from Hong Kong and her name was in fact on the list. Her parents had made the identification of the remains, before they had died.

I took this opportunity to present Austin's death certificate and our marriage licenses to be added into evidence. The great-grandmother slowly reached into her bag, as the tears started to stream down her face, and pulled out a hand full of letters that had been returned by the mail service to her granddaughter, that had never reached Austin in the United States. He knew nothing of the daughter that he had fathered. Austin had moved shortly after he returned from his Hong Kong conference trip, from California to Baltimore, Maryland where he had met me only a few months later. I then noticed the Chief of Police leaned over and whispered to the recorder who sat to his left and slightly behind him. I don't think he recognized me at first. The recorder confirmed that it was I with one single node of her head, while looking down and away from my direction. The Police Chief seemed to become very agitated as he figured out that Alex had more than likely been using his department's data bank to find these ladies and the lost child of his deceased brother. Gayle and I both noticed his disturbed body language and waited for him to find some reason to stop the procedures without tipping off the attorney and the rest of the panel. That very instance, his police-band radio beeped once very quietly. He sprang to his feet and bowed once to excuse himself as he raced for the door to take the counterfeit emergency call. The attorney stopped all statements as he used this time to go over the papers that had been entered into the records as evidence. "Please, everyone," stated the attorney. "We will now take a twenty minute recess, from these proceedings or until we have ascertained if the Chief of Police will be able to rejoin us at this time." Gayle and I looked at each other again and then towards the recorder as she looked away in an attempt to hide the fact that she had been a part of the Chief of Police's deceptive plan. Everyone began to take advantage of the large assortment of food that had been provided by the embassy's cafeteria staff. Gayle reached over and added a few extra selections of fruit to the great-grandmother's large bag that she was carrying, for later. She knew that the level of their poverty didn't allow them fresh fruit every day. A few minutes later, the Chief of Police returned with his story of why he had to leave. Something was happening in the city, which required his personal attention. Then he stepped back into the hallway to make another call. The attorney adjourned the panel and set a new date, for two months away. The American Ambassador was the first to leave the room.

"Please forgive me," said the attorney. "The Chief of Police has been called away suddenly. I believe I have enough paperwork to look into this matter more thoroughly. I will search the law books, pertaining to similar situations and present my finding to all appropriate parties. I will return all original documents to their owners, after I have copied them for the permanent file." Gayle sprang to her feet to challenge the attorney.

"Sir, I'm sorry, but no original American documents are allowed to leave the American Embassy without the approval of the Ambassador. What I can do for you, since he and the proper request forms are not available, is make copies of all the paperwork. Then you can witness that it is a true copy of the original and Miss Beasley can stamp it on behalf of the ambassador, to authenticate each document." The Asian attorney seemed to be a little put off by the aggressive nature of Gayle's tone, but soon realized that he didn't have the authority to dispute her position on the matter. After deep consideration, he agreed with a single nod of the head and a very shallow bow forward of the body. He retrieved all the letters, the police department's death list, my marriage license to Austin and Austin's death certificate from his briefcase and handed them all to Miss Beasley. She took them over to the copy machine and copied everything. Then she opened the letters one by one and spread then open and allowed them to pass through the copier. She stamped each item carefully in its margin and placed them on the large conference table for them to be reviewed and signed.

After all the signatures were collected on the papers, Miss Beasley stamped them with an American Embassy's seal. When the Chief of Police returned into the room, the second time, he had no idea what had taken place, while he had been in the hallway. The recorder updated him while the attorney dismissed the panel. I was pretty sure we were winning, by the look of disgust on the faces of the great-aunt and the Chief of Police. The great-grandmother was on our side and had proven this by turning over the unopened returned letters that her granddaughter had written to Austin, right after Milani was born. The Chief of Police was partially aware of Alex's monetary worth or of his pretense of wealth and I believe that he thought that Alex should pay dearly to take his niece out of the country, while being granted full custody. The aunt shared in his belief wholeheartedly and it showed outwardly by her greed facial expression.

The next few weeks ran like clockwork. One month later my father, Uncle Oscar, returned and provided me with a detailed update of how my foster-mother was recovering from my foster-dad's death. Slapp and his mother's relationship continued to improve as they spent more time together. Gayle spent a few nights at the resort with Max and I before my father returned, just for a change of pace and some girl talk.

A month after my father, Uncle Oscar, returned, Tate arrived and informed us that the three men had been caught. The son of the dead prisoner, that Miss Beasley had testified against, thirty plus years earlier; had been killed during a shootout with authorities. I was afraid to ask what authorities he might be referring to. The other two had been given twenty years each, after they had agreed to name the men responsible for the bombing, which had taken place in Clinton, Maryland less that a day before Alex was shot and Slapp had gone missing. It seems that they had mistaken Stacey's new boyfriend Thomas for Slapp and was shocked to see Slapp so far away on the other coast, only a day a so later. So they attacked him after they shot Alex. We were all relieved to know that these two incidents had nothing to do with the 'My Brother's Keeper' high-stakes bounty hunting service that the twelve of them had started ten years prior. The side business had now been dissolved as per contract between them and the bureau. Now all we had to do was to wait until all the dust had settled and see if we would be able to take Milani home to America with us.

Chapter Three

Tate's Passionate Return

The night that Tate arrived back on the islands of Hong Kong, it was very rainy and wet. It was the early fall of the year and the tourist season had dropped off a little, due to the weather. Tate had flown in around midnight and headed straight to the American Embassy to see Gayle. He wanted to surprise her, but felt that it might be impossible with Mr. Charlie making rounds and there was no telling where little Max had decided to sleep that night. It was a Friday night and on the weekends Maximilian had more freedom than through the week. As Tate retrieved his luggage from the airport's carrousel, he began to pray that Mr. Pauling had decided to work the weekend, that way he wouldn't have any problem getting into the embassy's gate without a third-degree of questioning. He had started to believe that Mr. Pauling had discovered who he and Slapp really were by all the freedoms that he had allowed both of them to enjoy, whenever he was on duty. It could have been something that he had overheard, during a conversation from the ambassador. Tate wasn't sure just what had caused Mr.

Pauling to grant him more access and had never stopped to question his reasoning—as it was customary and required for him to do.

Tate was now riding in a V.I.P. city company cab headed for the American Embassy's front entrance. He continued to play in his head, a possible scenario that would take place if Mr. Charlie and he had to cross paths this late at night. Tate was aware how seriously Mr. Charlie took his duties as the American Embassy's inside night roving patrol. He had witnessed how stern Charlie could be and how agitated he could become if he wasn't informed prior to an unscheduled arrival of anyone after the embassy's normal business hours. This applied to staff as well, in spite of the fact that they all had to be screened meticulously, before employment was even considered. The truth of the matter was that Mr. Charlie had been there for so long until he viewed the embassy as his own house. This was evident by the way he took each of his assignments as if it had a life-or-death attachment. This was very commendable, but had proven to be a pain in the ass for some of his fellow co-workers. Mr. Charlie had started out as a limo driver and then had been moved to night roving guard, when his eyes became too weak to see at night. Tate and Slapp never could figure out who had signed the paperwork for, who they referred to as, 'the blind bastard' to carry a weapon. Since they were new to the motor pool and had joined the security team, only as a granted temporary courtesy of the Ambassador, they had decided to back away from relieving Mr. Charlie of his weapons. However, they were able to implement a safety requirement that everyone that carried a weapon, on the

American Embassy's compound would be required to re-qualify every four months at a firing-range. Due to the fact that Mr. Charlie worked most nights, he had slipped through the cracks the last two times that the re-qualifying schedule had been posted. When the ambassador signed off on the archived rule, which subsequently reinstated it, he had forgotten all about Mr. Charlie's eyesight dilemma and was totally unaware that the agents where trying to trip-him-up, by using the power of the pen against Mr. Charlie. They felt that Mr. Charlie needed to be taken down a peg or two. He seemed to wear and use a portion of the ambassador's power at times, which in turn, sometimes, created a hostile working environment for a segment of the local contracted staff. Slapp was surprised that his mother didn't have a problem with the new rule and was usually the first person to bring back her results, even though she carried her weapon for a personal nature and not as part of her assignment at the American Embassy, as its language translator. All of this was running across Tate's mind, as he smiled to himself, while in the backseat of the taxi. When Tate arrived, there he immediately noticed Mr. Pauling standing tall and relaxed with his hand resting carefully on the handle of his sidearm. When Mr. Pauling noticed that it was Tate, he reached for his gate-key as Tate unloaded his luggage from the cab. Tate quickly paid the cab and walked inside the gate as Mr. Pauling locked the gate behind them. Mr. Pauling spoke first. "Hello Mr. Romano, welcome back. This was a long trip for you. I though at first that you had been reassigned somewhere else; then I noticed that your name was still on the board." Tate smiled briefly as he answered; while wondered just how much Mr. Pauling knew about him.

"Good evening sir, and how have you been?" replied Tate. "Yes that was a long trip, but a successful one if you will allow me to brag a little." Tate put his bags down on the top step of the front door landing as he turned to face Mr. Pauling who had followed him and was now standing on the same level. Tate continued the security process out of respect for the man and the sensitive nature of the position that he held. There were cameras everywhere and Tate wanted to support some of the very safety precautions that he had implemented, only months before. The new ruling stated that all bags are to be hand-searched plus x-rayed and at least two security guards shall be present at the gate when anyone arrives after normal business hours. Well, I'm sure that this midnight arrivals qualified and fell within the realm of the only recently adjusted security features. The only areas that were really new-and-improved was that now the staff could come in early and leave a little later, if they had obtained prior approval from security. Tate hesitated with a seemingly stressful facade as he asked his next question.

"Mr. Pauling, who did you request from the surveillance booth to check my bags," inquired Tate as he cringed at the thought that it might be Mr. Charlie? Mr. Pauling laughed because he knew precisely why Tate had asked that question. Tate removed his shades and looked up at a near-by camera monitor in hope that someone from the security booth had witness his return. He was also praying that whoever, would rush down to save him from a shakedown by Mr. Charlie. After that possible upsetting experience, Tate knew that there was no way he would be able to sneak into Gayle's quarters to surprise her, like he had planned during his returning flight. After Mr. Pauling had finished being amused, at Tate's expense, by hesitating to answer up quickly, he replied.

"I couldn't turn Mr. Charlie loose on you this late at night," said Mr. Pauling. "I called one of the guys from the security booth to come down and help me. Now all we have to do is hope Mr. Charlie didn't hear the gate's loud squeak when I opened it to let you in. You know that he is as blind as a bat, but he can hear a rat piss on a cotton ball, when he wants or has a mind to. I don't understand how the man sleeps," continued Mr. Pauling as he chuckled again while they waited. At that moment, a security man came into view as he walked swiftly towards Tate and Mr. Pauling. He spoke excitedly to both of them as he turned on the x-ray machine's motion belt. Tate placed two large bags on the moving counter. He then placed both of his weapons and three ammunition clips for each, in the basket that Mr. Pauling held in his hands, in front of him. Tate walked through the check arch security x-ray monitor and waited for his bags to emerge out the other side. The young man, who had been called down from the booth, wasn't sure if this was a test for him, so he nervously checked Tate's bags on the x-ray viewer very carefully. He saw the weapons that Tate was carrying and he knew they weren't standard issue; at least not for a rent-a-cop like himself. The dark blackout shades that Tate always wore didn't help either—when it came to putting his mind at ease. He had been in the room with Tate on several occasions, but since he was so junior on the job, no one had bothered to introduce him to Tate or Slapp directly. This was his limited mind-set or need-to-know level, but little did he know that Slapp and Tate knew more about him than his own mother. They had performed a full sweep on everyone on staff for their own exiled safety, more than for the ambassador's. Tate stood still and seemingly stared in the junior man's direction as the young security man glanced from Tate to Mr. Pauling and then back to the x-ray monitoring screen, as Mr. Pauling and Tate proceeded to engage in small talk, to fill in the time. The young security man was nervous to say the least; yet petrified would probably be a better word to use to describe his emotions. Tate had very unusual eyes that were piercing at times and some found them unnerving, until you got to know him better. This was probably one reason that they were almost always covered and the fact that he was a very private person and his eye-color was unusual for his hue. Mr. Pauling walked through the check arch a few seconds after Tate, distracted and without thinking apparently—when the arch sounded a quick alarm because of the weapon he was wearing and carrying in his hand. That mistake would have been fine except now everyone knew that Mr. Charlie would be coming around the corner at any second, if he were close enough to hear the alarm.

"Oh crap," said Mr. Pauling as he realized what he had done. Now Tate was laughing at Mr. Pauling as he stood waiting for someone to give his bags a quick hand-check. The young security guy turned off the belt and started to open Tate's bags. Mr. Pauling gave him back his weapons as Tate reattached them onto his body in their respective locations. The young security man turned to leave as Tate and Mr. Pauling prolonged their light informative conversation.

"Mr. Pauling, do you know if Mrs. Livingston is in-house tonight?" inquired Tate. Mr. Pauling answered quickly as he gave Tate his phone for him to check, to make sure.

"I believe she is in-house, here call her if you like." Mr. Pauling dialed in Gayle's berthing room number and handed the phone to Tate. He quickly walked away to give Tate a little impossible privacy, because every word echoed off the marble walls and floor, of the corridor where they both were now standing. Gayle picked up the phone on the second ring.

"Hello baby it's me," said Tate in that low sexy voice. Then he turned quickly and raised his eyes to see if Mr. Pauling was close enough to hear him address Gayle so affectionately. Mr. Pauling pretended that he didn't hear as he started the second verse of a little tune that he had now begun to whistle quietly to himself. In the room, Gayle became very excited that Tate was now calling and had possibly returned. "Where are you Tate, is everything alright?"

"Slow it down Paper Doll, everything is fine. I'm calling you from Mr. Pauling's phone at the front gate. I will be up in a moment." Tate hung up and walked towards Mr. Pauling to return his phone.

"Hey Mr. Pauling, thank you Sir for letting me use your phone."

"No Problem Mr. Romano, I'll see you next week." He took the phone from Tate's hand and attached it back to his belt. Tate walked away a few steps as Mr. Pauling headed in the other direction, back to his guardsmen's position, by the front iron-gate, in the little booth. Tate turned once more to thank Mr. Pauling again before getting on the elevator.

"Thanks again Mr. Pauling," said Tate.

"No problem Mr. Romano," replied Mr. Pauling as he gave him a thumbs-up sign. "Just go upstairs and handle your business." He smiled, just as the elevator doors close. Tate thought to himself that perhaps his and Gayle's relationship wasn't as secret as they had hoped. Now Tate's thoughts moved back to Mr. Charlie. He knew that Mr. Charlie had witnessed the sounds of some portion of his arrival. If he hadn't heard the gate, or observe the other watchman leave his post from the security viewing room, surely he had heard the alarm that Mr. Pauling had accidentally set off when he walked through the arch with his gun on while holding Tate's two weapons in a basket. There was only one deduction to draw from all of these facts and that was that Mr. Charlie had entered the surveillance booth the moment that the other young officer had come down to help Mr. Pauling and had watched the entire procedure over the monitors. This meant that he would now be shifting to the in-house lodging floor to observe where Tate was headed. Tate proceeded to the duty bunkroom where he found Slapp, in what appeared to be a snoring comma. He put his bags down and opened the one with his shaving kit and removed his body-wash and clippers. He trimmed his beard and then took a long steamy shower. He heard footsteps outside the door as he noticed something that caused a shadow to flicker underneath the door that connected the bunkroom to the hallway. Tate was positive that it was Mr. Charlie and he was also certain that Slapp was only pretending to be asleep. He strolled over to the bunkroom's door and locked it as he spoke to Slapp calmly.

"Hello Slapp, how has things been going? I know you probably haven't had a day off since I left. I promise to make it up to you."

"What's going on my brother," replied Slapp? "I heard when you called Gayle a few moments ago, next door. I think I heard her unlock the secret pass-through door right here between the two rooms. You know if you go out into the hall, to use her main room door access, Mr. Charlie will tie you up for at least twenty minutes or more, with his security crap. First he's going to refresh your memory on what is proper protocol, and the new rules about wondering around the embassy, after normal working hours, without his prior notification. Then he's going to remind you that it was you who implemented some of these upgrades to the house security plan, and that you should be setting a good example for the rest of us." Slapp was laughing the entire time while telling Tate this as Tate stood by the door in the dark; while he listened to Mr. Charlie's footsteps fade away down the hall. Tate was now wearing a pair of silk boxers and a robe. He quickly shoved his feet into his slippers as he gave his upper-body a one-shot spray of cologne. Slapp had now rolled to his side as he continued to watch Tate, by the dim light shinning through the crack of the bathroom door, as Tate continued to prepare himself for his late-night return-home rendezvous with his lady. Slapp just couldn't allow this opportunity to pass without antagonizing Tate about what he was planning. Tate was his senior in age and was from a different branch of special service. He knew Tate was a private man, with a very secretive personal life, but with Slapp, no one or nothing was off limits to his witty ridiculing sense of humor. Tate's personality also contained a peculiar wit. However, with his serious nature being the driving force, it sometimes revealed itself with a painful-truth undertone, as Slapp was about to experience, firsthand. "Damn Tate, you have to do all of that prep-work just to go next door to see a lady that you are already sexually involved with?" Tate laughed lightly as he tidied up the area and moved his luggage from the walking path of the room.

"I'm sorry Slapp, but I can't take any tips from you on how to keep a woman. And beside that, you have been guarding ass for the last two months that you don't even have access to." Slapp knew that Tate had punched him below the belt with his response. He also realized exactly what and whom Tate was referring to, in the past when Stacey had left him for Thomas. Now in the present, Slapp had been protecting Gayle, which was now Tate's own woman and that covered the 'ass' portion of Tate's statement, in which he was rudely highlighting.

"Screw you for that Tate; that's a low blow. There is no reason for you to be so cold and disrespectful to my feelings."

Tate replied instantly as he quickened his pace to exit the room from Slapp's immature jesting. "You know better than to speak out loudly about my personal affairs. Next time just make sure your house is in order, before you do; fair enough?" Slapp's pride had been bruised, so he didn't respond to Tate's last comment. Tate moved toward the secret wall-panel that connected the bunkroom to Gayle's sleeping quarters next door. Slapp gave him a finally tip, as Tate tapped faintly on the shifting door.

"Hey big guy," said Slapp. "Don't forget to lock the bathroom door between Gayle's room and Mrs. Carrington's room. I believe Max is in the house and you know how he can spoil a well-organized plan. He has ears like Mr. Charlie, if he hears any noise coming from Gayle's room, he will cut through the bathroom and knock on that door, which opens up into Gayle's room. I'll see you two tomorrow. Welcome back big guy, now I can get some deep sleep, that's if you and Gayle can keep the pleasure-sounds down to a respectable muffle. Just try not to give Mr. Charlie a reason to kick Gayle's door in and draw his weapon. The blind bastard is likely to shoot a couple of us, for no good reason, by the time we turn on a light bright enough for him to recognize us." They both laughed as Tate pushed against the section of the wall that moved inward. He found Gayle on the other side sitting up in bed with a wet face, from tears of joy, to see him. She leaped into his arms and Tate closed the panel of wall behind him and waited to hear it click back into its secretive place. Gayle was now making familiar sounds as she cried. She was kneeling on the bed as Tate stood on the floor beside it, while hugging her and kissing her face, cheeks, mouth, and neck. The passion instantly returned as he held her and rubbed her body calmly, while he waited for her to get control of her emotions. He brushed her uncontrollable wavy cotton candy like hair away from her face with both hands as he pulled away to take a good look at her for the first time by the dimly lit lamp placed next to the bed. He spoke easy in a whisper, as he remembered Slapp's warning, as it pertained to Max.

"Hey babe, how have you been? Wait, let me lock this door before a little unexpected visitor surprises us while we are in the act of pleasuring ourselves." He pulled away slowly from Gayle's stimulating clutches and walked over and listened for a few seconds before he turned the deadbolt lock on the door. Then he checked the lock on the door that opened into the corridor, as he lowered the temperature on the thermostat control. Gayle slid under the covers as she watched him. Then he walked back over to the bed to climb in with her.

"Tate, what are you doing?" asked Gayle. Tate smiled as he answered the wrong question, yet the one he understood her to be soliciting an answer for.

"I'm locking the doors so we can have a little privacy and I'm turning down the heat, because baby I'm all the heat you are going to need for the next few hours." Tate smiled, while filled with pride and believing that he had covered all the area of comfort for the two of them. Gayle looked on shockingly as he placed his gun on the nightstand, slid under the covers and moved closer to her.

"Tate you know security doesn't allow us to have over-night opposite sex visitors in the embassy's berthing quarters," whispered Gayle with a touch of panic in her voice.

"What about baby Max spending the night with Nana Carrington, the baby-sitter? That breaks that rule right there." They both paused as Gayle searched for another response to support her view on the matter. Tate spoke again, "Gayle, you have got to be joking right?" replied Tate in a lighthearted tone. "Relax baby, I am security, plus I got an okay from your bodyguard next door, and Mr. Pauling let me in the house without question," said Tate as he smirked in disbelief to Gayle's reaction and in a jesting manner. He now was laying flat on his back with his arms and robe wide open, waiting for Gayle to crawl into her favorite spot, which was on top of him, faced down. She was moving slowly towards him as she remembered that the next day was Saturday and only the essential staff would be around; one full staff of security, two cooks and two drivers from the motor pool. She leaned in over Tate for the first serious kiss since his arrival. He closed his arms around Gayle as he rolled her to her back while shifting himself partially on top. Gayle made a squeal noise of surprise, as she and Tate began to engage in frisky foreplay. The walls were much too thin for this type of activity, yet there they were testing an already proven theory. They were sure that Mrs. Beasley had taken her hearing aid out for the night and Slapp knew what would be going on next door to him. The only people they had to be concerned about was little Max, when he got up to go to the bathroom and that meddlesome Mr. Charlie, as he made rounds and would pass right by the door. Tate tried to cover-up her sounds with his mouth, as he applied some deep passionate kisses. Just about that time Slapp tapped on the wall just above their heads from the adjacent room. Judging from Tate's response, the tapping from

Slapp must have been in code, or had triggered a response from some distant-past training. Tate instantly broke off his seductive kiss; and then quickly slapped his hand over Gayle's mouth as he whispered to her.

"Shhhhhh Gayle, be quiet for a moment. Slapp is trying to tell us something." Tate listened intensely as Gayle tried to take in a full breath with Tate's hand clinched tightly over her mouth, as it almost closed off one of her nostrils as well. She squirmed a little, as Tate shifted his hand just a bit, so Gayle could take in a full breath. He had, no doubt, over-reacted to Slapp's thumping, because Slapp was only trying to warn Tate that Mr. Charlie was coming up the back-stairs and was headed in their direction. He stopped at the bunkroom's door first and knocked lightly. Slapp spring to his feet abruptly, as he checked his weapons status. He was wearing a gun and holster across his chest with only his maxi length robe on top. He also wore a pair of boxer shorts and socks with nonskid ribbed bottoms. His back-up weapon was attached to his right leg, just above his ankle, in a velcro-secured holster. He cracked the door a little as he pretended to have been asleep, as he rubbed his eyes while behaving as if the bright light from the hall was irritating to them.

"Yea Mr. Charlie, what can I do for you," said Slapp in a dry intolerant tone, as he leaned forward and up against the doorframe of the door. Mr. Charlie noticed his large gun strapped to his chest and the one that was attached to his right leg, in its own smaller holster. Slapp stood with his right leg stretched in front of the other, almost outside the door, as Mr.

Charlie stuttered while searching for appropriate words to explain himself. Mr. Charlie spoke nervously as he attempted to clarify why he had disturbed Slapp, in the middle of the night. The truth of the matter was that Slapp had only arrived an hour before Tate, from his final night's run.

"I'm sorry to bother you sir, but I heard a noise when I was coming up the back-stairs. I saw Mr. Romano come in about an hour ago. Is he in there with you?" asked Mr. Charlie. Then he tried to peep over Slapp's shoulder and through the narrow opening in the door that Slapp was protecting suspiciously, which was apparent by his stance.

"Yea, Tate did come in about an hour ago. Perhaps you heard us talking. I think he's in the back somewhere, getting out of the shower now. I'll tell you what I will do Mr. Charlie, since I'm not going to be able to go back to sleep anyway, I'll sit out here in the hallway for the rest of your watch; that way you can catch an earlier train home. I believe they run less frequently on the weekends." Slapp moved completely out into the hallway, as he continued to hide the fact that Tate was next door and not in the duty bunkroom with him, as he had stated. He pulled the door behind him as Mr. Charlie contemplated taking Slapp up on his appealing proposal. It had been a very wet and damp night. He knew the trains would be packed and no one would be walking, not even a few blocks, in this weather. In addition to the weather factor, Friday, Saturday and Sunday night were all high revenue times for the night markets. Hong Kong night-market shopping had given a whole new meaning to the phrase Kmart-blue-light-special. No other location came close to the merchandise that is sold nightly in this city. This is due partly to all the items available in a very small place, the prices, and the fact that bargaining is encouraged and respected. Slapp slithered away from the closed door of the bunkroom and slumped down in the chair right next to Gayle's door, as Mr. Charlie finally agreed to accept his offer.

"Well thank you Mr. Alvin, I will make one more full round and then I will go downstairs and start my log checkout early." Mr. Charlie continued his rounds on the floor; as Slapp listened to the sound of his footsteps as they became faint, as Mr. Charlie descended down the front stairwell. Slapp heard Tate remove his hand from over Gayle's mouth as she snickered a little while complaining. The idea of almost being caught had somehow given her a stimulated energy boost, which in turn had somehow made her more receptive to what Tate was suggesting. Tate heard Slapp take out his weapon from its shoulder holster, open the ammunition chamber and give it a hard spin. Tate smiled as he continued to kiss Gayle during their humorous foreplay.

"Gosh Thaddeus," said Gayle. "Were you trying to smother me?"

"No baby, I'm sorry about that. I guess I over-reacted. For a moment I thought that Slapp and I were out in the field. I'm so exhausted baby, so stop talking and make love to me—that way I can go to sleep a happy man." Tate held still to observe Gayle's response as he went on with his concept of 'cutting-to-the-chase'. "You do know that I love you right?" Gayle nodded her head yes. "And you do believe that

I will keep all the promises to you that I made in that vow, right?" She shook her head yes once more as she stared up at him while experiencing most of his weight pressing firmly and erotically against her body. "Then, please share your unrestricted sexual desires with me so I can go to sleep; then I will repeat all of these things to you tomorrow, with more conviction and passion; I promise." Tate said all of this while smiling and laughing in between each phrase or breath. Gayle opened up herself to his plea and he entered her slow and easy, as he applied a precise calm stroke to their intimate encounter. He rolled them to their sides as he pulled her top leg and thigh up to his waist level which allowed his manhood to enter her even deeper as she surrendered more to his aggressive pleasuring demands. He proceeded to orally massage her breasts, as she released a relaxing sigh. She lightly held his mouth to her nurturing mounds as she enjoyed every motion of pressure that he applied to her needy nipples. He pulled her into him with more force and commitment to pleasing her as he attempt to make the last several weeks, of missing him, just melt away from her body and memory. She was now moaning loudly enough for Slapp to hear them in the hallway. Tate didn't try to quiet Gayle as he continued to rub and massage her body into ecstasy. He rolled on top again as the stroke picked up to a different rhythm. Gayle answered his needs with needs of her own, while tightening her grasp and taking in more of him than she had ever been able to before. They didn't care, about the sounds that seem to be flooding the area or the fact that Slapp could hear them because this was something that he had heard before and understood rather well, as Tate's condo roommate. Slapp watched both ends of the corridor in hope that their coupling episode would be over by the time Mr. Charlie made his final round for the night. Slapp drew his weapon again and started to pace back and forth down the hall as he smiled to himself. The noise ended about twenty minutes later. He couldn't wait to blackmail Tate with this newly acquired knowledge. It was like being sixteen years old all over again and standing watch while your buddy crawled into his girlfriend's bedroom window.

A few hours later, the security staff changed and Slapp went back into the duty bunkroom. He washed his hands and face before going into the refrigerator for a bottle of orange juice. He was hoping that Tate would get up soon and relieve him from the task of keeping baby Max occupied or entertained, it depended on how you looked at it. They all felt sorry for him, because he didn't have a regular playmate, except for his little cousin Milani, but that was only through the week, after school. As Slapp climbed back into bed, he could hear Tate and Gayle speaking in a whisper. A few hours later, Tate woke up and reached over to slowly and gently shift Gayle back into his arms.

"Hey baby, come over here," said Tate. "I forgot to tell you that your clearance came in and you are now officially a member of the inner-circle. We assigned you a code name; 'Paper-Doll'." Gayle shifted over closer to Tate as she tried to wake-up more to respond to him, his morning conversation and affection. The words didn't sink in at first, as she snuggled for just a few more moments of satisfying comfort that her lover had returned safely. Tate spoke in a very quiet calm voice as he stroked her face, neck, shoulder, and back.

Chapter Four

Morning Afterglow

"Morning sweetie, it's amazing what one night with a wonderful woman can do. Did I tell you how glad I am to be back here with you? Did I tell you how much I love you and need you in my life?" He kissed the top of her head after each question. Meanwhile, Gayle continued to wake-up while embracing the fact of how unbelievably sore her personal was from their traumatic sexual encounter, only hours before. She moved around slowly to check to see just how painful it would be to get up and go to the restroom. Tate reached down and grabbed a handful of her butt cheek and pulled it upward playful like without realizing that the pull caused pain to her female counterpart. Gayle let out a suppressed pain response.

"Uhhh ouch, baby I'm sorry, but I'm a little sore down there." Tate immediately became very seriously concerned as all the joy that had been created the night before was sucked right out of him. He totally lost his morning erection as he sat up quickly in bed and reached to turn on the lamp on the nightstand. He cupped her face in one of his hands as he leaned up on one braced elbow, while staring very hurtful, down at her.

"Gayle, did I hurt you last night? Oh baby, I'm so sorry if I hurt you, why didn't you say something or tell me that it was too much pressure for you? What can I do? Just tell me. Will a cold compress help?" Gayle couldn't get in a word in to answer any of the questions that he was firing at her. He was almost in tears at this point. She tried to comfort him as she realized that this was a lot more serious for him mentally than it was for her physically. She instantly realized that his concern was coming from a phobia-level type root base. She attempted to do some damage control, unsuccessfully if I may add, as Tate's awareness moved to total distorted reasoning.

"Wait, Wait Tate, I will be fine after I take a shower and move around a bit. Please don't get upset. I didn't realize what had happened until I woke up just now. The discomfort wasn't that noticeable, while in the heat of the moment. Please don't get upset with me, I promise I will be fine. I know it was my fault, I should have said something."

Now Tate was treating her like a recovering surgery patient that had just awakened from a life threatening car accident where he had been the driver.

"Gayle, I am so, so sorry baby, I had no idea I was hurting you."

"Tate I have to get up and make sure that Max gets over to the resort to Helen," said Gayle.

"No, Gayle I will take him. You just stay in bed for a few more hours. I will be back to check-up on you. Do you want me to bring you some breakfast before I go?"

"No Tate, I promise you I will be fine." He kissed Gayle a few more times, with feather kisses like you would give a new-born that you didn't want to awaken and then got up and passed back through the secret panel, to the duty bunkroom. Slapp was already up and getting dressed for the day. It was now around 7:00 Saturday morning. Slapp could tell something had disturbed Tate, but he didn't feel comfortable enough to ask and probe deeper for an answer. When Gayle and Tate first became an item, he had told Gayle about parts of his childhood. It seemed that he had been born with a condition whereas ones reproduction organs grew and matured in a faster rate than the remainder of the body. He had been given hormonal shots and other therapies to control the growth. Now as an adult man, his male-hood was only slightly more endowed than the largest one in the general population. Yet this had haunted him all his life and had stunted his social skills development, because he was always in fear that someone would learn of his torturing secret. Of course, Gayle had no idea how severely damaging these childhood scars were to Tate that were caused by abnormality from birth or how they had affected his normal psychological growth maturity. Tate had explained it all to her at the very beginning, and she had listened to every painful detail, yet she never expected him to react this strongly to a little morning-after-aggressive-intimacy soreness.

"Hey big guy," said Slapp. "I thought you were going to sleep in. I got up to take Max back to the resort."

"Thanks Slapp, but that won't be necessary; I've already informed Gayle that I would take him back."

"Okay, fine with me," said Slapp. "I'll just take him down for some breakfast." Slapp left out of the bunkroom and walked two doors over to get Max up from where he had spent the night with Nana Carrington (Mrs. Beasley). He knocked on the door and Max ran to open it while wearing only his shirt, underwear and socks.

"Hey little man," said Slapp. "Where is the rest of your clothes, I hope Nana Carrington isn't running a nudist-camp up in here?" Max laughed as he closed the door and ran to get his pants, where Miss Beasley sat on the side of the bed, while so patiently holding them in her hands, for Max to step into them.

"Hurry up sweetie", said Miss Beasley. "Uncle Tate is waiting to take you back to the resort."

"Nana Carrington, what is a nudist camp?" asked Max as he stepped into his pants. Miss Beasley rolled her eyes sharply up in Slapp direction as Max stared downward while holding onto both of Nana Carrington arms at the wrist to balance and to make sure he was putting the correct leg in the appropriate pant-leg. She answered quickly and hoped that he wouldn't pressure her further.

"I don't rightly know too much about things like that Master Max, but if your Uncle Slapp mentioned it, it's probably something that children and ladies shouldn't know too much about." Slapp laughed slyly as his mother gave him the eye that only a child and their mother would understand. Max moved on from the subject. Then Max turned quickly as his face lit up with excitement as he inquired about his father to Slapp.

"I heard Uncle Tate come home last night; is my dad with him?"

"Sorry Sport, but Uncle Tate came back alone. You know the moment your father gets back, he will not stop until he finds you and hugs you." Max gathered up all his things and kissed Nana Carrington on the cheek as he rushed out the door towards the elevator. Slapp turned slowly to say good-bye to his mother.

"See you later, 'Nana Carrington'," said Slapp sarcastically. "I should be back in about an hour and a half." She didn't protest to his humor as he called her Nana Carrington. She knew that they had a lot more work to do on their relationship and all those years spent separated could never be recovered. The best she could hope for was possibly some of Slapp's numbing pain would subside and perhaps his wounds would finally stop reopening, everytime he learned more about the reason for his lonely past.

"Okay Alvin, I'll decide by then if I need to go out or over to my apartment."

In the room, immediately on the other side of the bathroom that connected the two berthing spaces, Gayle got up slowly to take a shower as she thought about whether or not if she should share with me what had happened to her in the heat of passion, the night before. She and I hadn't formed that type of relationship yet, where we talked about personal stuff, but we were both women with a common shared interest. She called about a half an hour after Tate had left her room, on his way to the resort, to deliver Max.

"Hello Helen, this is Gayle. I wanted to call you and let you know that Tate is back and he is on his way to you with Max."

"Hey lady, I know you are glad to have your man back safe. Thanks for calling me. I thought you would still be in bed, trying to catch up on lost time with that fine man of yours." The phone line was silent for a moment. I picked up on the tension. "So Gayle, what's wrong?"

"Oh nothing Helen, I think that Tate and I celebrated a little too intensely last night. I think we tried to make-up for lost time a little too aggressively, if you get my meaning? Now my, you-know-what is so tender, until I could hardly touch it to give it proper hygiene care." I suppressed my laughter, because I knew that all of us had been in that same situation, one time or another. I spoke up quickly and candidly.

"Listen Gayle, I have some cream that will fix that right-up, in no time. I will send it back by Tate. I will put a blouse or something in the bag, so he won't know what we are really doing. All you have to do is put a little inside and wear a panty-shield to bed and in no time you will be as good as new. To be honest, you might be better than new. This cream also has some side benefits that we don't like to talk about. If you want to become intimate while you have it on, that's no problem either. It won't hurt him; it might even help if he is suffering from the results of that same encounter. It has a pleasant aroma and it causes a tingling sensation, if it receives enough friction. It will also tighten things up a bit if you continue to use it after the soreness goes away."

I discovered later, through conversation that this was the last thing that she needed was a tighter vagina, while continuing her sexual relationship with thunder-thighs Tate.

"Thank you Helen, I'm so embarrassed to have brought this up. I will return the cream when I see you. Bye now."

Alex returned a few weeks after Tate and made his full report to the local Hong Kong police. He explained how the illegal tea was being shipped into the United States and other countries that had strict guidelines, regarding such exports. He also clarified that the additive wasn't added until it had reached its distributing point and that was the reason that each time the tea was tested in customs, it was always free of the euphoric agent. Alex was then released from his consulting contract with the Hong Kong police and was now in search of a new job to maintain his exiled cover.

Max continued to play with Milani, in the after-school-care program. I think the great-grandmother started to leave her there more often so she would have a chance to interact more with her little cousin Maximilian. When I discovered this, I decided to pay for some of the time that she was there, so the lady that worked there wouldn't get into trouble, for watching her for free. The new date arrived for the second meeting to discuss and decide who had the legal rights to Austin's daughter. Her grandparents were no longer alive in Thailand, but had given-up their legal rights in writing, prior to their death, for various custom related reasons; in which one was embarrassment. Since the great-grandmother was only viewed as a babysitter slash legal temporary guardian, and was willing to give up her legal rights to the child, by law the next blood relative, even one by marriage would have a strong case. In this case, that would be me since I was married to Austin at the time that her mother and father, Austin, had died. Milani's mother had died two years before her father, Austin. DNA testing was now possible and the child could be matched to Alex—Austin's twin brother, if the need arrived to do so. The letters that Milani's mother had written to Austin also proved that he was unaware of the child and that the mother wanted him to send for her, when she became old enough. Mix nationality children in certain providences weren't treated well; especially the ones that was conceived outside of wedlock and financially very poor.

Chapter Five

Slapp Reveals the Pain

My father, Uncle Oscar, returned about six weeks after my arrival back in Hong Kong. I moved back to Alex's and my condo, while Slapp moved in with Max and me for protection. Tate was now the guard for Miss Gayle and Miss Beasley inside the embassy's compound. He staged himself in the duty bunkroom, but by now everyone knew he spent most nights in the room with Miss Gayle. Max continued his routine of living wherever it gave him the most advantages. This allowed me to have some long serious talks with Slapp like I had promised his mother that I would, before I left for the states to check on my foster-parents.

Slapp's tolerance of me hadn't been the best since his accident. I would have to tread lightly, or I could cause more harm than good. Perhaps I would start off with our first meeting and then work slowly toward the present day. Slapp had never appeared to be the sentimental type, and I think that his past had a lot to do with that fact. One evening, I cooked some of his favorite foods and waited for him to come home. We had a quiet dinner and a few glasses of wine.

"So Helen, you never updated us on how your mother is holding up."

"Oh, Slapp I think she is doing well. I think she knew my foster-father was dying. My foster-father had been sick for a while. He retired a few years ago. Did you know that he was almost fifteen years older than my foster-mother? This was his second marriage." I leaned forward more now as I pushed my plate away and placed both of my elbows on the table. Slapp was staring at me intensely from across the other side of the table, as I replayed happy memories of my childhood in my head. Then I realized that this gave me the perfect entrance to ask Slapp how his relationship with his mother, Miss Beasley was coming along.

"So Alvin," I said to change the atmosphere and to get his full attention, even if it was mixed with anger for calling him Alvin and not Slapp like we in the inner-circle had always done. He stared in my direction with a quick-snap readjustment of his head as he wrinkled his brow just a little. I knew for sure that he was listening by his response and body language.

"How is the relationship between you and your mother coming along? You know I promised her that I would talk to you when I returned, if she promised not to be too pushy while I was gone." He looked on with a cold distant gaze as if I had just lost a few buddy-points with him. He seemed to shift more into his profiler's persona, as I continued to press forward with the new subject.

"Oh yea?" he replied as if I had no significant power over him, his action or emotions. "You told her that you would talk to me for her? And what exactly do you plan to say to me Lady Thore that will get me back in step or to reconsider my position on the matter?" He had flipped the script on me by calling me by my assigned agency-associated name, so I wouldn't have any doubt and to be forewarned that this conversation was not one between two old friends. His glaring stare also conveyed that this situation could get out of hand—if I pushed him too hard.

The room went silent for a full minute or more, as I waited and struggled to believe that Slapp was now remembering some bonding moments from our past. I knew he thought of Stacey and how he had reacted when she left him for Thomas. I had been there for him to help pick up the pieces. Surely that had to account for something in this friendship. He looked down and away as if he was trying to prevent me from reading him and his body language. Alex must have told him about my skills that he discovered, during his job interview for a consulting position with the Hong Kong Police Department. His demeanor and posture softened a bit, while he waited for me to make my next move; during this awkward and possibly friendship-damaging lecture.

Slapp slumped back in the chair and dropped one shoulder, as his initial anger response appeared to fade. I took this as a sign to continue the negotiating peace-talks between him and his mother. The process would have been much easier if the other party was present, but then again that could have presented itself as fuel for the fire. This was the same flame that was so fiercely burning inside Slapp about his past lonely abandoned childhood.

"Slapp, I think Mrs. Carrington is a very nice and caring person. I also believe, whatever her reasons were for not contacting you after all these years that she must have thought were strong grounds for her decision. I believe that you should hear her out and decide after you know the whole story." Slapp was now holding his head down, as he twirled the lightly soiled paper towel napkin around his fingers. For a few moments it was like scolding my son, William, that time I caught him and his friends smoking pot at sixteen years old. He was too old to spank, to innocent to have arrested and to young to give a full cussing-out. I almost smiled as I remembered that full-circle moment as I sat here with Slapp, who was now expressing the exact same body language. Slapp sat motionless as I wondered if he had heard everything that I had just said or if he was remembering something from his past and blocking me out. He then gave a sinister smile just seconds before he looked up at me. Then he put the napkin down, sat up tall, leaned forward and laced his fingers together as his forearm rested on the tabletop. He then gave me a more detailed look into his childhood past; as if I had earned the pain that he was about to share with me.

"You know Helen," he said as he tried to clear the painful lump from his throat. "I can't remember the exact day that I moved into the orphanage, but I do remember this old lady that took a special interest in me. I always wondered why I never got adopted. The old lady told me because of my respiratory problems that it was very expensive for someone to care for me. She assured me as soon as I was older and stronger that someone would love to have a young handsome man like myself, to join their family. That story appeased me for a while, but after I became older and my asthma attacks became less frequent, that explanation didn't work as well as she had hoped. It seems as if she started to work at the home a few weeks or so after I arrived. The way she had the run of the place, while she came and went as she pleased; I got the impression that she had worked there before, years back. During some major holidays or whenever I would get sick, she would take me home with her. Sometimes she took this other kid home also. Then she would call up this man to come and see me while I was there. I didn't put it all together for years that the same man that she called was Uncle Dexter Allen Burney. I never told anyone about this and I never told Uncle Dexter that I had put it all together years later when he had become one of my instructors for the secret service training. I thought he had taken a special interest in me because he knew my father or had made a promise to him to watch out for me. I figured that he had become his brother's keeper, by looking after the old lady and me. It was hard for me to make any sense or understand the subject matter as they conversed back and forth, while sitting around the kitchen table, all those nights. Perhaps I was too young or the medicine made me fade in and out. I'm not sure. It was as if they spoke in code or was just cautious, just in case I was listening. When I was sick the old lady would give me this breathing treatment and my inhaler. Then she would give me a liquid medicine that made me sleepy. Now that I remember, it was nasty tasting and the bottle didn't have a label on it. Knowing her, like I learned later, it was probably something that she mixed up herself for me and she took me home with her because it was illegal for her to give it to me at the orphanage." Then Slapp gave a sincere smile, as he gazed out into space and then went on.

"When Uncle Dexter arrived, he would come upstairs and get me out of my bed and hold me in his lap, while I was still wrapped in my blanket or sheet. He and the old lady would talk way into the night as I slept peacefully in his arms. Most times she would fix him something to eat, while they talked. Then the three of us would sit there in the eat-in kitchen, until the early morning, as they monitored my breathing. He would say, 'Ruth Ann do you think we should call the doctor for the little fella, he's looking mighty peak-it?' She would answer with a strong conviction, 'No Allen, he will be fine. He's to stubborn and quick tempered to get any worst. I think he just wore himself out coughing before I gave him the breathing treatment and the medicine to help him sleep. By tomorrow morning he will be up and raising hell like he always does.' 'Has he gotten a handle on that temper of his yet,' he would ask? She would answer quickly as if that was a standard question between the two of them." 'Hell no Allen!! Have you gotten a handle on yours?' She would answer firmly. Then they both would laugh out loudly as she reminded him that they were too loud and would wake me up. He would then give my head a couple of easy soft strokes, with those wide thick hands, as he looked down at me with such love and tenderness. It was almost worth getting sick, just to witness the two of them making such a fuss over me.

'Shhh shhh Allen, you will wake the boy up.' Then he would pull the blanket tighter around me as he kissed my forehead, while pretending to check my temperature with his cheek.

'I guess he gets that temper from his mother.' "Then Ole Lady Ruth Ann would interrupt him at that point and take up for my dead mother, or so I was led to believe and had been informed indirectly, without any explanation. 'Now stop right there Allen,' She would say. 'I can't allow you to talk about the woman when she is not present to defend herself.' Then they would snicker again quieter now, before moving on to another subject. After that I would fall back into a deeper sleep and I never seemed to remember when he had placed me back in my bed or when he had left. I guess that probably was best, for all parties concern. They told me that I would cry, at the drop of a hat, back then. I guess that was one of my coping mechanisms at the time." Then Slapp must have remembered his meltdown when Stacey left him for Thomas, "and now too, hum?" Slapp wiped the escaped tears from his eyes with his thumb as he tried to swallow pass that lump in his throat and take in a full lung of air, during the process. Then he went on. "That had to be when I was between the ages of three until I was about six or so. Yea, I guess that's about right."

I listened to Slapp's recounts of his early childhood and couldn't prevent myself from tearing up from the details. I was sure that his mother could fill in some of the holes that were now evident by his Swiss-cheese story that he had attempted to re-live. I sat up taller as he continued.

"Once Helen, when I was about four years old, I had made friends with this other kid. His name was Tommy. We were friends from the time we lay eyes on each other. At the time I was about four and about to have my fifth birthday. Tommy was two years older than I was. He left the home everyday to go to school. I followed him everywhere, once he came home, and that went on for the next three years. Now that same old lady, Miss Ruth Ann that worked at the home, always catered to Tommy and me. She watched over us like an old mother hen with brand new baby chicks. I think Tommy was from a battered home or something and the old lady wanted to make sure that he understood that it wasn't his fault. Sometimes on holidays and long weekends, she took us home with her. She lived alone in a large two-story house. It had a basement with a laundry room and all sort of stuff that two boys could explore. From some of the things we found, I concluded that the house had to have been in her family for at least three generations or more. We had the run of the place and got to stay up late and eat whatever we wanted. One afternoon Ruth Ann called both of us into the office area and told us that some of Tommy's other family had been found and that he was going to be adopted and would be leaving the home for good. My heart sank so deeply into my frail chest until I felt the air escape my lungs and I couldn't remember how to inhale. Of course, I had an asthma attack right there as I started to cry out of control. Ruth Ann grabbed an inhaler from the desk and coached me to breathe in as my friend Tommy stood by with his hand on my back and the other placed lightly on my chest, like he had seen the Ole Lady do a hundred times before. I couldn't decide if I wanted to cry or breath, but Ruth Ann and Tommy knew I couldn't do both—not at the same time. She kept on screaming at me and threatening me that she was going to have to call the doctor if I didn't calm down. 'Breathe and stop crying,' she yelled. I finally stop crying and took in a couple of deep breaths as I noticed Tommy was crying also. He was now so afraid for me until he was about to have a panic attack himself. Tommy then reached over and pulled the inhaler away from my mouth and pulled it quickly to his own. Miss Ruth Ann had remained holding the inhaler as Tommy grabbed for it to take a shot for himself. Well, that humorous gesture broke the tense moment as Miss Ruth Ann began to laugh out of control. We wasn't sure if Tommy was trying to help me calm down or if he had become so upset, by the way I had reacted to him leaving, that he believed that a shot from the inhaler would restore his breathing as well. Whatever his reasoning was, it tickled Miss Ruth Ann to the point that she appeared to be laughing and crying at the same time." I looked over at Slapp as he continued his story, while he mimicked ole Miss Ruth Ann's response of laughing and crying. I sat across the table while caught-up in the same dilemma, as we both dried our face with the napkins from our meal. I could tell that Slapp had never told anyone this story before and that we were now sharing, yet another, bonding moment of our uniquely foraged friendship. After a few minutes, as we regained our composure, Slapp continued on with his reflections. "I asked Miss Ruth Ann if she could ask his family to take both of us together. She answered no very harshly, as if there were other things that I didn't understand about my situation or my case. Neither Tommy nor I understood and I never became brave enough again to repeat the inquiry. I went home everyday with Ruth Ann for the next few weeks or so. I cried every night as she sat on the side of my bed talking to me about anything to get my mind off of being separated from my BFF, Tommy. With me there at the house with Miss Ruth Ann that meant that we had to get up earlier, travel across town to make sure that I arrived in time, to the orphanage, and early enough to walk to school with the other kids. A few weeks later, I mustered up the nerve to ask Miss Ruth Ann why she never adopted me. She looked at me and smiled widely. 'I would love to adopt you Alvin,' she said as her eyes lit up, 'but the truth of the matter is that I'm just too old and my health isn't strong enough to take care of you the way that one should take care a fine and handsome over-active boy like yourself.'"

By the time Slapp got to this part of the story, I had wet up all the paper towels within my reach. Slapp was now staring at his hands as he talked. I wasn't sure if I wanted him to continue to cleanse his soul or interrupt him with more reasons why he should ask Mrs. Carrington [Miss Beasley] his mother to explain how he had ended up at this point. I decided on the latter.

"Slapp, I believe that your mother has some information that will perhaps make your healing process a little easier." Then Slapp snapped at me without warning.

"So just how much do you know about this whole damn situation Helen? Have you been deceiving me all these months as well? Did you know about my mother and the fact that she was living out here all these years?" I answered calmly as I noticed the anger in him surface, but this time with a little pain mixed in as he turned his eyes away from my view, while waiting for me to respond.

"Slapp," I said calmly in a whisper. "I didn't know anything about this. I found out that she was your mother the same time you found out. It was early that morning in Gayle's office, just before I went home to bury my foster-father. I think Tate was the only one that knew her from before. He didn't put the pieces together about her until she told him who she was a few days before you went looking for Tate in Gayle's office and Miss Beasley was watching the desk for them. All I know about you is what you have told me from the time we first met, until now. I never asked anyone about any details about your personal life. I wasn't sure what part was a secret and what portion was personal, so I never bothered to ask. I found out a little more about Tate, on the flight over here to Hong Kong. However, the conversation had nothing to do with the rest of you, not even Alex." He glared over back in my direction across the table as he explored me with his profiling skills, to determine if I was lying. Slapp had been my profiler and I was sure that he could read me better than anyone else in the inner-circle of agents or friends. I broke off his gaze as I stood up to clear the table. He relaxed his body again to a slouched-down recline posture in the dinning room chair, as I made a couple of trips to clear the eating area. He was looking towards me, but I was convinced that his focus was on our conversation and the memories that had been stirred up by him reliving his story as he relayed it to me. It was now getting late and I was surprised that he didn't want to go and question his mother at that very moment. Slapp took the last swig of his wine, before I relieved him of his wine glass; he then seemed to rejoin me in the present time.

"Oh I'm sorry Helen, I guess the least I could have done was clear the table after you cooked some of my favorite foods." I laughed as I responded in jest.

"Slapp you don't have any favorite foods, you love all foods." He laughed as well.

"I guess you are right Helen, I do love to eat. I wasn't always a big eater. I can still remember; Miss Ruth Ann would tell me how worried she always was that I wasn't eating enough. She told me if I wanted to grow up and beat my illness I had to eat, exercise and take vitamins everyday. I guess she was right, because by the time I was fifteen, I was almost asthma free and after that I can't remember having another threatening attack. I had medication that I took everyday, but that wasn't a task." Slapp pushed his chair underneath the table as he thanked me again for the dinner and the conversation, or as Fred and the priest would have called it, 'A Lecture of Enlightenment.'

"Helen, can we leave early in the morning. I can drop you off at the resort. I have a few things to do before the first run."

"Sure Slapp, no problem. What time would you like to leave?" He hesitated before he responded as if he thought it would be an inconvenience to me, to leave so early.

"How about 4:30 a.m.?"

"That will be fine Slapp, I'll be ready." I went upstairs and Slapp moved to the sofa and turned on the television. I heard him check his weapon as I climbed the stairs. I was pretty confident that there would be no restful sleep for Slapp tonight. I only prayed that after he informed me of this segment of his childhood, perhaps Divine Intervention would take over and began the much-needed healing process. I took a shower and packed a few more things that I required to stay at my father's suite, at the resort. I moved to Max's room to select a few fresh items for him as well. That's when I realized that most of Max's clothes were either at the resort or at the embassy. I was hoping that someone had remembered to do laundry for the little fella, because he wasn't at the age to remind you, unless it was something special the guy wanted to wear. I smiled to myself as I turned off the light in his room. I got into bed around 11:00p.m.

Chapter Six

Slapp and Miss Beasley's Second Dance

The next morning arrived quickly. Slapp and I headed back towards downtown. He reached the embassy about 5:00 a.m. and Slapp set his path straight towards Miss Beasley's [Mrs. Carrington] sleeping quarters. Of course, Mr. Charlie, the faithful watch-hound was on duty. However Slapp was in no mood for his over-protective power-controlling crap. Just as Slapp reached the floor where most of the sleeping quarters were located, who came up the backstairs, none other than Mr. Charlie? Tate and Gayle were in her room just on the other side of bathroom that joined Miss Beasley's room to Gayle's with a double door cut-through. On the other side of Gayle's room and closer to the backstairs was the security duty bunkroom, where Tate was supposed to be sleeping. He had been assigned to watch over and protect both of the ladies. I assume he thought he could be more efficient if he moved to Gayle's room, which in fact was his girlfriend. Tate heard Slapp and recognized his footsteps coming up the front staircase. To confirm his belief, Tate pushed the call button on his communication pack once. Slapp in turn answered by pushing his communicator button twice, to signal that indeed it was he. Just before he reached the door to Miss Beasley's room, Mr. Charlie came racing down the hall speaking in a whispering yell. "Hey son, just where do you think you are going?" Tate knew if Slapp was at Miss Beasley's room door this time of morning, something had happened. Tate didn't want Mr. Charlie to know that he was in the room with Gayle, so he sprang up quickly and passed back through the secret panel access; that led from Gayle's room to the duty bunkroom. When Tate jumped up suddenly, it woke Gayle up in a panic.

"What's happening Tate," said Gayle in a startled whisper. Tate covered her mouth.

"Sssshhhh baby, Slapp came in early to see Mrs. Carrington and Mr. Charlie is about to delay him. I know Slapp is in no mind-set to accommodate Mr. Charlie's foolishness, this early in the morning. Helen obviously had a little talk with him and now he is coming to get some more answers from Mrs. Carrington. So I think I better get out there before someone pulls their gun and has an accident." Tate slipped back through the secret panel and walked out in the hall from the duty bunkroom.

"Hey everybody, what seems to be the problem?" There Slapp stood with his hand on the doorknob of Miss Beasley's living quarters. Mr. Charlie was about ten feet away trying to explain to Slapp why he shouldn't be on the berthing level that early in the morning, without prior permission. Mr. Charlie had taken the securing strap off of his weapon and had a tight grip around its handle. Tate moved slowly and cautiously between Slapp and the security guard as he noticed that Slapp had a dangerous piercing stare to his red puffy eyes. It looked as though he had been up all night, which was possible, because something more serious was on his mind. Tate knew, better than most, how unpredictable Slapp could be if cornered and even more so if he allowed his anger to take over. With Slapp, it was like having a blackout from too much alcohol. As an adult he had been able to mask that quick temper with his lightheartedness personality trait. This part of his behavior had been cultivated over time. Yet, since his last accident, he had lost some ground in the temper-control department. Once he had taught himself to shield out the pain that always seemed to be haunting him, when he was alone or if life became more stressful than usual. The priest had picked up on this and had made a lot of progress with this weakness in him, by teaching him how to stop looking back and revisiting the pain from the past. Now at this moment, he just wanted some answers so he could move on, possibly forward with less anxiety. Of course, Mr. Charlie had no way of knowing any of this and didn't have a clue of how much danger he was in by challenging Slapp in this manner, while Slapp was under this much stress. Tate held his hand up toward Mr. Charlie as he turned his back to Slapp. He felt safer with Slapp's gun at his back than blind-ass Mr. Charlie's weapon.

"Hey Mr. Charlie," Tate said real slowly with a little smirk as he spoke the words. "You do recognize Mr. Alvin don't you? He works in the motor pool and sometimes he drives in my place. He covered for you just the other night and allowed you to catch an earlier train home." Mr. Charlie removed his hand away from his gun and Tate held one hand down low and behind him to signal Slapp to stand still until he cleared this up.

"Yes, I know Mr. Alvin," said Mr. Charlie. "I just want to know why he is in the living quarters so early attempting to disturb Mrs. Carrington's sleep." Tate moved to the side of Mr. Charlie as both of them stared in Slapp's direction as he continued to stand with his hand on the door handle. At that moment, Miss Beasley (Mrs. Carrington) opened the door quickly to see what the noise was all about in the hallway, outside her door. Slapp spoke first as she opened the door.

"Morning Nana Carrington", said Slapp, as he looked back towards Tate and Mr. Charlie. Tate looked down with one arm across his chest that was supported by the other hand, which was now stroking his chin, as he refused to give Mr. Charlie eye contact, from his side-stance position.

"Can someone please tell me what the hell is going on," said Mr. Charlie as he spoke in a normal loud tone. Miss Beasley replied quickly as if she was irritated by Mr. Charlie's attitude. Her mother-bear protecting-her-cub anger surfaced quickly as she spoke in Slapp's defense.

"I'll tell you what's going on Mr. Charlie. Mr. Alvin is my son and he should be able to come and visit his mother anytime he likes, without being harassed right outside my door." Mr.

Charlie didn't believe a word of it. He just turned to walk away, as he waved his hand in their direction, displaying his disgust with the entire matter. He went down the front stairwell, from where Slapp had just arrived. He was mumbling to himself, like he often did when he discovered that things weren't the way he initially thought.

"I'm just trying to do my job and keep everybody safe while they sleep, but if every Tom, Dick and Harry are allowed to just stop by whenever they have a mind to do so, then I can be home sleeping in my own damn bed. I'm getting too old to be up this late at night anyhow. I will just have to talk to the boss about this. These last couple of guys has come in and just changed every damn thing up-in-here. I think the old boss is getting soft in his old age." Then his footsteps faded out completely. Tate retreated back into the duty bunkroom and through the secret panel, back into Gayle's room. Slapp walked inside the room and Miss Beasley closed the door behind him. She turned slowly to question him.

"Alvin, why are you here so early in the morning? I thought you were supposed to be protecting Miss Helen."

"I dropped her off at the resort with her father; beside she is packing a weapon just like you. I came to see you before my shift starts and I have some questions that couldn't wait." Miss Beasley moved to sit on the side of the bed. Slapp removed his jacket and his shoulder holster with his weapon still inside. He placed them on her dresser and then returned to sit at the foot of the bed in that familiar recliner that he had slept in a few times previously. Miss Beasley then realized that I must have talked with him, like I had promised, before I left for the States. She spoke with a very cautious tone as she addressed his demand.

"Alvin, this may not be a good time; for all the stuff I need to tell you son. It's Monday morning and the ambassador is not in-house, so I have a lot to do." Now Miss Beasley would observe that temper that she saw in Gayle's office that day when she was covering for her. Slapp's temper went from zero to a hundred in a single breath.

"I've waited for thirty five years, surely you can be late for work one damn day, mother," screamed Slapp. Her response was at the same tempo when she answered him as she sprang to her feet and moved in front of him, as he remained seated at the foot of her bed in the recliner.

"I dare you talk to me you in that tone, you little piss ant. Maybe I should have taken a chance and come back so I could have put more leather-to-that-ass of yours."

"And I dare you put me off for a minute longer after I have waited thirty-five years to put my past into clarity that I can grasp." She moved her face even closer to his. Even with her standing and him sitting, they were about eye-to-eye level in height.

"You aren't the only one that has suffered all these years. You think I left you behind because I wanted to. I left your little ass so you would be safe. People watched over you your whole entire life, you little ungrateful, selfish hot-tempered immature jack-ass."

"What are you talking about Mrs. Carrington?" screamed Slapp. "I was raised in an orphanage and I had nobody except for that old lady, Miss Ruth Ann, and that man that came around whenever I was sick to check in on us when I stayed over her house. I think he was the reason I joined the secret service, so I wouldn't loose sight of him as well." Miss Beasley walked away while looking down; slowly stroking her face with one hand while the other came to rest on her slim-hip frame, as the tears flooded her eyes. She turned her back to Slapp and walked toward the door that led out into the hall. He stood up as he watched her and waited for her next outburst. She was trying to think of a way to tell him without the information being such a shock. She was silently crying so hard until she became weak and had to lean against the door to steady herself. She was trembling with anger and disappointment that this was where her decisions had led the two of them. Slapp thought that he had caused her to become ill from all the excitement and rage that they were both experiencing and exhibiting. He rushed over to her and supported her from the back, as he grabbed her at the waist from both sides. His statue was so much longer than hers until his two hands almost fix the entire circumference of her tiny waist. He questioned her now with a lower softer and more concerned compassionate tone.

"Ma, what's wrong, I didn't mean to get you all worked up. I just wanted to know the whole story and I don't feel that I should have to wait any longer, that's all." He slowly turned her body around to face him as she continued to cry silently. Her body was jerking as thirty-five years worth of lies and secrets escaped her in the form of a flood of tears. It all came rushing in on her at once. Slapp was at least two feet taller than his mother, so he hugged her as he leaned down to kissed the top of her head. She wet the front of his shirt, just below his center chest level, as he continued to apologize for upsetting her. Slapp led her back to the bed where they both sat facing each other. Tate heard the noise and went through the bathroom and knocked on the door that opened into her room. Miss Beasley wiped her face with the back and sides of her hands, as she made her way over to open the door for Tate to enter from the bathroom that she share with Gayle next door. After all, Tate was on duty as the bodyguard. It was his job to check.

"Hey you two, is everything alright in here? You two are frightening our other in-house guests." Tate said in jest in an attempt to lighten the mood of the room. The truth was that he, Gayle, and Miss Beasley were the only in-house guest on the roster. Miss Beasley patted Tate on his bare chest as he stood in the doorway of the bathroom, with his opened robe, boxer shorts and slippers. He was caring his shoulder holster and weapon in his hand, while a velcro holster secured the back-up weapon to his right leg, just above the ankle. Tate continued his weak ploy to uplift the atmosphere of the room. Tate continued his jesting response to the situation.

"Mrs. Carrington, is this gentleman bothering you? I can have him removed, at your request." She stood closer to Tate, who had remained standing in the doorway of the bathroom, as they both looked in Slapp's direction. Miss Beasley almost smiled at Tate's humorous gesture, because she was familiar with him and his wit from their long ago past encounters. Slapp wasn't amused at all and viewed Tate's interruption as an intrusion on him and his mother's privacy. Then Tate turned to Slapp as he noticed that Miss Beasley didn't share Slapp's opinion of Tate's invasion of their high-volume conversation.

"Hey big guy, you can't expect to win the ladies over if you are going to make them cry. You have to speak calmly, like a gentleman. I'm telling you man, if you keep this up, there is no future for you with this fine woman. Believe me Mr. Alvin, this attractive, cultured, and well dress lady can have any man she wants to be her son. She can have the pick of the litter. As you know, I still have a mother, but I don't think having a second one would hurt me any."

Slapp stared at Tate like he wanted to put him in a chokehold. Slapp had heard every word, yet remained angry that Tate had taken some of the fire out of him with reasoning that his intellect couldn't ignore. Miss Beasley was smiling for sure now as the tears continued to flow down her face. Then she looked up at Tate.

"Oh, I'm sorry Tate if we woke you two up again. Alvin and I are having a conversation that we should have had years ago, at the very least, the moment he first arrived here in Hong Kong. I guess we didn't realize how loud we were getting while we expressed ourselves. Thirty-five years is a long time to keep things bottled up inside. Perhaps it coming out, all at once, was too much for the both of us to handle like civilized people." Tate realized then that Miss Beasley had figured out that he had been sleeping in Gayle's room all the time. Perhaps the fact that Tate came in through their bathroom, probably confirmed what she had suspected. During the excitement, Tate had forgotten to use the door from the hallway to enter Miss Beasley's berthing space, to protect the secret. Slapp questioned Miss Beasley again as if Tate wasn't standing there; after all, Tate had spent more time with her than he had.

"Ma, what did you mean when you said that someone has been watching over me my whole life?" She moved back to sit on the bed, as Tate stood still and quiet in his same position.

"You see Alvin, that lady that you are talking about, Miss Ruth Ann is your grandmother and Mr. Dexter Allen Burney is your father." Slapp jumped to his feet and walked over to the door that opened into the hallway. He turned quickly and pointed his disgusted finger at her and attempted to yell, but no sound came out as he broke down into tears. His face was all in a frown, his nose was running and all he could do was swing his arms, as he balled up his fists. Tate took this as a signal for him to back out and close the door. Slapp collapsed back into the big recliner that he had slept in only weeks before, at the foot end of her bed. He held his hand to his face and cried silently, as if he would never stop. He was angry and hurt that he had spent all that time believing that he was alone and no family members, who really cared about him or what he was doing with his life. She moved cautiously over to him and sat on one arm of the recliner and pulled his wet face to her breast. He pulled away slowly after a few minutes or so, and stared up at her.

"Ma, you are telling me that I had family around all those years and I never knew. Why didn't someone break the silence and tell me. I could have kept a secret as well as the next guy. I just can't believe that we have wasted all of this time apart."

"I know this is painful Alvin, but I promise to tell you everything tonight, when you get off from work. I will have one of the drivers take me to my apartment and I will bring back all the pictures. You won't believe the photograph shots I have. Please understand me son when I tell you that you were never alone, you just have to get pass all of this and let us openly love you now. I know we can't make up for lost time, but we can spend the rest of our lives trying. Some decisions that your father and I made before you were conceived is what has caused you all this pain and trouble in your life. We can't fix everything, but we can give you our reasons. All I ask is that you give us a chance. When you see all these pictures, you will see that you weren't as miserable, as you feel you were or remember." She then kissed Slapp's wet cheeks as she softly held his face in her hands, very close to her own. Slapp felt like he was eight years old again when his best friend at the orphanage had gotten adopted. Then, at that precise moment, time stood still as the memories of his mother's touch and the smell of her all came flooding back. It frightened him a little, but he couldn't allow the fear to be seen by her. He stood up from the chair and put back on his weapon and escaped in her bathroom to wash his face as he yelled back into the sleeping area. He felt lighter in his spirit and almost all of his anger was gone. He wanted to believe her words, but all the pain from his childhood had somehow given him strength that he couldn't put into words.

"Hey ma, which one of these towels is yours?" Miss Beasley answered as she smiled to herself. She never dreamed that she would ever hear those words in her only child's voice.

"They are all mind Alvin, Gayle hangs hers in her room. Use whichever one you prefer, I have more." Slapp left the room and Miss Beasley got ready for the day. The day passed slowly for her and Slapp, because they could hardly wait for the big talk. She sent him a message to meet her in the conference room. She didn't realize how much stuff she had gathered over the years. She also invited his circle of friends. She called Uncle Oscar and me. Gayle and Tate would already be in the house. She wanted to make the announcement that she had officially been reunited with her only son. She ordered snacks to be brought up to the conference room, before the kitchen closed and she invited the security guards to stop by on their rounds. She was so happy until it was hard for her to concentrate on her daily assignments, which included keeping a calendar for the ambassador, even though he wasn't in-house. She was also the language translator and was called on several times a day to provide the service.

That evening, after Slapp made his final pick up and delivery, he got back to the embassy around 7:00 p.m. His mother and the crew were waiting in the conference room for him to walk in. Mr. Pauling, at the front gate was already on duty for the night. Miss Beasley had instructed him to tell Slapp to meet her in the second floor conference room. He walked in and turned on the light and everyone yelled 'surprise!!!!' His mother grabbed around him and he leaned way down so she could kiss him on the corner of his lips, while he kept his eyes on everyone else in the room and tried to figure out what was going on and why were we all there.

"Hey you guys, what's going on? It's not my birthday or anything." There we all stood, Gayle and Tate in the back of the room at the far end of the long table. Uncle Oscar, my father, and little Max sat to Slapp's right near the light switches and other controls for the room. I had been standing next to his mother and was now moving closer to greet him with my approval that he had decided to talk to his mother. I spoke up quickly.

"Slapp your mother wanted to share this moment with us, since we have been your family for a while. I'm just sorry that Alex isn't here, but we will take pictures for him. I know we have to destroy them later. I haven't forgotten who we are or what we do." Slapp looked down at his mother who was still firmly holding on to him with all the strength in her little overjoyed body. Slapp finally spoke slowly and quietly.

"I want to think all of you for coming to celebrate this moment with me and my mother. We have some private talking to do. So please don't leave, and enjoy the pictures and the slide show from my childhood. We will be back shortly." Then Miss Beasley stepped away from Slapp and looked up at him as she spoke to the rest of us. She realized that she had gotten caught up in the moment and had not realized that this could possibly be an awkward and emotional situation for Slapp, in spite of the fact that these were his closest friends. It was definitely a personal and private moment between a mother and her son to be updated on thirty-five years of your past.

"Oh, I'm sorry Alvin; I had no idea that this would be embarrassing for you. I should have asked or had this little setting later on." Then she turned to all of us, as we looked on excited for the two of them, beyond belief. "I'm sorry everyone, we will have to excuse ourselves so we can talk, but please stay and look at the pictures and enjoy the food. If anyone else drops by please inform them that we will be back momentarily. I will have to fill in the time-line of the slideshow at a later date."

Miss Beasley and Slapp made their gracious exit, because she was very much the graceful lady, to an office down the hall. She was so happy until she almost pranced out of the room. When she and Slapp arrived in the other room, Slapp realized that he wanted to see the pictures as well and that his mother needed to be in the room with the others to explain the slides and inform then when the photo-shots were taken.

"Hey ma, I think we should go back. We can have the talk anytime. I waited thirty-five years, a few more days isn't going to kill me." He gave a big grin as he hugged her and told her that he didn't remember her being so small. She laughed as she responded to his comment about her size.

"Alvin, when we were separated, you were only two and a half, and underweight, if I may add; so everyone was a giant to you at that age silly boy. Now, just look at my tall, big and handsome son, all grown up and starting to heal. What more could a mother ask for from the Divine One."

"Ma, I just have one more question. Would you have shot me that day in Gayle's office when I came looking for Tate?" She looked at him and showed him a side of her that she knew was in him also.

"I wouldn't have killed you son, but I wouldn't have allowed you to hurt me with that temper of yours. You have gotten a lot better, but I think some of it has to do with all you've had to triumph over. All these years you have had to live with a heavy tormented heart; perhaps your father and me can change that a little. I believe in Divine Intervention. I know that the old priest has talked to you more than once about that very thing. Perhaps now more of his lectures will sink-in, now that you have more support and a better understanding of your past situation. Come on; let's go back to the party. Let's show them what we are made of." She grabbed Slapp's huge hand with her tiny fingers and led him back to the conference room. When they walked into the room, everyone was laughing very loudly as they saw Slapp as a scrawny under-weight baby. He was now six feet three inches tall, while weighing in at around two hundred forty-five pounds of pure danger. Tate spoke as Slapp and his mother entered the room.

"Now that is what I call a humble beginning," said Tate as everyone in the room laughed, including Slapp and his mother. Miss Beasley sat at the head of the table and explained the photos that appeared on the conference room's overhead projector screen. A couple of the guards stopped by during the presentation and got some food, while observing a few slides. There were scrapbooks all over the table and each photo confirmed that Slapp was never alone and was well cared for from the time he and Miss Beasley had been forced to separate, for safety reasons. We watched the slide-review of Slapp's younger years and we watched him as he seemed to have a roller-coaster of emotions that surfaced some times in the form of a silent cry and other times as loud laughter, yet other times in the form of a combination of the two. A lot of the pictures were taken at a great distance and Slapp had no idea that anyone was there, but now he felt good that he had been wrong all those years, about being alone.

After that night, Slapp and his mother spent as much time together as their jobs would allow. Most nights now, Slapp spent sleeping in the duty bunkroom, so he could be near his mother at night. Some nights he stayed in the room with her until she was ready to go to bed. Other nights he reclined in the big chair as she read or did some work in bed. If he fell asleep there, she would just cover him up and turn off the lights. She knew the rule also about going to sleep in the room with a jumpy agent. Move the gun from their reach before you move around the room in the dark.

Chapter Seven

The Counselor's Gift

A few weeks later, Alex came home and I was out-of-control with excitement. I couldn't wait to bring him up-to-date on everything and everybody. It was now time for the second meeting to discuss the fate of Milani. I was so happy that Alex was back to attend the proceedings. This time, both ambassadors were present, along with Gayle, Miss Beasley, and Alex, the great-grandmother, the great aunt, the recorder, the Chief of Police from before, the local attorney and myself.

Gayle and Miss Beasley arrived first with all the original documents in files. Just as we were about to start, another attorney arrived and moved to the space between Alex and me as he apologized for his tardiness. He was a, taller than expected, Asian man caring a briefcase so attractive that it alone told part of his very interesting story of success. He introduced himself before he came to stand between Alex and me.

"Please forgive me for being late to these proceedings; I flew all night to be here. I believe my licenses are still current to practice on this side of the world. My name is attorney Su Ki Chang senior and my son junior only called me about this case two months ago. Please forgive me if I need to be updated before we start." He bowed several times as he spoke, while holding his hands in a very humbling position in front of him. I would say that at the least a third of the people in the room's educational level had gone way beyond nonverbal communication 101, so no one was buying his poor little confused-lawyer act. He was dressed like a pure courtroom powerhouse and we all knew that some real cutthroat negotiating was about to be experienced in this small room. He was extremely well dressed in a tailor fitted navy-blue suite with a white shirt so bright and so sharply pressed until a warning label should have been attached, just as a safety courtesy to the people that would come into contact with him and/or his shirt. As a compliment, a red and blue power tie, pure silk of course had been selected, and a pair of shoes that had been made exclusively for him in Italian crock-skin leather. And just because he had the money to do so, he carried a one-of-a-kind tailor-made briefcase; that so happened to match his shoes, perfectly. No doubt he had ordered them as a pair. His hands were so well groomed until I hid my own underneath the table. Mr. Chang's hair appeared so freshly and flawlessly cut until I was willing to make a wager that the barber was still just outside the conference room door, while still putting away his clippers and sweeping up the hair-cutting from the floor. The cologne he wore was light, but very persuasive and unforgettably distinctive to him and his seemingly quiet demeanor. He had played this game before, no doubt, many times and had emerged victorious. When Mr. Chang first began to speak, he directed most of his eye contact to the two ambassadors and only looked towards the other attorney when he got to the part about perhaps needing to be brought up to speed on the case. The remainder of us in the room, at this point were treated like mere disregarded wallpaper just before a full renovation. We were seen, possibly noticed, but not required. The police chief was now staring with a very uncomfortable sneer on his face, as if he knew the attorney from long ago and wished to have never been in his company again.

The other attorney, representing the providence of Hong Kong, glanced up at him once and looked back down at the papers in front of him, in an attempt to hide his jealous disgusted contempt that he had for Counselor Su Ki, and for his presence in the room. Nether of the ambassadors seemed to be affected one way or the other by the new arrival. Mr. Chang finally sat down and whispered to Alex and me as he explained himself. Miss Beasley moved very slowly around the room, after she sprang to her feet to pass out some more folders that she had originally planned to give out later during the meeting, which allowed Mr. Chang sometime to talk to us privately and directly. Alex and I were in such shock that he was there and a part of our legal team, until we could hardly absorb what he was stating so eloquently, with passion and vigor. Miss Beasley was very polite and professional, as she stalled the proceedings by reaching over each person's shoulder to give them the file, as she manipulatively stalled the proceedings, while she explained the first page of it, in detail. She showed off her translation skills, while using her many language abilities, whenever she felt it was appropriate to do so. Mr. Chang continued his private briefing to Alex and me.

"My son, Su Ki called me and informed me about you and his relationship; and he also told me what you were trying to do for your deceased brother's daughter. I had been promising my son for a while that I would come home to see him and my family. I think he used this to lure me here. He's a smart young man, don't you think?" He almost smiled as he spoke the words relating to his son. We weren't sure if he was excited about the trickery of his son or the challenges he faced with our case. He was sort of hard to read, but we were certain that we were glad that he was defending our cause. He refocused before he proceeded.

"I did some preliminary research on past similar cases and I think you have a good chance. I know my culture will want to be compensated heavily and that's where my expertise is most valuable. Our countries have a letter-of-understanding about these matters that I'm sure that no one here is aware of, and if they were, they wouldn't share that information with you. The agreement limits the compensation amount that the law or the council can ask for in return. Then after you subtract all your fees, for example mine for this trip and others that we will discuss at a later time; it boils down to a fraction more than a tip that one would leave at a restaurant, when one desires to impress a first blind-date. Being that the child is a blood-shared relative, it's more like shifting custody and not like applying for a new adoption, of a stranger, to join your family. So your battle will be obtaining an American traveling visa and then a citizenship, for the child. Since you are here and have an inside track with the embassy, that should make the paperwork a lot easier to guide through the system and remain on the top of the pile, and not get lost in the political red-tape if you will."

Mr. Chang said all of this as the panel waited for him to end his whispers to us and explain how he became a member of our team. I imagine Gayle and Miss Beasley, without a doubt, were reading Mr. Chang's lips, as he continued his briefing to us. This was evident to me by the smiles that their faces maintained the entire time, while he was bringing us up to speed. Counselor Chang showing up at that very moment was more like Divine Intervention than just dumb luck, and I couldn't wait to thank God for his blessings and for being highly favored.

The recorder nodded once in the ambassadors' direction to signal that she was ready to take down everything that was spoken in the meeting. The first to stand and give his report of findings was the attorney from the previous session. Mr. Chang listened cautiously and made notes on a sheet of paper. The American ambassador leaned forward just a little as he observed the other members of the panel. The great-grandmother sat quietly as Miss Beasley translated, what the attorney was saying from English, into her language. She nodded her head a few times that she understood most of it. I was sure that Mr. Chang had invested more time into this case than he had let on or expressed to either of us. Counselor Chang sat very calmly and waited very patiently for his turn to speak. Alex and I were still in shock and found it very hard to listen with the intensity that was required for this precedent setting panel. Aware of a few laws pertaining to this matter we figured that at the very least some would be forced to be adjusted; that's if we had any chance of winning. We also knew that others, in our present situation, didn't have near the resources that had been made available to us.

After a few more minutes, the counselor gave a summary of the law as he understood it and then retired to his seat. Mr. Chang waited a few seconds as he peered in the direction of the ambassadors, for their permission for him to proceed. Counselor Su Ki Chang's first several statements to the panel virtually made the previous attorney's understanding of the law, null and void. Attorney Chang agreed that in fact the interpretation of the law was factual correct, yet outdated. Mr. Chang continued his briefing to the panel as he shared a little litigation history about previous cases, very similar to this one. He also explained to us of the trauma to the child if we decided to drag the proceedings out over a long period of time, consequently exposing the child to new surroundings, at an older age, which in turn would lengthen the adjustment time, to her new found family members. He used every opportunity during his monolog to reiterate that we already shared blood with this child and a portion of her already belonged to us, in spite of the outcome and final decision of the law. Mr. Chang elaborated on his thoughts and judgment, in which he assured all of us were law based, and within the guidelines of the letter of understanding between our two countries. Mr. Chang stood quickly to his feet, after receiving a nod from the American ambassador. He re-buttoned his jacket and gave a customary short bow from the waist.

"Ambassadors, fellow counselor, Chief of Police, our distinguished recorder and family members of the child in question, it is an honor to take part in these proceedings. I would also like to shed some light on the law, as it relates to this dilemma. The law states that if either of one's parents are an American citizen, then that child has the right to apply for citizenship in the country of choice, when they are old enough to do so, if all other decisive factors are met. What we are attempting to do is move this child to another environment until she is old enough to make that decision. There is no doubt that the people here are her family members and want the best for her. What we need to decide is how smoothly we are willing to make her transition. Her great-grandmother is willing to give her up, for financial reasons and personal health issues. We have the letters that prove that her mother was willing to send her to her father, at the proper time. We also have evidence that her father died without knowing that she had been born. So we don't have a situation where one parent abandoned the requirements of the child's basic needs. Therefore, I find, with the interpretation of the law, that this stepmother and uncle should be granted the right to provide a better life for this child that shares our blood and culture as well. I make a motion that we unite and help this family prepare the proper required forms and petition a hearing date for the courts to review this case and grant our request, as it relates to this family."

The great-grandmother was crying silently as Miss Beasley continued to translate to her. The little girl's aunt seemed emotionally unaffected by the proceedings. It remained clear that the monetary value was her only concern. The Chief of Police had nothing to add as he sat in amazement that we were able to obtain Mr. Chang as our counselor. Both ambassadors agreed that the best thing for the child was to move with her father's family to America, at this time. The American ambassador stood slowly and instructed the panel.

"I request that all words spoken be translated in the required languages and added to the files. If there are no more fact-findings to be heard, I am in agreement to filing the proper paperwork as a petition to the local court, that Milani Michelle Chang Jones be granted a travel visa under the law sanctioned by the letter-of-understanding between our courts. I would like to thank this panel for its research ground-work and I release this board, at this time." Everyone stood to their feet promptly as the two ambassadors shook hands and moved amiably towards the conference room door. Alex and I turned to hug each other as we forgot that counselor Chang had been seated between us.

"Oh, I'm so sorry Mr. Chang, I didn't mean to . . ." He spoke up quickly as though no harm had been done, as Alex and I retreated, in an attempt to allow him to move away from us to safety and out of harms way.

"No, no problem," replied Mr. Chang. "I totally understand your excitement as they relate to these proceedings. We still have much work to do on this matter. I will get back to you in a few days, you have my word." Then Mr. Chang gathered his papers and disappeared as mysteriously as he had arrived. I moved over to the great-grandmother and told her that when we received custody of Milani that we would take good care of her and if she wished, we would apply for her to receive a travel visa also, at our expense. The aunt looked on and listened, but no offer of restitution was made to her. The great-grandmother seemed to cheer up a little as we explained in detail of our plans. She had never been outside the country before, so a lot had to be done to prepare her for the long tedious trip, if nothing more.

* * *

That night Alex reserved the two of us a room at the resort to celebrate. It was a couple of doors down from my father's suite. We didn't want to drink and have to drive home to Stanley's Fort/Market area. We talked Miss Beasley into staying in my father's suite with Max. That meant that Slapp would be free for a change from bodyguard duty. Gayle had a date with Tate, but had agreed to have dinner with all of us. Everything was set; we would all be together for dinner. I made the reservation for 8:00 p.m. It was hard to get the seating for such a large group so late, but I told them that my father was Mr. Oscar Wiley. The maître d' then agreed to find us the space even if he had to set a table up in the lobby to accommodate our party of seven, that later turned into a party of eleven. Tate and

Slapp were both scheduled to be off for the weekend. Tate's last pick-up was at five. That would give him enough time to get back and dress for dinner. I had taken the afternoon off to attend the meeting in reference to Milani. Alex's position with the local police, as a consultant, had been terminated. Gayle and Miss Beasley were still not allowed in their apartments alone, so they got dressed at the embassy. After Alex and I picked Max up from after-school care, we headed to the condo to get dressed for the evening. I felt magic in the air and I wasn't sure why. I knew that the meeting went well, but there was something else. Alex was acting strangely everytime I looked in his direction. I knew he had a surprise for me, because he hadn't finished unpacking yet. I just thought it was a letter from my best friend Jean, or he had stopped by his apartment in the States and picked up something of mine that he knew I had been missing. It was something, but I just couldn't put my hand on it.

Alex, Max and I were the first to arrive at the resort for dinner. Max went up to my father's room to play a game and wait for the others to arrive. It was now seven-thirty and I saw Tate, Gayle, Miss Beasley, and Slapp arrive in a limo from the motor pool. I smiled to myself as I thought of how we use the limos as if they were our own. Everyone was dressed so handsomely and I knew the night would be just perfect. We greeted each other in the lobby near the bar entrance as we waited for the receptionist to call my father's room for Max to join us. Slapp was calm as he escorted his mother. He had a renewed spirit radiating from him and a lot of the pain that he had been carrying for years seemed to be melting away. Max came bursting around the corner from the elevators as if he had something to tell until he looked into my eyes. Then he just stopped, took a breath and swallowed whatever it was on the tip of his tongue. We moved to this large table and I was surprised that we had extra seats, after the reservation had been so difficult to book for seven. Then in the far distance I heard music and it sounded like my father. My father was back and I was sure that everyone knew except me. Everyone around the table started to laugh as I reached over to smack Alex for keeping it a secret from me. I stood up to go and see him.

"Alex, why didn't you tell me that my father was back? I have to go see him."

"No Helen, he promised that he would come over after just a few songs. He knows that we are here. Max talked to him up in the room." I looked over at Max and he was smiling from ear to ear as if the secret had almost finished him off, to keep quiet about it. I was sure by his busybody agitation, that there was more. Max explained the blame away from him.

"Auntie Ma, I almost told you when I first got off the elevator, but my dad shook his head no and I knew what he was trying to say. You should smack Uncle Tate too, because he was the one that picked grandpa up from the airport."

"Hey, hey little fella," said Tate defensively. "I just go where I'm told." We ordered our dinner's first course and waited for our drinks to arrive. The place was crowded and the delay was a little long. I heard my father excuse himself from his nightly audience and the bartender turned on the intermission music CD.

When my father, Uncle Oscar, came around the corner into view and into the dinning area, I sprang to my feet and slapped my hands to my face as I stared in shock and non-belief. My father was escorting my stepmother. She had traveled back with him. The tears started streaming down my face as Alex jumped up to comfort me. I was crying so hard until my body was jerking. I ran to hug my foster-mother and father, but I couldn't speak. The knot was too thick in my throat. Max was now tearing-up, and so was Miss Beasley. Gayle stood up and dried her tears with the linen dinner napkin. Tate stood with his arms around Gayle as Max reached up for Slapp to pick him up. They were all crying because I was crying.

"Hey big guy," said Slapp to Max. "Why are you crying? They are crying with tears of joy." Max didn't answer as he buried his wet face into Slapp's shoulder and neck as he held him tightly around the neck. Everyone was standing at the table when I finally released my parents and walked back towards them. My father kissed me on the forehead and told me that he had to get back to the piano. My foster-mother and I walked back to the table with our arms locked together. She looked so well, and it seemed as though she had gotten a makeover. My entire life, I never remembered my mother looking so sexy and youthful. She smiled charmingly and seemed to be doing better than I had expected. Slapp and Tate moved towards my mother to kiss her on the cheek as if they were sure that my father had told her exactly who they were, and they were correct. She smiled deeply as if she expected them to greet her in that manner. Slapp was able to pry Max loose from around his neck as his tears turned into an embarrassing moment for him. My mother coached him a little as she stroked his arm nearest to her.

"Oh Max, you met me upstairs. Surely, I can get a kiss after traveling all this way to see you and your parents." Max slowly released Slapp's neck as he dried his face with his hand while leaning in to kiss my mother with his eyes closed; their lips collided as everyone cheered very quietly. We all sat back down while Slapp placed Max in a chair next to him, as he spoke to him quietly and tidied up his clothes. I smiled as I introduced my foster-mother to Miss Beasley and Gayle.

"Mother, I would like for you to meet two of my friends that I have made since I arrived. This is Mrs. Becky Sue Carrington the translator for the American Embassy, here in Hong Kong and also Slapp's mother. And this is Miss Gayle Veronica Livingston-Langston who also works at the embassy as the security receptionist and Tate's lady, unadvertised ofcourse." Tate looked over and everyone at the table burst into laughter. My mother smiled strangely and looked around as if the joke was on her. "Don't worry mother, I'll explain later." Just as I thought that the night couldn't get any better, I heard Mr. Chang's voice talking to the waiter. I looked up and there he stood with his son Su Ki Jr. and in Su Ki's arms was little Milani all dressed for dinner. I was too weak to stand to my feet and cry. The men all stood as Su Ki put Milani down and she walked directly over to Max. He held out his arms to hug her and we all watched as he kissed her little face and talked to her as if we all had left the room. We knew there was somewhat of a language barrier, yet she was smiling as though she understood every word that Max spoke. We did notice that they seemed to have formed a bond that only family could share. Everyone bowed shallowly and sat down except Mr. Chang, his son, Su Ki and Alex.

"Miss Helen," said Mr. Chang very politely with his hands clasped in front of him. "Would you be kind enough to allow us to join you for dinner?" I dried my face and sprang to my feet as Alex and I returned his bow.

"Yes, please, oh please join us Mr. Chang and you also Su Ki; I would be honored." I held out my hand of hospitality and directed them to the unclaimed chairs at our table. Max and Milani continued to communicate with their little faces in close proximity. Slapp called her to him and she went without any reservation. We all looked on as he sat her in the chair next to him and called the waiter to request a booster seat. I started my introductions again as the waiter returned to the table to see if we needed more time. I was so overwhelmed with excitement and joy until I couldn't eat a thing. I just gazed around the table and tried again and again to stop crying. When I excused myself, all the men at the table stood up promptly, as Mr. Chang and his son, Su Ki dropped their hands in front of them and bowed in me and my foster-mother's direction. I instructed the men to please order for my mother and I as we headed for the ladies room. Milani was so beautiful and fearless. I knew she had to be a Jones, at least in spirit if not in blood. She had full round eyes with soft large looped curly hair. She had inherited dark pink lips, long eyelashes like the Jones clan and dimples in her cheeks deep enough for them to be seen from across the room, in spite of the evening's dimmed lighting. Milani giggled a lot as she and Max played a finger game that I'm sure they had engaged in many times before at the daycare center.

In the restroom, I hugged my mother again and tried to repair my make-up. That was the most joy that I had ever remembered feeling at one single moment. Then it hit me, how did Mr. Chang get Milani here and how did he know how to find her? I raced back to the table and found that everyone had ordered and that our drinks had finally arrived. When my foster-mother and I got closer to the table, all the men stood up to receive and welcome our return. I didn't want to insult Mr. Chang or Su Ki, his son. Everyone knew what I wanted to ask. Mr. Chang just smiled and stood up as I returned to my seat next to Alex.

"Miss Helen, forgive me please," he said with a strong Asian accent, that appeared a lot stronger than when he was in the meeting, only hours before. "Now I would like to introduce my guest." Counselor Su Ki smiled very pleasantly and then paused his monolog with a shallow humble bow. It was as though he could read my mind or perhaps they had discussed it while my foster-mother and I were away from the table. At any cost, he answered my question with his introduction. This is my son Su Ki Chang Jr. that most of you know and some have met before. Tonight we have the pleasure of escorting the little princess Miss Milani Michelle Acura Chang Jones, my grand niece and Su Ki's second cousin." Mr. Chang spoke every word slowly and with loving passion for both of his family members. I held my hands over my mouth in surprise as I quickly leaped from my chair and rushed around the table to hug Mr. Chang and Su Ki. Su Ki had been a victim of my uncontrollable affection before, however his father had only witnessed what happens when you stand between the person and I, in which the embrace is intended. I couldn't remember what to do to show my approval that our bloodline had been mixed. I knew that in this culture, open affection in public, especially between strangers, wasn't an everyday practice. I ran over and stopped quickly right in front of him, as all the others watched to see how I would handle myself. Su Ki was smiling shyly as if he was aware of his father's feelings and my uncontrollable excitement. I bowed deeply showing honor and respect and then I opened my arms to hug him with all the strength I could muster up. Everyone laughed as Mr. Chang stood stiff as a board and waited to be released. Mr. Chang stepped back one-step as he offered me his handkerchief to absorb my tears. He and his son remained standing until I returned to my seat. He smiled a little as he continued to nod his head that he understood what I was trying to convey without words. We all talked as we waited for our food to arrive. "Mr. and Mrs. Jones I must tell you now," said Mr. Chang. "My main reason for coming and being a part of the proceedings was to observe you very closely. I wanted to be sure that our little princess was in no danger and that you were honorable people. Please do not be angry with my son

Su Ki for not revealing what he had learned earlier about the location of Milani. He called me in the States and I instructed him to keep this information from you until I arrived." I looked over at Alex, then over at Milani and then back to Mr. Chang. His son nodded a couple of times as his father spoke these words. Su Ki placed his hands in a prayer position and nodded for us to forgive him for his deception. Mr. Chang continued, "Mr. Alex, I did an investigation on you and you are a very interesting man, if you would allow me to be so bold. I have many questions for you, but they are not suitable for dinner conversation; we must have a private moment soon. I believe I can assist you." Alex nodded his head as he held eye contact with the counselor. Our food arrived and Miss Beasley stood and offered grace for the entire table. Miss Beasley repeated in translation for Milani.

About half way through dinner, my father, Uncle Oscar, returned and seized the last available seat at our table. We all talked and laughed out loudly as the night faded closer into a new day. Milani had now crawled up into Slapp's arms and was totally asleep just as if she had done this ten times before. Max sat close as he played with her tiny hands and fingers, and now and again kissed her soft smooth cheeks. I couldn't believe, as I watched Slapp, that he didn't have any children of his own. He was a natural. His mother looked over at him several times and smiled as a proud happy tear escaped her eye. She noticed the passion and his child-like demeanor that lie slightly underneath Slapp's rough exterior and now understood why children always seemed to draw near to him. It appeared that their innocence didn't acknowledge the rough surface layer of Slapp's persona, yet their spirits only responded to whatever was flowing from the heart. Growing up in the orphanage had cultivated a protective and nurturing trait in Slapp. There was no denying that Slapp's heart was tender and sensitive—this alone made him dangerous and quick to anger.

Mr. Chang and Su Ki Jr. stood to their feet graciously and excused themselves to retire for the evening. Alex and I moved closer to hold Milani before passing her on to her second cousin Su Ki, as she maintained her limp rag-doll posture, while sleeping. My mother and I stayed in the room that Alex had pretended to reserve for the two of us. Alex slept in the suite with my father and Max. Tate and Gayle went to their room and Slapp took the limo back to the motor pool and spent the night in the duty bunkroom, one door down from his mother, Miss Beasley.

The next few days moved along like clockwork. Mr. Chang had a meeting with Alex and was relieved when Alex informed him that he would be retiring as soon as he returned back to the States. "Mr. Alex I know that you have a friend that is in a bind with the Los Angeles Police Department. I would like to offer my services in a goodwill gesture, in honor of our shared bloodline as a family through Milani." Alex spoke up quickly because he knew that we couldn't afford Mr. Chang's services any other way, even if he agreed to give us the family discount.

"Mr. Chang," said Alex. "You have no idea how much I appreciate your offer to help our friend. There is a chance that he may not need you, but I will speak with him and pass on your selfless generosity with admiration and pleasure."

Mr. Chang proved to be a man of his word and within two months after he returned to the States, the case was closed and the state and city regarded the incident as an accident, due to a leaky gas line. However, the bureau continued their investigation, full-steam ahead. They had their own deceptive reasons to maintain the probing, and Slapp was in the center of the crosshairs of the bull's eye target, as they say.

My foster-mother stayed in Hong Kong for a full month. She spent most of her time with my father and I started to question their relationship. I never asked my mother if my father, Uncle Oscar, ever repeated to her the words that my foster-father had said to him that night in the hospital, on his dying bed. I'm sure it had something to do with watching out for my foster-mother, and becoming a brother's keeper, so to speak. He couldn't have selected a better man for the job. My father, Uncle Oscar took better care of her than ever before. After a few months, I got the feeling that my father had become a little sweet on my foster-mother or perhaps the sugar from the past was now returning to the taste buds. He was very attentive to her and checked on her often. She traveled back and forth every three months to visit us. The live-in boarder that she and my foster-father had taken in was still there after all these years and looked after things in her absence.

Tate and Gayle were growing closer by the day. I continued to teach at the school. We got a chance to spend time with Milani on the weekends. She seemed to be fine as long as Max or Slapp was somewhere nearby. Miss Beasley taught us a few phrases of her dialect, to get us through on the weekends. Slapp for some reason didn't have any problem getting her to do whatever he wanted. He would just point and demonstrate and she would do it as if he had spoken the words.

We started the paperwork for Milani's great-grandmother and made sure that her health wouldn't be a problem. She was happier now that she knew that Mr. Chang would be there whenever she arrived, when or if she decided to return with us. Mr. Chang was the old lady's deceased granddaughter's husband's uncle; that meant that he was Milani's great uncle. Although Mr. Chang wasn't a blood relative to the old lady, he was family through the child and that proved to be sufficient enough to make her feel secure in taking an once-in-a-lifetime trip to America.

Slapp took a trip back to the States to rekindle the old flame with his girlfriend. He wasn't sure what kind of reception he would get because it had been almost a year since he had seen her. The only contact they had had was through Bruce the finance man and Father Caleb the priest. She had been outside the circle the entire time, as far as knowing what or who Slapp really was. He made sure that Bruce sent her something for all the major holidays. Her clearance had finally come back approved. They had discovered some shady characters in her personal associations, but what can one do about the family into which you are born? A blood transfusion is not an option, nor will it solve the problem. I felt in my heart that they had a chance for happiness. Now that Slapp had some answers to his past's burning questions, he seemed to thrive in a completely different direction. I wanted to believe that it speeded up his healing process from that beating that he took that night in the alley. I made it my concern to keep watch over Slapp and the relationship between him and his mother.

Chapter Eight

A Mid-morning Kiss

A full ten days had passed since Alex's return to Hong Kong, plus two and a half weeks had lapsed since Tate's arrival back. Gayle was extremely excited about spending more intimate time with her future spouse Tate, yet every since that first return sexual encounter, where things had gotten roughly out of hand, due to no fault of either of theirs; Tate had become very withdrawn in the sex department. He had taken full blame for the discomfort that Gayle had experienced during their last private merger. She had expressed to him more than once, since then, that she was fine and no serious damage had been done. He still refused to believe her. This was a mental issue that he had struggled with for most of his adult life, due to his more than normal size endowment. So Gayle had to be patient, until he reached his comfort zone with her in bed again. One morning after Tate's first pick-up from the embassy had been completed; he called Gayle at her desk. "Hello Gayle, this is Tate. How you doing?" he asked in his usual smooth seductive tone.

"Hello Mr. Tate, how may I help you?" Gayle replied in a very professional voice as though she had remained upset because of all the intimate rejection that she had endured from him in the last couple of weeks. It had even included the night that we all had gotten rooms at the resort, when my mother had surprisingly arrived with my father. Gayle and Tate had spent a lot of physical time together, since his return, but none of it had included intimacy, which she craved, after he had taken that last long mission trip, back to the States. She understood totally what he was dealing with emotionally because he had explained it to her at the beginning of their relationship. Gayle didn't want to push the issue, but she couldn't comprehend why he didn't trust her when she told him that she had made a full recovery from the trauma, during their lovemaking. Of course, the quick healing was due to a magic potion that I was more than happy to share with her.

I had purchased the original container in the States, but now over here I had to create my own concoction. I learned quickly that it was very easy to do, because in this part of the world it's effortless to get everything that one would need in its raw and purest form. That's because the Drug & Food administration laws are more relaxed. The formula included one part witch hazel, one part eucalyptus, two drops of peppermint oil, one part lanolin, one part glycerin and two parts alum powder, mix well and then let the good-times role.

Tate ignored Gayle's angry-masked professional tone as she answered the call, because Tate knew that she was aware that it was he, before she picked up the phone.

"Gayle, I have a break in my schedule and I was wondering if you would meet me in your private quarters, in about ten minutes?" Gayle hesitated as the phone went mute for at least twenty seconds. It was apparent to Gayle that they needed to talk about the situation and not only this, but also some trust issues. She took in a deep breath and responded as she exhaled.

"Sure Tate, I can get away for a few moments. Mr. Pauling has changed his hours this week and I'm sure he wouldn't mind assigning badges for a couple of minutes for me. I will see you shortly." Gayle locked her desk drawers at both locations as she took the login ledger and three visitor tags from her hallway desk drawer. She walked swiftly towards Mr. Pauling, who was standing at the front main-entrance, on the top step of the building's landing. Gayle approached him from behind as he paced leisurely back and forth, while keeping a watchful eye on the sidewalk and street, just outside the opened gate of the American Embassy, in Hong Kong. Gayle called out to him before she had arrived near him. "Mr. Pauling," she shouted as she walked closer. He turned quickly and instantly noticed that she seemed to be in a hurry. "Mr. Pauling," she continued. "Hello and how are you?" He smiled cautiously as he waited for her to come nearer.

"I'm fine Mrs. Livingston, and how have you been?" He laughed again as though he knew more than he wanted to disclose. Gayle returned his smile as she asked the favor.

"Mr. Pauling, would you mind covering for me for a few minutes while I go upstairs to my quarters? We aren't expecting anyone to arrive today that might require a badge, but a tourist might drop-in to visit the gift shop." Mr. Pauling lowered his eyesight to the logbook and the three visitor tags that she held tightly in her hand, while pointing in his receivable direction. Her gestures revealed that she never considered the fact that he might refuse to perform the favor she was asking of him.

"Sure Mrs. Livingston, that's no problem. I will be here until noon or until you return." He said all of this while still smirking suspiciously. He then brought his eyes up to make contact with hers as he asked a question since they were now standing only inches apart, while passing the log and tags.

"I just saw your man, Mr. Tate, return from his first run," broadcasted Mr. Pauling. "This wouldn't have anything to do with that fact, now would it?" Gayle smiled shyly as she tried to camouflage her body language from answering the question without the words being spoken.

"Now Mr. Pauling," she said as she continued to attempt to cover the exposure with a distressing smile. "What could you possible know about that?" Mr. Pauling stroked his chin a couple of times as he thought of just how he wanted to handle his reply to something of such a personal nature. He decided to show his hand.

"I know that he went up to your room the first night that he came back, because he asked me if you were in-house when he arrived. As a matter of fact, he used my cell phone to call your berthing quarters before he went up. We got a chance to talk a little, while waiting for someone to come from the security surveillance booth, to help me check his bags." He then held up one hand towards her face, palm facing forward while shaking it just a little, as a signal that she wasn't required to justify; confirm nor deny what he had just shared with her.

"Alright, alright little Lady if you want to play it close to the breast, that's fine with me. Sorry no pun intended. That's great if that's what makes you feel secure; just don't try to convince me that I'm blind," said Mr. Pauling with the smug confidence that he was right on target about these circumstances. Gayle felt spotlighted as she listened and speculated who else in the building had picked up on the romance between her and Tate. Mr. Pauling shifted gearing a little as he made an effort to put her mind at ease. "Don't be concerned about how much I know and notice around here. It's my job to be observant. Now you tell me, just what kind of security guard would I be if I wasn't able to make a few small deductions, on the side, with all the information that I gather while standing here day after day and sometimes at night?" He smiled again as his eyes indicated that her secret was safe with him, if that's the way she preferred. Gayle released her side of the logbook as he assured her that the favor was no problem.

"Thank you very much Mr. Pauling. I will remember your kindness and your discreetness." Mr. Pauling nodded his head once while giving a shallow bow from the waist; just a little something he had picked up after living in Asia all those years.

"You are more than welcome Mrs. Livingston; and let me speak for the record that I approve of the relationship. I hope everything works out for the two of you. If there is ever anything I can do, please call me anytime." He gave an authentic approving smile once more as he took the logbook and turned to place it inside the small gatehouse booth, located just inside the ten-foot full-perimeter iron fence gateway. It was located at the bottom of the seven steps where he had previously been pacing prior to Gayle calling out to him. Gayle retreated back passed her office and then across the wide corridor to the larger elevators. Tate was already in Gayle's sleeping quarters when she arrived. He had removed his primary weapon and jacket and hung it on the back of a straight chair. He was sitting on the foot portion of Gayle's bed, with his fingers laced together, leaning forward with his lower arm resting on top of his thighs, while in deep thought. Gayle opened the door slowly as he raised his eyes to her level. She was surprised that he had arrived before she could get upstairs. He stood slowly to his feet and walked towards her as she closed the door behind and leaned back against it while both hands remained clenched around the doorknob; which acted like a buffer cushion between her butt and the door handle. He spoke first as he moved closer to her.

"Hello Gayle, by your tone on the phone, I wasn't sure if you would come." He used his body to box her in as he placed both hands on either side of her. He leaned into the door with his forearms resting on either side of her head and shoulders. He slowly reached up with one hand and removed his shades and tossed them on Gayle's bed behind him. She instantly became aware of the essence of him as she enjoyed the familiar scent of his cologne. It was amazingly alluring and she was sure that he knew its affect on her and others like her. Gayle closed her eyes as Tate maneuvered his body forward and tilted his head to softly kiss her lips with passion that had made him famous in her eyesight and possibly in other women eyes as well. It's that type of kiss that a special man delivers while only making physical contact with your mouth at first, then slowly adding that firm grasp somewhere else to the body with strong powerful hands, to complete the erotic affect. Gayle inhaled a full lung of air through her nostrils, as she returned his affection, by slightly feeding him only a tip of her tongue. That gesture set off a chain of aggressive events within Tate's mood. He moved his huge soft right hand from lying flat against the door to behind her neck, as he added more pressure to the kiss while pressing his full body up against hers. She leisurely moved her arms up around his neck, as his embrace intensified with more weight and force. She felt his hunger that would turn into torment, if went unfed. He broke off the kiss and backed away quickly as he protested.

"Wait baby, this isn't the reason I called you up here. I called you to apologize for not believing you when you told me that you were feeling better. I guess I have some trust issues when it comes to my phobias. I just want to ask for your forgiveness and I hope that I wasn't too selfish by withholding myself from you. That night when I came back, I was so tired and sleep deprived until I wasn't paying attention to what I was doing. Later, I was angry with myself for hurting you and angry with you for not telling me that I was hurting you. Do you accept my apology?"

Gayle answered, "Yes" just before their lips met again. Tate was now kissing Gayle as he released his passion and sexual desires for her, in the form of a forceful unrestricted kiss. Gayle was hoping that this was a forecast of some promising aggressive intercourse, later on. Gayle could now feel the tears streaming down her cheeks as she waited for Tate to release her from the agonizing kiss of foreplay. He noticed the wetness on his face and pulled away quickly with serious concern.

"Gayle, baby what's wrong? Did I have too much weight pressing against you and the door?" He gently held her face between his soft hands as he spoke to her quietly, while waiting for her to respond. Gayle didn't have the courage to tell him the truth that she was horny beyond his understanding and was now elated that he had decided to believe her and resume their sexual activities. Perhaps now he would make love to her without allowing his fears and phobias of hurting her to intervene. Gayle had so deeply missed the intimacy between them until the hope of them making love had caused her to experience an emotional moment. She tried to gracefully recover and not show her embarrassment, by lying to him about the few tears.

"No Thaddeus," said Gayle as she pushed the tears to the side with her index fingers. I guess I had a flashback flood of emotions, of when you were on the mission and how grateful I was that you and the others weren't hurt." Tate smiled down at her as he stepped back and away a few more feet. He led her by the arm as he spoke in a hushed tone. He then sat on the foot-end of her bed again directly across from the door entrance to the room.

"Come here Paper Doll, sit on my lap and talk to me." He had only called her by her approved coded inner circle name, for the second time. Gayle smiled as she expressed that she sort of like it. Tate gave his watch a quick glance as he checked to see how much time he had left before his next run. Gayle kicked off her two and a half inch pumps by the door and walked over to sit on his lap while wearing one of her unmercifully tight skirts. She was well dressed as usual and coordinated to the tee. Tate now spoke quietly as though someone else might hear as he kissed her neck, top of her shoulders and upper breast area.

"So Miss Gayle, tell me, what do you want to do tonight? Do you want to go home with me or do you want to go to your apartment next door? Now that Alex has returned, you are my only responsibility as far as protection is concern. Please allow me to confess for the record that I sure enjoy looking after you. Nothing gives me more pleasure than guarding that fine body of yours," said Tate as he kissed her neck lightly and ran his fingers into the top of her revealing low-cut silk blouse. Gayle continued to hold him loosely around the neck and shoulder with one hand as she sat sidesaddle across his thick firm thighs. Tate balanced her, while holding her around the waist lightly with the other hand as he waited for her answer.

"Tate," she giggled. "You are so fresh." He quickly defended himself sarcastically.

"Not yet Baby, but I'm strongly leaning in that direction."

"Let's stay at my place," replied Gayle. "That way I can change out some of my clothes. I'm starting to repeat my outfits for the second time; besides there is never any food at your place."

"I know baby, I can't keep any food stocked up. Slapp eats like he is driving a delivery truck instead of a limo part-time. I've given up." They both laughed. Gayle stood up from Tate's lap and walked toward the shared bathroom between her and Mrs. Beasley's sleeping quarters. She had remembered how things had gotten out of hand in the forms-room closet, when Tate had decided that he needed a little romance from her in the middle of the day. A private kiss between two new lovers had turned into heated-out-of-controlled foreplay. This had left her unable to concentrate for the remainder of that day. Tate checked his watch for the second time, as he released his grip on her, while noticing how tight that skirt seemed.

"Tate, I have to go back downstairs. I left the log and guest badges with Mr. Pauling and I'm not sure what time he gets off. He seems to know all about us and our relationship." Tate let his hand slide across her smooth well-shaped buttock as she stood up to walk away. He looked down, in another direction and smiled as Gayle walked away. "What's so funny Thaddeus? Did you say something to him about us?"

"Don't worry about it Gayle, he probably figured some things out when I asked him one night if you were staying in-house, when I returned from that last trip I took. Don't concern yourself; he's a man of integrity." Tate followed Gayle into the restroom as she stood in front of the mirror to freshen up her make-up. Tate stood so close behind her until she could feel his hot aroused breath on the back of her neck and side of her face, as he shifted back and forth, while making small-talk. He eased his arms around her waist and crossed his hands at the wrists, just underneath her full shaped breast, as they seemed to escape the top of her low cut blouse. She pressed a fresh layer of powder over her face to cover the tear tracks. She was about to place a touch-up gloss to her lips when Tate stopped her, as he turned her around to face him.

"Wait baby," Tate insisted. "Give me another kiss before you put on your lip color." He was grabbing handfuls of her hips and butt as he asked for the final kiss. He took another passionate kiss as he moaned out loudly. He pulled away as he explained.

"Gayle, I'll see you tonight. Don't go to your apartment alone. Wait for me or get Slapp to go over there with you." He released his grip on her as he headed out the bathroom and back through the bedroom to the door that exited into the hallway. He grabbed his holstered weapon and jacket from the chair, then out the door and down the backstairs in route to the motor pool.

That night Slapp took Gayle to her apartment and stayed with her until Tate completed his last limo pick-up. This would be the first time that Gayle would be able to sleep in her own bed in over a month or more. When she and Slapp arrived, Slapp headed for the kitchen to find some food that hadn't spoiled.

Gayle went to her large closet to select some more clothes in case she had to stay at the embassy a few more weeks.

"Hey Gayle," yelled Slapp. "I can't find anything in here to eat. I'm going to call downstairs and order from the sushi bar. Do you know the number?"

"Slapp the number is on the refrigerator's door. Tell them that you are here and they will deliver it for free. Tell them to put it on my tab." Soon the food arrived. Slapp and Gayle finished eating and a few moments later Tate knocked on the door. Slapp drew his weapon and walked to the door. Tate gave the signal door tap and Slapp opened the door.

"Hey big guy," said Slapp. "I'm glad I didn't have to shoot you. I thought you were coming through the back closet door from inside the embassy?"

"Hello Slapp, thanks for seeing Gayle home for me. I owe you one. I started to come through the back door, but I left the limo right outside so you can take it back for me, if you don't mind."

"No problem Tate, I'll see you two tomorrow." Then Slapp looked at both of them as he gave a brief chuckle. "Or maybe I won't." Slapp laughed as he closed the door on his way out. Tate walked over to the chase lounge and leaned over to kiss Gayle as he pulled her to her feet.

"Hello sweetie, come take a shower with me. I need you to wash my back and my front and perhaps my sides." Tate smiled deviously as he pulled Gayle in closer to kiss her neck as his lips slid down to her shoulder and the top fleshy portion of her breasts.

"Tate you know how small that bathroom and shower stall is, we can't even move around in there."

"Gayle, listen, if we take our clothes off out here, we might have a chance. I'm willing to give it try if you are." Tate continued to kiss her gently as they slowly moved toward the shower. The water was now spraying them warmly as they lathered each other calmly while speaking nonspecifically.

"I noticed that you keep it smooth and hair-free above the knee sexy lady," said Tate as his hands traced every inch of her body that he could reach while standing up.

"Nothing seems to get pass you fresh and naughty agent man," replied Gayle with a giggle.

"What are you talking about? I just want my woman to know how much I appreciate her paying attention to small details. I love having a smooth-skin lady in my life, because you never know when the little details may become very important options."

"Ooooh Tate, you are so scandalous. I need to leave the light on so I can keep an eye on you."

"Baby what are you saying? Are you saying that you don't trust me in the dark?" She laughed before she answered as he continued to entertain himself by kissing her body and making small talk.

"I trust you with my life baby, when you are fully clothed with your weapons; I just need to keep the lights on when you are undressed while pleasuring my body, because I don't want to miss a moment of enjoyment that you might surprise me with."

"Sooo what you are saying is that you approve of my nature." Tate laughed a little, "Now look who's being cheap and nasty?" The water started to cool off as the hot water tank ran low. He remembered her telling him that she shared some utilities with the sushi bar underneath her small flat. A few moments later they were in bed sipping a glass of wine. Then Tate remembered what had happened a few weeks before, when their sexual encounter got a little out of hand.

"I think I've had enough of that Gayle. I want to make sure that I'm in control this time when I make love to you. I don't want to ever hurt you again. Will you promise to tell me if I do?"

"Please Tate, don't bring that up again. I told you that I was fine a couple of days later. I don't know why you didn't believe me."

"I know baby, but I only wanted to be sure." Tate pulled her closer and she rolled to her back as he leaned over her to kiss her and to start the intense humorous foreplay. He rubbed his open-palmed hands over her body as he made comments.

"I wasn't sure if I could control myself today when I saw you in that tight skirt. I wanted to ask you to give me a sample of you, to hold me over until tonight. I then remembered our little romance in the forms locker closet and the fact that that didn't go over so well. I didn't want to repeat that mistake again. How long did you stay mad with me anyway?" Tate continued to smooth her body with light brief kisses. She returned his affection as she reached between them and wrapped her cool hand around his warm unsuspecting male-hood. Tate flinched as he pulled away slightly in surprise to her cold hand.

"Wait; hold up lady, can you warm up your hands? I guess I got my answer. You only remained angry until you could fondle my manhood again. Gayle, babe sometimes you are a little too aggressive with him."

"Oh please stop being a baby. You know I just got out of the shower with you." The mood changed to a more serious nature as she stroked him while he started to enjoy her boldness. He pulled down the sheet to expose both of their nudity as he moved between Gayle thighs for better access to pleasure her. She held him lightly as he made the shift. He kissed her on the lips gently as he told her how he had missed her while he was on his last trip.

"Hey baby, I should have never approached you sexually that first night I was back. I was too tired to pay full attention to what we were doing. I promise I will never make that mistake again." He moved his kisses downward on her body and she allowed him to take his fill of her pleasure. Then he slowly position himself to enter her as she closed her eye in anticipation of how good all of him was going to feel, after such a length dry spell. She moaned out loudly as he entered her. He hesitated as he questioned her.

"Gayle, baby am I hurting you?"

"No Tate, please don't stop. I need to feel you. Please don't stop." They made love for what seemed like a long time as he methodically fed her sexual hunger easily while watching her closely. She closed her eyes again and returned his strokes forcefully, as he pulled away slightly. She locked her legs up around him as she attempted to take more of him inside her. She could tell that he was holding back and she knew and understood why.

"Tate, can I get on top?" He didn't answer, just shifted them into the new requested position. Gayle knew if she was in the superior arrangement, then perhaps she would have more control of the strokes and the penetration depth. She was right, but Tate didn't share in her excitement of her newly acquired control. He was so uncomfortable with the new position until it resulted in a deflated ego, unfortunately and inconveniently, right in the middle of the best part of the coupling session. Gayle discontinued her maneuvers to get more and lay still and quiet as he hugged her tightly. He spoke after a few moments as he reiterated what he had told her about that part of him at the very beginning of their relationship.

"I'm sorry about that baby, but my fears of hurting my companion are so strong until sometimes that happens. Give me a few minutes. In the mean time, we can discuss where we think we want to live, once all of this is over." Gayle snuggled even deeper into his arms as she took a deep breath in before she answered.

"Well, I would like to be near my daughter until she finishes school and get her life on track. After that, it doesn't really matter, as long as I'm with you." He pushed her away a little so he could see her face and eyes.

"Wow baby, those are some of the most comforting words that anyone has ever said to me." He then kissed her forehead as he slowly moved his focus to her lips. He titled her head upward by placing his curled fingers underneath her chin. The kiss aided in shortening the interlude recovery-time process. His ego began to re-inflate as he rolled on top of her again. Their second pleasuring episode faded into a restful sleep until morning. Their bodies remained enlaced during the night as they shifted to other positions of comfort, yet only briefly breaking the romantic embrace. It was as though they had been together for years, and that's always a good thing when you are trying to form a relationship, while in exile and trying to stay alive.

The following morning, Tate woke up first and held Gayle in his arms very loosely until she started to awaken. The alarm clock hadn't gone off yet, but they both knew that they only had about a half of an hour or so before it chimed. Gayle spoke first, “Hey baby, how did you sleep?” She hugged him tighter before he could answer.

“Good morning Paper-Doll, I slept well and I feel great. I always rest peaceful whenever I’m this close to a beautiful sexy woman.” Gayle smiled to herself as she pulled away to go to the bathroom. “I wish that I had a little more time to spend with you this morning,” said Tate as he released his weak hug from Gayle’s back and shoulders as his finger tips finally lost contact with her soft and warm body. Gayle disappeared into the bathroom and Tate reached for his communication pack to call Slapp. He knew that Slapp had spent the night in the duty bunkroom on protection duty of his mother, Mrs. Carrington (Miss Beasley). He thought that perhaps he could get Slapp to cover for him and give him a little more time with Gayle. Slapp answered the first beep of the communication-pack call.

“Yea Big Guy, what do you need?” Said Slapp in his usual playful arrogant way, when he feels that his mine is quicker acting than whomever he is talking to at the time.

“Hey Slapp, can you . . . ?” Slapp interrupted him with the answer that he was hoping for before he could ask the favor.

“Hey Big Guy, I’ve already got you covered. Your next run is at eleven this morning. Oh by the way, tell Miss Gayle that I could only get her two hours of coverage from Mr. Pauling, because he needs to get off before noon. I didn’t ask my mother; I meant to say Mrs. Carrington, to see if she could cover for an hour or so for Gayle, but I will if she wants me to ask the old battle axe." Tate tried to interrupt Slapp to thank him, but instead Slapp cut him off the second time.

"Slapp I really appreciate what . . . ."

"No problem Tate, I remember what it's like to get a new piece and them have to get up early the next morning before you get a chance to hit it again before you leave," said Slapp as he begin to laugh. Tate was sensitive and put off by Slapp's comment and how he had downgraded Tate's new relationship, with his future wife, while comparing it to just a fresh piece of ass. Tate became angry and he had no problem letting Slapp know just how he felt.

"Damn Slapp, man why do you have to make everything sound so cheap? This is my lady that you are referring to." Slapp replied without taking another breath and without giving his answer any thought. "The same reason you have to make things so serious all the time, Tate. I was just about to call you and tell you what I had set-up for you, when my com-pack beeped. I meant no disrespect to your woman or your relationship. To tell the truth, I'm glad that you have found someone to snuggle up with, because you are no fun to work with when you are alone. Besides, I like Gayle and I think she's really, really sexy," replied Slapp in a lustful tone.

"See that's the shit I mean Slapp, you always take shit to far," yelled Tate just as Gayle exited the small bathroom to crawl back in bed with Tate. Slapp was still laughing as Tate's temper flared.

"Hey Agent Thaddeus, we can finish this waltz later, I have to go now and cover for your ass on this first run." Slapp continued to smirk. "I can't believe I can still get a rise out of you, after all these years of you knowing me," replied Slapp as he disconnected the call from Tate on his com-pack.

"Tate, who is that and what was all that yelling about?"

"Oh, that was just Slapp covering for me. He said that he could only buy you two hours with Mr. Pauling, but if you needed more time, he can ask Mrs. Carrington to cover for an hour more."

"Well, I guess everyone knows about us now, if they are willing to work in our stead, to give us more time together." Tate went into the bathroom to freshen up and returned to their love nest. The alarm sounded a few minutes later and they laughed out loud as Tate reached over to turn it off. They spoke softly to each other with their faces close together, while sharing a pillow.

"Baby please don't let me forget to personally show Slapp my appreciation," said Gayle as she eased even deeper into Tate's warm pleasure-promising morning embrace.

"I will baby, but sometimes Slapp tends to take a few unnecessary liberties with our ladies—like that day at the meeting when he kissed you on the mouth, just to get a rise out of me."

"Oh Tate, Slapp and I have our own relationship now. I wasn't offended by that kiss or his comment. He's a big kid at heart.

We had a serious talk in the car that day that he came to pick me up and deliver me back over to your place. He's a twenty-year-old boy in a thirty-seven-year-old man's body. I think he acts the way that he does because he has had so many disappointments in his life until his maturing process has been delayed a little. His mother disappeared when he was only three or so, then they told him later that she was dead. Then at eight he lost his best friend at the orphanage. He never knew his father. I think that he tries to make himself seem happier than he really is to hide the pain he feels. He is a very intelligent man and he observes more than I believe you guys give him credit for. Didn't someone say that he was one of the best profilers that you have on your team right now? At any rate, I'm willing to bet that you will see a big improvement in his maturity level, now that his mother is back in his life. She is going to make up for all those lost years, one day at a time. I don't think he will even notice the changes in himself, at first. Then he will become aware of his new pulse heart rate and that warm fuzzy feeling that he will get everytime his mother hugs him around the neck and tells him how much she missed him all those years. Tate, you aren't going to believe the scrapbook that she has kept on Slapp. One day she's going to prove to him that a family member was standing in the shadows, in every important day of his life so far. What she showed us is only a sample of what she has collected over the years." Tate listened with the ear of a student on his first day of college. Then he spoke openly with admiration.

"Wow!! Gayle, how did you sort this all out, in such a short period of time?"

"Well," she said as she hesitated. "It's easy to see your reflection in the mirror, after you have been forced to refocus a few times, as you try to heal yourself from within. When I first met you a few months ago, I was terrified of giving up my comfort zone to date you because of all the trauma I have endured—I just thought that it wasn't worth it. Now you think back to that first night that you told me about your over-endowed male hood growth from birth. Don't you remember how you felt inside as the words left your mouth? You felt like you had to tell me, but you weren't sure how I would react, or how you would feel after you had. A part of you was willing to be alone even longer, so you wouldn't have to open up those old wounds to inform me. That's what being an adult and growing is all about, leaving your comfort zone to improve yourself. It's really not a big deal, now that you are a fully-grown adult. Most of the fears and phobias that you harbor, at this point, are from your childhood. See how that could have possibly delayed your maturity growth a little. That was considered a traumatic period during your childhood development. The only difference between you and Slapp is that he had more traumatic episodes in his young formative years. The same thing applies to me, except I had life disturbances closer to adulthood, in the form of bad choices. I believe that the pain intensity is the same in all of our cases. It's that some people retain more scars than others and that kind of hurt tends to linger longer, if there is no one around to help one through it. Just give him more time, be patient with him. You know he loves you like a brother, because he is always trying to do something for you, so you will except him and like him more. I say that you need to ease-up a little and concentrate on pleasing me with the time that Slapp has bought us." Gayle slowly raised her lips up from Tate's neck, then to his mouth, as she finished her train of thought on the subject, while exhaling into his mouth, as she spoke. "So you can see and understand how it's all good, Thaddeus; I found you, you found me and Slapp found his mother. I have no doubt that all of us will be fine. We just need a little time to adjust, as we learn to appreciate today, as I'm about to show you how much I appreciate you, again." They both laughed a little as they moved in, even deeper, into each other's arms. Then Tate pulled the covers up between them in jest.

"I really like the sound of that Gayle, but I wouldn't be totally honest if I didn't tell you that I'm a little scared. When you talk like that in that tone, I feel so cheap and used," said Tate as he laughed out loudly. Gayle pinched him to refocus him as she giggled.

They only used an hour and a half of the time that Slapp had negotiated for them. It proved to be more than enough time to enjoy another sexual encounter and its euphoria overcast.

Slapp picked Gayle up in the limo on the return of his first run to transport her to work one block away, for security reasons and Tate went out the back closet exit of her apartment, which opened up into the back portion of the embassy's compound, for personal and privacy. Nothing new or special happened for a few weeks, while we all continued to acquire Milani and her great-grandmother's proper paperwork, for the two of them to return home with us. Christmas time came and moved on and it became clearer that perhaps this season was the hardest time for all of us. My mother, that had reared me, came over during that time and we all had dinner together at Uncle Oscar, my father's resort. It was very nice. We took lots of pictures to start our new photo album to share, as a new eclectic family, whenever we were able to return to the States. Of course, the agents were left out of these photos for security purposes.

William, our adult son, was doing well, but had broken up with his girlfriend. Alex had promised to drop-in to check on him, during his next trip to the States.

Spring came soon that year, but not without a price. It rained almost every day for two month. The Cherry Blossom Festival was great, one of the best that the local people had seen in a few years. I think that the natives contributed it to the unusual weather pattern. Whatever the reason, the season had created these extremely beautiful flowers. It was a spring that I will never forget and I promised myself that I would return to the city of Hong Kong again, during this time of season. It took a long time for the weather to become warm enough to travel without a jacket of some kind. If the sun was warm, the wind prevented you from enjoying it totally. The tourist returned as expected, but less because of the flu virus that had taken over the city for an entire week, in the form of quarantine. Prices for most street vendors were down and the shop owners were barely able to hang on because of the overhead cost, due to their locations. I was informed that the city was well documented for making full recoveries, in spite of all devastation that the country's history revealed. I was hoping that this was one of those times.

My foster-mother came over for a visit, right after they lifted the inward flight band for tourist. She stayed a month and I believe it was to spend some quality time with my father, Uncle Oscar. I was glad that she was getting on with her life, and after all she and my father had known each other all my life. I knew that perhaps there was a little something more there than just a strong friendship that had been forged, due to my childhood rearing. I had my doubts if I wanted my father to get to know my foster-mother any better than he had at this point. My foster-mother had always seemed to be so private and evasive whenever anyone asked her questions. I knew my father was mature and intelligent enough to take care of himself; yet I still had reservations about him becoming more emotionally involved with her. I didn't trust her after learning that she never found an appropriate time to tell me about my past, and had prevented three other people that I cared about, from doing so as well. Now that I knew that I would be spending as much time with my newly discovered father that was possible, perhaps I just didn't want to share him with her. I realized that this was going to be a problem for the two of them and me, until I cleared the air. There was no time limit to this kind of discomfort, but the sooner you put it behind you the better. I decided to invite myself over to dad's place one night for dinner. I didn't want any interruptions, so I chose a night that he was off. The three of us agreed to have dinner in my father's room. My foster-mother had taken an adjoining room to my father's. They were both waiting when I arrived.

As I took the elevator to their floor, anger arose in me for no understandable reason. Perhaps it was nerves, or my way of placing a barrier up for my feelings to be protected, as I learned more about my past. I knocked on the door and my father answered quickly with a smile.

"Come in Baby Girl, we've been waiting for you. I just ordered some wine to be brought up, until we decide on a menu for dinner."

"Hello Dad, it's always good to see you and spend some time with you. I guess in my mind, I'm still catching up for lost time."

"Oh, don't worry about that Monique; I think we will have all the time that we need, once we clear up all the secrets." Then I saw my foster-mother come through the door that connected the two rooms, as I cleared the threshold.

"Hello Helen, I mean Monique," said my foster mother. "I guess I have to get use to your new name." I snapped back at her with the anger I had embraced in the elevator on my way up.

"Don't you mean my real name mother, before you saw the need to change it when you sent off for the second birth certificate?" My father broke the conversation trend with a lighthearted gesture.

"Ladies, ladies let's keep this civil. I know emotions are running high, but we did all agreed to clear this up without letting things get out of hand. I care deeply for both of you and I don't want any hostility between you two."

"Look dad, maybe this isn't a good idea. I think it might be a little too early to hash this all out. I thought I wanted to know everything, but now perhaps it's better if we just put this off for a while."

"No, Monique, I don't believe that will solve anything. We need to get it all out and put it behind us. We know that we were wrong for not telling you, but now we are willing to explain why. We thought if we all gave you enough love and stability, that when we did decide to enlighten you, that it wouldn't matter that much. I can see, by your anger, that we were wrong. Come in and have a seat, the wine will be up in a minute." I felt a little distant, because I believed that my father, Uncle Oscar, was taking my foster-mother's side of things. I figured he would try to block for her during the conversation that the three of us was about to have, that was long overdue. That conversation never took place. We had dinner and I left.

Chapter Nine

The Ambassador Takes a Stand

The cooler weather had finally arrived and it was a very windy season. The city of Hong Kong seemed a little quieter as the high volume tourist-season was slowly coming to a close. There were fewer street-vendors because of the strong gusts of wind and down pour of flash flood rains; that the weatherman was unable to correctly predict, had caused havoc for everyone concerned. The investigations relating to Milani's custody and the bombing back in the States were moving along well. Tate and Slapp had somehow managed not to upset the motor pool boss, with their unannounced and unapproved trade-offs, in over a month. Gayle had informed me that the embassy's regular doctor had taken leave and the administration had called in a local man to cover for him. The embassy's assigned doctor would be gone for a while, back to the States due to some personal family matters. The local Asian American man had covered before, so all his papers were in order. He had received his clearance and had been granted a permanent badge.

Mr. Charles, the American Embassy's night inside roving patrol, appeared to have a serious problem with this arrangement. For some strange unknown reason, Mr. Charlie didn't particularly care for him. Mr. Charlie expressed this dislike by questioning him each time he saw him in the halls alone, in spite of the fact that the Ambassador had issued him a special badge. The doctor had complained directly to the Ambassador about Mr. Charlie's behavior and how he seemed to over-react with the rule enforcements, whenever it was related to him. When Mr. Charlie was called in and questioned about his rudeness, he couldn't give a specific or justifiable reason why he didn't trust or personally care for the fill-in doctor.

As Mr. Charlie approached the open door of the ambassador's office, the emissary stood to his feet and held out a hand of welcome to Mr. Charlie. Mr. Charlie and the ambassador had a friendship, as well as a working relationship. They had worked together for many years. As a matter of fact, Mr. Charlie had been the ambassador's personal driver before his eyesight had become too weak to see well enough at night to remain safe. The emissary understood Mr. Charlie's temperament well and had been forced in the past to make some concessions to keep the peace within the embassy's supporting staff. For instance, Mr. Charlie usually arrived late in the afternoon and felt that he shouldn't be required to pay for his evening meal, since the kitchen was closed and they were putting away the leftovers or throwing them out. Most of the kitchen staff were locals and had been given strict orders to track all portions of food. The only person in the embassy that was allowed to eat free was the dinning-room staff and the ambassador himself. Everyone else qualified for a food allowance and was issued a code that they could use, if they didn't have the appropriate funds at the time. Then it was taken out of their pay at the next pay period. To satisfy Mr. Charlie's need to be extra-special, the ambassador had instructed the cafeteria staff to give Mr. Charlie whatever he wanted and charge it to the ambassador's quarters as a late night snack. The Ambassador had to bend the rules on another occasion when Mr. Charlie refused to leave the reception space during a diplomat's visit, because Mr. Charlie informed the ambassador that this was the precise time that he had scheduled the time to test an alarm in that room or whatever other routine maintenance requirements. This had caused the Ambassador to increase Mr. Charlie's security level, so it wouldn't be necessary to explain why the phrase "everyone out please" didn't apply to him. However, this time there could be no doubt who was in charge and running the American Embassy; because there was no way around maintaining this doctor to fill-in if Mr. Charlie continued to harass him, while the assigned doctor was temporarily away. The ambassador moved around to the front of his desk to receive Mr. Charlie and shook his hand as they sat in two chairs that had been positioned to face the big desk of power and diplomacy. Mr. Charlie spoke first as he pretended not to know why the ambassador had sent for him. The substitute doctor and Mr. Charlie had exchanged some aggressive body language and a few unpleasant words, two days before. The ambassador knew that he would need his political skills to deter Mr. Charlie's smoldering temper from becoming a burning flame of anger.

"Good morning Mr. Ambassador," said sly Mr. Charlie. "I was told that you needed to see me promptly. Is there something special that you needed?" The ambassador hesitated, as he seemed to be pondering just the right words to use. He knew that if he didn't choose his words carefully that Mr. Charlie would be angry for weeks and take it out on the other staff members, by applying the rules even more rigorously than was necessary for everything to run smoothly.

"Mr. Charlie," said the Ambassador as his face expressed a deep serious concern to alleviate any doubt that a problem had arisen. "It has come to my attention that you don't particularly care for the fill-in doctor that we have acquired. This wouldn't usually be a problem except the doctor has caught wind of it and we don't have another person in the pipeline if he decides to leave without notice. He has covered for us a few times before and if you remember, it took a lot of paperwork for us to be able to allow him the privilege to walk the halls, the way that it is required to get his job done. Now just lay it out for me Mr. Charlie, if you can—tell me why this elderly man seems to just rub you the wrong way? He's a very good doctor and we don't pay him nearly what he's worth. You could say that he works for us for a song and a dance, so to speak." The ambassador laughed a little to soften the mood before he went on with his inquiry. "We have a few people around here that falls into that category. For instance those last two drivers that we hired. They showed up looking for a job and they already had legal weapons and badges. Now I must agree that their shields are a little tarnished, but who am I to question such powerful help, or for that matter, question their motives. I'm trying to run this place and stay within budget, while keeping all the staff safe and working with minimum stress. We are a long ways from home sir and I can't afford to turn down any help that's coming our way so cheaply and with the devotion that those two have shown to our cause. So you see Mr. Charlie, I have to turn a blind eye, no pun intended, to some things to be able to enjoy some of their rewards. We know that the good doctor is qualified because he was educated in the States and moved back here to help his people and practice Western and Eastern medicine together. He has even doctored on me on several occasions and I would like to say, for the record, that I have no complaints."

Mr. Charlie stroked his poorly shaved face and looked down at the floor as the Ambassador reached a pause in his monolog. Mr. Charlie bobbed his head back and forth, in an agreeing motion, as the emissary spoke his words of fact. Charlie wanted to let the ambassador know that he was listening and understood his position, as the diplomat of power. Mr. Charlie then raised his eyes to the ambassador's level as he tried to explain. Then he took on that step-and-fetch persona that is commonly used when a person wants to hide the fact that they believe that they are smarter than the person they are addressing at the time. The ambassador knew and understood exactly what Mr. Charlie was doing. He had used the same identical tactic himself on several occasions when he believed that his power of position was too weak for the negotiations that he had gotten caught up in, while serving as the America Ambassador to China. In layman terms it's called 'live to fight another day.' Mr. Charlie paused before he answered. He knew in spite of their relationship that the ambassador was no one to be pushed around. "You know Sir that I would lie for you before I lie to you. However, to be perfectly honest, I'm not sure what it is that stirs me up about him. He just gets to me whenever he walks the halls bowing and smiling like he's up to something." Then Mr. Charlie went into his final act; the same one that he used the last time that his ass was in the hot seat. "I realize Sir that this is not a suitable answer to your question on the subject Mr. Ambassador and I don't want to be any trouble to you Sir; since you've been so considerate, while allowing me to stay on, even after my eyesight failed the last physical test requirements to work here. In addition, I really do appreciate the fact that you allowed me to keep my weapon, for my inside roving watch. It's hard to look official as a security guard and all without a weapon. Maybe it's nothing Sir. Perhaps he just reminds me of someone when I was fighting in the war." The ambassador cut Mr. Charlie off quickly as he took in a deep breath to start one of his war stories that the emissary had indulged him in many instances before, but didn't have time for this particular morning.

"Ah Mr. Charlie ah," he said as he held up his hand in a please-stop gesture, while swiftly standing to his feet. "What I need for you to do Charlie is take it easy on the good doctor, because we really do need the coverage and we can't afford to find someone else in such short notice." Mr. Charlie agreed as he stood up also to be dismissed from the office.

"Sure Mr. Ambassador, I can do that. I will just steer clear of the doctor, thank you sir."

"No, thank you Mr. Charlie for understanding the delicate position that I'm in," said the emissary. He walked Mr. Charlie part of the way to the door that connected his office to the hallway and then he spoke again. "Will you please ask Mrs. Carrington to come in on your way out?"

"No problem sir, I would be glad to," said Mr. Charlie as he checked his weapon and adjusted his ammunition clips in his belt. A few moments later, Mrs. Carrington stepped inside the office door that Mr. Charlie had left widely opened.

"Mrs. Carrington, will you inform the covering doctor that I have spoken with Mr. Charlie, the night roving guard, and that I don't believe that he will be having any more problems with him."

"Sure Sir, I will do that right now." Miss Beasley departed the office area and headed for the clinic to pass on the message to the fill-in Dr. San Won Li. Now Dr. Li was a very quiet man with deep traditional values. He had studied medicine in the United States and had opened up a practice there, right in the middle of China town, in Washington D.C. He and his wife had raised two daughters and put them through college. After both girls were doing so well, they decided to come home to Hong Kong. They opened a small practice over one of the pharmacy stores and had pledged to give back to the community. Money was not an issue and he routinely covered a few times per quarter for other American doctors when they went off island. In addition, to keep the assets building-up, in order to keep his practice free to the poor, he would work at large sporting events and conventions as the medic-on-call. He had his choice of when he wanted to work, because this city was always hosting something on a grand scale, in which a doctor was required.

Chapter Ten

The Quarantine

For the next few days, it rained every day. Everyone seemed to have a runny nose or red eyes. There was a strange type of dampness in the air that no one could explain. Late one evening Tate arrived at Gayle's flat. He had walked over from the American Embassy, which was next door. Usually Tate would use the back entrance that opened inside the American Embassy's compound. The back door's secret passage was used as an escape route for the ambassador and his staff, if and whenever the main entrance would become a problem. When Gayle heard the weak knock on the door, she thought to herself, how odd this seemed. Gayle opened the door quickly as Tate lost his balance a bit as he stumbled inside, through the narrow doorway.

"Hey Baby, what's wrong?" She grabbed around Tate to steady him as he attempted to catch his breath to answer.

"Gayle, there has been a flu epidemic out-break in the city and they are closing down some areas of the city. They have already quarantined all the various embassies in the city. I came to get you so you wouldn't be out here alone and unprotected."

"Tate, why didn't you come through the back way?"

"Gayle hurray, they have already locked down the backdoors and the fence, plus placed a chain on the gates. Mr. Pauling only allowed me to exit out the front gate to come and get you. I have to get back before the doctor makes his rounds and discovers that I'm missing. I was quarantined to my bunkroom quarters a couple of hours ago. Everyone that isn't showing signs of the illness have been instructed to take a vaccine shot and start a full course of antibiotics. Stop talking Gayle! And hurry baby. A community shutdown in this part of the world is a lot more serious than in the States. Mr. Pauling is standing at the front gate with a M16 and a sidearm as we speak. The gate is locked with barriers in place and a chain laced through the fence's web, plus a padlock. Local authorities will sound the all-city warning siren at 7:00 p.m. They are trying to give the people a chance to get off from work and not panic, while traveling to their homes. The only persons that are authorized to move around are medical personnel, police department, fire department and their version of the national guardsmen. To be honest, I think they are more like mercenaries with legal weapons. At any rate, after the siren sounds they will be in charge." Tate was now faintly leaning to one side, as he sat on the chase lounger, while Gayle quickly scurried around gathering her things. She began to hear people yelling outside and the siren screaming from a patrol car. Tate was panting for every breath and sweating as if someone had poured water over his head. They locked the front door of Gayle's flat and descended the few steps to the sidewalk. They walked quickly one block to the front gate of the American embassy. Mr. Pauling saw them coming towards the entrance, so he started to remove the locks and chains from the gate. Just as they reached the entrance, two cabs filled with American tourists pulled-up that were on their way to the airport when the news broke on the radio, about the city's situation. Apparently they had already checked out of the hotel and didn't have any other place to go. Gayle and Tate rushed inside and Mr. Pauling locked the gate back as he tried to explain why he couldn't allow them to come in. He spoke sternly as he held his rifle with a firm grip.

"I'm sorry, but the American Embassy has been closed until further notice. I can't let you in because a quarantine status has been placed on the city. The only people that are allowed in are the embassy' staff and local workers, that will be forced to stay until the quarantine has been lifted. Please look for shelter at another location. Here is a number to this embassy, if you have any trouble finding a room." Of course, the Americans were angry and one man attempted to storm the gate. "Please sir," Mr. Pauling went on to say. "Don't force me take deterrent measures. The American laws and rules only apply if you are on this side of the gate. Now please step back and get into your cab before you ruin the day for both of us. The city-wide siren is going to sound in exactly fifty minutes and I think you should spend that time more wisely looking for shelter and not arguing the laws of our country back home." The man jumped back into the cab as he screamed some obscenities back towards Mr. Pauling. Gayle and Tate proceeded into the building as they headed to Gayle's office. Her workspace had been turned into a makeshift pharmacy and a shot clinic. Everyone that came through the front gate entrance had to be examined and either given a shot or a series of antibiotics. Tate was now coughing out of control as he became weaker. Gayle was barely able to get him to a bench inside the door of the embassy before he collapsed from an episode of whatever was going on with his coughing attack. Dr. Li heard the two of them as they cleared the front door of the American Embassy and he then stepped out into the passageway with a look of unbelief that Tate had disobeyed his strict orders to stay in bed and not to come in contact with anyone, if all possible.

The doctor then raised his eyes to Mr. Pauling's level that was standing about fifty feet away looking on, while trying to ascertain just how much trouble he was in for opening the gate in the first place. Dr. Li stared at Mr. Pauling only briefly as he decided that perhaps he should get the entire story before he begin to chastise anyone, after all Mr. Pauling was carrying a couple of fully loaded weapons and he was sure that Tate was strapped with two or more as well.

"Hello Mrs. Livingston, it's nice to see you again and I'm happy to see that you are one of the few that is still on their feet. Let's move Mr. Tate to a chair in your office that has rollers and then you can use it like a wheel chair to get him back to his bed." Gayle could tell that Dr. Li was annoyed with Tate, so she just smiled as they assisted Tate to the chair that usually sat behind her desk.

"Hello Doctor, I didn't realize that you had begun your stay with us," replied Gayle with an innocent undertone, as if she was unaware that Tate had disobeyed the doctor's orders.

"Yes, I was asked to come in early and then the news broke about this outbreak of the flu this season. It's too soon to say how bad it's going to become. Until we know, quarantine has been set for the city." Dr. Li and Gayle propped Tate's weak limp body in the chair while the doctor examined Gayle and gave her the seasonal flu shot. "Well Mrs. Livingston, you don't appear to have any of the symptoms yet, so I will give you a shot. I know that you have been exposed to Mr. Tate, so the moment you feel different in any way, tell me so we can get ahead of some of the symptoms."

"Thank you doctor, I will try to get Tate back in bed." Gayle took her shot and the doctor gave her some medicine for Tate to take every six hours. She positioned herself behind the chair that Tate was slumped over in and attempted to push him towards the door. Tate protested as he weaved back and forth in an effort to stand to his feet.

"No, no wait, I can do this. I can make it back to the bunkroom," he insisted. Gayle spoke up firmly as she grabbed his upper arm to force him back into the chair.

"Tate, no you can't walk back. Your fever is too high and you can hardly stand. Stay in the chair, I will push you back. If you fall, I won't be able to help you up and there is no one else around to assist me." Tate leaned backwards in the chair again and did as he had been instructed. Dr. Li continued his briefing.

"Gayle, I need you to put him in a guest-quarter's room because when I make rounds I will need to hook up some oxygen for him and put in a catheter. He has too much fluid on his lungs and he will not be able to go to the bathroom alone. I can already tell that Mr. Tate is not accustomed to being sick and that he isn't going to be a very good patient." Gayle directed her path toward the large elevator, as Tate's feet drug along the floor. There was no one standing there like usual, so she assumed that the person had taken sick or had left the compound before the quarantine had been set. Just as she reached the doors of the elevators, she heard the loud scream of the citywide sirens going off from every direction. It startled Tate as he reached for his weapon. The doctor noticed Tate's response from across the corridor and yelled one last notation, to his list of instructions as they pertained to Tate.

"Oh yeah, please take his weapons, if he won't permit that, at least remove all the bullets." Tate instantly began to swear, complain and mumble to himself.

"No one is going to take my damn weapons. I'm on duty and I have people to protect. What the hell was that old doctor talking about, taking my weapons from me? I sure would like to see his old ass try. I think he should be the first one to catch a bullet, just for making the damn suggestion." Tate said all of this as he bobbed back and forth in the chair with his feet dragging as Gayle continued to struggle to get him back to bed. He was now wet from the preparation that had been caused by the high fever. He was weak from coughing; while gasping for air; yet he continued to believe that he was on duty and in charge of a protection detail. Gayle decided to put him in her room, because his things were already next-door and there was a secret pass-through shifting wall-panel between her quarters and the bunkroom. She managed to get Tate undressed, down to his boxer shorts and was even able to get his arms into a pajama top. She had a little trouble taking his primary weapon, but promised that he could keep the smaller back-up one that was attached with velcro to his ankle. Tate finally agreed after a few rounds of distrusting and nervous phrases had passed between the two of them. He continued to complain as he gasped for more air and coughed out of control.

"I don't know why the doctor insisted that you relieve me of my guns. It's not like I'm so sick that I would accidentally shoot someone that I know, by mistake. He should be trying to take Mr. blind-ass Charlie's gun. Now that is an accident waiting to happen. Who left the doctor in charge anyway? I'm secret service and I think that I out-rank him." Tate couldn't take in a full lung of air, yet he was fighting with all the strength he could muster-up to retain his dignity. He had no idea what was up ahead for him and we all knew that this was a good thing that he didn't. Gayle tried to calm him and make him comfortable, as she waited for the doctor to make his rounds, back to Tate.

Now at the front gate there was a new arrival. Mr. Pauling had continued his pacing watch at the front gate. He wasn't accustomed to walking around with the weight of a fully loaded M-16 riffle, while on duty, so he had placed it in the guard-shack. The little four-wall stand-alone building by the front gate was sometimes referred to as the guard's shack. When another taxicab pulled up in front of the American Embassy, he thought to himself that this perhaps would be a good time to retrieve his heavier weapon to bear. Once he noticed that a single passenger got out and that person was dressed as a priest, Mr. Pauling came to the conclusion that just maybe he didn't need all that firepower to deter the man. After all, if he had arrived with a mission from God, Mr. Pauling was sure that there was nothing he could do to keep him out. Mr. Pauling had never met Father Caleb, prior to that day and if he had, he couldn't recall. Father Caleb walked divinely and graceful towards the front iron gated entrance. He was dressed in his clergy attire and was carrying a medium sized piece of luggage. Mr. Pauling became very nervous at that point. Not only was the priest coming to the embassy and had broken curfew, but he had also broken the quarantine barriers by traveling after the citywide siren had sounded.

Father Caleb brought his gaze up to Mr. Pauling vision level, as he stared at him with those piercing green eyes. The priest walked to the gate and sat his bag on the sidewalk as if he knew he would have to wait for a higher authority to give Mr. Pauling permission to open the gate.

"Good evening Father Sir, how may I help you," said Mr. Pauling as his nerves caused him to stutter?" The priest smiled as though he knew that he had the upper hand or possibly to appear more charming. Mr. Pauling wasn't sure which had caused him to smile so profoundly and with so much confidence that he would be allowed entrance. All Mr. Pauling was sure of was that he was frightened by the priest's presence, even though he was carrying a weapon and behind a locked chained iron fence and gate. After a few more moments of discomfort to Mr. Pauling, the priest spoke. It was now almost dark and there were only minutes left before the armed forces took control of the streets and would be arresting whoever had not found shelter for the night.

"Hello my son, my name is Father Caleb and I believe that I am seriously needed inside." Mr. Pauling became very agitated because he was sure that someone had died or was near death and no one had bothered to inform the front-gate guard, which in this case was him. He knew that several people were sick and the doctor was moving as fast as he could to assist everyone with either a shot or medicine. There were two cooks in the cafeteria that had been off their feet since noon. The surveillance booth that was usually manned by four men was now down to one. The cleaning staff of three ladies had left early that morning after they caught wind [found out about] of what was going down [was happening] from a family member that worked at one of the near-by clinics. Mr. Charlie, the almost legally blind night roving-patrol guard was in house, but had been forced to become a runner for the doctor, since he carried keys to everything. The only other location that held a full-set of keys to every lock in the building was the master-key locker. If any door or desk arrived with two or more keys, you can believe that one was on Mr. Charlie's key ring. Slapp hadn't returned yet from his last airport drop-off run. With Tate sick in bed, the ambassador and the second in charge off island, this meant that the doctor was the man with the power, at least until Slapp arrived back to the compound. Mr. Pauling took a deep breath and swallowed before answering the impressive looking Godly man.

"Sir, I will have to get permission to open the gate, to let you in. Will you wait just a moment please?" The priest smiled again as he held his hands together in a prayerful clasp and bowed once.

"I figured as much my son," replied the priest with his very strong Ireland accent.

Mr. Pauling stepped back and then turned his back to the priest as he pulled out his phone to call the doctor, who he was sure was in Gayle's office that had now been turned into a makeshift shot clinic and pharmacy, as I said before. The doctor answered on the second ring as he tried to load up the cart with medicine for all the people that were too sick to come to him.

"Hello, this is Dr. Li."

"Dr. Li, this is Steve at the front gate. An American Catholic priest has just arrived and informed me that he believes that he is needed inside the embassy." The doctor spoke franticly and with a tone that relayed the irritation that plagued him when Mr. Pauling had called him with such a silly dilemma. After all, the man was a priest, and the gate guard had the weapon and he had the means to search him. The doctor felt that he was just too busy to be interrupted with something so petty. He snapped a little as he answered. "I'm not sure who called him, but I need all the help in here that I can get. Let him in Mr. Pauling. I will deal with the fall-out of doing so later." The doctor hung up the phone quickly and Mr. Pauling turned to face the priest, while walking back to the front gate. The guard removed his keys from his belt to take off the chain and then unlocked the gate with a different and very distinctive key. Father Caleb had maintained his smile the entire time he had been waiting. Mr. Pauling opened the gate and the priest picked up his suitcase and proceeded through the narrow space that Mr. Pauling had provided only briefly for him to enter. Then Father Caleb stood just inside the entrance as he waited for more instructions. It seemed as though he was familiar with the procedures for any guest arriving. The guard took his bag and carried it up the steps and placed it on the x-ray machine's motion belt. Then he turned to search the priest. When Mr. Pauling had completed his security check, which included only a quick glance and no physical contact, he motioned for the priest to walk through the arch and wait for his bag to appear at the other end of the counter.

"Please Father, walk to the end and wait for your bag." The priest did as he had been instructed. When Mr. Pauling lifted the bag from the motion belt of the x-ray machine, the priest placed is hand very gently on Mr. Pauling's shoulder and spoke these words of encouragement and truth into his spirit. Mr. Pauling was frozen in time for a moment as he respectfully listened. The priest's gift of discernment was at work, no doubt.

"Stephen," said the priest knowing that he preferred Steve. If it is all possible or whenever you get a few free moments and before I leave this island, I would like to spend some time with you, in private. You seem to have a very troubled spirit that you have been trying to free yourself from for a long time. I'm not sure if you are aware of it or remember when the haunting began. I promise you that I can help. You have a very good heart, but it appears to be burdened with something from your past. At any rate, please make time for me when this is over. I'm very easy to fine and so is our Father." The priest removed his hand from Mr. Pauling's shoulder and he instructed the priest to the next process area.

"Father Caleb, I'm going to need for you to stop in on the first door on the left and get a screening and a badge. If no one is there, please wait, we are very short handed and I can't abandon my post to assist you any further."

"Thank you and bless you my son, you are very kind and have been a great help to an old man of the cloth." That was one of the priest's favorite personas to project whenever he believed he had gotten his way, but only because of the robe he was wearing. He entered Gayle's office and found a seat to wait for the doctor to return to the room or area. It was possible that he would only come back soon, after he discovered he had forgotten to place something on that cart or perhaps when something had run out, that he needed. The priest had no way of knowing how long his wait would be. This gave him time to meditate.

At Uncle Oscar, my father's hotel room, Little Max was giving him hell because Uncle Oscar wouldn't allow Max to travel back to the embassy. Max heard that Tate was ill and that had caused him to have an anxiety attack slash flashback from when his mother died and he wasn't there to talk to her before.

"Max," yelled my father. "You cannot go to the embassy. The city is locked down and if we go out there we will be arrest." Max was crying out of control as he attempted to explain why he had to go and being arrested was the least of his fears.

"Grandpa Oscar, I just have to go and see if Uncle Tate is going to be alright. You don't understand Grandpa. When my mother died, I felt that I should have been there for her. I said that I would never let that happen again to anyone that I cared about. I just have to go and see if Uncle Tate is all right. I got to see him in case he dies or something."

"Listen to me Max; you can not leave the hotel. Your parents will never forgive me if anything happens to you." My father called the condo where Alex and I were held up until the city investigated the impact of the threat. Alex had some symptoms, but had taken the shot earlier in the season. I showed no signs of being infected.

"Hello Dad, are you two inside. We are here watching the news."

"We are fine Baby girl, but Max insists that he has to go to the embassy to check on his Uncle Tate. Will you talk to him, because I'm ready to give him a spanking?" Uncle Oscar passed the phone to Max as he tried to stop crying long enough to listen. I passed the phone to Alex, his father, on our end.

"Hello Max, what's wrong? The city is quarantined until tomorrow. If you go outside, you will be arrested." Max stopped crying long enough to plead his case to his father.

"I know dad, but I just have to go. He's very sick, I just know he is and I just got to see him in case he dies. The news says that the policemen can be on the street. Call Officer Su Ki and have him pick me up and take me over there. It will only take a few minutes dad. I promise to help Miss Gayle and be a good boy." Alex was sold and agreed to call Officer Su Ki. Mr. Su Ki had been his partner when he was hired as a consultant to trace the illegal tea that was being shipped out of Hong Kong. He was also Milani's second cousin's on her grandfather's side. "Stay by the phone, I will call you back. Listen to me carefully Max, if this doesn't work out and Officer Su Ki can't get to you, you have to promise not to give your grandfather any more trouble. If you do, I promise you that your punishment will be so severe, until there is a good chance you will apply to be adopted, by another family." Max agreed and hung up the phone. There was no uncertainty in Max's mind that Mr. Su ki wasn't coming to get him. He was so confident that he began to cram his things into his backpack, as he explained the plan to his grandfather.

"Grandpa, my dad is going to send Officer Su Ki to pick me up and take me to the embassy." "Max, what will you do if they won't let you in because of the quarantine?" Max continued to pack-up his things as he answered without a second thought.

"Well, Father Caleb always says that God takes special care of all babies and fools. So since I'm young and not scare I guess I will be okay. Because it's Mr. Pauling night to work, he will let me in—I just know he will." Uncle Oscar had to look away so Max wouldn't see him laugh about that last answer that he gave about babies and fools. Uncle Oscar picked up his keys and headed for the door to wait in the lobby with Max for Officer Su Ki to pick him up. Downstairs in the lobby of the resort there were people everywhere stranded, some sick, others angry and babies crying. People on the floor, others cursing at the counters. The hotel staff was trying to get control and calm everyone, but this had brought out the worst in everyone concerned. One of the staff recognized Uncle Oscar and hurried over to him to ask if she could sleep in his room that night. She was the same lady that came up at night to check on Max whenever he stayed overnight and my father had to perform in the lounge. Of course my father agreed because he was pretty sure that he would be working late to help keep the people calm. This meant that Max wouldn't be in the room alone if he returned.

Thirty minutes had now passed, but it seemed more like a few hours because of all the confusion and noise. Then Max heard a police-car siren pull up in front of the entrance. It was his ride, Officer Su Ki. Max ran out the door before his grandfather could say good-bye to him.

"Bye grandpa, I will call you in a few minutes from the embassy." He slammed the back door of the police car as a mob of people surrounded the vehicle with thousands of questions for the officer, in at least ten different languages. Officer Su Ki had to blow the horn and turn on the siren in short burst to force the people out of the way. Max noticed the top of a child's head sitting in the front seat. It was Milani. Officer Su Ki was taking her to the American Embassy so she could receive the flu vaccine. They had run-out of the vaccine in her area and the police department had refused to make an exception, since a second cousin was not considered immediate family. When Alex called the officer to transport Max to the embassy, Su Ki mentioned it and Alex informed him that they had more than enough of the vaccine at the embassy because only part of the staff was in-house and most of those were already sick and wouldn't be able to take the shot until they recovered.

Milani stood-up in the front seat of the car so she could see Max more clearly and to smile at him. She had learned a few words of English and was excited, to say the least. They arrived a few minutes later at the American Embassy and Officer Su Ki parked his patrol car up on the sidewalk in front of the gate, so the emergency vehicles could pass through the narrow street without any delays. Mr. Pauling recognized Max and Milani right away, but this was the first time he had ever seen Officer Su Ki in uniform. He opened the gate promptly as Officer Su Ki reached inside the car, to carry Milani in his arms. Then he opened the back door for Max, as he leaped out quickly. Mr. Pauling spoke to Max first, as he waited for the full explanation from the policeman.

"Hey Buddy, your parents are out in the country at their condo. Why are you here?"

"I came to see about Uncle Tate. He's very sick and I don't want him to die before I see him." Officer Su Ki gave Mr. Pauling a strange unexplainable look as he tried to explain his portion of the illegal protocol breach.

"How are you doing sir? This is Mr. Thornton Jones' niece Milani. I brought her here to get the flu vaccine inoculation. They ran out of it in her designated area and the police department wouldn't make an exception, because she is not considered immediate family. You can see why that could be a problem convincing them that she is." Milani held her cousin Su Ki firmly around the neck as she smiled at Mr. Pauling with those big round brown eyes. It was noticeable that she had a mixed heritage and it was also visibly obvious that she and Max were related as well. Mr. Pauling hesitated for only a second because he had learned his lesson well from the previous time when he had called the busy doctor to ask permission to open the gate for the priest. Given that Mr. Pauling knew Max very well because he was Max's ride to school, whenever his parents were off island, he decided to make a decision and if it was the wrong judgment call, then he would just have to 'take one for the team'. [Accept a blow of reprimand from the person in charge]

"Okay no problem, I will have to run Max's backpack through the machine, but other than that you should all be clear. You have to wait in Mrs. Livingston's office until the doctor returns from his rounds. The plan is to make sure that everyone is given the shot or start medication if any symptoms has surfaced that indicate you have been exposed." About that precise moment, the priest that had now been waiting for about an hour heard and recognized Max's voice as it echoed off the walls and floor of granite. The priest stepped out into the hall and called to Max. Max dropped his backpack and began to run towards Father Caleb, as he once more began to experience an emotional overload and began to cry.

"Maximilian Jones," questioned the priest. "What in heaven's name are you doing here my son and where are those fine parents of yours?" Max ran to the priest with so much force until he almost knocked him over as he placed a death grip around his waist to hug him. The Father leaned forward to receive him as he waited for Max to get a hold of himself and answer the question that the priest had just put to him. Max held onto the priest a few more moments. Mr. Pauling ran his bag through the x-ray machine and gave it to Officer Su Ki as he continued to hold Milani in his other arm. Everyone stood still for a minute or more to observe the reuniting moment that seemed to be taking place between old Father Caleb and Baby Max. Max tried to answer the priest's questions and explain why he was there, all at the same time, while unable to take in a full breath, due to his excitement and distraught feeling about Tate's ill condition.

"Father Caleb," sniffled Max. "I came to see about Uncle Tate because you told me when we were back home that I should look after them and I was at the hotel with my grandpa Oscar and he didn't want me to come and then I remembered what you said about God taking care of babies and fools, I told him that I should be okay and my dad called Milani's cousin, because he's a police and he picked me up and brought me here." Max said all of this without any respect to punctuation marks of language or rest breaths of speech. There was no doubting that he was upset and had mentally taken on the role of a much older person. Father Caleb attempted to calm him as he escorted Max into the waiting area, to wait for the doctor to return. The priest spoke now, directly to Mr. Pauling.

"I will keep an eye on the lad for you until we can sort this all out." Mr. Pauling returned to his post by the front gate and waited for another unpleasant situation to arise. He was sure that Slapp should have been back by now, so he took out his cell phone to give him a call in the limo. Slapp was only a block away when he answered.

"Mr. Alvin, this is Mr. Pauling at the front gate. Can you give me your ETA [estimated time of arrival]? All hell is breaking loose in this place. I believe you are the highest ranking person, still standing that hasn't shown any signs or symptoms to the virus yet." "Mr. Pauling, I'm only a block away. You should have the limo's headlights in your sight, as we speak. I will pull into the garage and lock the gate behind me, over and out." The doctor arrived from his rounds upstairs just as Slapp came through the side door, from a side entrance that lead to the motor pool's garage and duty driver's sleeping quarters. No one was stirring and Slapp knew this was a serious problem. He had only been gone a few hours and in that short period of time, it seemed like everything had gone from bad to worst.

He and the doctor came face to face as Slapp jokingly addressed him. The doctor was a very neat dresser by nature, but this flu outbreak had caused him to place his appearance on the back burner, as he tried to keep up with all the medical demands of the epidemic that had now shut down the city. Dr. Li's white shirtsleeves were now rolled up above his elbows and bottom tale portion was partially out of the rear of his pants' waistband. His collar was unbuttoned at the top and his necktie was just barely hanging on for dear life, around his neck. He was moistened from working quickly and worrying at the same time that things may become more critical before help arrive to inform him exactly what he was dealing with. He had already decided to use all the training and knowledge that had taken him a lifetime to acquire. He believed in Eastern and Western medicine and had studied both with passion and with a relentless pursuit.

Slapp addressed Dr. Li in his usual playful type attitude as they nearly collided in the main corridor, of the first floor.

"Hello Dr. Li, what's going on? What happened to you? Damn Doc, you look rough." The doctor snapped to make sure that Slapp understood that he didn't have time to play their usual word games that they sometimes engaged in to pass the time. If the truth were told, Dr. Li was quite fond of Slapp and had made an effort to befriend him, even at their first meeting. He told Slapp that he had the same temperament as one of his younger brothers—very playful yet deadly dangerous if crossed. His local Asian accent came to the forefront as he spoke the strong words of warning.

"Listen Mr. Alvin, I'm very busy man and if you are not going to be any help to me, then I would appreciate it very much, if you stayed out of my way. Tell me now sir, which is it going to be?" The doctor then stood motionless as he stared upward into Slapp's face with the seriousness of a ninja warrior about to go into battle for his instructor's honor. His instant anger had caused his eyes to close to an even more of a narrow slit as he waited for Slapp to respond, or come on board, so to speak. Dr. Li knew and understood that Slapp was willing to help in any way he could; he just needed Slapp to understand how much uncertainty and pressure that he was now operating under. Slapp answered up quickly to apologize, while maintaining his humorous wit.

"Sorry Dr. Li, I had no idea how bad it had gotten since I left earlier, but you do look like shit roasted in brown paper bag. Now tell me, what you want me to do, 'cause you know I'm your man." Slapp held up both of his hands above shoulder level, as though he was volunteering for whatever the doctor had in mind. The doctor almost smiled as he acknowledged that he did appreciate Slapp's unshakable lightheartedness.

"Mr. Alvin," said the doctor, as the strong local Asian accent, maintained its position as part of the doctor's speech. "I need you to stay as far away from the sick people as you can. You will need to relieve Mr. Pauling in a few hours and guard the front gate. When people get desperate, they do crazy things. There are a lot of Americans in the city and we don't want them to storm the gate. You know better than me how bold and selfish the Europeans act with their entitled arrogant attitudes. I'm pretty sure that your mother told me that you had some serious respiratory problems as a child, so we don't want you to come in contact with anyone that has been infected. Stay down here and manned the phones and then relieve Mr. Pauling so he can get some food and rest." Dr. Li gave Slapp his instructions as he and Slapp walked across the wide corridor and headed for Gayle's office, which now contained Father Caleb, Officer Su Ki, Max and little Milani. Slapp humorously responded to the doctor's last statement about not coming into contact with anyone that may be infected.

"Doc, does that include my mother? Because I know you heard that we are just getting back together after being separated for thirty-five years or more," said Slapp with a smirk. The doctor attacked Slapp again, but this time with more of his broken native tongue, which Slapp always found amusing and had secretly made it his goal, to cause to happen.

“Mr. Alvin, I hava no time ah for your ah crap. I’m ah to bizzee right now, so pleasa help ah me anna stoppa playing ah around. There is ah lot of ah sick people here to see about.” Of course, Slapp was enjoying every broken syllable that the doctor spoke.

They arrived at the door of Gayle’s office and Milani leaped from Officer Su Ki arms and lap, and ran to Slapp for him to pick her up and kiss her little cheeks, like he always did whenever he saw her.

“Hey Milani, how is my favorite girl?” The doctor turned to scold Slapp for the third time.

“Mr. Alvin, what did I just tell you? I haven’t examined anyone in here yet and you are sharing air with her already. Here, put on this mask please and wait over there with her.” Officer Su Ki explained his dilemma and informed the doctor why he had brought Max to the embassy. Next, the doctor directed his attention to the priest, Father Caleb.

“I’m not sure who called you Father, but I’m very glad you are here. I need all the help I can get. You can see what I’m dealing with here, with Mr. Alvin being in-charge. The most powerful man in the building, besides God of course, and he is a jokester. I will see how funny he remains when he comes to realize how sick his friend Tate is, upstairs.”

The Priest bowed gracefully once and removed his top cloak and jacket. He rolled up his sleeves and put on a mask. Dr.

Li drew up a shot for Milani and she began to hold Slapp even tighter around the neck as her cousin, Officer Su Ki, tried to explain what was about to take place, in their language. Then the doctor suggested that Max take the shot first. The doctor examined Max for any flu symptoms and then gave him the shot. Slapp placed Milani on the floor and Max led her over to the doctor. Max held her arm steady and placed his hand over her eyes. Officer Su Ki watched from a distance and was amazed at the level of trust that Milani had in Max. Milani tried to cry a little as Max leaned down to hug her.

"No Milani, don't cry, it only hurts a little bit. Then Max kissed the spot over the band-aide and Milani smiled through the tears. The doctor spoke again as he now placed a band-aide over Max's injection site. They found Gayle's cookie stash near the teapot area and appeared to be recovering quickly from the shots. The doctor turned to the officer.

"Officer Su Ki, has the remainder of your family received the flu vaccine this season yet," inquired the doctor?

"I have, but I'm not sure about Milani's great aunt and great-grandmother." The doctor spoke quickly.

"Very well, go and pick them up and bring them back here. If you can't return with them tonight, then, bring them first thing in the morning. I'm so sorry that I can't stay here and chat, because there are others in which I need to evaluate and treat. Father Caleb, will you please come with me."

Max spring to his feet, "What about me Father Caleb, I remember everything you taught me when the homeless people got sick that time at the soup kitchen. I can help, I know I can."

"Very well Max, but first go with your Uncle Alvin and cousins to the cafeteria and eat before time for Mr. Pauling to be relieved; by then the doctor will have an assigned job for you. I will put in a good word for you and tell him how much of a help you were to me." Then the Priest winked one eye in Max's direction.

Slapp, Officer Su Ki, Milani and Max headed towards the mess hall hoping that at least one cook was still on their feet and had not taken to their bed. When the four of them entered the cafeteria from the elevator, it was very quiet and they only heard one person moving around, way in the back of the kitchen. It was one of the old ladies that help the leading chef to prep the food and clean up afterwards. She was the only one that wasn't sick and had chosen to stay behind to help out when the news story broke about the flu virus. Officer Su Ki and Milani stopped just inside of the cafeteria's entrance, as they all four exited the elevators. Slapp and Max walked toward the large kitchen, as they usually had in the past, if it was near closing time for that shift. There they had found one old lady. She had started large pots of chicken soup from scratch. She had three pots and they all were set on a low simmer. Her name was Young Hwa, which means Shinning Glory. She had been working there for a long time.

She spoke English well and understood some of the nuances of the Western culture. She was the person who trained the newcomers about how the kitchen had to be run. Now she was running a solo gig (working alone) when we needed her most. Slapp and Max recognized her right away because she always saved them food and didn't charge it to Slapp's account as required. She would always say that it was 'something that we had to get rid of anyway, so why not let the little greedy people eat it instead of the garbage can'. She rushed over to the two of them as she spoke with a revived spirit and an open smile.

"Hi guys, I didn't expect you today. I thought everyone was told to go home before the big siren sounded. I live alone, so it no matter where I sleep," she said with a slight error in the translated speech.

Slapp spoke up quickly, "I'm sure glad that you decided to stay, because we have a lot of people who wasn't able to make it home. You think you can feed Little Max and me? Oh, I almost forgot about Officer Su Ki and Baby Milani. They are both out front. I will tell them that you will be right out to take their order."

The old lady smiled again, except this time with a little bit of an annoyed expression on her face. She looked to see if Slapp was teasing her as he usually did about one thing or another. Sometimes he would make her so angry until she wouldn't speak to him for a week or more. Slapp found this very amusing, for some strange reason. A couple of times, when he made comments about her food, she became so angry until she walked out in the middle of a shift. The Ambassador caught wind of what had happened and insisted that Slapp do whatever it would take to get her to come back. Slapp gave her a day to cool off and then he went to pick her up, very early one rainy wet morning, in one of the limos, as he pretended that he didn't know that she had quit. He told her the ambassador had agreed to give her a raise at the beginning of the next fiscal year. The extra dollar per hour was taken out of Slapp's pay. He didn't mind because most of the time, he ate free anyway, whenever she was in the kitchen. The other staff members that worked with her enjoyed the fights between her and Slapp. She would be cursing him out partly in her language and the remainder in English. They found it entertaining and a way to break up a long days.

Now Slapp noticed that look on her face as she turned to respond to him saying that she would go out front and take orders, when he knew that she was all alone in the kitchen, because everyone was either sick or had gone home.

"Are you crazy Mr. Alvin, I no go out front to take no damn order. You can eat ah from one of these ah pots or you can take your ah ass some place else. I'm ah cooking for the sick people. You no look ah sick to me, Mr. Alvin. So if ah you ah want something special order, then you can ah get the hell out of my ah kitchen."

Slapp started to laugh out of control as the old lady grabbed a large meat cleaver knife from side the wall that had been attached by a magnetized panel. Max became fearful and quickly backed up against the wall with his eyes stretched widely open.

“Put that knife down Old Lady, don’t make me shoot you. You know I will if I have to.”

“I’m no punk ass bitch, shoot me. I survived ten years in prison camp in my country.”

Then she realized that she was frightening Little Max, so she stuck the knife into the chopping block with a hard downward stroke and motioned for Max to come to her so she could explain. Slapp had continued to laugh as he looked behind and noticed that Officer Su Ki and Milani had now followed them into the kitchen, after they heard all the noise. The officer was still holding Milani tightly in his arms, as he entered the kitchen to investigate the ruckus between Slapp and the tiny old Asian woman. Max moved toward her and she bent down to hug him and kiss his cheek as she always had done, whenever she wasn’t too busy serving food. Now she was speaking directly to Max as she tried to calm herself down, because she was sure that Slapp was only teasing her and because she wasn’t sure in what capacity Officer Su Ki had entered the kitchen.

“Max, why do your parents allow you to spend time with this crazy man? He is too dangerous for a child to be alone with. He causes trouble wherever he goes. Now go out front Max and I will bring you something good. You will like it, you will see.” Max proceeded as he had been instructed and took Milani with him, while Slapp walked closer towards Miss Young Hwa to apologize for upsetting her.

"I was only teasing you Mama Son, will you forgive me again?" She yelled at him again as she turned her back to him to stir each of the three pots on the stove.

"You no call me that, if I was your mama, I would have drowned you at birth." This comment deeply hurt Slapp because he had lived without knowing his mother was alive for the passed thirty-five years. The old Asian woman turned just in time to see the pain, of a bad memory, wash over Slapp's face. He had spent the last thirty-five years without his mother or without any biological family, to his knowledge and she had just picked the worst possible thing to say to him. Slapp turned slowly and walked pass Officer Su Ki and waited at the table with Milani and Max, out front. Officer Su Ki spoke to Miss Young Hwa very calmly, in almost a whisper.

"You know that is Mrs. Carrington's only son and they have been separated for the last thirty five years," said Officer Su Ki in a low voice to make sure Slapp didn't hear him revealing this to the old lady. The old lady gave Officer Su Ki a shocked look as she slowly stirred the pots.

"I know Mrs. Carrington; she's a very nice lady. I like her a lot. She has been here for a very long time. She always gives me gifts for my birthday and for American Christmas, every year, she never forget, not one time do she forget." Miss Young Hwa started to tear up, now that she realized that she had hurt

Mrs. Carrington's son. She turned away quickly and dabbed the tears from her eyes, with the corner of her apron, as she scurried around to fix all of them a tray. She thought about what the officer had just revealed to her, before she responded again. "Okay, well, I'll tell him that I'm sorry, but not now because he will think I'm a punk-ass bitch." Her words were golden and she did apologize to Slapp, two days later.

Each pot had different ingredients, but the basic broth was the same chicken stock. Some had everything from scallions to noodles, the next pot had less spices and the third pot had all the flavorings, but she had trapped all the solids in a gauge, so it was only a liquid broth. She knew that some would have a hard time swallowing, because their throats would be too sore. The old lady had also made some pudding pops and jell-o cups with fruit cocktail. She had thought of everything and was only waiting around for her orders from the doctor, to serve her special magic soups. That's what she called it. The priest informed us later that she was a converted Christian and the magic that she spoke of was probably a little Lordy-Jesus that she had added in the form of a prayer. She also had a large kettle pot boiling for tea.

It was getting late and the winds had picked up again and it also had begun to rain. The sirens from the police cars, fire trucks, and rescue ambulances screamed in the vast darkness as the five of them sat and ate their fill while watching the latest reports, of the flu epidemic, broadcast over the huge flat screen television monitor. Miss Young Hwa served them, the soup of their choice; hot freshly baked rolls, white rice, and pickled ginger strips on the side. For dessert she served then freshly baked apple turnovers with French vanilla ice cream from Haagen-Dazs that the ambassador had had flown in for a special dinner. She laughed as she served the dessert, while she boasted that this occasion was special enough and if the leading chef had a problem with her decision, then he could just fire her, whenever he was back on his feet, or took a mind to do so. She repeated as she served, 'We are all still alive, dry and warm, that is a reason to celebrate.'

When the old lady moved around the table to serve the hot rolls, Slapp noticed that her eyes had been moistened and her nose was a deeper pink. He wondered what Officer Su Ki had said to her after he had walked out of the kitchen, but he didn't ask. Miss Young Hwa refused to give Slapp eye contact as she reached over the table with her tongs to pass out the hot rolls. Max and Milani sat next to each other and Officer Su Ki and Slapp sat on the other side. The old lady sat on the end of the table, in which was only designed for four, because she continued to jump up and bring more food out for them to consume. She served the kids over Slapp's shoulder and each time she would bump him side the head with her elbow as if she was still mad and then apologize so gracefully in a strange playful insincere voice, so the kids would laugh. Slapp pretended that it hurt more than it did and flinched to make it more realistic and entertaining for the kids. Even Officer Su Ki found it amusing, but he knew that the bumps side the head was only love taps that she couldn't put into words, yet. Slapp knew also, but never let on that he understood what the old lady was doing. She was trying to apologize and save face, (protect her pride).

Just as they finished their apple-turnover alamode', (with ice cream) the doctor called the cafeteria and ordered some food for three of the sick people in quarters. Officer Su Ki and Milani left and Max headed for Uncle Tate's room which in fact was Gayle's room that was located just on the other side of a bathroom that she shared with Miss Beasley. On the other side of Gayle's sleep in-house quarters was the duty bunkroom that was designed to sleep four. Slapp proceeded back up to the first floor to relieve Mr. Pauling, who had now been on duty and on his feet since early that morning.

In Gayle's room, there Tate lay wet with preparation, delirious from the fever, and hallucinating from the side effect of a local tea. The type of tea that would never had a chance of receiving the stamp-of-approval from the FDA, back in the States, or the CDC formulary for a legal cure.

The doctor's cart, with all the medicine neatly organized, was parked outside the room door in the opened passageway. There were small dosage cups displayed out in a tray. Some even had names and times written on them. The second level of the cart had a box of surgical masks, waterless hand sanitizer, syringes and vials of the flu vaccine. On the bottom level were small bottles of water and a clipboard holding a roster of names of people that had remained in the embassy after the final siren had sounded, announcing the time for everyone to be off the streets. When Max arrived from the back staircase, he noticed the cart and knew what to do. He sanitized his hands like the priest had taught him to do when the homeless people had gotten sick back home, at the soup kitchen. He put on a surgical mask and tied it tightly around his head covering his mouth and nose. He knew that the doctor or the priest would step out into the hallway from one of those rooms soon, and then he would ask if he could go in to see Uncle Tate. Max had never seen Uncle Tate sick before, except for the homeless people, he had never seen anyone very sick before. He didn't know any of the homeless people very well, but he was sure that the feelings would be different in his Uncle Tate's case.

A few moments later, the doctor appeared from a room across the hall from where Master Max stood near the medicine cart. The doctor spoke with renewed hope that he was about to get some more well needed help and a fresh pair of hands, even though they were a small pair and lacked some of the necessary training that was required for something so serious.

"Hello there Max, does your arm hurt where I gave you the shot?" The doctor smiled as he walked closer.

"It hurts a little," replied Max as he gave the area a couple of squeezes with the opposite hand."

"That's good," said Dr. Li. "Take this Tylenol and a bottle of water from the bottom of the cart. Now write your name on that bottle, because we don't want anyone else to drink from it, in case you need another sip from it later."

"You think I can go in now to see my Uncle Tate, doctor?" Max waited, as the doctor looked him over, and then spoke with ease.

"I think you should take one of these antibiotic pills to give your immune system a boost, after that and a short prayer from the priest, I think you will live through the night." Max remembered the priest favorite quote again and thought that this maybe a good time to share it with the doctor, as a repeat.

"Father Caleb always says that God takes special care of babies and fools and I believe him." The doctor laughed to himself and responded through the laughter that he was now suppressing inside.

"Well, why didn't you say so Max, then by all means, go right ahead on in. I have no doubt that you are protected, at least by some portion of that statement."

"Do you think that I will need a pair of gloves too Dr. Li?"

"No Master Max, just remember to wash your hands every time you think about it. I should say whenever you touch someone or something that a sick person has touched." The doctor had to remind himself that he was giving instructions to a seven-year-old boy. Max moved closer to the door of Gayle's room as he looked back at the doctor, who was now doing a inventory of the medicines, while trying to decide if he needed to go downstairs again, to replenish the cart. Max knocked softly on the door and waited for someone to come to the door or yell to him to come in. Inside the dimly lit room was Gayle standing next to Tate in bed as he was delirious with fever and side effects of the medicine, that was working much too slowly, for all parties concern. His attitude toward being sick wasn't helping matters any either. Father Caleb had made himself a little seat behind the bed on a simple stool and out of the path of traffic that had formed as the doctor passed back and forth through the secret paneled wall that led from Gayle's room to the duty bunkroom that contained three more sick staff members. The priest's gaze moved from Tate's weak face to the intravenous pole, which held two bags of fluids that the doctor had started in Tate's left arm. There was deep concern on the priest's face, but his faith was strong in the Spirit and the doctor's abilities, with the Divine One's guidance. The priest's sleeves had remained rolled up and he was wearing a mask. He moved around, throughout the building assisting the doctor, but every hour or so had returned to be near Tate, in case he asked for him.

Gayle answered the knock on her room door. "Please come in, it's open." In walked Max as he gave the room a quick once look-over. He walked over slowly to the bed where Gayle stood, as she held a cold compress to Tate's feverish forehead. She was surprise, to say the least that no one had told her that Max was in the embassy. The priest took this opportunity to go and help the doctor, as the doctor made his way to the next room that held yet another victim, of this strain of virus. He spoke to Max as he made his way from behind the tight space that the bed had created with the help of the wall and I.V. pole.

"Max, remember what the doctor and I taught you about washing your hands a lot. We don't want this to spread," said Father Caleb. Watch him closely Max and if you notice any changes, come and get me; just like I taught you to do at the soup kitchen when the homeless got sick last winter. Then the priest turned to Tate, but was pretty sure that Tate was totally unaware of his presence in the room. "Tate, my son, I will be right outside if you need me." Father washed his hands in the bathroom and left the room. Tate didn't respond or open his eyes when the priest's spoke. It was a good chance that Tate wasn't conscious enough to realize that the priest or Max was in the room.

"Miss Gayle can I help, let me do that," said Max as he moved closer. "I'm a good helper; just ask Father Caleb when he comes back." Gayle dipped the washcloth in the water and rubbing alcohol bath and wrung it out as dry as possible before passing it on to Max, then stepped back, so he could move even closer.

"Tate," whispered Gayle. "You have a little visitor. It's your buddy Max. I can't believe his parents agreed for him to come to see you." Tate didn't answer or move as he continued to struggle to breathe. Max held the wet cloth to his head and then leaned in to speak in his ear, as though he believed that he didn't hear Gayle announce his presence and his own voice would do a better job.

"Hey Uncle Tate, it's me, Max. My dad couldn't come to see about you because they are out at the condo and can't get a ride into the city. I was right down the street with Grandpa so I told them that I would come to check on you." He paused as he held the compress tightly to Tate's head. Then without warning, Tate began to cough again, out of control as he tried to sit up more to catch his breath and take in more air. Gayle moved back closer and held a tissue over his mouth as Tate attempted to roll to his right side to face them. Tate slowly opened his eyes and looked at Max little frightened face.

"Is he going to die, Miss Auntie Gayle," inquired Max?

"Oh no Max, we are just waiting for the fever to break. You know Max, for his body temperature to go down a bit. The doctor will be by soon from his rounds and to give your Uncle Tate some more medicine." Tate spoke for the first time since Max had arrived.

"Hey little buddy, I'm fine. I just need more rest. I promise not to die."

"Can I call my dad on your talking thing, Uncle Tate?"

"Sure you can use my communication pack. All you have to do is push one button and I promise that your mom or dad will answer." I answered my communication pack on the first beep.

"Hey Auntie Ma, can I speak to my dad?"

"Sure Max, he's sitting right here. How are you and how is your Uncle Tate?"

"He's very sick Ma, they say he's not going to die or anything, but I don't know. He looks real bad." I passed the communication pack to Alex. They talked for a moment and then signed off. It was now near midnight and the winds had picked up even more. Max listened to the howling whistling sound that the wind makes, as it passed between the buildings inside the embassy's compound. Then Max had this bright idea.

"I know what will help; I will go and get you some soup from the cafeteria. Miss Young Hwa says that it is magic because she puts so much love into it. Stay right here Uncle Tate, I will be back before you can take another ten minute nap." Max ran in the bathroom and washed his hands and ran out the door towards the elevators. He almost ran over the doctor as he stepped into the hallway from another room. "Sorry doctor," yelled Max. "I will be right back to help you, I promise." Max returned in about five minute or so with a bowl of clear broth soup. The bowl had a tight lid on it and next to it were two hot rolls and thin slices of pickled ginger. He sat the tray in a nearby chair, which accented the hallway and pulled a fresh mask from the medicine cart. He then picked up the tray and knocked on the door of Gayle's room with the toes of his foot.

"Miss Gayle, it's me Max. Open the door for me. I can't reach it—I'm holding the tray." Gayle opened the door and stepped back, so Max could move pass her. She cleared the top of the nightstand, next to the bed and Max sat the tray on top. He went in the bathroom to wash his hands and came out to feed Tate the clear broth.

He called softly, "Uncle Tate I'm back with the magic soup. Miss Young Hwa says that you have to drink at least half of it for it to work." Max placed the large white dinner-napkin under Tate's chin and across his chest. "Wait Uncle Tate, I have to say the blessing part thing." Gayle noticed that Tate almost smiled as he answered Max. He was probably remembering how Max's food grace usually consisted of a confusing mixture of a before-meal blessing and nightly prayers prior-to-bedtime prayer. The grace was always a little lengthy and slightly off target, yet in still, Tate was just glad that he remembered that it was necessary to thank God before eating. Besides, when you say grace or pray, you are talking to God, everyone else in the room are only extras, experiencing the spiritual moment. Tate was sure that God could figure it all out, even though we sometimes found his meal blessings and nightly prayers amusing, and was unable to.

"Max, make it quick, I feel another coughing attack coming on," said Tate in jest. Max pulled up his mask half way and took a bite from the first hot roll as though he thought that his Uncle Tate needed a demonstration or motivation. Then he gave Tate a spoonful of the magic clear-broth soup. Tate frowned a little.

"Oh, is it too hot, sorry Uncle Tate?" He stirred the soup slowly and fanned it with his other hand, back and forth over the bowel. Gayle and the priest looked on, but did not get involved with Max's recovery plan for his Uncle. Tate fell asleep for a few minutes and Max started to cry as he repeated over and over. "You have to wake up and drink some more Uncle Tate. The old lady said that it would only work if you drink at least half of it." Gayle knew that Max was getting tired from the long day and needed to rest. So she took over his feeding position and continued to hold the compress to Tate's head. Max moved around the bed and crawled up into the priest's lap to be comforted from his disappointment that his Uncle Tate was too sick to give him his full attention.

"Come around here, Master Max," instructed Father Caleb. You have had a very long day. I think you need to go to sleep. It is almost 1:00 in the morning and I'm sure that your father, Alex, would be very angry with us if he knew that we have allowed you to stay up so late. Don't worry Master Max, the Divine One has his own magic and I'm sure He knows how we feel about Mr. Tate and is willing to provide a little magic of his own, for Tate's recovery."

"You think so Father Caleb, do you think that God will give Uncle Tate some of his magic," inquired Max, with a heavy heart? The priest spoke up with confidence and with renewed hope, while smiling down at Max, but only slightly.

"Sure he will Max, besides Tate is a good fellow, why wouldn't He be willing to help us out. As a matter of fact, I'm counting on God to come through and do just that—send down some of His magic." Gayle smiled a little and continued to stroke Tate's face.

Father Caleb had been standing watch over Tate's condition. He had prayed because he and Tate had some unfinished business. Tate fell into a deep sleep and Gayle retired to the chair that was located at the foot of the bed. The rain and the wind continued to howl outside the window as they all listened to the emergency vehicle's sirens continue to scream throughout the rainy darkness. Max soon fell asleep as Father Caleb closed his eyes again to pray, while leaning his head back up-against the wall just behind the I.V. pole with the two bags of fluids that had remained attached to Tate. The two bags were almost empty, and Father Caleb knew that the doctor would be stopping by soon to check them. He placed Max on the bed next to Tate's lower leg and he adjusted Max surgical mask back into the proper position, for a safety barrier. The priest had to disturb Gayle in the recliner chair that she had borrowed from Miss Beasley's room next door, to squeeze from behind the bed, where Tate seemed now to be resting peacefully. It had been a long night, but the doctor was still on his feet and Father Caleb wanted to go help him, now that he was pretty sure that Tate was out of danger, from the need of being hospitalized.

"Excuse me my child, I have to make rounds with the doctor and to make sure that I can spread a little more of God's magic." Gayle smiled for she knew that the priest was making fun of Max's understanding of Divine Intervention.

"Sure Father, no problem, I didn't mean to block you in back there." The priest placed his hand on her shoulder as he slid pass her in the chair and made a request.

"Mrs. Livingston, will you keep an eye on him for me until the doctor or I get back?" Gayle answered with spunk as she peered over in Tate's direction. Max had moved over closer and was now sleeping on top of Tate's lower left leg while holding on to it as though he didn't want him to make a move without him knowing. The priest washed his hands in the bathroom and walked out into the hallway to wait for the doctor to appear from one of the five berthing rooms on that floor.

Back at the condo, near Stanley's Market area, Alex and I had spent a restless night on the long sofa. Alex was facing up on his back, while I rested on top. We had placed both, the communication packs and the portable house phone within reach, waiting for a call from anyone at the embassy who had a mind and give us an update. We had left the television on all night, turned down low, so we could track the weather and the epidemic of the virus. They hadn't given it a name yet. Different people seem to have conflicting symptoms. So now we were playing the waiting game. It had currently been hours since our last call from the embassy. We knew that Max was okay and in his element after being forced to live at the embassy for a month or more when we had gone off island to see about my foster-father, who had later died during my visit. Our only concern was how many rules of quarantine had he broken or if he was in the way of the people requiring treatment.

It was now 5:00 in the morning and I got up off the sofa to turn on the coffee pot. I was wondering if Slapp would be able to come and pick us up. Living at the resort with my father would make things a lot easier for us if the quarantine lasted a few more days. Then I remembered that Alex had mentioned that his former partner from the Hong Kong police department, Officer Su Ki would give us a ride later. Officer Su Ki was considered family since he was Milani's second cousin who was our niece by way of Alex's deceased twin brother. The house phone rang about 5:30 a.m.—it was Gayle with the morning report.

"Hello Helen, this is Gayle." Gayle was whispering so I assumed that she was in the room with someone who was asleep. No doubt it was Tate and possibly Max, as well. "I'm only calling you to inform you that little Max is fine and that he is still asleep. Tate seems to be resting better and the doctor removed his intravenous fluids a few minutes ago. I think his fever has broken, but he is still coughing a lot and fading in and out of sleep. I think the doctor wants to make sure he can contain his movement. I believe he added a little something extra to the I. V. bag."

"Hey Gayle, we are so glad that you called us. We wanted to call earlier, but we knew that everyone would be busy, asleep or taking care of the sick. How is the doctor holding up? Was Milani able to get her shot?"

"Yes she received her shot and the doctor ordered Mr. Su Ki to bring Milani's great aunt and great-grandmother in today, whenever time permits, so they can receive a shot as well; compliments of the American Embassy." "Thanks for calling with the updates. We will try to come into town as soon as we can and take Max off of your hands. Bye." Gayle hung up. I relayed all the information to Alex and then I started breakfast.

Back in Gayle's sleeping quarters, Tate started to move around a bit more and open his eyes. The only people that he could remember, before becoming delirious, was the doctor instructing Gayle to take his weapons and Gayle struggling to remove his clothes, before putting him in bed. He didn't remember the doctor putting in an I.V. or a catheter. Neither did he remember Max, forcing soup down his throat. He vaguely recalled the priest's arrival, his low voice and mute presence. He called out to Gayle before he opened his eyes. Our deductions later were confirmed by the conversation with Tate, that the local medicine side effects included the mixing of dreams with reality.

"Gayle," called Tate with a weak raspy breath voice. Gayle sprang to her feet from the recliner from Miss Beasley's room and rushed over to Tate's bedside.

"Hey you," replied Gayle as she stroked his forehead while checking to see if his fever had lowered. "You gave us quiet a scare last night." Tate opened his eyes slowly and reached out for Gayle's hand.

"Hey Baby, I need some water." Gayle poured a half a cup of water in a styrofoam cup and added a straw. Tate took a few full sips and then swallowed. Gayle questioned him.

"So how do you feel Thaddeus? Is anything hurting you? Does your body still ache?"

"I still ache a little all over, but something is wrong with my left leg. I can't seem to move it." Gayle could see the deep concern on Tate's face as he continued to speculate the problem with his left leg. "You think that maybe it's a side effect from some of the medicine that the doctor gave me." He turned his head to look over at the I.V. pole that had remained in place with the two empty bags. The doctor had come in a couple hours before and removed Tate's I.V., but didn't have the time to move the I.V. pole set-up. "You think there was something in the I.V. solution that has caused this to happen on just one side?" He closed his eyes again. Gayle began to question him more.

"Thaddeus, explain to me how does it feel?"

"It just feels real heavy and there is sharp pin-sticking like sensations running through it. I just don't have enough strength to move it like the right leg." Gayle looked down at his leg and began to laugh and tear-up at the same time. Tate became more disturbed by his personal dilemma and very excited as he spoke. Gayle was now holding her hand to her face as a single tear escaped each eye as she laughed more. She couldn't answer yet; her mixed emotions of relief wouldn't allow it. She was to choked-up to speak.

"Gayle what's wrong with me? Are you laughing or crying? Say something Gayle, you are scaring me!" Replied Tate as he became even more agitated and emotional.

"Baby, I think I know what is wrong with your left leg, Little Max has been sleeping on top of it, most of the night." Tate lifted his head up more off his pillow to look down at his legs, as Gayle continued to laugh and cry at the same time.

"What the hell!" said Tate as he expressed relief that nothing was seriously wrong with his leg and infuriated that someone had allowed little Max near him, while knowing he was so sick, and no doubt infectious. Gayle became aware instantly of his dual emotions of concern and started to explain, in hope he wouldn't become too wound up and start to cough again. Tate's raised voice and his jerking reaction to his legs; woke Max up.

"Thaddeus, there was nothing we could do to keep him away. He had a temper tantrum at the resort with Uncle Oscar, when he informed him that he couldn't come over here. Then Alex called his former partner on the local police force, Mr. Su Ki, and asked him to drop Max off with us. Max was afraid you were going to die, like his mother and he wouldn't be able to see you again. Don't be mad with us, Max took his flu shot last night and the doctor put him on a series of antibiotic, to be on the safe side of this unknown danger."

Tate's anger decreased a little as Max became aware where he was and that Tate was now awake and talking. He became very excited as he rolled off of Tate's lower leg and began his crawling ascend up the front of Tate's weak achy body. With no respect to Tate's condition, Max moved upward so quickly, until neither Gayle nor Tate could prevent the damages that was about to take place. Knee to groan, open hand to the stomach and chest were all mishaps that Tate sustained as Max made his way up to Uncle Tate's face, now that he had discovered that Tate had lived through the night. Tate was screaming from sheer pain as Max crawled up the front of his exhausted and pain throbbing body.

"Ouch, oh God, wait Max, oh please do something Gayle, he's killing me," said Tate as he tried to deter Max's path to top of the bed, which was straight up the front of him. Gayle reached for Max quickly as she tried to explain the pain and discomfort that he was causing to his uncle.

"Wait Max, Uncle Tate's body hurts and is too sore to support your weight." She pulled Max off of Tate quickly and stood him on the floor, as Tate tried to recover after being trampled.

"Hello Uncle Tate, do you feel better. I stayed with you all night and fed you some magic soup from downstairs. The lady told me that it would work, but at first I thought that I didn't give you enough. Do you remember?" Max held his face so closely to his uncle's face until it was impossible for Tate to focus well enough to see Max clearly. He was still wearing his mask, but it was twisted out of place and torn on one side. Tate answered slowly.

"Hey Buddy, they told me that you stayed to look after me in your father's place. I'm glad I didn't make you sick. I don't remember much from last night. I guess my fever was too high and the medicine was stronger than I thought." Tate rubbed Max's smiling face and head to reassure him that he was feeling better. Gayle looked on and laughed to herself. She had no idea what strong bonds had been forged between Max and his father's friends.

"Uncle Tate, can I use your phone thing to call auntie-ma and dad? I told them that I would call them and tell them how you were doing. I forgot to call again last night and I fell asleep." That was Max's name for me, other times it was Auntie Helen.

"Sure Max," replied Tate. "It's next door in the bunkroom. It should be next to my shades." Max ran off to get the communication pack. "I know Uncle Tate, I used it last night; don't you remember?"

Tate questioned Gayle further, "What time is it and why is it so dark in here?"

"It's still pretty early in the morning Thaddeus; we are under a weather condition warning. There was no moon and it rained off and on all night." Gayle then reached over and turned the lamp light to a brighter level and then went to the wall switch by the door and turned the dimmer up, so the room became brighter.

"Gayle, I need to get up, I need to take a shower. I need to shave."

"I don't think the doctor want you to get out of bed until he makes his rounds and that may take a while. You are not as strong as you think you are. Your temperature has gone down a bit, but you haven't eaten in a while. Besides, the doctor put in a catheter. You have to wait until he takes it out Tate." Tate reflected before he responded to Gayle's last statement.

"Max crawled all over the catheter tube, I would be surprise if it is still in. I was wondering why my loins were on fire." Tate made a strange face as he remembered that the doctor must have discovered his birth abnormality when he placed the catheter. Tate was too out of it to remember, but he still felt embarrassed. Now he would be fully aware whenever the doctor returned to remove it. The doctor came through the door as the thoughts were still running through Tate's mind.

"Hello Mr. Tate, I see you are looking better. I guess you are ready to eat and get cleaned up. I have a confession to make, if you promise not to shoot me. I gave you some stronger extra sleeping meds in your I.V. to make sure that I could keep you in bed. I know you are ready for me to take out that catheter." Dr. Li turned to Gayle slowly.

"Miss Gayle do you mind excusing us for a moment. I would like to exam him and remove the catheter." Gayle and Max prepared to leave the room.

"Sure doctor, by all means. I will just go downstairs and get him some breakfast." The doctor and Tate made eye contact as the doctor listened to his heart and then his lungs, front and back. Then he asked him to open his mouth wide and held his throat as Tate attempted to swallow. Then he walked away to the bathroom to wash his hands, before gloving up to remove the catheter.

"You know Mr. Tate I didn't remember who you were when I first met you. I remembered your name and I couldn't for the life of me remember why it was so familiar. Almost fifty years ago I was a student at John Hopkins, and I was on my pediatric rotation when a case came in. It was your case Thaddeus and the birth anomaly that you have. A new hormonal drug was being introduced and you and a few others were the pilot cases. I came in contact with you again when you were about two years old. As a matter of fact, I gave you one or two of your injections. The Privacy Act wasn't in full compliance like it is now, so I shadowed your case after I finished my rotation there. I remember that I had to check your name against the vial three times before I drew the medicine and then the instructor had to check it and ask me to identify you in three different ways. You all were taking the same basic drug, but you were all different ages and each vial was designed strictly for each patient. I remembered you because of your name and those unusual eye colors for your mixed ethnicity. I wanted to know what happened to the six of you. Your family must have move around a bit, because I lost track of you when you were about nine. I never forgot your name or those eyes. So you see Tate, there is no reason for you to be embarrassed of me; I was your student doctor fifty years ago. This is what some people like to call, 'life doing a full circle on the two of us'. When you feel up to it, I would like to ask you some questions, so I can make notes and catch up on results of the treatment. If this is too much of an intrusion into your privacy, I will understand. I came home to help my people. You can help me in this area, if that's not asking too much. I promise to be discrete; if that will help you make up your mind. I just need to collect some raw data, from the patient's perspective." Dr. Li finished his hand washing procedure and then removed Tate's catheter. Tate never answered the doctor about allowing him to interview him later. He just listened to what the doctor had to say about his past and realized, from the tone of the monolog, that he knew other things about his family dynamics. Tate was from a broken home and carried a last name that didn't biologically belong to him. He knew that with all the blood work that the hospital had to draw, while keeping track of the results, for a pilot case study such as his, the subject must had come up that his father was only his stepfather and there wasn't a chance of his younger brother having the same birth irregularity. He knew that his biological father was contacted and a medical profile had been performed on him as well. No one outside his agency, other than Alex, knew who Tate's biological father was. He felt that he should tell Gayle, but it could wait a few more days, he thought, until he was back on his feet.

Dr. Li exited the room and informed Gayle that Tate could take a shower, but with only lukewarm water and that he wouldn't be able to stand very long without help. Gayle entered the room and found Tate sitting up on the side of the bed in deep thought. He started to cough again and lean forward, as though he was protecting some sore ribs or an old previous injury that had been irritated by the traumatic cough.

"I guess this isn't attractive to see your man sick," said Tate in between episodes. Gayle didn't hesitate a second before she responded to his pity sarcasm.

"What's really unattractive is to see such a big handsome man feeling sorry for himself when there are so many others around him that will be bedridden, for at least a week if not more. I know that's not what's bothering you. What did the doctor say to you? Are you upset about the catheter thing or did the two of you cross paths before? You know he had a practice in Washington D.C.'s Chinatown for years and I know how you guys like to stay-under the radar, when you all are out of your element or get hurt." Tate looked up at Gayle as she stood just inside the door, but never responded to any of her comments or questions. "Tate, can you move over to the recliner, I want to strip the bed and put on some fresh linen? The doctor has given you the okay to take a shower, but he said that you would need help. Alex and Helen are headed into the city in a few hours to pick up Max, would you like Alex to assist you then?" Tate answered slowly as he stood to his feet to move over to the recliner.

"That will be fine, baby. I will just brush my teeth and wash up a bit; because I'm sure Max will be back any moment with my breakfast."

"No, I have it. It's right outside on a cart."

Later that day, Officer Su Ki arrived with Milani's great aunt and great-grandmother. Dr. Li administered the shot to each of them and Officer Su Ki took them back home after they all made a stop in the cafeteria to eat. Miss Young Hwa was in her comfort-zone whenever she was given the opportunity to serve some of her own without asking permission and filling out a triple copy request form, to justify the food usage later. She was a gracious hostess by any standards and an excellent cook. She had prepared breakfast food and had placed the three chicken based broths back on, for the sick people that wouldn't be able to tolerate solid food. Until further notice, she was considered as the one in charge of the mess deck. Around noon, Officer Su Ki delivered Alex and me to the embassy. We arrived and went to work for Dr. Li. Slapp was now off duty and Mr. Pauling had taken over the front gate watch again. A few of the regular employees returned, but Mr. Pauling refused to let them back onto the compound. They had all left the day before without checking out with anyone. Now that they had realized that the various embassies had the best survival plans in the city, they reached the conclusion that they would fair-out better if they were quarantined at work. The workers also learned that they were now off the payroll's clock and was now burning annual leave during the quarantine period.

Gayle spent the day between her office answering the six-line phone and hovering over Tate, as he continued to recover in her bed. The message traffic came in through Miss Beasley's office and reported that it was a very deadly strain of the flu virus and that the shot that was prepared for this season was not the right strength or anti-viral mixture. More vaccine was being flown in and would arrive the next morning. Each distribution location was advised to report to the CDC's warehouse with the proper paperwork to receive its allotment. Miss Beasley rushed the message down to Gayle's office to give it to the doctor. There was no one in-house authorized to sign the paperwork. This was the first time that the ambassador and the second in charge had ever been off island the same time and leaving behind a fill-in doctor.

Usually when they were both gone, the doctor was in charge and had the power to sign the paperwork in their stead. Dr. Li was only there, as a cover-doctor and that power had not been extended to him, which had been a mere oversight. So the fact remained that Slapp was the most powerful badge on the compound, in spite of the fact that he was in reality a fugitive from justice. Gayle and Miss Beasley knew exactly what paperwork was required; but they were hoping that the person on sight wouldn't question the signature. The authentic seal would be proof that the request was coming from the American Embassy, but would that be enough? There would be absolute chaos surrounding the area, because there wouldn't be enough vaccine to go around in the first shipment, plus there would be black-market concession being made, before the inventory could be matched up with the paperwork.

Alex decided that he, Officer Su Ki and Slapp should go the next morning to retrieve the American Embassy's portion of the first shipment of the replacement vaccine. They discussed it with Tate, who agreed that they should go locked-and-loaded. The rules of engagement were different in this part of the world and they decided if anything went wrong that they wanted to be the ones helping the authority to fill out the investigation reports. In some parts of the city, corruption was spelled with a capitalized "C" and the black-market was corruption's twin brother. The National Guard that the U.S. uses to keep the peace on the home front was more like rebels for hire in this part of the world. Who knew better than a group of renegades, on how to deal with them?

Now that the message had confirmed that the vaccine was very little help or protection from the present stain of the virus, Dr. Li decided that he should revert back to Eastern medicine, at least until the new vaccine arrived. The doctor had already mixed Tate's treatment between the two disciplines of studies. This risk had been taken because they didn't want Tate to have to go to the hospital. The hospital fills-out forms and make computer entries and they can be traced. Tate and the remainder of us were all living under an exile status. Now the doctor would kick it up a notch to include the other's treatment as well. He knew that one of the locals that worked in the kitchen would have something that he could use. A few tea combinations might work he thought, perhaps a root or even a couple of petrified animal organs that he could crush and create an elixir. He just needed something that would give him an edge, to boost their immune system. His patients needed something to restore their hope. The doctor knew that nothing boost-s hope like a few restful hours of sleep, while under a restful and caring eye. The priest showing up had surely activated the belief in Divine Intervention even more. Yet all of his patients weren't Christians or had even chosen a spiritual guide for their life. Some viewed the priest's presence as an omen of something bad to come. The doctor checked his bag to make sure he had enough acupuncture needles. He knew that everyone wouldn't consent to their use, but for the ones that wanted to give it a try, he felt that he needed to be prepared.

Chapter Eleven

The Vaccine Heist

Later that afternoon, Alex and Slapp put on surgical masks and went in to visit Tate. When they arrived, Gayle left the room. Slapp spoke first as he entered the dimly lit space. The drapes were drawn and the area was a little warmer than in the hallway outside.

“Hey man, how do you feel,” said Slapp with a touch of humor? “I hope you feel better than you look.” Alex turned to Slapp quickly with a harsh tone.

“Slapp, if I ever get sick, do me a favor, send flowers or candy or something; just please don’t bother to visit me. Can you do that for me,” said Alex with a serious face? Tate smiled a little as he made an effort to sit up on the side of the bed. Alex moved over to him quickly, to shake his hand and pull Tate firmly to a sitting position. He grabbed Tate’s upper arm as Tate held his left hand over his mouth to cough, then returned it to his rib cage, in a protective manner.

"I do feel a little better than I look," said Tate as he adjusted his oxygen nasal cannula. "I just can't get enough air in and the cough has my lower back, rib cage and sides hurting. The doctor says that it's more than the seasonal flu." Slapp kept his distance, as he stood just inside the door. The doctor had instructed Slapp not to even go into the room, where Tate was, because of his childhood history. Alex sat on the foot-end of the bed as the three of them devised a plan to acquire the revised flu vaccine, without causing an unpleasant national incident. All of them had a handle on physical confrontation, but Fred had always handled the political aspects of the missions; whenever finesse was required. Fred was another one of their friends that had gone into the side business with them. He and Alex were from the same branch of the secret service. They had enough time to retire, but had stayed on to help the younger guys out, like Slapp and a few of the others.

The second best person for the job was Tate, when it came to a cool head prevailing, but Tate was too sick to occupy a position on the team and its illegal mission. Tate opened the floor for discussion as he leaned forward on the side of the bed, waiting for another coughing-attack to wave over him, and then subside.

"So what is the plan, fellows? I'm sorry that I can't go with you." Slapp answered.

"I think we should go early in the morning and just wait for the shipment to arrive at the CDC's warehouse," said Slapp. Then Tate turned to Alex, who sat only two feet away.

"What are your thoughts on the subject Alex," inquired Tate as he maintained his bent over posture?

"I'm not sure which approach we should use, but I do think that we should go with our weapons in plain-sight. Tate, do you remember what happen to us that time when we were hiding out on the back forty of Cambodia for two years? Remember how things got out of hand when that shipment of drinking water was trucked into the outline villages when they discovered that the local water supply had been tainted? Some rebels wanted to intercept the trucks and sell the water to the people who couldn't afford to pay. Well, I believe that this is going to be one of those same situations with the vaccine."

Slapp stood up taller now as he interjected into the conversation, "Hey guys you never told me about that." Alex looked over at Slapp, and then back towards Tate as he smiled at him.

"And we don't have time to enlighten you about it now, so concentrate on the problem that we have at hand." Tate took a sip of that specially brewed tea that the doctor had made. It smelt like animal urine and probably tasted even worst, but Alex didn't want to judge. However, that wasn't Slapp's style or position on the matter, as he noticed how Tate would frown-up his face each time he took a sip.

"Tate man, what the hell are you drinking? From where I'm standing, it looks and smells like some three-day-old dishwater that someone left in the sink, before going on vacation. Is it expected to help with your flu symptoms or finish you off?" Alex and Tate both looked over at Slapp and spoke the words together as they tried to suppress their laughter.

"Slapp shut the hell up." Slapp tried to recover as he always had managed to do.

"I'm just saying that it looks and smells like something that you shouldn't be drinking. Maybe he meant for you to pour some on a gauge and place it on your chest while you slept or something. I'm not too up on this Eastern medicine; most of my assignments have been in South America and South of the border. I just want to survive over here and then take my ass back to the States. I do think you need to ask my mother about that concoction before you drink anymore of that. Everything that is given to you in a dish isn't designed to be taken internally, for instance, when they bring you out that finger bowl to wash your finger tips." Slapp continued to babble and make unrelated remarks until Alex gave Slapp the evil eye and Slapp backed down from his criticizing mode.

"I think a better plan would be to meet the airplane," said Alex. "And act as an escort from there through customs, and then to the CDC's warehouse; that way it will be understood that we are a part of the distribution team, since there are a lot of Americans in the city right now, for one reason or another and won't be able to leave for at least a few more days."

"That's a good idea Alex," said Tate. "Here take my American Embassy's badge, Slapp has his own badge and tell Officer Su

Ki that he should wear his local police uniform and transport you guys in a squad car tomorrow. You should also hang your U.S. Secret Service departmental badges outside the front of your shirt's pockets, when you go to the airport. They will believe that the United States is providing extra protection for the short supply of vaccine and more control on the streets, if needed. They will look at this as a good-will gesture by our government. That little display of power might confuse the airport staff long enough for you to exit the area. One more thing, Slapp I need you as Mr. Alvin on this mission, not Slapp. You know as Slapp, you are unpredictable and even harder to control. Just remember, we are going on an assignment for the American Embassy and we want to remain under the radar while doing so. No heroics, understand?" Tate had struck a few of Slapp's sensitive nerve areas, while giving his input to the stratagem and also with his insulting personal instructions to him. However, Slapp was willing to let Tate slide for now. Slapp understood that Tate was sick and was probably feeling slightly depressed because he was too-under-the-weather to tag along. Nevertheless, Slapp had to make it clear where he stood, on the matter of Tate's tone.

"Tate," said Slapp in a warning tone, as he focused more in Tate's direction, while moving closer to where he and Alex had remained sitting on opposite ends of the bed. "I'm going to let your tone of voice take a pass this time, but we will need to finish this waltz (clear up the way he addressed him) when I get back, or whenever you are feeling better and not under the influence of that piss-in-a-cup that the doctor is passing off as a medicinal tea." Alex wanted to get involved, but opted out for the sake of time and argument that he knew would incur, if he shared his views. Tate gave Slapp a strong glance of agreement with a single deliberate fearless backward node of the head. Tate then continued with his contribution to the task force and to assure Slapp that he heard and accepted the later-date challenge of hashing out their differences.

"Duly noted my brother;" said Tate as his green eyes appeared to pierce through Slapp's eyes to the back of his head. "I also need you Slapp, to retrieve the key to the embassy's armory and draw two long range rifles with a full assignment of ammunition."

"I can do that," said Slapp with the excitement in his voice that made Alex nervous.

"Wait you two," replied Alex. "We are only going to escort some flu vaccine from the airport to the Hong Kong's Department of Health's warehouse. Do you really think that we need all that firepower?" Slapp and Tate gave each other eye contact as if they believed that Alex was completely out of touch of what was about to take place the following morning. Tate thought it was his duty to give Alex an update or a refresher course on the overall mission and possibly open his eyes to what they were up against.

"Alex," said Tate as he regained his composure after yet another coughing attack. "Think about it, you are going tomorrow to retrieve a portion of a short-supply flu vaccine, without the proper signature, on a form that was designed by another country. The first shipment of the vaccine won't be enough and the city is already in a panic. Martial Law is possibly in effect, due to the quarantine. Now given everything that I have just said, to be indeed a fact, do you still believe you can get the medicine without a show of force?" Alex dropped his head and stared at his hands as he pondered the words that Tate had just spoken. He knew that this had always been Tate's strong area, as it pertained to each mission. He was their weapons specialist, in spite of the fact that he hated violence of any kind, yet loved life twice as much. His favorite quote was 'If anyone is going to assist the officials with the investigation of what happened, when there is blood found on the sidewalk, due to a death, let it be me.' The room went mute. Then after at least a full two minutes or more, Alex responded.

"Hey man, are you sure that those guns in the embassy's armory still operates properly, they are pretty old and out dated," said Alex with deep concerns in his voice? Tate spoke up quickly as Slapp smiled and looked on, while waiting for them to come to an agreement.

"Oh please don't concern yourself about that Alex, I took care of that the moment I was hired," assured Tate. "I cleaned, oiled and fired every weapon in that armory. I used up so much ammo at the local firing-range until it threw the embassy's budget off that month, so I agreed to take a pay cut for a couple of months, to replace it." Slapp laughed out now because he knew how phobic Tate was about getting hurt or dying. Slapp, on the other hand, was fearless and felt that since he had no family to speak of, until lately when he found his mother, that any day was a good day to die, if it was for a noble cause. Of course, Alex thought that both of them was a little off the center of a healthy awareness, because for him this was just a promotion to make more money. All the secret service had done for him, in the way of self-gratification, was giving him a bigger paycheck than the police department, while taking down some bad guys, which he felt, was his civic-duty to do.

"Okay Tate," said Alex. "We'll do it your way. Who is going to man one of the long distance rifles?"

"I'm glad that you asked," replied Tate. "That's where Mr. Pauling will come in handy. He was in the military and I'm sure he would love to go on this mission with you two."

Alex objected, "I don't know about that Tate. What will happen if we get into some real trouble? Like a gun fight."

"Alex, the man works at the American Embassy as a night front gate guard. His job is to shoot people if the need arises," said Tate with an unremorseful smirk on his face. Besides, I want you to position him on the rooftop of the airport with a telescopic lens attachment. No one will know that he's up there, except the team members. All of you will be wearing ear communication plugs so you can hear everything each man on the team says. He will know when to give you strong-arm back up from the chatter. Oh yea, issue everyone a vest, just incase". Alex didn't like the sound of that.

Slapp used this moment to leave the room and go to the weapons locker to draw two rifles and the ammunition. After a few more minutes of planning, Tate took a big gulp of the doctor's special formulated tea and lay back down. Alex came to find me in Gayle's office slash pharmacy shot clinic. I called my father, Uncle Oscar, to check to see if he was having any symptoms. He informed me that he had stayed up all night, entertaining all the misplaced people that had gotten caught without a room and had spent the night in the lobby. He was now headed to bed. Miss Beasley had steered clear of all the sick people and had only traveled from her room to her office to answer the phone and to retrieve message traffic. She informed us that the ambassador was scheduled to arrive the next morning on an early flight. It was a good chance that he would be at the airport the exact same time as the guys would be there on their high jacking mission of the revised flu vaccine. Alex thought that perhaps if the ambassador's plane landed earlier than the vaccine, they would be able to get him to sign the requisition order to legally draw their allotted quantity of vaccine for the American Embassy's personnel. The plan could possibly shift a little, but, of course, Slapp and Tate still believed that the original plan was the best; just go in with guns blazing and take what was rightfully ours.

The day went by quickly, and then we heard the loud siren scream again telling everyone to find shelter. The weather remained rainy, damp and windy. This would be the second moonless night in Hong Kong for us; and one that we would always remember and relive in the future.

The next morning the men geared up to intercept the plane that was due to arrive with the new and improved flu vaccine. Gayle and I both prayed that the plane carrying the ambassador would land first. If this happened then there wouldn't be any reason for the guys to show a sign of force when they went to the warehouse to pick up our portion of the first shipment of the vaccine. During the night, Tate's fever had risen again and the doctor had changed his regiment of medication for the second time. The priest, Father Caleb, seemed very concerned, a little more than we believed he had shown in the past when others from the renegade outfit had gotten shot or worst. I had stayed in the embassy and spent the night in the room with Mrs. Carrington. Max had bunked in Gayle's office slash pharmacy with his Uncle Slapp and Mr. Pauling. Gayle spent another night in the recliner that she had borrowed from Miss Beasley's room. Father Caleb took his usual position behind the bed, where Tate had spent another night gasping for a full breath. There we all waited and watched closely for Tate's fever to break. I had spent sometime with the priest, back in the States, when I had taken Tate's deceased wife's position as a part-time assistant to the priest. This was the first time that I remembered him looking so inconsolable. As I watched the priest's face, I became more convinced that he and Tate's paths had crossed before the priest had become their office manager for the "My Brother's Keeper" side high-stakes bounty hunting venture. He stared at Tate with a mournful nature. It made me wonder if the doctor was keeping something from the rest of us; like how badly Tate's condition had become. I stood, leaning up against the dresser, next to Gayle as we made small talk, but I never took my eyes from the priest as he gazed in Tate's direction. The doctor still had him attached to a tank of oxygen with a nose cannula. His breathing was shallow and the short amount of sleep he was getting, in between the coughing episodes, was disturbing. He continued to show signs of restlessness, as he mentioned in a dream-like state someone that we assumed was his father. The priest stood to his feet a few times and leaned in closely with no reservations of becoming infected by Tate's feverish panting breath. Their faces were almost touching as the priest stroked Take's brow to calm him. Father Caleb had now removed his mask; after the doctor had instructed us to make sure they stayed in place. Gayle and I took turns holding the cold wet compress to his forehead and the back of his neck, as he stared at us as if he didn't know us at all. A few times, during that early morning, Gayle and I stop talking, because we were sure that the priest was praying and we wanted to be respectful, as he discussed our desperate situation with God.

The men were now in position, waiting for the planes to land. Mr. Pauling had been instructed to go on the roof of the airport, with one of the long-range rifle and keep watch. When Alex and Slapp arrived inside airport, the first person that they saw was Miss Beasley, Slapp's recently reunited mother. She was wearing those same half-calf cut boots, so they were pretty confident that she was packing a weapon as usual. Slapp became instantly angry that she was in the area, after being informed of their plans, the night before. Alex quickly grabbed his upper arm to retain him from approaching her as she stood waiting patiently, thirty yards or more away.

"Damn it Alex, what the hell is she doing here?" asked Slapp, as he changed direction to approach her. Alex pulled him back, as he tried to reason with him.

"Wait Slapp, she doesn't see us and that's good. Besides, what can you do? She is already here. Do you really think you can go over there and force her to go back to the embassy? Remember her position and the fact that she has lived over her for years. I'm sure that the local authority recognizes her and will protect her if anything gets out of hand. We could jeopardize her safety by association. Stand-down Big Guy, we might need her later to translate for us."

Slapp took a slow look around the vast space of the Hong Kong airport. It was huge to say the least. There were people sitting and lying all over the place, where they had became stranded, because of the quarantine. There must have been a couple of thousand people in the entrance lobby alone. There was no way of knowing how many were at the seventy-five or more departure gates. There were the usual armed guards walking their beat, plus the militia in a different uniform, and a third unit with other markings was placed to maintain crowd control. Now people were moving around more because they were now waking up from where they had spent another night in the airport. Most of them were trying to obtain some information about when departure flights would resume.

Miss Beasley had arrived early to meet the ambassador when he returned from his trip. The only security guard that had remained on his feet from the American Embassy's staff, from the security booth was now her driver. The sun was peeping up from behind some rain-clouds that had stayed in the area for the last two days. Alex and Slapp proceeded to the exits that led to the arrival gates. This area was restricted and they knew that this would be their first obstacle in obtaining access, while escorting the vaccine. Alex stepped quickly in front of Slapp when this short older Asian security man pushed Slapp back from the entrance using the mobile guardrail. The two of them stared each other down as Alex reached into his blazer to show the man the paperwork from the embassy and his American Embassy medallion. Alex could now feel Slapp hyperventilating breaths on the back of his neck as he continued to block Slapp, with his body from attacking the little mean-spirited man.

“Your badge no good here,” said the man as he continued to leave out parts of a correct sentence. “Where is your ah escort? How did you get to the airport with no escort? The streets and city is under quarantine.” He said in a broken and choppy version of the English language.

“We are from the American Embassy,” said Alex with this wide counterfeit smile. Alex stood at least a foot and a half taller than the man he was addressing. Two other young and taller armed security guards noticed the raised voices and rushed over to backup the shorter guy. They were both so young looking until Alex was sure they hadn’t started shaving yet. Slapp backed away from Alex a couple of steps and pumped his rifle handle to place a round of ammo in the firing chamber. Alex turned quickly and snatched the gun from Slapp’s hands and began to chastise him.

"What the hell are you doing, Alvin? Have you noticed how much coverage of firepower they have in here? Just please let me handle this." The old man was smiling now because Alex had taken Slapp's weapon away. Miss Beasley heard the ruckus as it rang out through the crowd and looked over to see Alex and Slapp in confrontation with the local. She walked over to them and offered her assistance. First she bowed gracefully before addressing the man. She noticed that he was mature and assumed that he would respect her more if she seemed to know a little about him and the old ways. (Local customs and culture)

"I'm a translator and personal assistant to the American Ambassador. I arrived earlier with a driver to pick up the Ambassador from his trip. These men are in our employ and have been instructed to guard and escort the new arriving flu vaccine to the distribution center as a good-will courtesy, requested by your Ambassador Qu' Lui."

Miss Beasley stood very near the short man while speaking so soft and eloquently until it made one forget the disagreement completely. Slapp was shocked by his mother's diplomacy abilities. He and Alex had no idea the power she had obtained in a culture that had appeared to be so secretive and occasionally anti-American. They remained motionless as Miss Beasley continued to speak in a low non-threatening tone. Her body stance was straight, yet relaxed. Slapp felt that she knew this man, but didn't want anyone else around to realize that and diminish any power that he was demonstrating by being the gatekeeper of all the arriving flights. When Miss

Beasley finished speaking, she timidly bowed again slowly, with just a node of the head. Then she spoke a few word of respect in his language and waited for a reply. She had studied the culture well and had learned to play the game like a professional; after all she was an expert in her field and a whole lot more. The man returned her bow and then spoke words of greeting, in his dialect as he seemed to stall while deciding just how he wanted to handle the situation and retain his power and standing in the eyes of his subordinates. Miss Beasley was aware of this, so she waited with her eyes slightly focused below the level of his. The two guards, that had remain standing closely behind him, brought their weapons back up to the vertical stand-down position, as their faces reflected the disappointment that they wouldn't be given the opportunity to shoot someone or just fire off a round or two to exhibit evidence of control. Then he confirmed what Slapp had suspected, for it was customary for the male to acknowledge the female first, if and only if he so desired.

"Hello Mrs. Carrington," he said with another slight shallow bow-of-the-head. "It is nice to see you again. Please explain in detail why I should allow these men to pass through this gate without an escort."

"Oh Mr. Peter Lui, they have an escort. He is parking the car as we speak." At that very moment, almost as if we had rehearsed Officer Su Ki's entrance timing the night before, he appeared at the gate with a lost look on his face, as he pushed his way through the angry crowd that were demanding answers from whomever they saw in a local police uniform.

"Sorry it took me so long to park the squad car, but I wanted to park it near the exit gate that the transportation for the vaccine will be taking when it departs the airport," said Officer Su Ki to Alex as he approached him from the side. Officer Su Ki didn't realize it at the time, but he had managed to reiterate the very lie that we had been trying to sell the gatekeeper guard for the last few minutes. The Asian man's posture softened a bit and we knew we had a chance of pulling this ruse off. It didn't hurt that he recognized Officer Su Ki and in fact had attended grade school with Su Ki's father, who was now a practicing Asian-American attorney, in the States.

"Sure, I know Officer Su Ki very well. If my memory hasn't started to fail me, I believe Officer Su Ki's father is a lawyer in America. I saw him the last time he was on island here. It is good to see you again and to see that you are doing so well." The old man spoke the words of honor and respect, but his body language and tone of voice conveyed something totally different to us. He had identified the young lad Officer Su Ki correctly, but it was clear to us that he was deceitful by implying that he was one of Su Ki's father's friends or even being an associate of his. At that moment, Slapp nervously checked his watch because he knew that they had a few more people to convince before they would be allowed to go out on the flight line with the luggage crew, while they unloaded the plane's cargo bay. Now as Officer Su Ki responded to the man, while the two guards, which stood behind him, faces reflected more anxiety that they wouldn't be needed to kill something; Officer Su Ki gave a quick nervous customary bow, and then answered.

"Yes Sir, your memory is as sharp as ever. That is indeed my father and I am his son." For a split second Alex and Slapp thought that Su Ki's American wit was surfacing, but then they realized that he was just shook-up by the fact that out of all the possible gates in this mega international airport, Alex and Slapp had chosen this one to pass through, to reach the tarmac. Officer Su Ki knew that the guard was well acquainted with his boss, the Chief of Police and that he didn't trust either of them. Su Ki was also aware that as soon as they were around the corner, the gatekeeper would call the Chief and ask him about their fraudulent flu vaccine escort detail. Officer Su Ki knew that the flight wasn't due to land for another fifteen minutes. He knew this to be a fact, because he had checked the arrival board on his way to Alex and Slapp's location. Su Ki figured if he stalled a little longer that perhaps that would buy them enough time to exit the airport before the security guard could get a call through to the Chief of Police or enough time before the chief could react to information that he was sure that the little man would be more than happy to inform him of. We all knew that on this side of the world having all the information was the only thing that gave you an edge for whatever type of business you were in. This included black-market, blackmail and underground deals, which always made the top five on the chart of corruption. Officer Su Ki turned slowly to Miss Beasley and smiled gently.

"Mrs. Carrington, aren't you going to introduce Mr. Lui to your son, Mr. Alvin?" Miss Beasley knew immediately that Officer Su Ki was trying to stall, but she didn't understand why. So she decided to just go along, and play her part in the floorshow.

"You are correct Officer Su Ki," said Miss Beasley as she ended her words with a devious smile. "Just where have my social graces gone?" She reached back and pulled Slapp from behind Alex and drew him near as she made the introduction. "Sir, I would like you to meet my son, Mr. Alvin." They all knew that the local man couldn't see any resemblance between Slapp and his mother and would probably confirm in his mind that we were up to something for sure. Miss Beasley had also taken that class about never giving too much information. It was evident when she introduced Slapp by his first name only and no title or job position, back in the States. Slapp was in his profiling mode as he tried to smile, but was unable to pull it off. He kept his right hand on his side arm as he gave a backward node of the head in Mr. Lui's direction. Then Slapp moved his gaze over the top of Mr. Lui's head to give the two young guards a threatening eye contact stare. They leaned in toward each other and whispered something then they walked away. Miss Beasley continued to babble on, in an effort to use up the waiting time they had left, before the plane arrived carrying the flu vaccine. At this point, she had no idea if the Ambassador's arrival would be delayed as well.

"Yes, this is my big handsome son," said Miss Beasley as she held onto Slapp's left arm. Alex was looking around behind then and had noticed that the sun was now up in full view while shinning through the huge building's front entrance that was almost completely constructed of tinted panels of glass. No one else in their party had noticed the sun's new position because from where they were standing, approximately fifty meters away from the front entrance windows with their backs facing in that direction; the sun had provided no additional light or warmth for them. The ceiling in that area had been dropped down to a seven-foot clearance as the passengers were forced to be huddled together in dim lighting, just before exiting into this vast space with hundreds, if not thousands, of others all at once.

Alex realized that now that the sun was up, he would be able to view at least three or more of the inbound plane's luggage belts as they unloaded. The container would be massive and would be marked with something that would be impossible to confuse with anything else on the flight. He realized that Mr. Pauling was in place by now and would be watching everyone's moves closely.

Mr. Pauling had only been stopped and questioned twice, while he moved into his assigned location. There was so much security around until no one bothered to question one more person with a long-range weapon wearing a secret service badge and an American Embassy employee's I.D. tag hanging around his neck. In his pocket, he also carried a copy of an itinerary that stated that the Ambassador was due to return and a copy of the message that included the arrival of the revised vaccine.

With the two formed memos, any lie that Mr. Pauling decided to tell, about why he was walking the top deck of the airport's international arrivals' roof, he felt that he was covered. He had already determined if the paperwork or the two badges didn't appease whomever, then a non-life threatening bullet would be his final answer to their meddlesome questions. The flight line was in total chaos to say the least. Mr. Pauling assumed that the usual people that worked there, at least a major portion of them, had succumbed to the deadly flu virus that now had all of Hong Kong city in its grips. As he looked down onto the international tarmac, he was convinced that this crew wasn't the first-string staff. There were people running all over and screaming in at least three different dialects. Mr. Pauling became so amused and distracted that he didn't notice an armed guard, who had gotten the drop on him with his weapon at the ready. The man yelled at Mr. Pauling as he stood close to the edge of the roof with one foot propped upon the shallow rain-gutter like ledge. The man had approached Mr. Pauling from the side and was very nervous.

"Hey you," screamed the man. "What are you doing up here? They told me that no one is supposed to be up here." Mr. Pauling slowly raised his hands as he gripped the long-range rifle midway the shaft. He then slowly turned to face the man, who now began to shake and stutter as he spoke. "Who are you? You don't work for any of the airlines." The moment Mr. Pauling saw the man's face he knew exactly who he was. He was one of the deliverymen who delivery food to the embassy and to Mr. Pauling's small restaurant.

His name was Mr. Ming Yue Lee. Mr. Lee was an elderly man that had worked long passed his prime and was only functioning to be unavailable for his grandchildren-babysitting duties. He was a short man with bowlegs and thinning salt and pepper hairline. He knew everyone that was worthwhile knowing in Hong Kong and where all the bodies were buried, in a manner of speaking. His father, who was now deceased, but had dedicated his entire life to the police department, had passed that on to him. Since Mr. Lee was his only son, his father had spent countless hours showing and explaining various case files to him almost every night, when he was a child growing up. He had photos and family layouts of how all the different influential families, which in some way or another affected their day-to-day lives. As a matter of fact, Mr. Pauling was now remembering how much Mr. Lee had been so helpful when he first tried to break into the restaurant business, as he prayed that the old man would recognize him before he pulled the trigger of his weapon.

"Gosh damn it, Mr. Pauling," yelled Mr. Lee as he lowered his weapon by his side. "What the ah hell ah you doing up ah here? You scared the crap out of me. I'm ah old man and my heart is not too strong any longer. Who knows for sure how much ah time I have left. I'm sure that seeing you up ah here has taken away a few of my days." Mr. Pauling slowly lowered his arms and began to smile, because of Mr. Lee's choppy English.

"I'm sorry Mr. Lee. I'm just glad that it is you and I don't have to shoot anybody."

"What the ah hell you are ah talking about? I had my gun pointed at you first." Then Mr. Lee took in a full breath for the first time since he had climbed to the roof. He and Mr. Pauling were wearing those large ear muffles as protection against the noise of the jumbo jets engines.

"So tell Mr. Lee, what is going on around here? No one down there seems to know what to do next. You still didn't answer my question, why are you here?"

"You no funny Mr. Pauling, that was my ah question to you." Mr. Pauling was playing a word game with Mr. Lee because he was old and his attention span, no doubt was short.

"Okay Mr. Lee, I'm here because the Ambassador is due to return on one of these morning flights. My team was sent to safeguard the new flu vaccine that is due to arrive today also. We are to escort it to the warehouse. This is the first shipment and they knew that it won't be nearly enough for all the people that's right here in the city. A second shipment is also due later on today from another location. Now tell me, why are you here?" Mr. Lee slowly brought his gun back up to point it in Mr. Pauling direction as he began his answer.

"Mr. Lee, what the hell are you doing now?"

"I'm protecting myself from a vaccine thief."

"So are you saying that you know some people who will try to steal part of this first shipment? Who are they? I have to warn the other members of my team." Mr. Lee became very tense as he stared in Mr. Pauling's direction.

"You stand right there I have to think. I overheard this conversation on my way up here. Some people came and asked me did I want to do a security job at the airport. They didn't say what it was for. I think they sent me up on the roof so I will be out of their way. I took the job because I wanted to have extra money to pay for my family to get the flu shot." Mr. Pauling stood motionless, with his hand held above his head, as Mr. Lee continued to sort things out in his mind. "If I tell you everything that I know about this job and promise not to shoot you, will you promise that my family will all get the flu shot vaccine?" Mr. Lee hesitated as he waited for Mr. Pauling's response.

"I can't make any promises like that, I only work at the embassy part-time and I don't know what the protocol is for things like this." Mr. Pauling almost smiled as he answered. This angered Mr. Lee. "How many people are we talking about Mr. Lee?" Mr. Lee answered quickly as though he had already counted everyone before he took the assignment.

"There are ah twenty-five people, in my house."

"Damn Lee," said Mr. Pauling. "That's not a household, that's a small village." Then Mr. Pauling smiled more as he started to lower his arms a bit.

"Put your hands ah back up," yelled Mr. Lee. "I'm a very disparate man, you no laugh at me, I will shoot you." Mr. Pauling gave the old man his full attention as he calculated in his head just how many doses the embassy would need before the second shipment arrived. He knew that the total staff, excluding the deliverymen and couriers, was approximately sixty. Half of the staff had walk off the job, or left early that day before the quarantine was announced. The people that had already started to show signs or symptoms of exposure would be advised to wait. The sick people wouldn't need to take it until they had recovered. That meant that if Mr. Pauling counted his family and included Alex, my father Uncle Oscar, the priest plus the covering doctor's family and myself, it might just be enough. Besides, Mr. Pauling felt that his mathematic ability wasn't a significant matter at that precise moment. Instead, telling a man that was holding a gun to your stomach, something that he wanted to hear, took top priority for sure. So Mr. Pauling agreed to inform the fill-in doctor that he might be taking a field trip, to the village [house] of Mr. Lee.

"Look Mr. Lee," said Mr. Pauling with a more serious attitude laced with just a tad of anger. "Believe me when I tell you that I understand your position. I have family members also that I'm hoping will be able to come to the American Embassy and receive a flu vaccine. Okay, I will talk to the people in charge and see if your family can be included in the count, since you do make deliveries to the American Embassy's compound. I'm sure that qualifies you for some kind special consideration. Now put that gun down before someone gets seriously hurt, in this case, probably me." Mr. Lee lowered his weapon and told Mr. Pauling everything that he knew to be fact as it pertained to what he had overheard. Mr. Pauling called Alex, who was now being escorted to the gate by the security guard, Officer Su Ki and Slapp. Miss Beasley lagged behind them by thirty paces or more, because she was scheduled to meet the ambassador at another gate. Two airplanes were now taxiing in to park at a different gate. The new gate arrival was at least a five-minute jog from where Mr. Pauling and Lee were perched on the roof of the arrival gate. They didn't have time to climb down and then run over to the next terminal, and then climb back up. Furthermore, someone might see them together and realize that they had become allies or partners-in-crime, depending on how you wanted to analyze the situation. Either way this would, without a doubt, place Mr. Lee in more danger. Besides, running on top was a straight shot and a much shorter distance.

Mr. Pauling and Mr. Lee scurried to their new location, while they remained on the roof of the airport. Now they positioned themselves just above the mobile walkway arm that extends to the plane for the passengers to disembark. They were both out of breath and breathing hard as they fell to their stomachs to lay flat and stay out of view of the baggage crew. Suddenly this out-of-place truck came rushing up and hit its brakes and slid right underneath the cargo and luggage door of the plane. Mr. Pauling used the scope on his rifle to get a closer look. Mr. Lee had remained lying next to him while still trying to catch his breath. Mr. Pauling began to taunt Mr. Lee so he would talk and possibly take in more air in the process.

"Mr. Lee, if you want to become a successful criminal element, then you are going to have to get in better shape old man," said Mr. Pauling as he gazed down at the men below in the mystery truck. Mr. Lee became angry and more frightened by the predicament that the two of them were now engaged in.

"What did you say to me? I took this job to help my family. We came to Hong Kong very poor and now fifty years later, we are still poor and don't have enough money to go back home. I'm no bad person. I'm just trying to survive." Mr. Lee was talking loudly and the pilot was shutting down the planes engines.

"Keep your voice down Mr. Lee, the wind is blowing from our direction and they might hear you, Sssshhhh." Then Mr. Pauling noticed a man leap from the strange unauthorized delivery truck. Mr. Pauling began to give Alex and Slapp a step-by-step update on everything that was taking place through their earpiece communicators, at the gate where they all believed the vaccine had just arrived. Alex and Slapp increased their speed on their approach to the gate that Mr. Pauling was now directing them towards. When they arrived at the gate, the old man from the first security gate began to explain, in their language of course, to the flight attendant why they should be allowed to descend down the walkway to the plane and then out onto the flight line with the baggage crew. Slapp was a quick study like his mother and realized that the security guard was doing a poor job of explaining their mission. The gate attendant pretended not to comprehend the information fast enough for Slapp so he snatched his rifle from Alex hands and demanded that the female attendant open the door. Slapp was reading into her body language, while listening to Mr. Pauling, as he described what was taking place on the flight line, and decided that she was stalling, and was possibly in on the black-market vaccine heist, as well. The mature lady moved quickly to the door panel and punched in her code for the door to open. Slapp stormed down the walkway arm and to the side door and made his escape to the ground. Mr. Pauling was now screaming into their ear communicators his updates from the roof of the area where Slapp had just leaped. Mr. Pauling's voice was filled with panic, as Slapp and Alex could both hear his weapon being fired. Alex was traveling about three paces behind Slapp as Officer Su Ki brought up the rear, with his sidearm drawn to the ready. The door of the plane had remained strangely closed. The plane by this time had already been on the ground twenty minutes and had been at the gate, for at least seven of those minutes. There was a young man at the end of the mobile walkway arm waiting for the door of the plane to open. He backed up against the opposite wall, with fear on his face as Slapp, Alex and then Officer Su Ki all stormed pass and out the side employee's-only baggage crew exit. Immediately outside, just as Slapp's feet made a thumping noise as they came into contact with flight line's tarmac, Mr. Pauling fired a warning shot next to the man's feet that had gotten out of the illegal transport truck. The man had pinned one of the baggage crewmembers up against the luggage belt. Mr. Pauling was unable to hear what the man was saying, but he knew that this was no way to behave toward the luggage crewmen and that no one should be allowed to claim any baggage before it had cleared customs.

The other members of the crew, stood their ground, but were unable to help because the man was holding a knife on the man in question. Slapp ran around the side of the plane, in view of the man holding the blade on the crewmen, which placed his back to Mr. Pauling and his long-range weapon. People on the plane were now observing what was happening and began to scream. Slapp continued to walk towards the man screaming for him to release the baggage man. Mr. Pauling fired another warning shot next to the man's feet and he dropped the knife and pulled his sidearm weapon. Officer Su Ki shot the man in the shoulder and he fell to the ground. The driver spring from the truck and held up his hands high above his head, while trembling. Officer Su Ki arrested the two men and airport's security drove the truck off the flight line. The second plane had just begun to approach the gate, at another arm of the terminal. Miss Beasley had continued on, to her gate to welcome and update the ambassador. By the time the police secured the first plane and released all its passengers, Miss Beasley was able to acquire the Ambassador's signature on the proper paperwork, which authorized the American Embassy to draw sixty doses of the revised flu vaccine.

Back at the American Embassy, one of the monitor-booth security guard, that had been sick in the bunkroom, had allowed some of the workers, that Mr. Pauling had previously turned away a couple of days before, to enter the compound and report to their stations. The security guard, who had temporarily taken Mr. Pauling's position at the front gate, was unaware of who had left without authorization and who had been released early in preparation of the quarantine. Mr. Pauling, on the other hand, knew exactly who they were because the first thing he had been instructed to do was place a chain on all the entrances and exits except the one that he was controlling at the front of the compound. The last person who had received approval to exit the front gate was Tate when he staggered one block to escort Gayle back to the embassy. The last person to return, before the siren sounded, was Slapp in one of the limos. The doctor's log and notes would give proper account of everyone else that might have been overlooked. Mr. Pauling had already made peace with all those other decisions that he had made alone and was willing to take one for the team when he allowed Max, Father Caleb, Milani and Officer Su Ki to cross the threshold, after the siren had been sounded. The only numbers that were important to Mr. Pauling, now more than ever were the ones in his promise to Mr. Lee. Mr. Pauling wanted to be able to keep his pledge to Mr. Lee in reward for not shooting him on the roof of the airport. Even though Mr. Pauling was wearing a bulletproof vest and the fact that the gun that Mr. Lee held looked too old and required too much maintenance to do any serious damage, he was in fear that it just might backfire and hurt the old man, when and if he pulled the trigger. He wanted to keep the arrangement that he had made with Mr. Lee, about giving his family of twenty-five the vaccine shots, between him and the doctor, but he was willing to tell the whole story to the ambassador, if it became necessary and the only way that he could keep his word. After all, Mr. Pauling was a small businessman out in this town and he didn't want the expression to get around that he wasn't honest, or a man without scruples.

The swat-team, as they were affectionately referred to later on for their daring vaccine heist, all returned that morning with the sixty doses of the flu vaccine and with the American Ambassador's name unblemished. Slapp sprained his ankle when he leaped from a flight of steps that he should have taken, perhaps no more than two at a time, but other than that, there were no injuries or fatalities to report.

Chapter Twelve

A Priestly Confession

In Gayle's sleeping quarters, Tate was presently coming around and recovering from his third night of incapacitation, caused by the flu that had turned into a mild case of pneumonia. He could hear the priest's voice as he explained some facts about how his and the priest's life secretly intertwined. Behind the bed where the priest sat, there was a narrow slither gap between the two-panel drapes that allowed Tate a glimpse of an early morning sunrise, which by the way looked promising to be a very clear and pleasant day.

Tate continued to lie there as he realized that he was unable to take in a full lung of air without some discomfort or possibly causing another coughing episode. He could barely see the sun coming up as he thanked the Divine One that he had survived another sleepless night, while the flu continued to hold him in its clutches. The sound of Father Caleb's voice was no doubt very soothing to Tate, because even Gayle and I were hanging on his every word and had been drawn into the narrative, as he revealed the secret. His Ireland accent was very strong as he searched for just the right words to portrait, what would turn out to be a soul-stirring tale for us. At first Gayle and I thought that it was a story that he had been entrusted with during a confessional contact, after all he was a Catholic priest. Yet, as he went on we realized that the story appeared to be too old and detailed for him to remember with such sharp clarity. Next we assumed that only part of the story was true and the remainder was just thrown in for our entertainment, to pass the time of a dreadful dreary night. The priest stared over at Gayle and me with those piercing green eyes for perhaps five minutes or more. The two of us had been babbling about nothing in particular for at least the last hour or more, as we continued to swap positions, from the head of the bed to the chair, while holding the medicated compress to Tate's head and neck, for comfort and support, if for no other reason. Gayle and I both, being mothers, deeply believed that there were healing powers in the human touch. No doubt Father Caleb agreed with us, because intermittently he would reach over to stroke Tate's arm or forehead. Now with Father Caleb in the room, praying non-stop, we were just waiting for God's grace and mercy to show us a sign, like we knew that He would. We all had faith it was coming, we just didn't want God to believe we were impatient, in case he was a little busy, with something else more pressing. Surely I jest. Father Caleb gave another quicker glance to Tate's face before he began, while the strong Ireland accent remained in the forefront of his speech.

"Ladies," said the priest to get our full attention and in a low volume tone, as if he was trying not to disturb Tate's ten minute catnaps. "Have I ever told you the story of this lad that I have the pleasure of knowing; quite well as a matter of fact? It seems that this very young man had reached a milestone or crossroad in his life and was unable to decide which fork in the path to take, as it were. For some reason or other he found it too painful to discuss it with his parents, for they had high hopes for him and he didn't want to break their heart, you see. So he thought that if he just waited and prayed, like he had been taught to do, that an answer would come or the confusing moment in judgment would pass. This was his first summer out of upper secondary school and the dilemma was what classes he would enroll into for college in the fall, as it were. Up until now he had lived a very strict life and he wanted to put higher education off for a couple of years. He wanted to travel back home and spend some time with his cousins, if you will. But his parents wouldn't hear of it and when the subject came up one night at the evening meal, an unforgettable commotion broke out about it, right there at the supper table, as fate would have it. The family of five was split down the middle as each took an opposing position-of-argument, you understand. The mother understood the son's point of view, but the father was remembering when his older son had reached a cross road in his life, only two years before and had taken the wrong fork, for sure. The mother of these two lads maintained her stance to her husband that the two sons were different in every way and that he shouldn't be so stern with his children, after they reach a certain age of maturity. Dinnertime was never quite the same after that night, to say the least and the young lad took the blame for it to heart, you might say. A few nights later, his rebellious spirit surfaced strongly again as he decided to see more of the world's night-life and what it had to offer to such a confused and distraught youngling, like himself. He made his way into this bar nearby and had his first drink and then he had another. He was carrying such a heavy heart, and the spirits of fire [alcohol] didn't help atall [at all] I might add. Soon after he arrived, this beautiful girl approached him as fate would have it and asked if she could sit with him for a spell. He noticed that she was lonely, the night was still in its prime, what could it hurt, he thought? They ordered another round of drinks and they shared their life stories with each other, which didn't take very long. You see both of them were still 'wet behind the ears' as they say; while wearing milk mustaches, as others prefer to comment to their youth."

The priest turned his head in our direction, yet smiled profoundly to himself as he glanced down at his hand that had just given Tate's arm a long affectionate stroke, as Tate lie motionless and breathing much easier now. The priest went on.

"A storm came up around midnight and began to blow something fierce, as fate would have it. The bartender changed the station on the tiny television, which sat clearly between the Jack Daniels and Makers Mark bottles on the second shelf of the three level tiers of liquors, to the local news station. There had been a storm warning put into place earlier that day, but with a stronger storm raging inside of the young lad, he had forgotten all about the pending weather conditions. The bartender lived outside of the city you see, so he made an announcement to the staff that they could go home early, because he wanted to close up. By this time, the young lad was more intoxicated than he realized until he stood up to depart the reaping-with-smoke stench filled establishment. He knew that he couldn't go home to his father's house without causing his father's doors-of-hell rage from opening up upon him, and sucking him in, in a manner of speaking. So he took the offer of the kind beautiful girl and agreed to dry out in her basement. By the time they reached her house, which was only ten blocks away, they were soaked to the marrow of their bones, if you will. It was still an early warm fall, as luck would have it, but with the hard storm rain plus the wee morning hours of the night, upon them, it was quite chilly to say the least. After they arrived at her house, with the help of God, as he realized later; she took him to the basement to dry out. She brought him some dry clothes and some hot coffee spiked with brandy. He found that strange considering he was already three sheets-to-wind, as they say. He thought to himself, 'what did he know'? He was just a snotty nose kid that had gotten caught in a rain storm and was too afraid of his father to go home, and face the music."

The Ireland accent became even stronger as he continued with the saga. Gayle and I both noticed that Tate was fully awake now and listening to the tale, as well. The priest had now leaned his head back against the wall, as he sat behind the bed, with his eyes lightly shut. He was now speaking in a tone that made me wonder if this wasn't some kind of therapeutic healing for him to tell the story once more and that it was more for his benefit than for ours, to pass the time. Tate looked over at Father Caleb a couple of times and then looked down to the foot of the bed where Gayle and I had remained motionless, for twenty minutes or more, as we listened intensely to the priest's re-count of an event that we were both confident, had taken place several decades before. We were tormented by the decision if we should interrupt the priest's story with the encouraging observation that Tate appeared to be making a turn for the best. If it had not been for the fact that Tate appeared to need to hear the ending to the story as well, the choice wouldn't have been a dilemma at all. So we all stood our ground, as the priest went on with his monolog, while totally unaware of the nonverbal communication glances, between Gayle and me, which now included Tate, as well. The priest smiled again as he took in a deep cleansing breath and let it out slowly, as if the memory of the story always provided him with a spiritual euphoric moment, or so we assumed by the calmness that he displayed as he told the story. Father Caleb then continued on.

"The two of them sat up the remainder of the night, as they continued to trade their life stories. They hung his clothes up to dry and added more coal to the old furnace, as they paused every now and again to listen to the howling winds of the short-lived storm. Somewhere during one of their stories, he fell fast asleep and she went upstairs to her bed. The next morning the lad was awakened by her uncle as he came downstairs to reflect on what stray his niece had brought home with her. He recognized the young man instantly and found it amusing that his niece, who lived in the next town over, had brought home someone that they knew. The young lady, his niece, had come over to spend a few days with her sick aunt and to send her younger cousins to school, while her uncle worked. Now that school was out for the summer, and her aunt was recovering nicely; this meant that she would be traveling back home soon, as fate would have it. Well the young lad was smitten by her, her beauty and fearlessness, to say the least and he spent every moment he could with her. She had no idea how strongly he felt at this point about her and it never even occurred to her to inquire. She was three years older and more experienced with life, you understand. They spent some private time together, but for the young lad, this was his first introduction to how powerful the sinful desires of the flesh can be. For her it was merely an intimate encounter with an admirer.

Three weeks later she returned to her home and the lad's very soul became ill, due to her departure. He was inconsolable for months and his parents even took him to the doctors. He himself was unaware that he had been so deeply affected by her leaving. The power of love or lust of this kind was totally new to the young lad, and quickly became clear to him to have taken no prisoners, in regards to his emotions or understandings of life. The following summer the beautiful young lady returned and by then the young lad had decided on what fork in the road that he wanted to take. He knew that he never wanted to feel that pain and emptiness that he felt when the girl left him behind that summer. So he chose the fork in the road that he thought would prevent that portion of his life from ever repeating itself again. He was now in school full time and had seemed to find a soothing distraction for his pain. That following fall the beautiful girl had moved back in with her aunt and uncle, for a longer spell, to be closer to the clinic where her son was now receiving experiment drugs for his rare birth abnormality.

The young lad questioned her about the baby's father because he knew that it could have easily been his, after their close interactions, you see. She refused to give a for-sure answer and he pressured her to allow him to see the handsome child. She was now engaged to her boyfriend of three years. She and the boyfriend got married that fall and the young lad continued to see her around because they now lived in the same parish. The young lad became aware the moment he lay eyes on the infant that it was in fact his and not her husband's. What could he possibly do? He shared the information with his mother about what had happened that early fall before and explained to her his painful beliefs about the child's identity. The young woman and her husband tried to make a go of it; I mean of the relationship and even had another child that next year. Unfortunately some wounds of the heart never heals, or so I'm told on many occasions, during my confessional duties."

The priest opened his eyes only briefly in Gayle and I direction, while he remained unaware that Tate had now awakened. Then he closed his eyes again as he continued the tale. "She and here husband were now living together in their own apartment and the young lad continued to befriend her and help with the two young boys. Their dad wasn't much of a father to them, so she welcomed and was grateful for the help. They never spoke of that stormy night or what had happened between them that late summer or early fall, if you will. A lie of secrecy and deception was born and soon took on a life of its own, so to speak. When the lad finished school he took a position at a local church as a youth counselor. That assignment lasted three years. During that time, the young lad took the child for many of his appointments, because the mother was unable to get the time off from work, as destiny would have it. The child was given an injection at each visit, which caused him to cry very sadly. It hurt the young man's very soul each time the baby cried and had to be comforted by him and not by his dear sweet mother, as it should be. Yet the young man and the little boy seemed to get along just dandy as God would have it and there appeared to be a serious bond that had been forged between them, one might be inclined to say. This arrangement lasted until the boy was three years old or a wee bit more. The husband was moving further and further away from his responsibilities, it seemed. The next job the young lad took, after the one at the church as a youth counselor, was a few states away and the next time he saw that child, the boy was twelve and his parents, well, I'm sad to say, were divorced."

The priest slowly opened his eye and looked over at Tate, and then he quickly sprang to his feet. His reaction was caused by the surprise that Tate was so alert and apparently better than the priest had expected. More than an hour had passed since the priest had began his enlightening tale, as we waited for him to explain why he felt that we needed to hear this story or why he had such a strong compulsion to repeat it, at this precise moment, with a passion that we had never experienced before.

"Thaddeus my boy," said the priest as he bowed down over him. "Tell the old father how you feel and why did you allow me to go on so long, without giving me a sign that you were improving a tad." He stroked Tate's forehead, from just above his brow to the top of his head, ever so gently as he stood over him, leaning down with his face immeasurably near Tate's. He wiped a tear from the corner of Tate's eye with his thumb and then repeated the same motion to his own. Now for the first time I realized that I had observed some affection between them before. The night that the others, including the priest, had all arrived to Hong Kong to join Tate and me. I recalled how Tate and the priest had walked away from the group that night to have a private conversation. I said to myself that evening that it was more to their affiliation than the rest of us knew. I also remembered thinking that the moment would present itself that would allow me to understand or provide an opportunity for me to ask some very in-depth questions, about that night and also their connection. Perhaps becoming aware of the priest's story would answer my inquiry of why this man had decided to team-up with this renegade outfit. I knew that it wasn't for the money, because the priest had used his cut of the takes [rewards], from the side business, to open and operate this soup kitchen, which was now feeding more than two hundred a day, two full meals. I now believed that this was going to be that instance in time that I had so patiently awaited to arrive. Tate responded to the priest.

"I feel a lot better Father, I need something to eat. Do you think I could have a few sips of water? Oh, and about the story that you were so eloquently recalling, I just thought perhaps hearing it once more wouldn't hurt. I was sort of relieved that you were brave enough to tell it to my friend Helen and future wife Gayle." The father and Tate both smiled privately, as if the old priest had left out one important detail, of the account. Then Father Caleb stood up straight and moved towards Gayle and me to escape his confinement; that had been created by the two of us and the bed.

"Sure Thaddeus," said the priest with a revived joy in his body language. "I will go right now down to the cafeteria and see if any of that magic soup is left. I will be right back." The priest was almost giddy as he scrambled pass Gayle and me.

I looked over at Gayle and she was crying now as if she had extracted something more from the story that I had totally missed. I have to agree that the story was touchingly sad and a tearjerker in some spots, but I wasn't sure why it had almost paralyzed Gayle, as she stared into Tate's weak moistened eyes. I moved aside as I asked the priest whatever happened to the people in the story.

"I'll be right back Helen," said the priest. "I will tell you more when I come back. Better yet, ask Tate. He knows the story quite well, if I may add. I've shared that story with him on a few occasions over the years, when he expressed to me that his path wasn't clear. Of course there were various portions of the story that were emphasized more to fit the need at the time, but other than that, the story is true and has not changed."

Tate glanced in my direction as Gayle continued to stack more pillows up behind his back, so he could sit up more easily. By the time Father Caleb returned with the soup, I was convinced that I was the only one in the room that didn't know what had happened to the young man, the lady and the child in question. I had continued to stand at the foot portion of the bed, as the priest gave the bowl of soup to Gayle, so she could assist Tate in consuming the tasty magic broth. The priest stood back a little and smiled as he held his hands in that divine pose of gratitude. I repeated my question to the priest that I had asked before he departed the room, to retrieve the food.

"So Father Caleb, whatever happened to the young man and the boy in the story," I inquired with a curious look on my face? The priest moved slowly over to me as Tate and Gayle peered in my direction as well. The Father placed his arm slowly around my neck and shoulders, as he stood to the side of me and leaned in to kiss the side of my face very gently, while smiling. Tate and Gayle were now smiling also, as only a couple of tears escaped their eyes. While the priest's Ireland accent remained in the forefront, the Old Catholic Priest answered with pride, as his volume increased and filled the small room with joy and laughter as he responded.

"The man in that tale my child," said the priest. "Is none other than yours truly and the boy is one who we all know and love desperately, if I may add, is none other than Thaddeus Bernard Romano who is my one and only child and a truly gratifying connection to this world and a joy that this life has to offer." He bowed his head for a quick second as if he had just finished a prayer and considered adding an amen to the end of that heartwarming statement, then he brought his head back up with a wide and pleasing smile. Now for the first time everything made sense. That day when we had the meeting at Alex's place, back in Maryland before we were on the run, the priest had arrived in a taxicab. Tate ran down the steps to give Alex all the money he had in his pockets, to pay for the cab that the priest had hired. He felt an obligation, since this was his father. Then later, during the early portion of the meeting when Tate just opened the priest's briefcase and started to take everything out and stack it up, the priest never gave him any instructions, nor did anyone question Tate's actions. The reason this elderly man had agreed to spend so much time with this group of outlaws, was because he wanted, and was willing to do whatever it took, to spend some more time with his only son, and to protect him in any way that he could.

My mouth flew open as I gasped and realized that with all the time that I had spent with the two of them, I had never put it all together. Tate always treated him like any other member of the group. He always addressed him as Father Caleb, like most of us. Occasionally Tate would leave off the priest's name and only address him as father. Father Caleb always smiled warmly, but other than that, he showed no peculiar response that would give the secret away. I thought it was because of his position in the church. I couldn't recall a single time that I had witness an added touch of affection between them. The priest was a very hands-on person whenever he would talk to you or offered a blessing. He would hug the men briefly and kiss the women and children on the foreheads often. However, Tate wasn't the type to display much affection to anyone in public, outside of a handshake, shoulder tap or a quick kiss on the cheek of a pretty lady. We were all surprised when he allowed us to see him stand so closely to Gayle that evening at the meeting when she had become emotional about her secret. This had been the same secret that she had shared about spending a short lifetime with Thomas, which was one of the men that had gotten killed in the bombing with Max's mother Stacey.

When Tate had given me a portion of his history on the plane, on our initial trip to Hong Kong, he had completely left this segment out about the priest being his biological father. Except for the green eyes and the fact that both were very handsome men, there was little resemblance at all.

"Father Caleb, please continue," I pleaded. "As you know, Tate is a very private person and somewhat of a mystery to us all." Gayle agreed with me with a mere node of her head, as Tate continued to eat his soup and pretend not to be in the room, entirely. He was embarrassed to say the least and the priest knew why. The priest wasn't sure if Gayle and Tate had taken their relationship to the next adult level. Besides, the priest didn't want to have to explain those shots or the birth defects that he had so quickly glazed over, during the very informative story. He insisted that he should end the story at that point.

"No, no my children, perhaps another time would be best," said the priest as he bowed out gracefully. "Due to the nature of it all, I believe that Thaddeus should be the one to tell the painful secrets of that period, to his friends and my future daughter-in-law, as it were. I have revealed too much already and have possibly damaged the relationship that it has taken me years to build with Thaddeus, with him having such a tender heart and a deep passion for privacy." Tate took another full spoonful of his soup as he studied Gayle's and I face closely. He then responded in a tone that made us believe that he had wanted to tell us before, but the right moment had never presented itself, prior to this moment.

"Go on father," said Tate. "They should have been told before now. The story isn't as painful to me anymore, as it once was. Perhaps the therapy of hearing it all again was more healing than I initially realized." I turned to Father Caleb to ask another question, as he had remained standing next to me with his arm draped gently around my shoulders.

"Does anyone else know about this?" Tate looked up in my direction, just as the priest was about to take in a full breath to answer.

"Yes Helen, Alex knows everything about me. We exchanged histories when we first decided to be friends. I guess that's why I'm so sensitive to him when we have a disagreement about anything. Excluding my father here, my grandmother and my wife Brenda, Alex has been my closest friend and more like a brother than my biological one. Now that I have the love and support of you two ladies, I think that maybe I will be given the chance to heal completely from my traumatic childhood. My only brother and I aren't close because he blames me for the breaking-up of the family. It is true that the fights that my mother and stepfather had, were mostly about me and the fact that I wasn't his biological son. Yet you all must agree that this was a heavy burden for a young male to carry who already had diminished self-esteem and sublevel social skills to start. Oh I forgot, Dr. Li knows part of the story, it was during his internship nearly fifty years ago when my father here took me in for my experimental hormonal shots."

The priest moved away from me a little, as he seemed to remember more details about that period in their lives. He pinched his bottom lip between his thumb and index finger as his face took on a serious appearance. Then he spoke to Tate as the memory re-appeared in his thoughts.

"You know Thaddeus, my boy, you are absolutely right. I didn't remember the fact that Dr. Li was working there at the time. I did recall that there was an Oriental man in the clinic, but not for the life of me did I consider it was he. Ladies will you please excuse me while I go and find the good doctor and ask him to forgive an old man of the cloth, for not remembering such generous and gentle acts of kindness that he showed the both of us? As I recall now, he was extra compassionate and considerate to us both. More than a few times, we were late for the appointment, but he never made us wait because he knew that I had to get back to work, at the church and he always gave you a lollipop. The red ones did appear to be your favorite, back then Tate. I distinctly remember that you always seemed to get more of it on your clothes and my white collar than in your mouth, of course. When I would returned to the office, the younger children thought I had cut myself shaving or worst, by becoming a victim of a neck stabbing."

We all laughed out loudly as the priest left the room to locate the doctor who was making rounds to make sure that everyone ate something before their next dose of medicine was administered. I departed the room as well, so Tate and Gayle could be alone and Gayle could possibly retrieve a little more of the story, while Tate seemed to be in an unusual talkative mood. I was correct; Tate started the story right where the priest had left off and Tate's grandmother influences had begun.

Chapter Thirteen

Tea for Two

"Well Gayle," began Tate. "My grandmother told me about my father, the priest, when he came to visit one summer when I was about twelve. I was almost four when he took another job in another state that first time he disappeared from my life. For a four year old kid, when no one speaks of that person, it seems like that person just faded away into your memory or become locked behind some other stuff. Perhaps I believed that it was a nice long dream that I later had awakened from. I don't know; it's hard to explain. After a while of not seeing him, he just turned into a dream more or less to me. Remember, I told you I was very shy and withdrawn? I never questioned anyone about him, so no one thought to mention him to me, except my Nana. Back then I just thought she was babbling about something that I was too young to understand. Then one summer he just suddenly appeared around the corner of our street and walked right up to me. 'Hello my son', he said to me. He was dressed like a priest so I thought his greeting was pertaining to his position and not our relationship. I answered slowly as I could almost remember the sound of his voice, from a previous time. He sat on the step next to me and soon my grandmother came to the door to see to whom I was speaking. At first she just listened to the two of us. She stood quietly in the doorway, but we both knew she was there. After a few moments, which seemed like a long time, my grandmother came out and greeted the cleric.

'Hello Father Caleb, I didn't know you were back in town,' she said as she reached to shake his hand.

'Actually I'm not;' he answered quickly. 'I just thought I might stop in to see how my boy was doing.'

'Oh that's very nice of you Father, but I don't think he remembers you as well as you remember him' said my grandmother as she stepped out onto the landing. 'I've spoken of you many times to him Father Caleb and how you had taken him to his shot appointments as a baby and young child, but I didn't get much emotion out of him. Perhaps in his heart he's still a little upset by your leaving. You know he waited for you everyday, at the door that first two weeks when you moved away. A few times he had silent tears in his eyes as I tried to distract him. He was very young and unable to express his feelings,' she went on to say.

"I knew the moment that she said that, that Father Caleb knew of my private and personal condition and I became very embarrassed, once again, to learn that yet another person knew. After that I sort of shutdown from the conversation, in which the father and I had been engaged in up until that point. He decided not to push, since he knew better than most the reason why. He gave me a phone number to where he would be staying in the city for a few more days and a number to where he was assigned, once he went back. Locally, the area was close enough for me to ride my bike there, and I'm sure that my grandmother wouldn't have had any problem with that, but I never got up the courage to go and see him. He stopped by again before he left town that time. 'Here Laddie,' he said as he gave my head one last stroke of affection, while kissing my forehead. Then he held my head on both sides as he held our foreheads in light contact. 'Perhaps later you will remember me better, I guess I should have called ahead, but I became so excited to see how you and your mother were doing, I forgot my social graces, as it were.' "His Ireland accent was even stronger back then and I had no idea that he was my biological father, at the time. After that my Nana told me about the checks that he had been sending for years to her mailbox and then she would give the money to my mother to help us out. My stepfather was gone by now, so we moved in with Nana. I was already being teased about my tanned skin and green eyes. My grandmother has green eyes, but they are a different shade. She has fairer skin than my mother and I. No one believed that she was my grandmother. Along with this appearance feature combination and my personal secret, I became the poster-child for mental confusion and loneliness. My grandfather was Portuguese or something. That was my grandmother's first husband, and my mother's father. He got himself killed while my mother was very young. My grandmother got married the second time and birthed two more children. I was the first and only one to take on my grandfather's hue, so I always felt out of place. My shyness and my birth defect didn't help much either."

Tate smiled again profoundly as he took another sip of that tea that the doctor had mixed for him. The tea was now cold and had been sitting in that cup all night.

"Damn Gayle, that is really nasty. I must have been pretty sick and desperate for the doctor to talk me into drinking this elixir that he calls tea, and on top of that, with no sugar."

Then they both noticed a noise outside in the hallway. It was Alex and Slapp coming to tell Tate how the vaccine heist had gone at the airport. There were no other words to describe what they had planned the night before. Gayle met them at the door and excused herself, so they could talk more openly, like men will do sometimes when the ladies aren't around. Alex entered first.

"Hey big guy, you are looking better than you did last night. I thought that perhaps I was going to need my black suit pressed," said Alex as he walked over to the bed to get a closer look. Tate ignored Alex's comment.

"Come in Alex and tell me how did the mission go? I was about to get up and take a shower." Slapp walked in and answered in jest.

"Hey my brother, now that is good news about that shower, because it smells a little stale in here." Alex and Tate ignored

Slapp as he continued. "I can't hang out with you now. I have to relieve the security guy at the front gate so Mr. Pauling can go home to check on his family. Now go ahead and get that shower, because my nose is sensitive. The weekend is coming and there is no way you will get a date if you hold on to that look and smell."

"Okay Slapp, no problem," replied Tate. "I will be able to walk around a little. I'll see you in a couple of hours, downstairs. Slapp backed out of the room and Alex could tell that Tate was preoccupied with a more serious subject matter, when he didn't attempt to defend himself from Slapp's needling.

"Alex, did you ever tell Slapp that Father Caleb was my father?"

Alex laughed. "Are you joking Tate? You are kidding me, right? Do you think that if Slapp knew he wouldn't be calling you half-bred, baby holy man or something worst? No, I've never told him anything about you. I know how private you are. Why did you ask me about this, after all this time? Please tell me that you didn't have a near-death experience last night."

"No, nothing like that, Alex. Well, when I woke up this morning, Father Caleb was telling Gayle and Helen everything."

"Damn man, you mean all your personal shit too? Wow, about you know . . . ?"

"Well, Gayle already knew about the personal stuff, because you know . . ."

"Yea, right, right. I guess she would have to know by now, if you two have been . . ."

"What she didn't know was that Father Caleb is my father."

"Did that bother either of them, when they learned the truth?"

"No Alex, of course not, why would it bother either of them. Helen still doesn't know about the personal stuff. I thought for sure that you or Gayle would have told her by now."

"No Tate," replied Alex. I can't think of any reason for that to come up in general conversation, can you? I try to leave out all the personal crap out of my reports and conversation, and I noticed that you do the same. I guess that answers my question about whether or not you slept with my wife while the two of you were over here alone those three and a half months. Did Father mention the trips to the shot-clinic?"

Alex paused with a baffled expression on his face, as he waited for an answer to the question. Tate's mind had already drifted off into another direction as he noticed that Alex had hid the doubt in his heart about his loyalty to him as a friend. Alex had suspicions about whether or not Tate and I had become intimate. Tate had guarded me for almost four months and now Alex's mistrust surfaced in a light unrelated conversation. Tate just listened as Alex unknowingly revealed his true colors, so to speak.

"Tate, I knew how you felt about Helen back then, when I asked you to be her bodyguard. I am rather surprised that she didn't ask about the shot therapy that you received as a baby and young child. Perhaps it will never come up again. How long did you have to take those shots anyway?"

Tate was relatively surprised that Alex had even brought up the subject of him and me alone in Hong Kong, together. It was kind of a sore subject between them. With this being a fact, it sort of made Tate angry to the point that he wanted to retaliate, just to see the look on Alex's face or how he would react when the conversation unexpectedly took an unusual sensitive turn. Tate eased into his mean-spirited mode, as he answered the question that had been a prelude to what had stirred his anger.

"I took them frequently, as a baby, because the dosages were small and because that is a very rapid growth stage. Then later on the treatments were spaced out more, when a larger time-released dosage could be administered. Oh, and by the way, for the record, I did in fact sleep with your wife every night for those three and a half months. How was I supposed to be her bodyguard, without doing so? That was the way you use to do it whenever you were asked to protect the females, right Bro." Then Tate hesitated to observe Alex's response. "I have to confess, while we are on the subject, that this was one of the best field assignments I ever had. Anyway, you shouldn't be jealous or angry with me; you should be interrogating Tye for that escort mission to Hawaii when you got shot in the shoulder that time, right after you and Helen first began seeing each other. The way I heard, it was some close quarters in the backseat of that limo ride to the airport. Tye's wife almost left him behind that gig [job assignment]."

Alex became real quiet and motionless while Tate laughed and taunted him a little more. Alex found no humor in Tate's recall of the limo event, to say the least. Tate continued.

"Besides Alex, you know I would never make a move on your woman without giving you a heads up first. That's where you and I split the row [are different]." He paused again as he watched the anger build in Alex's facial expression and body language. Tate decided to give a quick recap-highlight to drive his point home of how Alex was unable to do anything about what had taken place in the past. "Now there was an incident, while she was under the influence of some tea she was given," continued Tate in a jesting spirit. Alex wrinkled his bow and waited for Tate to give a more detail focus to that introductory phrase. Tate hesitated longer than was necessary, for a dramatic affect and to allow Alex's imagination to run-amok about Tate's meaning.

"What the f—k are you talking about Tate? Did you make inappropriate advances towards my wife?" Tate giggled again as he took another sip of that cold tea that had somehow now turned into a truth-serum elixir. It wasn't in Tate's nature to be cruel, but for some reason, his medical condition, mixed with a little sleep deprivation and that illegal tea, which he had now been sipping on for two days or more, had in some way forced a few things to the surface of his personality that we were all unaware existed.

"No, no Alex, that's not what I'm saying at all cuz", said Tate with a slow malicious twitch of a smile. "I'm only informing you that she made a few under-the-influence advances towards me and now that I look back, [Tate paused] perhaps I didn't resist her as strongly . . . or as quickly, as I should have, if you know what I mean."

Alex sprang to his feet and walked closer and stood over Tate as he remain sitting on the side of the bed, still holding his cup, with a very weak and nonchalant grasp.

"Tate are you telling me that you got my wife drunk and took advantage of her," yelled Alex. Alex had now balled up his fists in rage as he felt that Tate was taking too long to explain exactly what he meant. Tate on the other hand was only having a little fun at Alex's expense and didn't notice how angry Alex had become. Tate had unfortunately forgotten all the details that had stirred Alex to this point before and had caused him to have an unannounced anxiety attack. Then it became clear to Tate that Alex was leaning closer towards out-of-control when he detected Alex with a tightly clenched hand. Tate's humor became even more enjoyable to himself, as he responded to Alex aggression with disrespect to his emotions, with an added off-the-cuff wit.

"Let me see if I understand where this conversation is going, and has possibly experienced a derailment, for like of a better term," said Tate as he snickered almost uncontrollably. "So now you are going to punch out a sick friend, because your wife left out part of the details of her story that she felt inclined to tell to you, about the three and a half months she spent with me, upon your insisting request? Did I get that right, Mr. Jones?" Then Tate gave Alex a dangerous stare before he continued. "Don't let my seemingly weak and frayed condition give you a false sense of security that you can beat the rest of the details out of me. I know interrogation is what you bring to the table, for our little side business and the bureau also, no doubt. However, Alex, don't let your anger misguide you into thinking that I'm going to allow you to whip my ass so you can feel better about a bad decision that you made, almost a year and a half ago. And whatever you do, don't let this cold cup of tea, that I've been sipping on, be any indication of my strength and health level; this was the only remedy left that the doctor hadn't tried to control my cough."

Once again the tea, identified as Hong Kong Moonlight, had now revealed other properties of influence that one should be aware of—like unforgivable wit exploits. Tate became angry as he spoke the words of warning to his long time friend Alex, which was in fact more like a brother that Tate believed his real brother should have been. Alex moved away slowly and now sat in the recliner placed at the foot of the bed, in which Gayle had failed to return to Miss Beasley's room, next door. Alex was breathing heavily now and Tate suddenly remembered Alex's medical history and how he had recently begun to suffer from anxiety attacks. The doctor had placed him on some nitro tabs to regulate his heart. Alex leaned back deeper in the recliner and Tate quickly put down his cup. He then sprang to his feet to make sure that Alex wasn't having one of his apprehension-onsets; similar to the one which he had experienced that day at Gayle's hallway-desk when he first found out about Milani, his orphaned niece. Tate instantly sobered up from the side effects of the addictive inhibition suppressing tea as he rushed over to see if Alex was okay. Alex continued to breathe heavily and now he had placed his hand on his chest, as if that was going to be some type of aid to his difficulty. Tate spoke to Alex aggressively in a panic, as he grabbed his wrist to take his pulse.

"Hey Big guy, are you alright? Is your chest tightening up again? Wait right here, don't move, I will call for the doctor!" Tate rushed over and picked up his com-pack and called Slapp. He knew that Slapp was at the front-gate and would be able to locate the doctor pretty quickly, by using the surveillance-fed monitor in Gayle's office that had access to most of the in-house security cameras.

"Hey Slapp, this is Tate. Get the doctor up here. Alex is having chest pains, over and out."

"No problem Tate, right away." Slapp locked the front gate of the American Embassy and ran into Gayle's office. She located the doctor and called the room that he was now in. He was in the conference room, next to Miss Beasley's office that the ambassador had given him to set up as the new location for pharmacy slash shot clinic until the flu crisis had been resolved. The doctor was only one floor below, but the medicine cart had remained on the berthing level only two doors away from where Alex and Tate were now waiting, because that was where most of the sick people were lodged. The doctor arrived only minutes later with his portable defibrillator. Tate had already given Alex one of his pills that he was carrying and it seemed to be working. Slapp returned to the front-gate and then called me and informed me of what had happened in Gayle's quarters. I had been in the embassy's basement cafeteria eating slowly while waiting for Alex to join me, after returning the weapons to the armory.

"Helen," said Slapp in a clearly warning tone. "Something has happened to Alex; he's in the room with Tate. I can't leave the front-gate, over and out." I left the tray on the table and rushed out to go to Gayle's in-house sleeping area. I arrived about ten minutes after the doctor because the maintenance crew had taken control of the one and only elevator that goes to the basement, for supply transport. When I arrived, Alex was sitting up with the blood pressure cuff on his arm as the doctor had decided to take a third reading to make sure the medicine was working. I instantly turned to Tate to question him.

"Tate, what happened to Alex?" Tate dropped his glance to the floor and then back up as he turned his head in Alex's direction; as Alex answered instead.

"Oh nothing major happened, Helen. It was crazy on my part. We were just talking and I got a little too excited, that's all." I pressed the issue for a more thorough explanation.

"What could you two possibly be talking about that would have caused you to get so upset that it brought on another anxiety attack? You two have been together as friends for the last twenty years. Somebody better start telling me something truthfully, up in here." The doctor took off the cuff and used this as his cue to leave the room quickly. He heard the angry tone in my voice and decided that he should be somewhere else, which was sure to be safer than in that room. Gayle arrived about that time and performed an eye sweep of each face in the room.

"Well Mr. Jones," said the doctor as he interrupted me. "I think the medicine has started to work and I believe you will be fine. If you haven't had breakfast, I suggest that you eat real soon." Gayle stared at Tate as if she had figured a few things out on her own. She remained leaning up against the doorframe as Tate had refused to look in her direction. Then she spoke directly to Alex before she left the room.

"Alex, I will check on you later. I can have some food delivered up here, if you would like." Alex answered quickly in refusal.

"No Gayle, that won't be necessary. I will go down in a moment." Gayle gave Tate one more harsh glance before she turned to walk away. Now there were only the three of us left in the room, Tate, Alex and me.

"So who wants to tell me what happened in here?" Tate took a deep stalling breath before he began.

"Helen, I was just having a little fun at Alex's expense. I was about to tell him what happened between us when the lady gave you that tea at the massage parlor. Alex became so angry too—quickly, before I could explain, that's all."

"Damn it Tate, what was so amusing about that?"

"I'm sorry Helen, I forgot about his heart and that anxiety thing. I guess the tea made me a little giddy and I just forgot. I said I was sorry." I turned to Alex as I tried to hide my anger, with Tate.

"Baby, Alex, how do you feel now? I will tell you everything later, I promise." I then walked over and punched Tate in the arm, with my fist. "I thought you were my friend Tate, how could you do this to him." Tate was still smiling a little.

"Ouch Helen, I said that I was sorry, that included you also. I wasn't trying to create a problem between you two. I was only trying to come clean and put his mind at ease about us. Then he became all mad and everything, like he believed that I would take advantage of you and betray our friendship. Both of us should be upset with him for not believing us when we tell him that we are only friends. As a matter of fact, he was the one that brought it up in the form of mistrust that he had for both of us." Alex just listened as he lay back in the recliner while trying to lower his heart rate and disperse his anger. He knew Tate pretty well and he realized that he was a stand-up kind of guy. After all, who was Alex to question anyone about his or her activities? Whenever he was out of the sight of others, he was the poster-child for deception, hands down.

"I'm going to leave you two alone to fix this; whatever the hell it is or was." I closed the door behind me, but the truth was that I didn't want either of them to see the guilt on my face. Tate continued with his own personal story again just where he had left off, like nothing had happened, before shit had hit the fan about him and I, while he was my bodyguard. Alex seemed to be okay with that arrangement. I knew he would ask me about it later, when he thought that his heart was strong enough for the facts, undiluted of course.

"Anyway Alex," continued Tate. "By the time I was twelve, it was more like once a month that I had to take those shots. You know that Dr. Li was an internist at John Hopkins, during that time and remembered me when he went to put in my foli-catheter, the other day. He was there when I was very young, so I don't remember him at all."

"Get the hell out of here," said Alex as he expressed disbelief. "I guess that means that everyone knows except Slapp. I'm sure the girls will keep your secret, because they know how insensitive Slapp can be. Listen Tate; I will get out of here so you can get that shower. Do you need me to stay, or do you think you can handle it?"

"No thanks Alex, I think I'm strong enough to do it alone this time. The doctor told me to stay out of very hot water. I think that this tea helped a lot, but there are other side effects that the good doctor conveniently forgot to mention. I know he did it on purpose. I still have questions about what he put in that

I.V. bag. I had some strange-ass dreams and hallucination." Alex laughed just as he stood up to leave.

"Hey Tate, I'm sorry that I got all worked up about that thing with you and Helen."

"No problem Alex, I'm just glad that you didn't choke me out. I guess that was the wrong thing for me to joke about, given you two's history. By the way, there is nothing between us. Yes it's true that I think she is sexy as hell, but my feelings for her were misplaced because she reminded me of my deceased wife. Other than that, there is no real attraction. Well, there is the sexy part, after all I'm still a health male." Tate laughed just before Alex closed the door with his final words, laced with a sarcastic warning for his friend.

"I think that the doctor needs to take you off of that tea, before I have to whip your old sick ass about my wife."

"Damn it Alex, how many times do I have to say I'm sorry? Are we good or do you need more time?"

"No Tate, we are good."

Chapter Fourteen

The Emissary Meets the Cleric

Now that the ambassador was back and a few of the staff members had returned, in spite of the quarantine status, which had remained in affect; the embassy began to recover. It was now around noon and one of the cooks, that had remained in-house sick with the virus, was now back on his feet, wearing a surgical mask for the safety of others. He was able to work and give the old lady down there in the cafeteria, a hand. The ambassador made no demands on any of the staff to get back up to full speed, but Gayle and Miss Beasley was working plenty hard. The American Embassy had remained closed to visitor and was only available for urgent business. Gayle was helping the security department with the logbooks and accounts for everyone and everything that had happened in the last three days. Everyone knew how important the logbooks were so they had little sticky notes all over the place. Gayle and Miss Beasley's job was to make sense of it all and get it into the logs in chronological order. Gayle and Miss Beasley met in the conference room right next to the ambassador's office, which was now the new pharmacy slash shot clinic and called everyone in to turn in all the notes and scraps of paper that they had been making little reminders on. Gayle and Miss Beasley agreed that some of the pieces of paper needed to be handled while wearing cloves for sanitations purposes if for no other reasons. The strangest report was made when one employee had written the time down on his pant leg when he had discovered that the seal had been broken on the armory's locker and two rifles were missing. He had gone back to retrieve his reading-glasses so he could read the next time that the doctor had written for him to take another dose of medicine. He had now worn the smelly, no doubt three day old germ-infected pants into Miss Beasley office so the two of them could decipher what else he had written while delirious from the fever. Miss Beasley was able to put his mind at ease, because she knew that Slapp had drew the weapons and what they were used for. It was going to take at least a page to explain the reason that the armory's seal had been broken and weapons issued to an only part-time employee. The ambassador had already heard about the incident at the front gate when Mr. Pauling had threatened to shoot two carloads of Americans. The part where one man tried to storm the gate had been omitted from the report that the ambassador had received and just like most of the time, ethnicity came into play and was later deemed the main reason, for that oversight.

The citywide quarantine lasted three more days after the American Ambassador had arrived back on island. Slowly the staff returned and things started to get back to normal. The second evening after the ambassador's arrival back, he called in Miss Beasley to his office. He pushed the call button on his phone.

"Mrs. Carrington, will you come into my office please?"

"Sure Sir, no problem." Miss Beasley stood to her feet and picked up her steno notepad and turned it to a fresh sheet. She tapped on the door that separated the two rooms, softly and waited for a reply. The ambassador was standing near the door, so he opened it quickly for her to enter.

"Mrs. Carrington, do you know if the priest has remained in-house and is possibly available to speak with me? I've been very rude to him by not calling him in earlier. I do remember in your briefing that you mentioned that he was our guest. It's that with all the paperwork and the quarantine, I completely forgot about him and my social position. Will you check to see if he can speak with me now? If he has continued to assist the fine doctor, please tell him I will receive him at his earliest convenience. Do you have any idea if his business was urgent, if that is the case, I will apologize the moment he arrives? Keeping a priest waiting is no way to accumulate brownie-points with God." Then he chuckled as Miss Beasley shyly smiled. That was the ambassador's attempt to make a funny, as Miss Beasley like to call his spontaneous wit, which she found most of the time, totally un-amusing. The ambassador was similar to Tate in that respect. He was smart, but he also had learned late in life about humor and its proper place in casual conversation and the timely delivery of a punch line. "I shouldn't keep a man of the cloth waiting and not showing him the courtesy he deserves. By any means necessary Mrs. Carrington, I would like to see him before I retire for the evening."

Miss Beasley stood tall with her notepad clasped closely to her breast with her hands overlapping at the wrist, while she listened purposely to the ambassador's every word. She then responded very professionally.

"I will go and locate him this moment and inform him of your request, Sir. If he is available Sir, are you prepared to receive him now?"

The ambassador spoke up quickly as he waved his hand in a submissive fashion, of not wanting to be a bother.

"Yes, I will see him, but only if he's not engaged in a task for the good doctor." The priest, Father Caleb returned promptly a few moments later with Miss Beasley bringing up the rear. She escorted him into the ambassador's office, where the ambassador now stood to his feet, to greet the priest.

"Please Father, come in. Is there anything that we can get for you? Have you eaten your evening meal? You may join me if you like." The priest bowed gracefully to satisfy the local custom and to give honor to the power of the office. He then sat in the chair that the ambassador presented with an opened palm-up hand gesture. The ambassador sat across from him as they both sat on the opposite side of the big desk's power chair, which faced them on the other side. The ambassador spoke first again.

“Please Father Caleb forgive my manners. Mrs. Carrington promptly informed me that you were our guest during these troubling times and I totally forgot. Now please tell me, how can I help? Enlighten me of the reason for your visit.” The priest brought his piercing green, sometimes teal, eyes up to the ambassador’s level and divinely placed his hands together, as his Ireland accent moved to the forefront, once more, of his speech.

“Mr. Ambassador Sir, it was extremely compassionate of you to take the time to receive and old man, while on such a personal mission. I came to Hong Kong to visit my dear friends and when I arrived . . . .” The priest stopped suddenly, because Mr. Charlie walked into the room, unannounced and without knocking, to make his weekly checks of the thermostat control, the fire extinguisher box, and the windows to see if any of them were leaking from the extremely wet weather season we were having.

“Oh, I’m sorry Sir; I didn’t expect anyone to be in here,” said Mr. Charlie with a sincere apology. “I know this is about the time that you usually take your evening meal, Sir. I can come back later, if now is not a good time.” Mr. Charlie stood motionless while waiting for an answer. The ambassador spoke quickly as he turned back to Father Caleb to explain.

“Mr. Charlie is one of our night roving guards and a personal aid to me when required. You can continue; his clearance is sufficient, since he was once my driver, for many years.” The priest looked over suspiciously in Mr. Charlie’s direction and then took a breath to continue his conversation with the ambassador.

"As I was saying Mr. Ambassador, this was a personal visit. When I arrived and became victim of the quarantine, I learned that my son was also very sick." The ambassador looked very puzzled as he wrinkled his brow to reflect his confusion. Mr. Charlie was headed towards the door to exit the room, while walking slowly so he wouldn't miss the punch line of the priest's open-ended statement, about having a son in these distant lands.

"Father Caleb", inquired the ambassador. "Who is your son? Do I know him?" The emissary maintained his bewildered facial expression as the priest prepared to jog his recollection.

"Yes, I believe you know him. Mr. Thaddeus Romano is my son and my only child." Mr. Charlie heard the words just before he closed the door. The ambassador was stunned to say the least, and was unable to hide that fact, as his facial expression conveyed that precise emotion, to the priest. He jumped to his feet and reached to shake the priest's hand and pulled him to his feet as well.

"I apologize for acting so shocked Sir, but I had no idea and would never have put the two of you together because of . . ." He hesitated to find just the right words and refrain from embarrassing himself again or possibly insulting the priest further with an uncontrollable response.

"Oh I know," interrupted the priest to let the ambassador off the hook. It's because of the race variance and the fact that you know that unmarried priest normally shouldn't have any children." The priest smiled forgivingly as the ambassador continued to hold in his breath the entire time the priest was speaking his last proud words of fact. Then the ambassador exhaled loudly as he agreed, with a single nod of the head. The priest spoke again to improve the clarification that he had attempted to make on behalf of his life.

"You do realize Ambassador, I wasn't born a priest. I was also very young once and traveled the road of life with some confusion and uncertainty, you might say.

"Huh! Yes, I guess that's what I was thinking. Well at any rate, Mr. Romano is a fine man and we are glad to have him on our team. I know he has some personal stuff going on, back in the States. I didn't want to pry. I figured the less I knew about the details, of why they are out here, the better it would be for a man in my position. They are extremely over-qualified for the services they provide for us and their names haven't appeared on any search-and-report list, their passports are current, so that's good enough for me. I gave them the run of the place, by not restricting any area to them on the compound. The truth is, with their combined security clearances, and the fact that they are from different agencies, they out-rank me in power in some arenas. Other than disturbing the motor pool boss, when they trade positions without his approval, I haven't had a moment of trouble out of the three of them. On occasions, Mr. Alvin the youngest one of the trio finds creative ways to amuse himself, by irritating random members of my staff. It's all in fun I'm sure. Their friend, Alexander Jones, visits them on the compound frequently, and that is the reason I said three. As a matter of fact he got himself a short-term consulting gig [position] with the local police department, a few months back. You can never have too many strategic eyes working in your favor and you can never have enough security on the payroll, whenever you are this far away from your homeland. Very few people here on the compound are aware of who they are or what they do. I promised them that I would protect that information, for their safety as well as the rest of ours." The priest smiled warmly as he agreed.

"I understand your position completely Mr. Ambassador and I'm grateful that you have befriended the lot of them. I'm sure that you are also aware that Mrs. Carrington's son is his friend. You know him as Mr. Alvin from the motor pool."

"Yes, I was informed of that little detail only a few weeks ago." The ambassador paused for a moment as he stroked his chin with two fingers while focusing his gaze downward, trying to remember more details about that situation or perhaps waiting for the priest to volunteer more information, to fill in the gaps. He continued.

"Well, at any rate, will you please agree to join me for the evening meal; that's if you don't have any other plans? Then, after that, perhaps we can share a nightcap or two?" The ambassador hesitated for a second as he realized what his last sentence had been to a priest. "I hope I haven't offended you by offering you spirits." The priest smiled and stroked his five o'clock-shadow beard that was probably leaning more towards a medium Miami-Vice look, while he very reservedly answered the question. He thought to himself, what could it possible hurt; this man already knew his most guarded and personal secrets?

"No sir, no harm atall [at all] has been done. I'm a brandy man myself, but I have been known to change my libation if so encouraged to do so, to whatever the host is inclined to contribute to the cause." Then the priest lightened the moment by following-up his response with a gracious wide smile, as the ambassador let out a hardy chuckle.

"Very well, then it is all settled; we will dine and afterwards a night-cap. You must fill-in the holes of that passionate story that you just intrigued me with, but only if you feel that it's not too personal for me to inquire." The old priest smiled again and felt calm that the ambassador seemed to not have a problem with the facts of his earlier life. That night, after it became later than the two of them had planned to stay up, their relationship somehow shifted from a chance meeting to a beginning of friendship worthy of pursuing and encouraging for a lifetime, and that's exactly what happened.

Chapter Fifteen

Mr. Charlie's Story

The finance guy, Mr. Bruce, forwarded a message from the bureau that Alex, Tate, and Slapp needed to return to the States. No doubt for debriefing and to face some charges that had surfaced during an investigation of the man that had been killed in the house fire. The guys knew what this meant, so they waited a few more days before answering, to give Tate more time to recover from the flu virus.

The fill-in doctor moved Tate to Gayle's apartment next door from the embassy's compound and instructed him to take off another week, to regain his strength. Dr. Li didn't want to have to treat him for a relapse of his condition. In spite of the fact, that the quarantine had been lifted there had been reports of new outbreaks of the flu all over the city.

One morning, just before Mr. Charlie was due to get off watch, Gayle asked him to go over to her place to check on Tate.

Gayle chased Mr. Charlie to the front entrance as he shuffled passed her office door.

"I'll see to you tonight Miss Livingston," called out Mr. Charlie as he made his way towards the front entrance. He was walking swiftly as if he was trying to catch the next metro rail, two blocks away.

"Wait, wait Mr. Charlie I need you to do a favor for me, if it won't put you out too much." Mr. Charlie really liked Gayle and would do just about anything for her. He thought she was very sexy and had told her on several occasions that he would have pursued her if he was only twenty years younger and wasn't married to the love-of-his-life. He stopped short of the embassy's front door to allow Gayle to catch up to him. She was wearing one of her lord-have-mercy tight skirts; that was what Mr. Charlie would say, whenever she wore one that he believed she put on, just to stimulate the staff more than was professionally required. The skirt was light summer wool-blended sage colored tweed with a hint of gold threads, which perfectly matched her gold silk cleavage-revealing blouse. It was one of her favorite outfits. There was no argument from me or from anyone else for that matter, who worked there at the American Embassy, that Gayle had all the right curves to wear the wardrobe that she had so meticulously put together. However, I was torn to agree with Mr. Charlie's assessment of the reason she had created it.

"Mr. Charlie, I need a big favor. I know that it's time for you to clock out, but I need you to go over to my apartment, next door and check on Mr. Tate for me. I can't get away and the doctor wants to make sure that he continues to take his medicine on time and drink that tea. If you do this for me, I will get Mr. Alvin to take you home on his next run. He's covering for Mr. Tate until he gets better." That was more information than was needed for Mr. Charlie to agree do whatever Gayle had requested; but now she had to listen to his spiel for a moment, so he wouldn't appear to be a pushover for a pretty girl. We had all been in that position, one time or another, whenever we had to deal with Mr. Charlie. If you hadn't been a victim yet, just stand by because your number was sure to come up. This guy had a story for everything or a monolog that you had to endure, if you asked him a question or if you wanted him to do anything out of the norm. He preferred to call it 'outside my job description'. That meant that the payback was sure to become an issue in the near future. It worked out a lot better for you if you suggested something right up front, during the negotiation of the favor. Gayle had learn this the hard way, yet again lessons in life and a street education is never obtained for a cheap price. He listened carefully as Gayle went on while giving him the whole big picture of why she couldn't do what she was now asking of him. He stroked his stubby whiskered face and answered with one request.

"Sure no problem, Miss Gayle, but you have to make some kind of arrangements for me to eat breakfast somewhere.

"That's not a dilemma Mr. Charlie, I will call the cafeteria right now and tell them to give you whatever you want and charge it to my account. That's the least I can do for you, since you are agreeing to go and check on Mr. Tate. And could you pick up something for him as well; I'm pretty sure he is tired of that soup?" Gayle almost made a successful escape from one of Mr. Charlie's soapbox editorial speeches, but the God of Divine Mercy chose not to spare her this time.

"Here Mr. Charlie, take my key for the back entrance. I believe Mr. Pauling has removed the chains and locks from the private rear tunnel gate. You do know how to get there through the back way," asked Gayle?

"Sure I do Miss Gayle; I was once the Ambassador's personal driver, before my eyes became too weak to see at night. You do realize that those spaces use to be his private quarters and an escape and entrance route, if the front door wasn't a safe option. I don't know how many times I've gone through that tunnel to that sushi bar, just beneath the place. I even had a running tab there, once, back when my lunches were mainly liquid, so to speak." He chuckled as he looked towards the ceiling as if he hadn't thought of those times in years. Gayle interrupted him with a repeat and a few more instructions, in hope that he would lose his train of thought.

"Now here is the key to get in my back door, Mr. Charlie. It will open up into the closet. I will call ahead and tell Tate you are coming, so you won't startle him. He might have drifted off to asleep again from the medicine or that tea."

"You know Miss Gayle, I'm not sure if that tea is legal inside the compound and all. This is considered American soil you know and I have heard of some strange going-ons after a few sips of that brand. Hong Kong Moonlight was the tea that appeared in the message traffic a few weeks ago . . ." Gayle stopped Mr. Charlie in mid sentence because she wasn't sure if he was privileged to all the information about Tate and his associates or the fact that Alex had worked part-time for the local police department. His subject matter shifted after the interruption.

"You do realize Miss Gayle that this is a special favor just for you? Personally I don't particularly care for him or his friend Mr. Alex. They always seem so smug when they strut around the hallways flashing their badges of authority. I know that the ambassador gave them the run of the place, since they are here helping us out and taking minimal wages and all. It's just that they don't seem to respect their elders." Gayle tried to stop Mr. Charlie's opinionated monolog, by clearing her throat, but he was too involved with his caught-up-in-the-moment sermon to notice Gayle's subtle gesture. He continued.

"Now for example, Mr. Alvin, I can deal with him a little better than those other two. He's younger and we still have time to save him from himself. I know he's Mrs. Carrington's long lost son and all and I'm glad they finally got back together. I can deal with him a little better because you know that boy isn't too bright. He's a couple of cans short of a six-pack, if you understand my meaning."

Gayle knew that this was just the opposite when it came to Slapp. Tate had told her more than once to not be taken in by his child-like demeanor and humor. He was a profiler for the team and had probably already figured Mr. Charlie out and knew how to get around him and all his made-up house rules. At any rate, she had to listen as Mr. Charlie carried on. He waved his hands dramatically as if it helped him make his point.

“I know, I know that God loves us all and I try to do the same thing pretty lady, but I really have to search my soul to warm up to those other two. I know Mr. Tate is your boyfriend and all Miss Gayle, and he’s a handsome fella too, but he could stand to be taken down a peg or two, if someone had a mind to ask me. He’s a slick one, the way he’s always hiding behind those dark shaded glasses. I can’t believe the ambassador allows him to wear those inside all the time. They aren’t prescription are they baby, because that would explain everything, if they were? The boy isn’t going blind is he? I show can tell you a thing or two about failing eyesight. It’s no fun.” Mr. Pauling, who had been standing right outside Gayle’s office door listening and trying not to make a sound, while he laughed at the craziness of Mr. Charlie’s babbling; suddenly entered the area to rescue Gayle from Mr. Charlie’s torment.

“Excuse me Mr. Charlie sir”, said Mr. Pauling as he attempted to hide the fact that he had been listening the entire time. “I need Mrs. Livingston to help me fill-out this log before I get off my watch.”

“Sure thing young fella, I was just about to go and do a favor for Miss Gayle myself. I’ll talk to you two a little bit later.” Mr. Charlie walked away talking to himself as he crossed the corridor to take the elevators to the basement level that housed the cafeteria and other areas that was required to assist in the smooth running compound. Gayle spoke to Mr. Pauling with deep gratitude.

"Thank you so much Mr. Pauling for rescuing me from, yet, another one of Mr. Charlie's long drawn out history lessons. I do enjoy some of his stories, but occasionally they aren't time appropriate. I owe you a favor Mr. Pauling for liberating me or should I say freeing me?"

"Yes you do Miss Gayle," replied Mr. Pauling as he smiled. "But I will add this favor to your boyfriend's tab, and give the nice pretty lady a break." Mr. Pauling's relief watch showed up a few moments later and he passed on the log. Gayle's office was now being transformed back to its original state, after the ambassador informed the doctor that he could use one of the conference rooms on the second floor as his makeshift clinic. Gayle called the lunch area and told the staff that Mr. Charlie was on his way down and to serve him breakfast and allow a take-out tray for Mr. Tate, the driver. She informed them that the charges should be applied to her account and that she would come down to pay as soon as she got a moment to spare. Then she called Tate that was now between naps, in her apartment next door. He answered on the third ring.

"Hello, this is Mr. Romano, go ahead." Even with a cold, his voice was so deep and sexy. Gayle was happy to hear that he was sounding a lot stronger and clearer. If it weren't for that cough, he would almost be back to at least eighty percent.

"Hello sweetie, this is Gayle. I'm sending Mr. Charlie over with a tray of food. I can't get away right now and it's almost time for you to take your medicine again." Tate raised his voice.

"You did what Gayle? You are sending Mr. Charlie over here! Why didn't you send one of the guys from the security booth? I'm not in the mood to deal with him. You do want me to get better don't you Gayle?"

"Yes Thaddeus, don't be silly. I didn't think about the guys in the booth, besides the shift is changing and all of them aren't in yet. I caught Mr. Charlie on his way out the front door. Mr. Pauling's relief hadn't shown up yet, at the time. What's wrong with Mr. Charlie? He's a nice old man until you break one of the house rules."

"You mean one of his rules, don't you?"

"Oh Tate, just try not to shoot the man when he comes in the back door to bring your tray. Will you do that for me please? Perhaps I can come over on my lunch-break and check on you then. Will that be okay?" She was speaking in the softest and most seductive way she knew how and it worked like a charm.

"Sure Gayle, I'll be here. Call me back later. Love ya."

"I love you too, um bye." Tate hung up the phone and lay back down to wait. About ten minutes later he heard Mr. Charlie, the night roving patrol guard, coming in the back door that entered in through the huge closet.

"Hello Mr. Romano, it's only me, the night guard, Mr. Charlie. I'm coming in the back with your breakfast." He appeared in the doorway of the closet that led into the sleeping area of Gayle's flat. Tate yelled back his answer.

"Come on in Mr. Charlie, Mrs. Livingston called me and told me that you would be bringing my breakfast because she couldn't get away. I really appreciate you doing this for us. I know that it's at the end of your shift."

"No problem young buck, I was glad to do a favor for Miss Gayle. You know I really do like that gal. If I was only twenty years younger and unmarried, I would give you some competition for her affection." Ha Ha Ha ha he laughed as he sat the tray in a nearby chair. He was limping a little on one side; this caused Tate to become curious.

"Yea, yea I know what you mean Mr. Charlie. I'm sure glad you aren't twenty years younger, because then I might have to put a bullet in you." The room went quiet as Mr. Charlie and Tate made eye contact for the second time, as Tate reached for his robe. Then Mr. Charlie broke the silence with his laugh as he responded, but Tate maintained his poker face and never cracked a smile to lighten the moment.

"Oh young buck," said Mr. Charlie as he continued to laugh even more. "I'm sure that it wouldn't have come to that, besides I was only teasing you. Don't get your boxer all in a bunch." Tate stood and went into the bathroom to wash his face and brush his teeth. Mr. Charlie found a folding single tray-table in the kitchen, between the wall and the refrigerator for Tate's breakfast tray. He turned on the coffee pot and poured Tate a half of a glass of orange juice and had it all set up on the tray by the time Tate immerged from the tiny bathroom. Mr. Charlie was now sitting in the chair with his back to the door of the closet that he had just entered through. Tate took his position back on the side of the bed and pulled the tray table closer. He took a sip of orange juice to possibly get rid of the toothpaste taste. Mr. Charlie sprang to his feet as Tate made a face from mixing the juice with the toothpaste remains.

"Oh, sorry about that Mr. Romano, I brought the juice for the medicine. I have some coffee brewing. Sit right there, I'll get it for you." Mr. Charlie returned with the coffee and took his seat again facing Tate, as he made his selections of food.

"So Mr. Charlie, what's wrong with your leg? I noticed you limping when you came in".

"Oh, it's just an old war injury son. Whenever the weather is wet or damp, it acts up a bit".

Mr. Charlie then leaned back in the chair and lifted his bad leg with one hand and placed it across the stronger one, at the knee. He stroked it from mid-thigh to just below the knee, as if that helped with relieving the pain. Tate ate his hot breakfast and glanced up at Mr. Charlie's face every few seconds or so.

"So tell me something young buck, how did you get those green eyes? I always wondered why you wore those shades all the time. Is it to hide those unusual eyes? You know that it is rare for a mixed raced man, like yourself, to have green eyes." Tate was surprise that Mr. Charlie took such liberties with him. The two of them made stabbing-eye contact again as Tate chewed his food and reminded himself that Mr. Charlie was an old man that his fiancé liked and respected to some degree. Tate took a deep breath and let it out quickly before he answered.

"I always tell people, whenever they ask me, that they were passed on to me from my grandmother and it's true that her eyes are green as well, but to be honest, I inherited them from my father. Why do you ask Mr. Charlie, is it that strange? Or is it because my eye color doesn't match my hue?" Mr. Charlie, looked away from Tate's harsh piercing stare as if he was about to lie or feared he might reveal too much of what he had overheard in a private conversation the evening before between the priest and the ambassador; that in fact the priest was Tate's biological father. Tate found out later that the latter had been the case. The priest had informed the ambassador that he had come over to check on his friends and when he arrived, he found his son seriously ill with the flu virus. Tate took this time to change the subject.

"So what are you doing over here, old man? I think that it is peculiar also that the likes of you are so far from home and out of place, so to speak."

"I beg to differ," swiftly replied Mr. Charlie as he shifted his posture by uncrossing his leg and leaning forward in the armless chair. Now Mr. Charlie was only twelve inches away from the other side of the tray table as he rested his elbows and upper arms on his thighs, just above the knee. He laced his fingers together as he looked down at the space between his feet as if he was deciding where would be an appropriate place in his life's story, to start his tale. He decided on just before he had left home more than forty-years before.

"You see Young Buck." Tate interrupted Mr. Charlie abruptly about his title that he seemed to give everyone that appeared to be younger than he was.

"Mr. Charlie, why do you do that? You know, call everyone 'young buck'. I don't remember anyone introducing me to you as 'young buck'. My name is Mr. Thaddeus Bernard Romano Senior and any portion or part of that title I will be more than pleased to answer to." Mr. Charlie instantly went into a rage as Tate looked on and laughed lightly as he waited for Mr. Charlie to realize that it wasn't that serious.

"See; see that's what I mean. You young bucks have no respect for your elders and always looking for ways to push them aside or prove that they are wrong about something or other. I know what your damn name is and when I have to fill-out my reports, I don't call you young buck either. Now stop being rude, you almost caused me to lose my train of thought defending myself. I know what you young bucks want, yea I know. You need somebody to bus' a cap up in your asses and see how you like that for starters. You are always going around changing shit and correcting people. Don't you know that it's impolite boy, didn't your daddy teach you anything?" Tate laughed more wholeheartedly as he attempted to correct Mr. Charlie now from calling him boy. The laughter's excitement cause Tate to have another coughing episode and Mr. Charlie sprang nervously to his feet, while almost turning the eating tray table over, in the process. Then he began to slap Tate in the back to assist him in getting his breathing under control again. The body-jerking cough that Tate produced had frightened Mr. Charlie a bit and forced him to change his aggressive attitude to a more compassionate one as he continued to pound Tate forcefully in the back. Mr. Charlie started to back-peddle from his stern stance of chastising Tate on his manners, to one of concern about his ill condition.

"Now look what you have gone and done; started your coughing up again. I'm sorry Mr. Tate that I got you all worked up. I would hate for something to happen to you while I'm here and have been entrusted to look after you for a spell. Mrs. Livingston would never forgive me if you had a relapse because of my lack of judgment." Tate finally caught his breath and held up his hand so Mr. Charlie could stop thrashing him in the back. Mr. Charlie quickly moved the tray and took it back to the kitchen. Then he returned with a glass of water and another half of a glass of juice. Mr. Charlie reverted back to a harsher tone as he instructed Tate about the next phase of his care. "Come on now son, you have to take this medicine and drink all of this water. When Mrs. Livingston asks me did you take it, I refuse to lie for the likes of you, so take it and just be done with it; that's all I'm asking of ya."

Tate took the medicine, removed his robe and lay back down on the bed. Mr. Charlie limped backwards to the chair and sat down again. "Now where was I? Oh I was about to tell you the story that landed me way out here in Asia. Here, spray some of this on the back of your throat, it will help your cough a bit," insisted Mr. Charlie, as if he had just become a new member of 'Old Folk Medicine' chapter. Tate did as he had been instructed, while he remained in a jesting mood and continued to badger the old man, just to amuse himself. We were all convinced that as long as Tate continued to drink that tea, it would have some affect on his congenital personality traits. I'm sure that the elixir had once again played a role into Tate's strange flippant nature that he had only recently revealed. Tate began to see why Gayle liked the old guy. He had a rough and stern talk exterior, but he had a marshmallow for a heart. Tate couldn't wait to tell Alex about Mr. Charlie because he was pretty sure that Slapp had already figured him out, with Slapp being an exceptional profiler and all. Tate continued his harassing pretence.

"When are you going to tell me the story old man, the medicine is started to make me sleepy," said Tate as he laughed out again.

"Listen son, if you interrupt me one more time, I'm going to have to take my knife out. You aren't well or strong enough for me to shoot you in the ass yet. Damn kids, always playing around. Who story is it anyway? Don't be rushing me." Then Mr. Charlie leaned back in the chair again and began to stare at the ceiling and laugh profoundly. "You see Son;"

Then he stopped suddenly and leaned way forward to ask the question. “It is alright for me to call you son, or is that going to be a problem between us too?” Tate smiled widely before he answered as the old man waited for his response.

“Yes Mr. Charlie, it’s alright in this setting.” The old man’s temper flared once more.

“See what I mean, what the hell is that suppose to mean, ‘in this setting’. All I need is a simple yes or no. What other setting could we possibly be in where you might change your mind about it?”

“Sure Mr. Charlie, yes, call me whatever.” Mr. Charlie gave Tate one more annoyed glance before he began again.

“You see it was the early part of 1968. I was sixteen years old when my parents received the second service-draft notice for my brother, who was two years older, to report to the local recruiting station for the Vietnam War. My mother was inconsolable and cried every night for weeks. My father didn’t know what to do. My brother was a big strong guy, but he had no survival skills, you see. He was just too easy going. We both were good in school, but he was our best hope to escape the poverty that we had endured for years as sharecroppers. One night I got this bright idea that I could go in his place. I wrote my parents a note, took the letter that had come in the mail about the draft and stole my brother’s birth certificate. We were living in Mississippi at the time on twenty-five acres of farmland. The only predicament with our plot was that water was a problem. Anyhow, after I had been gone a week or a little more, I wrote home and told my family that I was all right. I guess that's the day I became my brother's keeper, so to speak. I'm not going to lie to you junior; I was frightened near to death. This was the first time that I had ever left home and went some place where I didn't know anybody. I think I silently cried the first few nights to myself."

Then Mr. Charlie looked up to make sure Tate was listening and to be certain he hadn't insulted him again by calling him 'junior', before he went on. "After basic training, everyone was headed to the frontline. We were giving as well as we were taking, as I remember it, when I got hurt. They shipped me out and checked me into the hospital to fix my leg, you see. It was never the same after that and it took some time to heal. I went into therapy and I saw men every day with a lot more serious injuries than I had. Some of them were depressed and when you looked into their eyes you could see it. They had that far away stare. Everybody recognized that gaze that's hard to come back from, even if your injuries are minor. But you see young fella I didn't have that problem. Death was all around us. Almost every night we lost someone from one of the wards. I think some died because they just gave up on the will to live or that's what I heard one of the doctors say to the nurse. I had my own problem and that was the secret that I had taken my brother's place. I was praying every night that the war would be over or at least they would close the draft board. I knew that if my mother had to be separated from both of her sons in the war fighting, it would kill her for sure. So you see Junior, I was on a mission. I was trying to protect my brother and save my mother from a pain that I knew she would never recover from, unless God decided to work his magic. You know God can do whatever he pleases. That's one of the things I like about him. That's another story I need to tell you young buck about, but that will get me off the subject a bit, and besides, I am a little pressed for time." Mr. Charlie laughed out loudly as if his last statement was an unplanned punch line to a joke or witty play on words. Tate smiled only briefly.

Mr. Charlie rubbed his hands together methodically while he gazed out into space and smiled to himself as he remembered the next portion of this tale.

"I was able to get some R&R in Hong Kong; you know, rest and relaxation is what it was called. But with all the partying that was going on in this town, every damn night, it was hard to get either. I was still having problems with my leg, so when I returned to my unit, the doctor said I wasn't well enough to rejoin my platoon in the field. They shipped me off to Honolulu, Hawaii to the Tripler Army Hospital and I received some more surgeries on my leg. Boy, let me tell you, there was a party every night at the Pearl Harbor Base Enlisted club. God only knows what was going on at the officers club, probably nothing exciting. Back then; the officers were all cultured and uppity or at least they tried to appear to be, until they got a few drinks in them. After a few drinks, I was told that they became twice a bad as any of us, I think that's why they wanted to keep the two clubs separated. The most action and the best parties were always at the chief's club. As a junior enlisted man you only got invited over there if you were a new young female. They had more money to through around and the local girls knew it. During that time it was an unwritten rule that an officer couldn't have an ugly wife. Pearl Harbor was another R&R [rest and relaxation] stop for the troops. Every military branch of the services was represented there on that island and at any given moment a fight would breakout over some local woman or another. Liquor was cheap and the women were pretty, then after a few drinks, perhaps it was the other way around, I forget." Mr. Charlie laughed out real loudly, clapped his hands together as if he was enjoying remembering the story's flashbacks more than he did telling Tate about them. He collected his composure and went on with the explicit recollection. "During that time and years later, so I'm told, they had topless dancing ladies on base at the cantina, for the duration of lunch time; so you can only imagine what it was like around supper time. The lunch menu was mostly beer and burgers, but who gave a damn about that; most guys went there for the naked girls and latest sounds in music. Motown Record studio back then was producing a top-of-the-chart hit every week, or so it seemed to us so far away from home." Mr. Charlie paused again and clapped his hands together and giggled again, like it had happened the day before and Tate was an old barracks roommate that had missed the excitement because he had to stand a security watch, which made the cantina off limits to him, for that day, unless he had to go inside to arrest somebody. "And if that wasn't your fancy," Mr. Charlie went on to say, "there was Hotel Street; some called it Shit Street, because there were ladies-of-the-evening on every corner for blocks." Mr. Charlie hesitated again as Tate smirked a little and began to cough, only slightly. This alarmed Mr. Charlie a tad, as he stood up and moved to lean over Tate once more, as he continued to lie in bed listening intensely to the story.

"Wait a minute there young fella," said Mr. Charlie with the look of concern in his eyes, that just maybe he had cross the line once again with his labeling-name he used to address Tate. "Are you sure you are well enough to hear the rest of this story? If not, I can tell you the rest of it some other time. Because when you are telling the truth, the story doesn't vary. Oh it's true that some of the parts maybe more highlighted than others, but the story never changes." Tate pushed himself up in bed as Mr. Charlie place another pillow underneath his head and shoulders as he patted both sides of the cushion down with his hands, to make the adjustments.

"Now, that's better for you junior," said Mr. Charlie as he shuffled backwards to his chair and landed hard on the seat, due to the weak leg. "Now where was I, let me think? Oh, oh yea," he said as he held up one finger like an old person would do to excuse himself from a Southern church congregation when it was inappropriate to move around, but was urgently necessary. "I remember now, I was telling you about Pearl Harbor at night. 'Cause night time was the right time," he said in a joking manner, while looking pleased with himself that he had made a rhyme of his statement. "Well, while I was there, my discharge papers were served. I was having such a good time until I wasn't ready to go home yet. I sent my discharge papers home and told my mama to send me my birth certificate, because I wanted to apply for a passport.

While I was on active duty, I didn't need one. I knew once my military paperwork expired, I wouldn't be able to go back overseas without one. I had fallen in love with Hong Kong and all the pretty girls, you understand. I got me a job at the Tripler Army hospital as a janitor, for a while. I saved my money and applied for my passport. I was now nineteen and hadn't been home in almost three years. I bought a ticket back to Hong Kong and I lived at the USO for a spell. I got a job at the Fenwick Pier and quickly learned that this was where the action was for all the sailors coming through. Now they were a different breed, let me tell you. They drank, partied and fought. I'm sure at least a hundred of them were thrown in the brig every Friday, Saturday or Sunday night. The locals loved them though, because they spent money like God himself had already canceled tomorrow, without prior notice, if I may say without angering God. Back then, I worked as a short-order cook in the little greasy-spoon snack bar they had there. This was years before they allowed McDonalds to add their flavor to the place. When money got tight once, they even found a place for me to sleep in one of the storerooms. I was like a live-in security guard. I guess you could say that this was my calling. It seems that I've been guarding something or someone all my life. First my brother, then the cantina; after that a bodyguard for the American Ambassador and then the job I have now. To tell truth about the matter, I was more like a fire-watch back then. It wasn't as though I could stop anyone who might have a mind to break in and steal some stuff. The local franchise owners really appreciated me being in the place at night, even though it was illegal. Every now and again they would give me a few dollars to help me out. This old Master Chief knew I didn't want to go home yet, so he looked after me and then when he transferred, he told his relief [the person that replaced him] about me and he agreed to look-out for me as well. Then one day this young girl came in with her father to shop at the Fenwick Pier. I was sitting outside soaking up a little sun, smoking a cigarette. She smiled at me as she passed and I knew she was the one for me. Her father was an American and her mother was local. The next time I saw the man come in to be fitted for his suit by Mr. Tony upstairs, I asked him about his pretty daughter. He gave me a deadly look and I backed off. I saw her a few months later and asked her out. The rest is history. A few months later, I overheard two men talking one day and they said that the American Embassy was looking for drivers. I had a military license to drive around, but had never owned a civilian driver's license. So I had the old Master Chief to type me up some paperwork so I could fly to Hawaii on a military airlift and get some civilian license. I think he made a phone call to one of his buddies, because the paperwork and identification didn't look that impressive; even to me. After I returned I got my girlfriend to teach me the layout of the city. I bought the maps and she and her mother, whom I told you was a local lady, taught me everything I needed to know about the beautiful breath-taking island city of Hong Kong. Even back then the city was unbelievable and filled with life and an energy that I can't put words to. I got the job and began driving for the ambassador. When the ambassador changed, I still was the best man for the job, because I had learned all the short cuts and truly became invaluable as a tour guide whenever VIP's came to visit. My girlfriend went to the States to go to school. Her mother took sick shortly after, so after only two years, she had to come home. She was the oldest and her father had to work even though he had retired from the military. The war was over and we got married and got our own place. Her mother never got better and after a few years, she died. So now we had to help raise her sister and brother. They finished school and their father traveled back to the States so they could go to college in the States. My wife and I stayed here and have been here ever since."

By the time Mr. Charlie finished vicariously reliving his life story, Tate was fast asleep. The old man hadn't noticed exactly when Tate had stopped listening, but the story was true and therefore could always be repeated if necessary. Mr. Charlie stood slowly to his feet as he shook his head in unbelief that his story had lasted so long until it had relaxed Tate into a deep sleep. He mumbled to himself as he meticulously and sympathetically pulled the covers up onto Tate's chest, as he appeared to sleep unhindered by his agonizing intermittent coughing episodes. Mr. Charlie began to think out loudly as he prepared to leave.

"Poor fella, I was wrong about him. He's a nice man after all. How could I have been so misguided? Well Lord, perhaps I'm getting old and set in my ways. Next time, I pray, I will remember to do more soul searching before I make my decision about a man that I don't know very well. Yea, that's what I need to do, just to be on the safe side, amen."

Chapter Sixteen

A Holiday to Remember

A few days later, Tate was back on his feet. Father Caleb left the island, but he promised to return for the big party, in which the American Embassy had been selected and had accepted the challenge, to co-sponsor. This was a huge event and very important to the surrounding ally relationships. The American Embassy's staff was much too small to successfully prepare for such a large gala. So the ambassador arranged to borrow help from whichever U.S. Naval Vessel was in port at the time, to assist. He was praying that one of the larger ships, perhaps an aircraft carrier, would be in port during that time of the embassy's great need of help. We required at least seventy-five people to be assigned to us for ten days or more. For the men or women selected, it would be like a vacation because the American Embassy had decided to put them up somewhere in the city. The Ambassador wanted to make sure that they remained motivated to do their best and be a little creative at the same time. They would have to share rooms, to cut the cost, but other than that it would be like an all inclusive get-a-way with a little work added on. As payment to the ship and its crew, the top brass would receive extra ten tickets to be awarded to the crew, as they saw fit. The only stipulation that the ambassador had was that the ten passes should be awarded to ten of the recipients, that had volunteered and that the selections were to be made from the enlisted ranks.

The party was set up as a good-will event, but Of course, politics was always at the top of the occasion's agenda or under-currant, depending how one wanted to view the situation. It was a black-tie affair and this year's event would be held in the New World Renaissance Hotel and Resort's ballroom, which was located downtown Kowloon, Hong Kong. The guys all had tuxedos tailor made by none other than the infamous 'Tony', of Fu Shing and Sons second-generation tailors, at the Fenwick pier. Mr. Tony had to order in black fabric to accommodate the demands of this occasion. Gayle and I decided that this would be the perfect time to have a new outfit made as well. We all met in Miss Beasley's office one afternoon to discuss the details. Although the ball was three months away, there was a lot of planning and preparations to be done. The guest list alone would take weeks to construct and then update all the names. The Ambassador had business cards in his personal rolodex that required sorting and then the persons had to be located, in case they had changed jobs, titles, or physical location. Meetings had to be held to select food that would be added to the standard menu and make sure that it wouldn't clash with other items that was required, just as a diplomatic courtesy if nothing more. All of these issues took time and Miss Beasley was so glad that she had Gayle and me to help. Alex would be brought on staff for a few weeks as another pair of eyes as security, for the event. Slapp and Tate would show him around the embassy's compound and teach him a little more about the city. There was no serious pay in it for Alex, but that was fine because now he would qualify for a few guest tickets for the event. My father, Uncle Oscar, had been asked to perform part of the music during dinner, with his seven-piece orchestra. When Uncle Oscar divulged to us that he had been indeed hired, he used the words 'commissioned and acquired' to enlighten us of his proud moment. He said that it sounded more personal and dignified, the way he informed us. This sort of followed suit for him, because he never allowed any of us to use the word 'band' while referring to his back-up instrumental group.

After dinner the entertainment would consist of local talent. First the children would perform a routine from their martial art gyms, and then a drum and warrior group of about two hundred would perform something with a traditional nuance. After that, the last performance would be a group of about three hundred and fifty that would be broken down into ten groupings of thirty-five. Each group would be dressed to represent the top ten tea flavors in the regional area. When each group came into view of the audience, they would be introduced as a tea and the area in which it was grown. Each costume was unique and the colors were chosen to represent something very distinctive about the tea, or where it had been grown. Pale colors represented the mildness, dark colors such as brown, black, or burnt orange meant that it had a strong robust or dominating flavor. The standard primary colors signified the color that the tea was identified by on the market or its packaging. Each performer wore a costume that came apart and off in many areas from the body. First each group of tea-dancers would come out and dance according to what they felt would describe their flavor of tea. Examples would be ballet, salsa, tango, waltz, rumba, tap and so on. The announcer would then ask someone in the audience to come over to the microphone and read a predetermined premix name of two or more teas. These performers would then exchange parts of their costumes with another tea dancer from the other group that was named and then perform a blend of the two dances, therefore representing the blending of tea that the two created by being combined. The performance was breath taking to say the least. It was called the Festival of the Blending Teas Ballet. This worked out great, because this year's theme slogan was 'Contributions Great and Small'. Gayle and I got a chance to see the dress rehearsal of the dancing teas one evening when we went into the ballroom to check the dignitaries seating chart, one last time.

Mr. Tony from Fu Shing and Sons Tailoring called us in for our final fitting. Gayle had selected a strapless maxi length black dress with a short waist long sleeve open front jacket to cover. The skirt portion over lapped in the front, but when she walked it was more like an opening that swung open just shy of the crouch. Of course, it was in her standard Lord-help-me tightness and Tony had added more weight in the hem of the dress to give it more of a dramatic swing. The cuffs on the sleeves of the jacket were trimmed with a braided black and cream silk fabric with a hint of pure gold thread mixed into each of the colors. The gown was a masterpiece and Gayle had all the right curves to make it a head-turner. We weren't sure how Tate was going to react to this dress. He wasn't an 'in-the-spotlight' kind of a guy. The only saving grace for Gayle was the fact that he would be partially working that night and we would possibly be on our own. There was no doubt in my mind that the men in the room would be talking about that dress for months, after the event.

My dress was black as well, spaghetti straps with gold woven into them. It had a short midriff jacket with the high Asian cut stand-up collar, with eighteen carat gold thread embroidered double-headed dragon with two heads that face each other under my throat, just shy of the gold clasp that held it together, which resembled a dragon's tongue. The sleeve cuffs also carried a smaller dual-headed dragon while its tail stretch all the way around my wrists. The split opening on the lower dress half was on the front and over the left thigh. The slit opened up four inches above the knee. It was you-may-want-to-consider-standing-all-night tight, maxi length with double headed dragon diamond studded pin at the top of the gap, to absorb some of the pressure from the seam. After losing twenty-five pounds, when I first arrived in Hong Kong, I was modeling runway material, hands down. We both wore fire-engine red lipstick and black accessories. Milani's outfit was an all-white dress with white lotus flowers outlined in black satin, at the hemline. Maximilian wore black slacks with a white tuxedo jacket with black satin mat-finished lapels and bowtie.

Father Caleb arrived two days before the event. Slapp was our escort that night. We were able to get a table together. So there we all sat, Max, Father Caleb, Gayle, Slapp plus Milani who sat mostly on Slapp's lap, and me. My father didn't join us until much later because he was playing soft music the entire time during the dinner hour. Alex and Tate were security guards for the American Ambassador and his second in charge. The doctor, Miss Beasley and Father Caleb had been invited to sit with them. The Emissary had sent Tate over to ask the priest to join them at their table. Now we were down by one, from the original table count. We weren't able to see them because the room was so large and so many people were there. The guys were all wearing their ear communicators so we were able to get an update of what was happening at the grown-ups table, so to speak. The evening was long and by the time we moved the entourage to my father's hotel for a nightcap and relive the highlights of the evening, Max and Milani were out cold. Slapp and Tate carried them while Alex escorted the ambassador and his immediate-staff back to the American Embassy. Mr. Pauling was on duty as usual, at the front gate when we all arrived. We all agreed that that evening was unforgettable and we knew years from now we would remember the details of that night with a deep fondness and no regrets.

* * *

The winter weather was setting in as the rain continued. The holidays were rapidly approaching and this meant that this would be our second major holiday season away from home and on the run. My father, Uncle Oscar, had given notice to his contractors that he would be retiring and permanently moving back to the United States to lessen his workload. He was giving them a full year's notice, so they would have time to find someone else to fill the musical gap that he had created by retiring. His sponsors came up with an idea to bridge the space by filming my father and possibly use the videos after he was gone to fill in some empty areas that he would leave in the entertainment area, on this side of the world. My father agreed and his schedule became more demanding than before. He was now working and filming on his off time. Some of the recordings were made on location, while others were taped in a studio setting. This required him to travel to some of the spots that he hadn't performed at in years. The pay was very good and they gave him free range on the music selection. I took a few trips with him when he decided to record our song as a duo. I don't think I have a pleasing voice, but each time we appeared together, the audience seemed to enjoy it. Lucky for me, because when it came to music, my father was a slave driver, putting it mildly.

Milani was spending more time with us and was learning the English language quickly. Uncle Slapp had remained her favorite person from the group even though he talked to her forcefully all the time. He didn't yell at her loudly, it was just a certain tone that he used, only with her. We believed that she was able to read his facial expressions, more than understanding the words that he spoke, because they were usual mixed with his strange flavor of wit. Whatever the case may have been, there was no denying that there was a bond that none of the remainder of us completely understood.

Miss Beasley, Gayle and I decided to make this a special holiday season; one that we would always remember. If things worked out the way we had planned, this would be our final Christmas in Hong Kong. The guys had made the decision that they would return, right after the holidays to answer all the bureau's questions about their ten-year side business, and possibly face charges that had arose, during their venture. There was also the minor issue of explaining about the house fire, which had killed the informant, which was originally their hired watchman. Plus, of course, there was the bombing that they had devoted a lot of time into discovering who were involved. The bureau had run into some walls and would surely want them to share the information that they had gathered, about the incident. Being a renegade outfit did have its advantages and the bureau wanted to cash in on these perks in exchange for some leniency during their investigation, of the so called misfits.

The men had been around the different agencies long enough to know how all the games were played, from the inside when no one was watching. They understood also that many times, things that happened behind closed doors were mere paper-drills to make everything look legit on file. However, now and again you would have some overachiever, in the ranks. A person that apparently would be trying to get some brownie points to move up to the next level up on the food chain. He or she would pull out the rulebooks and make everyone else's life, that was involved, a living hell. This was their only fear about the whole ordeal of going back and turning themselves in to be lightly interrogated. These urchin-types usually made it their personal mission to make the environment unbearable. Frequently, these by-the-book people have something missing in the social or power arena that makes them feel as though they need to compensate for their shortcomings in other areas. Personally the most common one found to support this syndrome, in men, has been the Lil' Penis Syndrome. While others around them are just as intelligent as they are, they frequently feel the need to point out every petite flaw in everyone around them, or find fault in the process. It's an unwritten rule that when you are trying to accomplish a task that you can't achieve alone, one should chose their battles and move on. Obviously, these busy little people missed that groundbreaking training completely, because they spend countless hours making sure their presence is always felt, by quoting a rule that probably has out lived its usefulness. However, these individuals do serve a very important position in any task force, but someone is always needed around to keep them on a short leash. These individuals are excellent people to leave in-charge, when you have to be out of the office, but only for a short period of time. They appear to have huge gonads and always up for a challenge, they just have a problem when it comes to the fact that someone else's hanging-and-swinging might be superior to theirs in some form or fashion. I believe the socially accepted term is called 'Alpha male.' However, this man wants to be the Alpha male, but he's not. This person may also be referred to as 'the Company Man'. Sometimes he may be the one with the Neapolitan Complex, or the 'Short Man Syndrome'. Slapp preferred the term 'Baby D—k Syndrome', so no one will be confused about the way he felt about the ass-wipe in question.

This man is always needed and serves a very important role in any arena, it's just that he doesn't play well with others because he has memorized the rulebook and feels that it is his calling from some lesser god, to enforce them on everyone concerned. Other members of the staff, unknowingly to them in most cases, frequently use them. This is the individual that the men feared the most, because this character always found some way to add weeks, if not months, onto any investigation, as others on the team try to appease his irritating and mentally abusive nature. One of Murphy's Laws is that if you search for something wrong long enough, you will find it. In Alex and Slapp's branch, this man was named Sheppard Chesterfield Munson. Oh there were others that wanted his position and lobbied heavily for it, and on a frequent basis, I was told. Yet the guys felt that the kissing-ass-award, with trophy, had to be awarded to, without a doubt Agent Sheppard Chesterfield Munson.

Alex had strategized ways to get around the man, whenever he had been forced to deal with him, whereas Slapp loathed the man with a passion so deeply until he couldn't even explain it. Slapp had once promised the supervisor that if he were ever forced to go out into the field with agent Munson, he would more than likely shoot him his self. The only thing that saved Slapp's career after that statement, when he had only recently joined the force, was Agent Dexter Allen Burney, whom he fondly called Uncle Burney. He had been Slapp's deceased father's partner, or so Slapp understood at this point. Agent Burney convinced the powers that be that Slapp was speaking out from his anger when he had made the threat and that he and agent Munson had been in a turf-war, since Slapp's arrival. Slapp always seemed to have an under-current of anger brewing. Over the years it had seriously improved, but now after his recent beating in the alley, the side business being shut down, learning the truth about his mother, living in exile for safety, and losing Max's mother; we weren't sure how close Slapp was to the breaking point or edge of a melt-down.

Alex had expressed to Tate, since he was from another branch, about Slapp's feeling towards Agent Munson, more than once. To be truthful about the matter, whenever they wanted to get a rise or the best of Slapp, by teasing him about an issue, all they had to say was 'I think Agent Munson would have another opinion'. Just that simple phrase would send Slapp's temper right off the chart. Then they would laugh and apologize real sincere like, until the next time they wanted to be entertained. Of course, Slapp would start swearing, while using every four-letter word that he could chain together. The funniest part was when Slapp would join profanity phrases together that were never designed to be linked. I personally couldn't believe how often the repeated teasing worked on Slapp and provoked the same zest response as the last time. Slapp would turn all red and saliva would be spraying whoever was near. He would be waving his hand and placing the other one on his gun as if he expected Agent Munson to enter the room, on cue and add in his two cents. Personally, I had never laughed so hard before, without purchasing a comedy-club ticket. From listening to the details, I gathered that Slapp didn't like him because of his demeanor. Agent Munson was from wealth and everyone knew this. He and Slapp were both profilers and damn good ones, I was told. They had both been trained and had spent some countless hours under the tutelage of the infamous Agent Dexter Allen Burney. Agent Munson was a few years older and had been a part of the bureau for about four years before Slapp arrived. Agent Munson always made it a point to talk about breeding and coming up in the right environment, etc. How one's upbringing [rearing] and social status, always weighed heavily on one's outcome. He always took the scientific approach. We all recognize this man; he's the one that reads everything that has been printed on the subject, before he gives his opinion. Slapp on the other hand believed in science also, but only up to a point and then he felt that some things were in a person from birth, his or her DNA, if you will. Slapp had been given an opportunity that very few people get a chance to observe, up close and personal, and that was young children from all walks of life, in an orphanage. Slapp claimed that no matter how much money your family has or opportunities they can afford to purchase on your behalf, you were just going to be a useless piece of shit, if you weren't taught, at a really young age, the golden rules of nature. Of course, Agent Munson grew up with a silver spoon, trimmed in platinum with a diamond-studded handle, in his mouth and made it one of his daily functions to remind everyone around him, of this fact. Slapp on the other hand, had been raised in an orphanage and Agent Munson knew this and had made a comment once about Slapp's short temper and a lack of his social graces, due this fact. This was a very sore subject with Slapp and after that he never had much to say to Agent Munson, outside of work, again.

The guys knew that this was going to be a problem whenever they returned for questioning. Alex, Tate and Fred had been brought in a few times before and questioned about their actions in the field, during their lengthy careers, but this was the first time for Slapp. So now they had to brief Slapp, or perhaps rehearse would be a better term, for the interrogation that they knew that the bureau was setting up, whenever they turned themselves in. No doubt Agent Munson would be leading the investigation, just to make things interesting. After all, who would enjoy gunpowder-moments more than a fellow agent that you loathe?

Chapter Seventeen

Father Caleb and Slapp's Mission

During Father Caleb's trip back to the States, Alex had asked the priest to stop in San Diego, California to see if he could find the man that had saved his life that was working at the Hotel Del Coronado, at the time. This was the spring that Alex had gotten shot and Slapp was beaten up in the ally, while in San Diego on that simple bounty pick-up mission. Alex knew it would be a long shot trying to find this man, because he was working that weekend with an expired work-visa. He was attempting to stay under-the-radar, while he and his illegal brother made a few extra dollars. Alex only had a first name of the man and with his work-permit status being what it was; he wasn't even sure that the man had given him his correct first name. It had been almost eighteen months since that incident; Alex getting shot and being able to reach the parking lot of the hotel, before passing out. Jose' had found him and had recruited his illegal brother and a couple of other special weekend employees, from Tijuana no doubt, to help him with this delicate rescue. Alex did reward him a couple of days later, before all of us left the hotel, but after deeper thought, felt that he should do more. That day the doctor listened to the man's story as Alex questioned him intensely to ascertain if he could be trusted. Jose' checked on Alex at least twice daily, until he was able to get back on his feet. He had even taken a big risk by leaving the resort's grounds to make a couple of runs, to a nearby drug store, to pick up a few things that the doctor needed to treat Alex, when his wound started to seep blood through the first layers of bandages that the doctor had applied. The doctor had also put himself and his license in jeopardy, by not reporting the incident to local authorities, which is required by law. The reason that he didn't report it was because Alex and his friend Tye had both showed him their official federal badges and he was afraid that he might blow their cover. Secondly, they all pleaded with doctor to refrain from calling it in because Slapp was still on the streets and had missed two check-in times and had disappeared off the radar tracking device that Linda, their attorney friend and associated, had been assigned to operate. Tye explained that they had to wait until backup could arrive to help them, due to the fact that this was a side-job that they were working and wasn't sure of the nature or the origin of the threat.

The doctor grudgingly agreed, but gave them a limited time to wrap things up and move out of the hotel. He was operating under an-all-expense-paid guest status at the hotel and resort in return for agreeing to be the doctor-on-call for the exclusive sinful event, identified as the Gentlemen's Conference. It was merely a group of rich older men sneaking away from their wives to sleep with younger women they didn't know.

At any rate, Alex had given Jose' a few dollars, but after thinking about it later decided that Jose's quick judgment call and response should receive a much greater reward. Alex understood to well that once he went back to the States, to turn himself in to the bureau, all his powers would be stripped away the moment when he accepted retirement. This would probably be his last act as a 'brother's keeper', by getting Jose's family out, that would be in his power to perform, while using his influence as a special agent. Yet, before this could happen, Father Caleb had to find the man and make sure he was the correct person. Alex gave the priest a list of questions to ask Jose' that only he would know the answers. Alex felt that Father Caleb was the best man for the job because who would fear coming forward, if a priest ask about your whereabouts?

Father Caleb arrived at the front desk of the hotel and resort around 9:00 one morning. There he approached a man that appeared to be in his early forties. The priest stared in his direction as the male receptionist returned the gaze. The clerk rendered a big smile as the priest casually confronted him. He appeared to be of India decent. His accent was very thick and the speed, in which he spoke didn't help matters either. He addressed Father Caleb very calmly with the appropriate respect for his attire, but he made the priest feel uncomfortable right away. The father smiled and clenched his hands together in that divine pose, as he offered a return greeting. Father Caleb now partially closed his eyes to that probing slit that he always used, when he felt that other avenues of his life-long training were required to better deal with the matters at hand. The priest somehow knew that this guy was a slick one, but that didn't bother the priest in the least, because he had written a few chapters in the book of 'How to be Slick' and had a back-up degree in body language, better known as nonverbal communication, when and if the first superior talent would prove not to be enough. Now the father introduced himself graciously, as usual and stated his business and concerns, with his Ireland accent out front of his speech.

"Good morning Sir, my name is Father Caleb and I have come to attempt to locate a gentleman that possibly worked here almost eighteen months ago, during one of your seasonal special events. I understand that he is a Hispanic young man from Tijuana. I'm sorry to report that I only have a first name, of the man in question. My friend informed me that he was very helpful to him when he was here for a few days and had promised to reward him later for his kindness." The moment the priest spoke the word 'reward' the man's eyes became wider and his pupils dilated, ever so slightly.

"Reward," the man repeated the word with deep curiosity. "If you leave it here we will do everything in our power to locate the man, by checking our files, and passing it on to him." The priest slowly lowered his head as though he had to think about the man's proposal. Then he brought it back up with the same slow speed as he spoke and pretended to be confused by the suggestion.

"Well, I don't know . . ." said the priest as he continued the ploy to get the information on Jose'. "I'm not sure. Those weren't my instruction, if I was successful in finding the right person. I realize Jose' is a very common name and all, you see, but there must be something in your files that will help me out a bit." It was obvious to the man now, and to everyone else that was close enough to overhear, that the priest didn't trust him. The clerk then became annoyed and short patient with Father Caleb.

"When exactly did you say that your friend was here and what was the man's employment time frame?" The man listened and made a few notes on a piece of paper as Father Caleb told him what he knew, as his Ireland accent remained in the forefront of his verbal communication.

"I believe it was early spring, two years ago if I'm not mistaken. So that would make it around April or May, no doubt. The resort would have been holding an annual special event I believe." The man interrupted him quickly.

"I'm so sorry Sir, but two years ago I wasn't working here at that time. Perhaps one of my clerks may be able to help you. Wait right here; I will call the office." A few moments later a lady came from the back, walked up to the counter and offered her help. The man explained to her their previous conversation and the lady began to inform them of the well-documented facts.

"I've been working here for the past ten years. We have two special events, which are held in the spring. One is the Gentlemen's Convention that lasts around a week with some stragglers that stay-over, of course. Then we host the annual Coronado Rose Garden Club Extravaganza. Sorry boss for the drama, but the ladies informed the staff to always use that word at the end of the title or they would find some other location to hold their event."

The priest was quite sure that it was during the Gentlemen's week because there is no way a group of ladies would have allowed a bleeding man to pass through the lobby without all hell breaking lose. Knowing how some eccentric old crazy ladies can be, it would have been a good chance that Alex would have bled to death in the lobby, while the old bats denied treatment until all their questions were answered. The three of them continued to zero-in closer to the information that the priest needed. The man from India never moved an inch as he continued to believe that if any reward was going to be left for the man that it would have to pass through his hands, or be taken into his care.

"I'm sure that it was during the time of the Gentlemen's Convention", said Father Caleb politely.

"No problem," said the lady. "I'll just go and get the file that has a listing of all our part-time help, during those time periods. Please wait right here." The priest and the male clerk gave each other eye contact a couple of time, but no words passed between them. The lady returned with the file and there were two Jose's listed so she gave the information to the priest, as the man from India body language protested.

"So Sir, now that we know the two possible people that it may have been, we will be more than happy to deliver the reward." The priest paused.

"Well, usually we like to give the meager Divine Blessings in person, if possible. Would you like for me to write it out for you? It has proven to be a lot more effective, if it is delivered precisely the way it is received."

"Whichever way you do it will be fine," replied the man. The man was sure that the priest was referring to a monetary reward. Now that the reward would be placed in written form, from cash to a check, the man was sure the amount would be greater than he initially thought, or so the man from India speculated and hoped.

"If you insist, I think it will be okay this time, for I believe that God knows the heart of every man." The priest reached into his inner pocket and pulled out a long sash, he kissed it in the center and then placed it around his neck. The man looked on in shock and the woman stood quietly still as the priest spoke. "Very well then, bow your head and close your eyes." The man didn't respond as he looked over at the female clerk as she did as the priest had requested. Then the priest quickly reached up and grabbed the man's head and forcefully pulled it forward and down towards the counter top. He frightened the man as he quickly pulled away and questioned the priest in an angry tone, with a thick accent as well.

"Sir stop please, sir what the hell are you doing to me?" The priest spoke very calmly; while it took everything that he had inside of him not to laugh at the man's response.

"I'm giving you a blessing reward for you to pass on to Jose'. Whichever one it might be or you can give this reward to both, if you are so inclined to do." The woman laughed out and then covered her mouth as the man dismissed her very rudely, as his thick accent remained in place.

"Go; go back to your work. I am able to handle it from here, go." She gave the full names and address of both men to the priest and turned to leave as she laughed out even more. She knew that her boss was a man who had succumbed to greed and it was evident by his over-eagerness to collect the reward without being sure that they would be able to locate the man in question. She was sure that Jose', whoever he was would never receive a monetary reward, if it had to pass through his hands.

"I'm sorry Mr. Holy Man that we have wasted your time and couldn't be of more assistance to you. Now if you will please excuse me, I have other paying customers waiting for my attention." While painfully holding in his laughter, Father Caleb bowed gracefully, quickly turned and walked out the front door of the hotel and resort. Outside he laughed as he prayed that God would forgive him for embarrassing the man. Two days later, the priest crossed the border and went to the local large Catholic Cathedral and asked the priest to help him locate the men. The community priest agreed and Father Caleb spent two more days in the city of Tijuana, Mexico, as his guest.

On the second day, after the local priest had put out the word in every mass why Father Caleb was there, three men with the first name Jose' showed up to stake a claim on the reward. The first one to speak with Father Caleb was an elderly gentleman and he had indeed worked that week, at the Hotel Del Coronado, unfortunately he was one of the cooking staff. Father Caleb felt pity for the older man, so he wrote him a check out of the petty cash fund from the 'My Brother's Keeper' foundation. The second man to come forward spoke very little English and was surely a scam artist. The priest gave him a prayer blessing and told him that he perhaps should spend a little more time in the confession booth. He didn't know any of the answers to the questions that Alex had instructed Father Caleb to ask, but tried to pretend that he did and that his memory had now confused the details a little, because of all the time that had passed. His confusion was a fact, but only as it pertained to him trying to trick the priest.

The third man to arrive was traveling with his brother, no doubt the same one that he had brought illegally with him those two weeks, in question. They both came in very slow and fearful as they tried to example the expired work-visa dilemma, before anyone asked them a question. Father Caleb knew the moment they started to speak that they were the ones he had been looking to reward. They both entered the back room suspiciously while holding their caps in their hands. The oldest brother continued to run the brim of the cap through his curled fingers, as though it was a nervous twitch.

"Yes Father, you wanted to see me. This is my brother Geraldo. He's my younger brother and I look out for him. Most of the time, I do a real good job, but sometimes I don't think things through, so here we are. My sister came to your morning mass and told me that a priest from across the border was looking for me. I brought my brother because I thought that it had something to do with us going to San Diego to work that weekend, without the proper paperwork. I have corrected the problem with my work-visa since that time, but on that trip I took my younger brother here and he has never had a work permit because he don't speak English so good. He's kind of slow Father, but he's a real good person in his heart. So I took him with me that time and we both promised the border patrol that we would return after two weeks, and we did, just like I had promised. I also promised him half of whatever money my younger brother made. A deep sadness washed over his face as he continued the tale. "But when we came back, the man took all of my brother's money and my brother got mad and challenged the man. Then I had to give him half of my money also, to keep him from throwing my younger brother in jail. He's a very bad man Father. Now he has been blackmailing my family for more money. I'm sorry Father; I'm a good person. I was only trying to make a little extra money so my family can eat." Both priest stared at the man as he confessed all his sins without using the confession booth. His brother stood next to him, not making a sound of any kind, while staring at the floor. They were both dressed in tattered clothing and a soaking bath wouldn't have hurt either of them in the least. Father Caleb got that big choked-up feeling in his throat as Jose' went on with his story.

The local priest seemed to be somewhat unaffected by the recall. Father Caleb believed that the local clergy knew and had heard tales worst than the one they both were so patiently listening to now. Whatever the case was, Father Caleb had to wait before he could stop Jose' and tell him the good news that his ship-of-mercy and divine-favor had just docked into the harbor. Father Caleb stood to his feet as he stared in Jose's direction. He walked towards him and placed one hand softly on his shoulder. Jose's brother Geraldo turned slightly as he looked over and upward into Father Caleb eyes as Jose' continued to look down at the floor while waiting for more bad news.

"It's true Father," said Geraldo. "My brother took me with him only because I begged him to take me. I didn't have a problem with the police at the border taking half of my money. It was all worth it just to see America; for me, this was my first time." Geraldo smiled as if he had to do it all over again and give up his pay; he would without a second thought. Father Caleb watched Geraldo as he fidgeted around while adding in his little part to the historical moment. Then he turned back to look at the top of Jose's head as he kept it bowed and tried to stop his brother from talking.

"No Jose'", said Father Caleb. "That's not why I'm here. Mr. Alex sent me to fine you." Jose' snapped his head upward now and became very nervous again as he interrupted the priest with a question, with renewed hope that the priest's visit was for something good. His south-of-the-border accent dominated his speech as he became very excited when the priest mentioned Alex's name.

"Mr. Alex? You know him Father? How is Mr. Alex doing? I was so scared for him when I found him in that car bleeding.

He had lost a lot of blood. He is a nice man. Is he still alive?" Father Caleb smiled as a tear escaped his eye that Jose' had so much compassion for a man he barely knew.

"Yes, I know him quite well, as a matter of fact. He is a friend of mind." Jose' interrupted the father again with the same excitement in his voice.

"Wow, Mr. Alex is one lucky man Father, to have you, a priest as a friend. I am sure you get extra points with God for having a priest as a friend." Then he turned quickly to his brother. "Did you here that Geraldo? Mr. Alex has a priest for a friend? That means that someone is praying for him all the time." The priest smiled deeply now because he knew that Jose' had no way of knowing how closely to the true his statement was about Father Caleb and Alex's relationship.

"As a matter of fact Jose', Mr. Alex sent me to find you and to offer you a reward for your kindness when he was hurt. He told me to ask you three questions when I found you to make sure that it was you. I don't think that will be necessary, because you brought your brother along and he said that you mentioned your brother a few times. I think he became very fond of you because he had a brother that he loved fearlessly, but his brother died. They were twins and now Alex sometimes feels alone. Alex was very impressed with the way that you take care of your brother and he wants to show his appreciation to you for saving his life."

Jose' and Geraldo's eyes lit up as they looked over at each other and started to laugh with giddiness.

“Are you sure Father”, said Jose’? “He gave me some money the day he left the hotel, even though the man at the border took most of it. I guess that’s why he started blackmailing my family members and me. He thinks that I have some kind of connection in America, because I came back with so much money after only two weeks of work.”

“Yes, I’m sure Jose’. He sent me to find you and tell you again how grateful he is that you were the one that found him that day.” Then Father Caleb turned to the other local priest. “Father Fernando will you be so kind, along with Geraldo to excuse Jose’ and me for a little private heart-to-heart? I promise not to use your office much longer. Father Fernando and Geraldo left the room.

“Sure Father Caleb, it will be no problem. Please use the room as long as you like. I will go to the basement and put a few things together for them, from the clothes closet.” Father Caleb moved to a nearby chair as Jose’ sat in a chair across from him. Father leaned in closer, even though the stench of him in that small room was almost unbearable. Father thought to himself that this perhaps was as an appropriate time as any to bring up the fact that he was odorous, but with tact that the priest had mastered.

“You know Jose’, cleanliness is next to Godliness.” Jose’ instantly defended himself.

“I am sorry about the smell Father, but a few weeks ago, because of my blackmailing problem, my water was turned off.

Now I have to bring in water from a community well or go over to my sisters. I realize I'm a little smelly, but I came straight here from work, as soon as my sister informed me that a priest was possibly looking for me."

"Very well, enough said," responded the priest. "I want you to listen very closely and you must never repeat anything that I'm about to tell you in this room. I didn't want your brother to hear, because I'm not sure how well he can keep a secret when he gets excited. Then there is the priest, well let's just say that I don't know him very well and I would feel better if we kept this between the two of us." Jose' was bobbing his head continuously, in agreement, as Father Caleb spoke the words of understanding of a secret, into his spirit. They were both leaning in forward while sitting on the edge of their chairs, as the priest continued. "Mr. Alexander Jones, that's his full name you know, will be returning to the United States soon and he wants to know if you and your family would like to make a new start in America, with his help of course." Jose' became so emotional until he couldn't answer the priest as he sat waiting for a response. The priest went on with the briefing. "I'll take your tears of joy as a yes, my son. What you need to do is keep this to yourself and tell no one. Now tell me whom you would like to take with you?" Jose' wiped his nose and eyes on the sleeve of his dirty smelly shirt as he tried to pull himself together. He reached over to hug the priest as he tried to contain his tears.

"There are only three of us. Our parents are dead. They died when we were very young. I am the oldest. I have my brother Geraldo and a sister Maria. Maria has a husband and two children. Her husband is lazy, but I know that she is going to want to take him along. I will only talk to her about this, I don't trust him."

"Good", said Father Caleb. "The least amount of people that knows the better it will be. All you have to do is keep on working and don't change your habits. Everyone will be watching to see why I wanted to talk to you. I have some money for you, please spend it slowly and don't bring any attention to yourself or your family members. I need you to write down your family members' full name, date of birth and anything else you can think of that will be an identifying item for them. Now, write down the names of the men at the border that has been blackmailing you. The next time you see them, don't give them eye contact. They will be able to read your body language that something good has happened to you. If any of them roughs you up a bit, don't fight back. We don't want their warning, which they will be receiving from Alex's friends, to be linked to you in anyway. I'm sure that there are other people that they are shaking down for money as well. Jose' can you do that for us? It might take a few months or even a year, but please know that we are not going to leave you over here, in these conditions, after you saved a federal agent's life."

Jose' was crying the entire time as he erroneously wrote the names on a piece of paper, from Father Fernando's desk. He wrote down what he believed was true and correct.

"Please pull yourself together my son, the priest will be back at any moment now and I won't be able to explain all those tears, son." Jose' gave his nose one last wipe with the now dirty and wet sleeve. Then he gave a big smile as he tried to tell a little more of his story and his life-long dream.

"I have wanted to move to America all my life, since I was a boy. One of best days of my life was when I got a work-visa that allowed me to go there and work. When I got to stay for two weeks or more, I always cried when I had to return. Sometimes I would get drunk for two days. I was so down. How do you say the word, Father?"

"You were depressed Jose'," said the priest.

"Si', si', that is the word I was trying to say; I was depressed. Now that I know that I will be given a chance for a better life, I will never be depressed again, I promise Father. I will go to confession and pray everyday that you and Mr. Alex won't forget about me here, across the border."

"Very good Jose', but you have to keep all of this a secret. Trust no one. The only person that may come looking for you now is a man name Alvin. He is like a brother to Mr. Alex. We call him Slapp for short. Can you remember that name Jose'?"

"Si, sure Father, I can remember that and more if you tell me to." The priest reached into his pocket as he held eye contact with his new acquired friend.

"Here is some money, spend it very slowly. We will take care of the border patrol in about two weeks or a little more."

Father Fernando knocked on the door and then entered with Jose's brother Geraldo. "I am done with our chat," said Father Caleb. "Thank you so much for allowing me to use your spaces." Father Caleb and Jose' stood to their feet and headed for the door. They walked outside the small room and reunited with Jose's brother Geraldo, where he was standing holding two bags of fresh clothing—one for each of them. Father Caleb shook Father Fernando's hand and informed him that he would be leaving the next day, but wanted to walk around to see some more of the city. Then he gave one last warning to Jose'.

"Remember what I said my son and take care of yourself and your brother."

"I will remember Father everything you say Father, I promise," yelled Jose' as he and his brother stepped through the side exit of the church, onto the street.

Meanwhile, back in Hong Kong Alex and Tate was attempting to come up with a plan that Slapp would support without losing his temper initially, as usual. They wanted to travel back to the States ahead of Slapp and more or less lay down the ground work, for all the little details that they were planning to leave out of their reports and verbal accounts. Tate was from another branch of the secret service than Alex, Slapp and Fred plus a few others and he had already submitted his paperwork to retire, during his last trip back to the States. Alex, on the other hand, only had one other task that he wanted to accomplish, before he turned in his badge; and that was to award Jose' and his family members an application to become American citizens, for saving his life and not blowing his cover. He needed someone to casually drift across the border and tighten up the assholes [stop the shake-down] of the border patrolmen that were blackmailing Jose's family. The best man for the job was none other than Alex's partner-in-crime, as he was affectionately called, Slapp. This arrangement would also allow Alex and Tate a chance to go back early to get a feel for the investigation and the direction in which it was moving, as it pertained to them and their illegal side-business team. They had a few bargaining chips in their files and some pretty creditable witnesses, if their word was no longer any good with the bureau. All they had to do was get Slapp and his temper onboard; because if it was left up to him, he wanted to just stroll in and tell the lot of them to kiss his a— and be done with it. The rest of us had other people to think about and didn't want to spend our final days looking over our shoulder or exiled to some God-forsaken place without our families. Alex called a meeting at our place one night, while the girls and I continued to plan for the holiday festivities. What we were arranging went way beyond a simple holiday celebration. The only thing that was placing restrictions on our dream was time and funds. There were plenty of money available, but we couldn't draw any from our accounts, back in the States, because that would alert everyone to where we had been hiding out for the past year and a half. We had been living out of a suitcase of funds that we had brought over with us. Everyone that came to visit, for example my mother, our son William, the priest or my father whenever he made a trip back; would all add a little more to the pot. Then we would give them our checks, to hold for collateral. I didn't have a problem, because my name had changed and no one was looking for me, not as Monique Yvonne Coleman. At any cost, this was just one more thing of many, in which we did to stay under the radar.

Alex wanted my father, Uncle Oscar, there at the meeting in case they needed a neutral party. He would mostly listen, but had proven to be a fair man, voiceless or even while voicing his opinion, yet always speaking from the heart. Slapp respected him for being a man of few words and always to the point, with nothing watered down. Slapp had expressed to Uncle Oscar on several occasions that he would have made a great field operative. His body language was hard to read and he paid attention to details, especially while others didn't share his views that any little item could become important. Slapp liked this in him because his style was different, but the same conclusion could be reached, nevertheless; they both believed that everything was important. Alex and Tate continued to wait for my father and Slapp to arrive as they designed an approach to recruit Slapp for this on-the-side detour mission.

"So what do you think Tate? Do you believe Slapp will cross the Mexican border, if I explain to him how important this is to me? After all, the guy indirectly saved his life as well. If he would have called the police instead of the doctor for me, Slapp wouldn't have lasted another couple of days in that bar's storeroom, waiting for one of us to find him."

"Perhaps you need to state the facts to him in that manner. Maybe it will convince him that this is something that both of you need to have a joint concern about. The man did come through for the two of you, even though he had ulterior motives. One phone call to anyone else instead of that doctor, and all of this could have turned out totally different; do you agree?" Alex titled his head down in deep thought before he answered, while both of them continued to wait for Slapp and Uncle Oscar to arrive.

"You just may have something there, Tate. If I approach Slapp in the method that he has an invested interest in the plan, perhaps he will see it more like both of us owing this debt. If he agrees, then all we have to do is continue to wait for Father Caleb to deliver the information that he has gathered, when he visits us during the holidays. We don't want anyone tracking the priest and putting his life in any more danger than it already has been in, in the past and probably will continue to be, by his association with us."

The doorbell rang. It was Slapp and Uncle Oscar—Alex greeted then at the entrance of our condo.

"Hello you two, Tate and I have been waiting for you both to show up. Has everyone eaten; Helen prepared a few things for us?" Uncle Oscar and Slapp entered quickly and closed the door. Slapp headed straight for the kitchen while Uncle Oscar removed his cap and jacket and tossed it on the arm of the sofa, as he walked pass. The four of them sat at the table for the discussion. Alex began first.

"Mr. Wiley, we asked you to come to this meeting because after the holidays the three of us will have to go back and answer some questions, from the bureau, about our activities these passed ten years. I believe they are more concerned with the past three years, since that's when shit started to hit the fan, so to speak. We would like for you to look after the girls for us, and little max of course. We are planning to leave Hong Kong with a list of people that you may or may not be aware. I'm sure that you are familiar with the fact that we are trying to get the paperwork together to take our niece and your granddaughter Milani back with us. That includes her great-grandmother, if she agrees. I haven't spoken to Mr. Charlie about his family. I think it's time for his old ass to go home also. I understand that it's just him and his brother that are still alive. I understand that his only brother is married and has only one adult son. Mr. Pauling may not be ready yet, but I will lend the offer to him as well and inform him that we will back him with some money, interest fee, to start up his catering business, back in the States, if that's his only dilemma for staying over here."

Alex then turned slowly towards Slapp as Tate sat motionless while hiding behind those shades of his. Slapp had his mouth filled with a bite from his sandwich, as Alex called his name before addressing him.

"Slapp, I'm pretty sure your mother, Mrs. Carrington has decided to return to the States with us. Do you know of anyone else that she may be concerned about leaving behind?" Slapp continued to chew his mouthful of food down to a reasonable amount that allowed him to answer, as the three of them waited. Uncle Oscar smiled to himself, lowered his head and shook it from side to side in disbelief that each time he had ever been in Slapp's presence; he had always been eating something or other.

"I'm not sure Alex, but I will ask my mother the next time we talk and brief her on what we are planning to do," said Slapp as he swallowed a couple of times. Alex couldn't allow this opportunity to escape him to pry and ask Slapp about his and his mother's renewed relationship.

"Oh, so how is that thing with you and Mrs. Carrington coming along Slapp? Do you address her as mother now or are you still playing the role of the disgruntle son?" Slapp had remained real touchy about the subject and therefore had refused to keep them updated on the matter. He also took offence to the question, since he believed that everyone knew before him that Mrs. Carrington was indeed his estranged mother. He answered Alex with an annoyed tone and was surprised that he had taken such liberties with him, while in an open forum.

"Bad choice of words my brother—it's not a thing, it's a painful relationship trying to repair itself. And to answer your question, I only refer to her as mother when she's not in the room. Most of the time, I call her an old wasp, whenever we disagree. Sometimes I kiss her on the cheeks to say good-bye or goodnight, but I talk pretty stern to her because I don't want her to forget that I'm angry with her and that I still carry the pain from her earlier selfish decisions." Alex spoke up quickly with a resolution, without thinking, because that was what he had been trained to do by the agency. Alex had always had a hard time separating his personal relationships with the work related ones. This was his biggest problem between him and me. Sometimes he treated me like an agent and not his wife.

"Sorry about my selection of words Mr. Alvin, but I think you two should get some counseling so this can be put behind you." My father dropped his head quickly again because he was very observant and knew that Alex's suggestion wasn't going to sit well with Slapp at this round-table setting. My father was remembering that at each meeting, that he had been invited to attend; someone had lost his or her temper about something. In view of their claim, to be all brothers-of-a-common-cause, he wondered how their friendship had lasted this long without one of them shooting one another, since everyone strapped on their guns everyday like their weapons were a fresh pair of underwear. Slapp retaliated without taking in a full breath.

"Excuse me Mr. Jones, but I'm sure you didn't call this meeting to discuss my feelings and relationship with my alienated mother or to strategize our reconciliation"?

"As a matter of fact, I didn't. I called us together to plan for our return to answer for our alleged misconduct. As you know or may not be aware of Tate here has already filed to retire from his branch of the bureau, but because we had this side business, in play, he may be called upon to collaborate on a few missions, on our behalf." Slapp looked over quickly in Tate's direction as if he felt that he had been betrayed once more for not being told sooner about his retirement. Tate returned his disappointed gaze as Slapp spoke.

"So what do you have to say for yourself, for not telling me before now," roared Slapp?

"Mr. Alvin, I let my gun do most of my talking these, days, when it comes to people with unpredictable rage outbursts."

"Wait; let me see if I have this straight, because everyone here knows that I can be a little slow at times. So what you are implying Mr. Tate, is that I have anger management issues?"

"Yea, that's what I'm saying and a whole lot more if you are willing to listen right now." Alex spoke up loudly to Tate, because he believed that he would be speaking to the least angry one out of the two.

"Stand down Tate; this is not a good time for a soul-cleansing moment." Tate quickly pushed away from the table and stood up very slowly and purposely to address Alex and his tone. He removed his shades before he spoke.

"Alex, I think I told you before about interrupting Slapp and I when we are having a one-on-one disagreement. Do I need to remind you of that again and of the fact that my beef [disagreement] with Slapp isn't the same as yours?" Alex stood to his feet to defend himself, if the moment arrived. He then spoke in a calming tone to allow the meeting to progress towards its goal.

"No Tate, there is no need. I was only trying to get a feel for Slapp's frame of mind, before we, I mean before I send him back out into the field." Tate pulled his chair closer and sat back down. Alex repeated his moves as Uncle Oscar sat motionless with his fingers laced together, as his forearms rested flat on the table in front of him. Slapp spoke up again with just a slight new hope of being a full member of the team once more, in spite of his weak eye and the plot he had set into motion, by arranging the killing of the trader surveillance security guy that they had hired to watch out for their families, via computer cameras.

"So tell me Alex, what do you want me to do? I've had all the baby-sitting gigs I can tolerate in this lifetime."

"No, no nothing like that. Remember the man I told you about that called the doctor when he found me bleeding-out in the garage of the Hotel Del Coronado. Well he is having some troubles and I want to help him out, if I can."

"Yes, I remember you telling me about him. I think his name was Jose' or something like that".

"Yes, that's right. I need you to go across the Mexican border from San Diego and gather some Intel [intelligence] for me. I sent Father Caleb down there to find the man and I promised Jose' that in two weeks or a little more, after we identified the corrupt ones, the border patrols would stop blackmailing him. I'm waiting on the priest to contact me and inform me if he was able to find Jose' and if Jose' gave him the name of the greed-infected Mexican border patrolmen. I know you have to go in for your eye surgery, so I just thought while you was healing you could do it south of the border. I just need you to give them a strong warning, that way they will leave Jose' and his family alone until we can process their paperwork to make them U.S. citizens."

Everyone looked in Slapp's direction, including my father, as he slid down more into the chair and leaned far over to one side like a street thud that had just been asked to go straight. He then gave a misleading half-cocked lip smile, as he seemed to be getting his thoughts together to answer Alex with simple and precise words that would explain his feelings and thoughts on the matter.

"You know Alex that I'm not in the habit of taking prisoners or leaving enemies behind. With that being stated as fact perhaps I'm not the right man for the job; that's if you only want me to tune his ass up [show him the error of his ways]. Now if you want something a little more permanent, then I'm your man." Alex sprang up from his chair quickly and went into a rage, while slamming his fist loudly on the table towards Slapp.

"Listen closely and lets be clear about this Slapp; I do-not-want the man killed. I only want him to stop jacking Jose' up and shaking him down when he comes across the border with his paycheck from his U.S. work-visa job. I'm asking you because I know you did some work down there before and your language abilities are still intact. I know you remember your way around and the locals will remember you." Slapp corrected his posture by sitting up straighter and leaning in with his hands and lower arms on the table, bent at the elbows. He now remembered Alex's health condition and didn't want to excite him to the breaking point of another anxiety attack. Alex was now twitching as he tried to calm himself while explaining how important it was for them not to get into more trouble before appearing back at the bureau, for questioning.

"Okay Alex, we'll do it your way this time, since it's a personal favor to you."

"What do you mean, 'personal favor to me? If Jose' would have called the police and not a doctor, I wouldn't have been able to get to you as soon as I did." Uncle Oscar interrupted by putting his hand high in the air like a first grader, with the belief that he might have the correct answer.

"Can I say something please," asked Uncle Oscar, as his serious down-home country-twang moved to the forefront of his dialect?

"Sure Mr. Wiley, say whatever you like. We need your help as well."

"I've been listening intensely, at all these meetings and I'm not thoroughly convinced that each of you wouldn't seriously benefit from some counseling. Look, I don't claim to know anything about the inward workings of the secret service, by any means, but don't they have some kind of program in place, whenever you guys start to turn on each other? Never mind listening to me, because I'm the only one in the room without a gun or two. Pretend, if you will that I'm only talking out loudly to myself, if that's what it takes for me to leave later on without a bullet hole or something to its equivalence".

Everyone looked around at each other and then in Uncle Oscar's direction, as they agreed and attempted to conduct themselves better, by correcting their posture. Then Uncle Oscar continued.

"Now Alvin, let's take you for an example. Your mother is a very nice lady and a fine woman to-boot. I know you love her. I can just tell. By the way, that's my gift and what I bring to the table, 'insight'" said Uncle Oscar real arrogantly. "So why don't you just stop trying to push her away with your pretend indifferences and spend every moment with her that the two of you have left in this life, however long the Divine One sees fit to grant you. Ah, and you Mr. Tate, please tell your fellow-men-in-arms your real plans. Why you are giving up this life entirely and stop trying to convince them that you are retiring because you no longer want to deal with them or have the stomach for what you all do. What about you there Alex, retire and take your hypertensive ass on home and get your health back on track. You don't need this stressful job. My daughter has enough money for you to walk away tomorrow and if she won't give you any of hers, I have the money that I was sending her foster-mother for twenty-five year. She never spent a dime of it out of guilt for not giving Monique back to me like she had promised, when I came to pick her up all those times. It seems to me, that you all apparently have had a good run at this job, by the fact that you are all still alive. Just place this entire portion, of your lives behind you and don't look back. Life if too short; besides at this point you should all be getting drunk on the weekends while trying to remember all the details to the missions you went on together and how you could have done it better; if you were given another chance to do it again, now that you have the hang of it. It's not like you have enough time left to make new friends with this level of commitment. Making friends takes a lot of work and it takes time to get all the hard feelings ironed out, so to speak. You know what I mean, a friendship that you can trust with all your secrets and the cloak-and-dagger crap of the job. It is like that in life. Just about the time you get a task down perfect, in your own eyes of course, your time is up and you have to move on. Now this is some important stuff that I'm talking about right here. The rest of that stuff is merely nonsense; you should just let it go. Take my life for example. It went by so fast until I never took time out to consider my priorities or how my decisions had affected others around me. It wasn't the money or the traveling—I just really loved music and the thrill of performing in front of an audience, night after night. It wasn't work for me, because I enjoyed it so much. Look at the cost I had to pay. I lost Monique's mother and Monique all those years. My mother will probably die of a broken and lonely heart, because I was too selfish to understand that she needed her baby boy to come home and stay a little longer than a week, every few years, if I was lucky enough to talk the sponsors into letting me off." Then Uncle Oscar slowly brought his head back up to their eye level as he continued his 'come-to-Jesus soapbox editorial moment, as he smiled slightly due to their response.

The guys were all passively smiling because of the way my father spoke with wisdom and passion, while he believed in his heart-of-hearts that he was telling them off, as he laid it all out for them, in his own country way. He was from the city, but in his soul he had always been a pure country bumpkin. He had never spoken to any of them in that manner before. Yet my father, Uncle Oscar, felt that this light ass chewing, that he was so eloquently applying, was long overdue. To be totally honest, he had always kept the interactions with them unobtrusive and cordial. Outside the normal greetings, Uncle Oscar only conversed when he was asked a question or replied when his help was requested. He was in rare form at this meeting and they were all listening carefully, because what my daddy was saying was all true. When my father completed his sobering monolog, the meeting resumed with a different and in a more structured atmosphere. All their anger seemed to take a backseat as they continued to plan and strategize their return and Slapp's solo mission to Tijuana, Mexico. Tate was the first to verbally agree with Uncle Oscar's open-heart all-cards-facing-up suggestion. He removed his shades and sat up taller and straighter at the table.

"You are right Mr. Oscar, we should all concentrate and be focused on the same goals, and that is to stay alive while we solve the mysteries. I would like to just tell all of you something that I'm planning. I plan to go back to finish my education. Before I met any of you and before I joined the bureau, I was attending a religious seminary to become a priest." Slapp was the first to spring to his feet and loudly respond.

"Get the F—k out of here; are you kidding me? You are telling us that you detoured from the divine-calling path to join the forces-that-be and become a part of one of the most corrupted boy-clubs that has ever been organized, well except for the mafia. But we all know that there are a few with a dual membership of both clubs. Excuse me brother for cursing, I just want to be the first to congratulate you on your decision." Slapp then reached over to shake Tate's hand and give him one of those one-arm hugs and shoulder-to-shoulder taps. Tate was smiling widely as Alex and Uncle Oscar followed in the gesture.

"Hey big guy," said Slapp. "Did you tell Gayle yet? I didn't know that priests could have a wife.

"They can, if you chose the correct order. No one knows about this yet, so keep it under wraps until I get a chance to tell the ladies, agreed?"

"Sure Tate, no problem, after all we are secret servicemen," replied Alex and Slapp.

"I had already been informed about your decision," said Uncle Oscar. "I had the pleasure of speaking with your father before he went back to the States." Slapp peered across the table very sternly in Uncle Oscar's direction, as he spoke the words with confidence and pride for knowing earlier than the others, about Tate's plans to return to the order.

"Did you say that you spoke to Tate's father? I didn't know that your father came to Hong Kong Tate. Why didn't we all get together? Why didn't we have a party or something? You've never talked about your father; what's he like?" The room went totally quiet as Slapp searched each face and realized that he was the only person that didn't know about Tate's father coming to visit. Tate put his glasses back on to hide and Uncle Oscar became very interested in his fingertips, as he stared at them and refused to comment. Alex answered the call of Slapp's plea of a clearer understanding of what was now being said.

"Slapp," said Alex real quietly as if the information would be more receptive if whispered. "Father Caleb is Tate's biological father. He joined forces with our outfit to be near Tate and to spend as much time with him now as he could. Tate grew up with his mother and stepfather and his grandmother helped out mostly."

"No way," responded Slapp in non-belief. "There is no way I could have missed that. Perhaps the race difference thing could have thrown me off my game, but there is no way I could have missed all the other nuances." Then Slapp turned slowly towards Tate, while still in shock, but with a very calm and hurt demeanor. "So why didn't you tell me Big Dogg? How long have we known each other?" Tate never looked over at Slapp or made an effort to answer him. "Okay, no problem. Let's get back to the meeting," said Slapp as more of the hurt feelings move even closer to the surface of his tone.

"Right," said Alex. "Where were we?"

"You was about to give me the details on what you wanted me to do about the man that's blackmailing Jose'," reminded Slapp.

"Oh yea, that's right. I just want you to cross the border as a retired military man. That way you will be able to live without getting a job. We will age you some and let your hair grow, plus your beard. Once you get in the country, I will mail you your weapons and whatever else you may need."

"How long do you think this sting operation will take, Alex? Where will I meet back up with you and Tate?"

"We are hoping that it doesn't take more than six weeks. I have already ordered you a cover identity as an old retired disabled veteran. I want you to walk across the border every day and go to the banks' automatic machine outside (ATM), on the U.S. side of the border. The corrupted guys will be watching you the same way they do all the others with a U.S. work-visa, whenever someone uses that teller machine. Sooner or later they will find some reason to hassle you and take a part of your money, when you try to re-enter Mexico. Don't fight with them; just give it to them. After a week or so, they will pass the word that you are an easy mark. That is what we want so we can identify all the rotten eggs at one time. Try to go at different times of the day or evenings, so you will come into contact with other shifts of patrolmen. We want to shut all of them down at once and force their government to replace them with some new people on the border crossing or we will get our government to place Tijuana on the restricted list, while we conduct a deeper investigation of the border's corruption. This will mean no shopping across the border, no crossing to buy gas, no soldier traffic from the local military bases. We only have the power to enforce this for ten days or less, if no death is involved, because of the memorandum of understanding between their government, and us but that should be enough to let them know that we mean business. This would have a greater impact if we pick one of their busiest times. Unfortunately, this will be right after the holidays, everyone's pockets will still be fat. I will check their holiday schedule. At any rate, you have to be patient and wait for the proper time. I will mail you your weapons, once you are in place. After the warning contact, I want you to melt them down and bury them. You won't be able to cross the border with them and you won't have time to mail them back. Make sure you have plenty of gloves with you and cover your finger pads. We don't want anyone tracking you. Sandpaper them off before you leave. You know what to do. Tate and I are going to turn ourselves in first, to test the waters, back at the bureau. The bureau will know that you are on convalescent leave, for your eye surgery and that will give us more time to see what they are really searching for. It may be just some information that we have stumbled across that will help them with their active cases. If that turns out to be correct, then I will trade what we have to get Jose' and his family's paperwork expedited, before I get a date on my retirement. If it turns out to be more, then we will lawyer-up and hold everything that we have until they put it all in writing. Does this sound like a plan?" Slapp answered slowly as though he had something to add to the negotiation treaty that Alex would be trying to implement, between the now closed My-Brother's-Keeper high-stakes bounty hunting business and the bureau, which had allowed them to illegally set it up, in the first place.

"It sounds like a good 'A' plan, but what's plan 'B' if they don't want to play ball with us? What are we going to do if they found out how I was involved with the gas house-fire?"

"That's a good question Slapp. If that happens, we still have all the tapes that will provide evidence that the surveillance man, that we hired, was responsible for getting those three agents and Stacey killed, at that satellite office. If they want more, then I think we should lawyer-up and see what witnesses they can come up with to testify about our alleged misconduct. After all, he was the one that broke the code and his agreement of employment. I think blackmail is still a crime. His only problem was that he chose the wrong people to blackmail—us. Tate, do you have anything you would like to add?"

"No Alex," replied Tate as he continued to hide behind those shades. "Not at this time."

"Then all we have to do is brief you Mr. Oscar." Uncle Oscar turned to Alex with his full attention. "I know that you have put in your paperwork to retire from the music arena, over on this side. We want you to check on the girls, keep your eyes opened and deliver a message from our families whenever you travel back and forth to see Miss Buddy. By the way, what is Monique's foster-mothers' name again?" The guys all started to laugh and Uncle Oscar gave an ear-to-ear smile.

"Her name will soon be Mrs. Wiley if I have anything to do with it. She was fine forty-five years ago and she is still beautiful to me today." The boys all started to yell and make those encouraging playboy player noises.

"You are the man, Mr. Wiley", said Slapp as he stood up to give him a handshake and shoulder tap.

"My man, Uncle Oscar, you go son," replied Alex. Everyone was laughing.

"Perhaps you can marry us Tate, when you complete your training, that's if she will have me"?

"That would be great. I would be honored to perform the ceremony. I think she's a great catch." They all had a drink of wine to toast my father's announcement, celebrate Tate's news and to hopefully salute a more open and honest relationship between them. I think this was the best meeting ever, but then again I could be bias, since the room was filled with men that I truly love and adore.

We continued with all the preparation work for the Christmas-to-remember gathering as we waited for our day in court to arrive. We had collected all the files that we needed to petition the Hong Kong courts to allow Milani, our mixed heritage niece and daughter, to travel back to the States with us. We wouldn't dream of appearing in court without Counselor Su Ki Chang sir, because the paperwork stated precise and complicated conditions and due to the fact that she wasn't old enough to make such a permanent decision on her life. We were granted a dual citizenship certificate for her and a permit to apply for her passport to travel. All of this paperwork would expire when she reached the legal age of adult consent. Then Milani would have a few options in which to choose from about where she wanted to live. Her great-grandmother's paperwork was a little less complicated. It was merely a matter of one of us becoming her sponsor, applying for a passport and requesting a work-visa, as a reason for travel for the lengthy stay. She would have to return every two years or so to renew the request. We all knew with her being such an elderly woman that there were ways to get around that long flight. On the other hand, if she wanted to come back we would pay for it, without question. She and Milani were joined at the hip, so to speak. We wanted Milani's transition to be as smooth as possible. We all agreed that this was the best way to go.

We spent the Thanksgiving holiday weekend at the Hong Kong's Disney resort and theme park and the kids had a blast. The girls and I continued to plan the Christmas activities. My foster-mother was planning to come for a longer stay than usual and I knew this would be great. Before she arrived she shipped a few cooking items that I couldn't find on the island. Oh I'm sure they were here, but I didn't have time to locate them. We decided to have the gathering at Alex's and my place. We would invite Mr. Charlie and his family, plus

Mr. Pauling's family, a couple of men from the motor pool and the security booth. Before we realized what we had started, the head count for Christmas dinner had already reached twenty-one or more. We made a plan to rent more tables and chairs and; moved the living room furniture to our guest bedroom upstairs. It would be a task, but it would all be worth it. My father had to work Christmas Eve, so we rented rooms at the resort, so we could all be together, the night before.

Alex informed me that he had also talked Mr. Dexter Allen Burney into making that long flight to be with all of us, as well. The truth was that he had already planned to make the trip because he tried to spend that time with Miss Beasley every year. This would be the first time that Slapp would be spending the holidays with both of his biological parents. He didn't know how he would react with both of them in the room. He grew up with Mr. Burney around, but he didn't know him as his father. Miss Beasley on the other hand, was a new discovery totally because he thought for sure that she didn't want him or was dead. Everyone recalled the early morning when he was told that she was his mother. We all were convinced that it would be a touching moment for him once more, we just weren't sure which emotion would surface, or dominate the reaction and possibly spoil the Christmas that we had all worked so hard to make special and unforgettable.

Chapter Eighteen

Phone call from Sam

Early one Sunday afternoon Tate called Gayle from the motor pool and asked if he could spend some time with her at her apartment. She agreed without hesitation because it had been a few days since she had been able to interact with him, except in a professional setting. Slapp had traveled back to the States to see his girlfriend; this had caused Tate to work two positions in Slapp's absence. Considering all the times Slapp had covered for him, Tate felt that this was the least he could do. Now, after a week and a half, Tate finally got an afternoon off, plus the following Monday. Gayle packed a few of her soiled clothing and waited near the back tunnel entrance of the embassy. As I mentioned before, this tunnel began at the embassy's escape-route and ended up in her large walk-in closet of her efficiency apartment; located over the sushi bar a block and a half away from the front entrance of the America Embassy, if the distance traveled was from the front entrance. Tate arrived from the back staircase of the embassy with laundry of his own while they made small talk as they journey the back passageway's maze that finally reached the stairs that led to the secret closet entrance. Gayle was excited to be in her place for the evening and night because her daughter usually tried to call her from college every Sunday evening. However, for the last couple of months Gayle had been instructed to stay at the embassy and was forced to miss the usual call from her daughter, Samantha. Tate was exhausted and was looking forward to a full night's sleep while being concern with only one other person's safety, besides his own. The evening breeze was blowing steady and he was pretty sure that he could convince Gayle to open the windows, which faced the front noisy street, for a couple of hours, before they retired for the night.

When they arrived, Tate headed straight for the shower as Gayle collected fresh and alternative outfits for her return to the embassy's birthing quarters the following day. Tate emerged refreshed as Gayle went into the bathroom to perform her body maintenance as well. When she came out, Tate was lying face down on her bed and almost asleep. She selected a book and went into the living area, which was just on the other side of this large folding Asian shoji screen, to wait for the call from her daughter. Tate roused up and realized that she was now out of the tiny bathroom. He then heard her turning the pages of a book while she waited in the upper corner of the long curved-back-chase lounger. Tate wanted to be near her so he followed her with a pillow in hand to lay his head in her lap, while she read. The light wind mysteriously cause the thin Asian printed curtains to dance at the window, facing the front street as Tate made himself comfortable on the long chase lounger, with his head and pillow across Gayle's lap. She never once took her eyes from the pages of her book, as she raised her hand and arm out of his way, as Tate searched for that perfect spot across her thighs. Then she slowly draped her hand down to his head and began to stroke his thick wavy hair as she wondered when had been the last time he had received a haircut. Tate face was now pressed up against her stomach as he closed his eyes once more. She could hear and feel him as he took full breaths while sinking deeper into a restful sleep. She glanced over and down at him for the first time, as she reached up with her hand to turn the page of her book. Gayle smiled to herself as she noticed what he was wearing. Tate had slipped into a pair of cotton pajamas with no shirt, a pair of slippers that was hanging onto his feet for dear life where they had slid away from the proper position on his feet, and his back-up weapon in its velcro attached holster, secured firmly around his leg, just above his right ankle. She turned the page and moved her hand back to him, but now had decided to rub his back instead. He shifted more of his body across her knees as he hugged her around the waist with the top arm as the other slid around the other side. The pillow and his head were hanging more off her lap onto the seat of the lounger, as his upper body replaced its previous position. Tate was now motionless again as Gayle continued to read. An hour or more passed before Tate finally began to squirm around. He reached up the front and between her breasts to check to see if she was wearing the ring-set that he had given her a few weeks before, with his promise to make her his legal wife. The only thing that was holding up the process was the predicament he and the others were in as renegades from the bureau. Tate held the rings in his hand for a few seconds and then allowed his hand to slide back down to its location, around her waist. Gayle watched him as she realized that he was still asleep and must have been dreaming.

Then the phone rang and startled Tate as he flinched and reached for his gun that was attached to his leg. In a matter of a few seconds, Tate had released the securing strap on his weapon and drawn it to the ready before he became aware of where he was or the fact that he had fallen asleep in Gayle's arms.

Gayle answered the call on the second ring and didn't realize that the volume on the ringer had been turned up so loudly. Tate slowly sat up and placed his gun back in its holster. Gayle watched him, as he headed for the kitchen, while she spoke cheerfully to her daughter, Samantha.

"Hello Sweetie," said Gayle. "I know you have been trying to call me for a few weeks now, but I've been living inside the embassy in my assigned quarters. I think I told you about that a few weeks ago. So tell your mother all about your life at school.

"Hello mother, why do you have to stay at the embassy? Has there been some trouble in the area", inquired Samantha?

"No serious problems, nothing like that. There has been an investigation going on and the Ambassador thinks that it will be best if all of us stay inside the walls for a while. You have my number to the office and my berthing area; don't be afraid to use it."

"Okay Mother, I'll remember. Did you talk to Mr. Tate lately? My classmates and my friends really think he's hot."

"Oh Samantha, I don't believe you and the others should be talking about a man that you know so little about."

"Of course, I know that mother, but he ass is fine. Is he there with you now, is that the reason you are acting so stuffy?"

"Samantha, stop, that will be enough of that from you, young lady. I understand that he has stopped by your school on a couple of occasions to see you. I'm sure he was a perfect gentleman."

"Unfortunately he was Mother, is he there? I know he is there. I wanted to ask him something. Oh, by the way, I returned your money to your account for my tuition. When I went to pay it, the finance counselor said that some foundation had already sent a check to the school and have paid for everything. I'm pretty sure that it has something to do with your Mr. Thaddeus."

Gayle turned her head quickly to look in Tate's direction as he stood in the doorway of the kitchen attempting to look completely innocent, while appearing sexier than was necessary or required. Gayle continued to stare at Tate as Samantha repeated her request to speak with him.

"Sure, no problem Samantha, he's standing near-by."

Gayle called Tate to the phone with a wave of her hand and then she placed her hand over the receiver.

"Thaddeus, I think Samantha wants to question you about the money that suddenly appeared in her school account", said Gayle in a whisper.

Tate walked over to take the phone and then held it to his ear.

"Hello Miss Samantha, how are you and is everything alright at school?"

"Hi there Mr. Tate" she replied in a sultry like voice. I just wanted to know if you had someone following me or watching me. It's a new young man on campus and he seems to show up everywhere I am. I know what my father did as a career. So I don't have to tell you that this has happened to me before. I recognize all the signs."

Tate spoke up quickly as Gayle looked on with a puzzled expression on her face. Gayle was sure that Sam wanted to ask him about the money, but it seemed as though the subject had changed. Tate held up the standard wait-a-minute finger towards Gayle as he answered Samantha's last question.

"Yes Samantha, I did put a watch on you for a few weeks. We are in the process of investigating your father's death. I wanted you to be safe and I didn't want it to interrupt your education so I paid for my nephew to take a few classes on your campus. I hope he didn't disturb you. I told him to keep his distance, so your boyfriend wouldn't become suspicious or jealous."

"Well Mr. Tate, whatever you told him; it didn't work out very well. I knew it had to be your arrangement because he is so handsome and he looks so much like you. I also figured out that you are responsible for that money in my school account. My father, Thomas, was well known for the same stunts, when I was younger. My mother opened me a bank account when I was about eight years old and money would just magically appear. What is it with you secret service men, always lurking in the shadows?"

Tate smiled to himself as he took a full breath to answer her.

"Well Samantha, I hadn't planned on you spotting my nephew. I forgot to tell your mother about the money, so she could in turn inform you. I called the foundation after our first meeting, but I wasn't sure when they would release the money to your account. I've been very busy; I guess it slipped my mind. I will call my nephew and tell him that you know about him. I assume he found you very attractive also, if not he wouldn't have gotten close enough for you to notice him." Samantha giggled as she listened.

"Hold on Samantha, I will give the phone back to your mother. I will talk to you later. Please be safe and don't make any new friends. Don't speak about any of this to anyone."

“Okay, Papa Tate lighten-up, I know the drill, and please keep working on my mother. She can be such a prude sometimes,” replied Samantha. Tate passed the phone receiver back to Gayle as she smiled.

“Okay Baby, thanks for putting the money back. I will try to save a little more and then perhaps I can come for a visit, or perhaps you can come here for Christmas. I’ll talk to you next week. Bye, bye”.

Gayle hung up the phone as Tate sat next to her waiting for all the questions to start about the money and the bodyguard that had been assigned to her daughter. He decided it would be better if he just volunteered the information and save some time.

“Gayle, I know you have questions; please let me explain. I placed a watch on your daughter for a couple of months, because I wasn’t sure who was watching me when I went to visit her. As for the money, I turned her name into Father Caleb for a scholarship from our foundation. There are guidelines and he never called me back to tell me if she would receive the money. I guess I should have told you what I had done; I didn’t want you to be disappointed if she didn’t get it. A few of the other agents have used the fund for their children or grand children; this was my first time nominating anyone. I promise that the watch will be taken off of her at the end of this semester. Besides, it’s only my nephew. The most danger she is in from him would probably be a blind-date gone bad. He’s a little older than she is, but I’m sure that he is attracted to her, otherwise she would have never noticed him watching her."

Gayle listened to Tate's explanation, and she did believe that he was telling the truth. She spoke slowly during her reply.

"Well, I guess all I can do is thank you for looking after my baby girl and for making sure she has the money that she needs. I promise you that I will encourage her to give the money back when she starts working. I'm sure that she will, if I explain to her how it perhaps will be able to help some other needy-soul in the future.

One night after a meeting and before Christmas, Tate was able to, once again, get a couple of days off consecutively. With the holidays so closely upon us, this was a very rare occasion for any of the staff. So many people were putting in for holiday leave until it was a standard occurrence for one to work two or more positions on the same shift. This was also a true statement of infrequency because Tate and Slapp were always doing something to disorganize the schedule, or that's the way the pit boss felt and had expressed his feelings about the matter, up the chain of command, regularly. We all remained confident that he was unaware of what their occupations were back in the States.

Tate got off from work around six and went over to Gayle's apartment next door and waited for her to arrive. It was a cold and very wet Friday, but this had not put a damper on the holiday spirit in the least. As a matter of fact, this had lead

Tate to remember some things about his childhood that he hadn't thought of in a long time. As he took the short stole over to Gayle's place, he noticed that there were people everywhere and traffic was the worst that Tate could recall since we all had arrived in Hong Kong, the Beautiful City by the Sea. His thoughts of home were always more haunting this time of year as he reminisced. His mother was a mature woman now and his grandmother had long since passed on, years before. His grandmother was and shall forever be the first love of his life. She understood him better than anyone. When he was growing up, he would have sworn that each time he felt pain, of any kind, that her heart would receive a stinging prick as well. His brother and his brother's children had always stayed around to help their mother to celebrate the holidays, but for the pass number of years Tate had been missing from all the festive photos. Tate always sent very nice gifts, yet most of the time an appearance was out of the question. When it was possible, it had to be done in the cloak of night and only for a few hours, which seemed to do more harm than good to the holiday cheer-meter of all concerned.

Tate loved the holidays as a child because his grandmother always made sure that they had a great one, even if she had to borrow the money from a friend to make it happen. During most of the early years, that's exactly what had taken place. Tate didn't discover this little detail until years later and had done everything in his power to repay his grandmother's friend's family for their kindness to him and his family. It so happens that his grandmother was best friends with the little Jewish lady whose husband owned the building where they lived for almost thirty years. After Tate's mother and stepfather got a divorce, they moved in with his grandmother. Each year, just before the holidays, the Jewish lady would lend his grandmother money interest free, in turn she would spend the next six months paying it back. It was never a lot of money to the old rich lady, but to Tate and his brother it was the difference between jumping up on Christmas morning to open gifts or sleeping in and pretending it was just another day with a special meal. She could lend it from her household money and the husband was never the wiser, after all those years. He had passed away long while back and left his wife even richer. Tate's grandmother and the little Jewish woman spent even more time together. She was a few years older than Tate's grandmother and her health had started to fail early in life. Before Tate's nana had passed on, his family including his grandmother, mother, brother and his family had gone over to the lady's huge house every year for the holiday celebration. Tate had even started to have the gifts that he sent, delivered over there to save time and effort of the transport. Once Tate and his brother became adults, there weren't any reason for the lady to continue to lend the family money, but she insisted and Tate's grandmother accepted it, for the sake of argument. The old lady would said, 'what the devil can I do with all this money now? You guys are all the family that I have left.' Then on the first day after the holidays my grandmother would pay it all back, every dime. The old lady was so wealthy that she wouldn't notice. She hired a financial advisor to come over once a month to go over all her transactions and make sure that each of her charities received their proper portion. Tate and his other family members believed that she just wanted him to come by for company. It was always a drawn out process, each time he came. She would instruct her live-in cook to prepare his favorite cookie or coffee cake and a full meal. They would sit and talk for hours, as she would pull out the picture books. That's what she called her library of photo albums. Of course over the years Tate's family had been added to those photo albums and the will as well. To Tate, it was more like a history class or a documentary from her old country, with the pictures as documentation that all of it was true. Tate was sure that any museum would have loved to get their hands on only half of all the stuff that had been left in this woman's care. She had picture, of when her grandmother was an infant.

As the years passed on, the advisor was able to name more of the people in the pictures than she was able to. When she couldn't remember a name of someone she would just laugh and say that they probably weren't worthwhile remembering anyway, as she turned the pages and move on to the next person or event, which was reflected in the next photo. The advisor listened to the stories over and over just like Tate and his brother had been forced to do when their grandmother had left them over there when it was too cold for them to tag alone with her and their mother was working. The financial advisor was paid handsomely so why not listen attentively just one more time, to her stories, for clarity. The question was now whose clarity was in doubt.

Tate laid across Gayle's bed very quiet and motionless as all these memories of his child and young manhood flooded his thoughts. This was the first time in years that he felt that he had missed out on a lot, by not being able to spend more time with his family. He smiled to himself a few times as a single tear escaped his eyes, while he remembered other happy times from his childhood. Ole Lady Rosenthal had made a greater impact on his early life than he had realized. He wanted to go back to thank her in person. Even though she was dead, a graveside visit would be the best he could do and would possibly give him some closure to his regrets for not doing it while she was still alive.

Gayle came through the front door and called out to Tate as she entered, while removing her shoes. This was a highly practiced custom on this side of the world and one that she had embraced for her own personal reasons. She placed her purse on a small table by the door as she noticed Tate's shoes.

"Tate, are you here"? She called calmly in case he was asleep. He sprang to his feet to meet her near the door, as he responded.

"Yea baby, I'm here. I've been waiting for you to come home. Why are you so late? I started to worry a little."

"Oh, I was talking to Helen and Mrs. Carrington about our holiday plans and I lost track of time. Are you hungry? Do you want to go out or call out for delivery"? Tate had now met her at the door and was holding and kissing her as he buried his face into her neck and shoulder. Gayle politely attempted to squirm away. He mumbled something as he shifted his face into the upper portion of her breast area.

“It doesn’t matter Gayle baby, whatever you decide will be fine.” She noticed something different in his mood, but decided not to spotlight it for conversation.

“Tate, I think that we should get dress and go to the resort and catch Uncle Oscar’s second set tonight. They will be taping it—Helen and her father will be singing that song that he wrote for her when she was six.”

“Gayle, I don’t have any clothes on this side of town formal enough to be out after 5:00 in the evening.” She gave in with an agreeable response.

“I guess you are right,” agreed Gayle. “Traffic there and back can be very slow and tedious this time of evening. We can stay in, I’m sure that there will be other tapings of Helen and her father, Uncle Oscar.”

Chapter Nineteen

Healing Time with Father

At the resort, my father had just finished his first evening dinner-set and we decided to eat in between. He approached my table where I sat waiting for him. I spoke and smiled widely as he came near.

"Hello daddy, I see that my timing was perfect. How are you?" He leaned in to kiss the corner of my lips and cheek before he answered.

"Hello baby girl, your timing is great. Your father is very well and even better now that his favorite girl has arrived." We both laughed as the staff looked on. "You know Monique [Helen] everyone doesn't know that you are my daughter. Some of the ladies here are very jealous of you. Some have known me for years and they are wondering how can I allow you to show up and lock-up all my time every Friday night?"

"You're joking, right daddy?" He turned to face me again as he tried to convince me what he was saying was, indeed, a fact.

"No, no Monique I wouldn't tease you about a thing like that. The word is out that I plan to leave soon and you won't believe how much attention I've been getting lately. I get more play than a pitcher in a warm-up box, during the last tiebreaker game at the end of the season. I know what their plans are, but I only have eyes for one lady. That reminds me; I need to talk to you about something. Let's order our food and then eat it upstairs in my suite. I have at least and hour and a half before my next set. I have a menu in my room. We can call it in." We took the closest elevator and entered my father's room. He removed his coat and tie, and hung them in the closet, by the door. I went into the sitting area to find the menu. He proceeded into the bathroom to wash his hands as I called out to him.

"Hey daddy, what do you want me to order for you"? He answered quickly.

"It doesn't matter baby girl, I have had everything on that menu at least forty times or more, surprise me. Just make sure that it doesn't include anything with acid—like tomatoes or vinegar." We made small talk as we waited for the food to arrive.

"Dad I need to ask you something. You can answer only if you want to." He smiled as he turned to face me more on the sofa, while placing his arm behind me on the back of the couch.

"Ask me anything that you want, I at least owe you that. No more secrets. Just shoot."

"Well daddy, I wanted to ask you about what my foster-father said to you when he called you into the hospital room, just before he died. I got the feeling that he didn't want me and my foster-mother to be there." My father looked down as if that was the last thing that he thought that I would ask him about. I didn't get the feeling that he wanted to lie or keep it a secret from me. I felt like he was embarrassed to talk about it out loud and probably for the first time, since he had left my dying foster-father's bedside. I waited as he got his thoughts together. There came a knock at the door and he seemed relieved that the arrival of the food had interrupted our little talk. He sprang to his feet.

"Excuse me baby girl, I think that's our food arriving. What did you order us anyway"? He smiled back at me as he raced for the door. He opened the door and the man pushed in the cart. My father instructed him to leave it, that we could set it up. I made my selection as I waited for my father to answer my question.

"Well Monique, the night your foster-father called me in, he made me promise to look after you and your foster-mother. He revealed to me that he knew that I was attracted to her and that she told him how she felt about another man when he first started to date her, years before. At first he didn't know that the man was I, the little baby's father. He didn't see it as a problem for him because he figured once he married her;

that would be that. You were still a newborn at the time and I came back to visit as much as I could, but it wasn't enough for her to remain alone, or keep hope alive. After all, I never told her how I felt and I always had some wild story to relay to her about some woman that I was acquainted with at the time. My sexual conquests you might say. Now I realize that she was laughing on the outside, but was feeling hurt as I told her about the other women in my life. At first, I thought that my feelings for her had been misplaced, and had been based on the gratitude for her doing such a good job of caring for you and keeping my secret. She never gave me any clue that she was attracted to me. When she met your foster-father, she explained to him how it came about that she ended up taking care of you. What she didn't tell him was that the man that she was carrying a torch for and the baby's father was the same person. There was no way for me to know what parts she had told him or what portions she had omitted. I was so appreciative that the man trusted me enough to stay under the same roof with my little girl whenever I came home to visit, until I wasn't about to rock the boat by asking questions about the arrangements that the two of them had worked out. I sent your foster-mother money almost every month, just like I had promised, but she never spent any of it because of the guilty conscious that haunted her for not keeping her word about giving you back to me. As the years rolled on, very quickly if I may add, I became afraid to tell you the truth. That played into Buddy's hand because by then she found out that she was unable to bare any children of her own. Your foster-father had become very fond of you as well and I'm sure if I had taken you, he would have died years before he did. The stress would have been too much. You know that he had ulcers and a weak heart. Later on, the ulcers turned into stomach cancer.

After I came back the second time, she had become involved with your foster-father and seemed to be moving forward with the relationship. I had nothing to offer her and I still wanted to pursue my musical dream. That night I went into talk to your foster-father, at the hospital, he told me that he believed that she held on to you to make sure that she would still see me from time to time, even though we couldn't be together. It was hard for me to call a dying man a liar—after all, what would be his motive? He even provided me with a little proof by telling me some dates of my first few visits. When he called me in that night at the hospital, he talked about you as if you were nine years old. I think those memories were the strongest and had surfaced in his weakened medicated state because that's the age you were when I came to get you that night that we sang that song that I had written for you when you were six. He told me that this had been one of the most frightening nights of his life. If you remember, he and his friends got drunk and spent a lot of time in the kitchen doorway, while yelling from the back of the room when we finished our song. He wasn't suppose to be drinking. After that night, the fear of losing you stayed with him for a long time, and he continued to drink more than he should have. I know that you were too young to grasp what was happening and I'm glad that you were. Anyway Baby Girl, I'm just trying to keep my promise to a dying man. Please don't doubt that I have carried a torch for your foster-mother all these years, so keeping this pledge is going to be an easy one." Then my father smiled widely as he reached over to grab and squeeze both of my hands as he held them together.

Thirty minutes had now passed, the food was now getting cold and it was almost time for my father to go back downstairs. He seemed a little choked-up a few times as he told the story and I knew then that he had regrets about the decisions that he had make in his life. I knew exactly how he felt, because the lump was so hard in my throat until I couldn't swallow enough to ask the next question as I had planned to do. The tears were too close to the surface for me to hold them back and speak at that moment, so I just listened. He held one of my hands the entire time as he relived the events that had brought all of us to this point. I finally was able to speak as I broke his concentration and deja vu affixation with another question, as he stared down at our enlaced fingers.

"So daddy, what are you going to do about it?" He looked up and attempted to smile through the sadness caused by the regrets. He swallowed hard as he took in a breath to get to the part, of why he had asked me to come for a special talk.

"I'm glad that you asked me that baby girl. I realize that you are a grown woman, but I want your honest opinion on something that is very important to me. What do you think about me pursuing your foster-mother's affection?" He quickly dropped his head and looked away for a quick moment as if he didn't want to see the expression on my face, in case it wasn't good. Then he continued, "I know this is awkward for me to ask, but I wanted to talk it over with you before I decide."

“That’s fine with me daddy, I’m not sure what you want me to say. I just want you to be happy. I always knew that you two cared for each other.”

“Was it that obvious baby girl?” Daddy then smiled real big and gave a players giggle.

“Yes daddy, especially after I got old enough to understand relationships a little. I always wondered why my foster-father wasn’t jealous of you two.”

“Oh, you are so smart. I think he was a little envious at first, but later on he just couldn’t take a chance of losing her and you. After all, she did tell him up front, she just left out the part that it was I. He really loved you Monique; he told me more than once or twice. I wished I wouldn’t have wasted so much time keeping this a secret. You have a whole other family that you don’t know.”

“Well Daddy, I wouldn’t be so sure about that.” He quickly checked his watch and stood up to put back on his tie and dinner jacket.

“Wow, look at the time and we didn’t even get a chance to eat. I have to go baby girl. Come downstairs and sing that song with your father for the cameras. By the way, you look great. We will have to eat later. The show must to go on, as they say.” Then he winked one eye and smile like the professional performer that he had proven to be.

"Sure daddy, you go down and warm up the crowd for us. I will be down in a minute; just a soon as I freshen up my make up." We made eye contact as he kissed my face just below that single tear that had some how escaped my eye without me noticing.

"You hurry now, don't disappoint me. Once I tell the audience about you, they will expect a performance of our song, 'When Monique Came Out to Play.' See you in the lounge." He closed the door as I headed into the bathroom. A few moments later I made my grand entrance from the back of the dimly lit lounge room, just as my father finished the second song and were standing to take a bow. We sang our special song and later that night we got a bite to eat at the bar. I stayed at the resort with my father that night and we sat up late and talked way into the early morning. We sat back deeply into the couch as he sat with his arms around my shoulders while resting the side of his face on the top of my head. He kissed my forehead a couple of times as we talked. We fell asleep in those positions, but before that occurred somewhere during one of the rims of sleep, I became nine years old again and realized that this had happened before. Once before, when Uncle Oscar, had come home and we sang our song, for family and friends. As the memory occurred in a dream-like state, it seemed that my foster-mother had gone into the kitchen to clean up after the party was over and the entire guest group had left. My foster-father had fallen asleep in his favorite chair, because he had had too much to drink. My biological father, Uncle Oscar, and I had settled down on the sofa as we played our song that we had tape-recorded earlier that night during the dinner party. We heard it for the tenth time before I passed out that night from pure exhaustion from the excitement of my Uncle Oscar coming home, once more. Now thirty-nine years later, here we sat in the same position, except now I was a middle-aged woman, he was a mature man and I knew him as my biological father and not Uncle Oscar, my foster-mother's friend. Whichever title one chooses to use, during this enlightenment, I thought of him as a wonderful dad and one that I loved with every fiber of my being. He had always been my hero and nothing anyone could tell me would change that fact; not even a shift in his title from uncle to dad.

* * *

The end

Edwards Brothers Malloy
Thorofare, NJ USA
March 27, 2013